Penitence

Books by Dale E. Lehman

Howard County Mysteries

The Fibonacci Murders
True Death
Ice on the Bay
A Day for Bones

Bernard and Melody Capers

Weasel Words
Rooftop Sonata

Science Fiction

Space Operatic
The Belt
Penitence

Short Story Collections

The Realm of Tiny Giants
Found by the Road
Manifest Secrets

PENITENCE

DALE E. LEHMAN

RED TALES

Chase, Maryland

Penitence
Dale E. Lehman

Cover art by Proi

Book design by Dale E. Lehman
Book set in 11-pt. Calluna

Published by Red Tales, 2024
Baltimore, Maryland
United States of America
https://www.DaleELehman.com

Trade paperback: 978-1-958906-08-8
Ebook: 978-1-958906-09-5

For Kathleen. I finally finished it. I so wish you were here to read it.

No AI tools were used in the crafting of this story. Seriously, where would be the fun in *that*?

Part 1:

Death

1

"**G**OD GRANTS you one day to relive. Which—"

"He doesn't."

"But if He did—"

"If God existed, this wouldn't have happened."

The universe arched overhead, a coal-black vault painted in star-light, embracing mountains, cathedral spire pines, moon-sparkled snow. To the west, a frozen tidal wave swept the Interstate, blocking the ProMaster cargo van's advance. Behind, its tire tracks had been obliterated. The van jutted above the motionless river of white, a gray boulder defying its power.

The atheist, Will, tried to erase the question from his mind but couldn't. In truth, there was a day. No power in or beyond the universe could reset the clock, but there was a day, another last day, the day his life ended at seven forty-five P.M. when the truth finally sank in.

"The day Sarah left," he said, aged beyond years.

In the driver's seat, the believer, Jesse Markakis, didn't react at once. He ran his hand over the steering wheel while the stars twinkled in the black of his eyes. Then he shifted as though waking from a long sleep. "Why that day?"

"It was the last day I felt loved."

Jesse wouldn't understand. Jesse didn't understand anything. He was as black as this night, not quite poor but nowhere near rich, and too young, barely twenty-five circuits about the sun. He'd almost been married, but not quite. In fact, he'd never quite lived.

How had they been thrown together, these antipodes? Will—legally William James Bancroft III, though legal counted for nothing now—wasn't just white. He was pale from life in the great indoors. His hair had begun to gray, as though absorbing the pallor of his flesh. Still, in the mirror he'd never seemed a poor specimen. Once suitably perched on the corporate ladder, he had strength and looks and money—commodities now as valuable as ash. Planted in the passenger seat, he was fifty-three going on dead.

Will tugged up the zipper on his blue Chinese-made coat. They had that in common now, anyway: clothing raided from Walmarts along the way. Easy to find along Interstates, Walmarts. Infinitely easier than Bergdorf Goodman.

"I'd want the day I met Lynn," Jesse said.

Of course.

"What the hell day is it, anyway?" he continued. "We shoulda been married by now." Jesse pinched his eyes shut. "She coulda survived. I shoulda—"

"For God's sake!" If anything had immortality, it was grief. Will knew that. He understood denial, too, up to a point. For an hour after he discovered Sarah and her things gone, he spun every possible scenario except the obvious. But Lynn wasn't a mere day dead. It had been a month.

Jesse crossed his arms over his chest. "Ha. You *do* believe in God."

"I only believe in two things."

"Yeah? Like what?"

"Myself, for one. For the other..." Will imagined himself running free among the stars, a giant striding through the cosmos, hopping stepping-stone galaxies, roaming forever and ever and ever, finally free of everything. "We have forty hours of fuel. After that, we freeze."

"Oh, but Mr. Manager's got a plan," Jesse sneered. "Always does, don't he?"

"Yes. He does."

Not that it would likely help. But he had one.

2

WILL HADN'T dug that forty-hour figure from the snow. His cell phone plucked two bars of signal from the frigid air, enough to scrounge up a formula for gas consumption while idling, enough to download—slowly—the ProMaster's specs. Using all that and the gas gauge and his calculator app, forty and a fraction spilled out.

Not much time, but time. With luck, the night's falling temperatures and rising winds would yield to better weather come daylight. According to his maps app, a cluster of houses huddled the south side of the Interstate a mile, mile and a half ahead. Not too bad a walk on a good day.

Not that it would be a good day. Not that Will and Jesse could survive a frozen wilderness with only their wits and a cell phone to guide them. Will couldn't factor in the snow and the cold and the wind chill. Maybe that mile, mile and a half would do them in. Oh sure, they'd made it farther than the Donner party, but these mountains could kill. They'd done it before. They wouldn't hesitate to do it again.

The ProMaster was his fallback. If they began to feel the elements while shelter remained out of reach, they could return. But the van couldn't save them. The cold would stalk them, waiting as the gas supply dwindled. And then...what? Would it gently rock them into oblivion, children in the arms of Mother Universe? Or would they linger for days in half-conscious terror? Will didn't know. He knew finance and management, mobile devices and Manhattan. He might as well have been on Mars.

He didn't want to die. Of course not. And yet, bathed in the uncaring light of the stars, it seemed the only life left lay in the past, and much of that life he now regretted. He'd spent far too long pursing wealth, thinking mostly of himself, ignoring if not looking down on the Jesses of the world.

"Do you still think I'm a racist?" he asked.

With his index finger, Jesse drew a stick figure in the window fog. "You care what I think?"

"If I didn't, I wouldn't have asked."

Jesse added a happy face to the figure. "Nah, I never thought that."

"It sure sounded like it."

"Just prejudiced. You got stereotypes stuck in your head. But everyone's got those."

"Even you?"

Regarding his drawing like an art critic examining a Rafael, Jesse didn't answer. After a brief silence, he changed the subject. "I oughta tell you something," he said. Then he didn't tell Will anything.

Jesse's secrets couldn't amount to much. Not anymore. Or ever, really. The kid had worked a loading dock in the vicinity of the U.N. building where his live-in girlfriend Lynn was an insignificant secretary to some insignificant manager. They'd been happy and devoted to each other, but nothing more.

No, wait. What had Will just told himself about himself? Nothing *less*. Happy and devoted and nothing *less*.

Still Jesse offered no answer.

"Tell me, already," Will said.

"I think I'm a carrier."

Will leaned into the cold door, drawing back from Jesse in a flush of primal fear. "Don't be paranoid," he said, but maybe not for Jesse's benefit. Probably he meant it for himself.

"Yeah, I guess we'd know by now. You'd of caught it."

Who knew? What was it Daffodil had said? Something about sites of infection and sites of action and the length of the incubation period. She'd been a nurse, so she would have known. Not that it mattered. Once the disease went to work, it burned through the population, engulfing the city. The state. Probably the whole world. News outlets fell silent within days, leaving the scattered survivors in ignorance.

"Why do you think so?" Will asked.

Jesse added a second stick figure with long hair. She was holding hands with the first. "I got sick that morning," he said. "Sore throat. Lynn told me to stay home, but a day's pay's a day's pay, you know?" He glanced at Will, who couldn't even pretend to know. Will had never lived paycheck to paycheck. "We rode the subway together, as usual. She went her way, I went mine. By the time I got to work, it was worse. Weakness. Dizzy spells. An hour of that, and my boss said go home."

Will blew on his window to thicken the fog and started a stick figure of his own. "Probably just a cold."

"Yeah, 'cept I wanted to strangle the bastard. I needed the money. He didn't care. He just didn't want me breathing on him."

"So?"

"Strangling him. For real. I wanted to feel my fingers squeeze his neck." He illustrated, hands over the steering wheel, straining at someone who wasn't there. "Pull his damn head right off his shoulders."

Will finished his drawing. Just one stick figure, no companion. "Did you try?"

"Almost."

"Why didn't you?" He pivoted to see Jesse's face. It seemed an important question, although the answer would tell him nothing.

Jesse stared at the stars. "Don't know. The feeling passed."

They'd talked about this before. Not *this* this, but in general. Why hadn't they caught the bug? Daffodil had an explanation for that, too. Some people, she said, stored more antibodies than others. Some fought off diseases before they turned symptomatic. Maybe that was Jesse. And Will. Hell, maybe the whole thing was just a nightmare. Maybe they'd wake back in their own beds, back in their old lives.

If only.

"You're fine," Will assured him. "You'd be psycho by now if you weren't."

"How do we know? We got nothing to go on."

Fair point. They only knew the world had gone mad, and now here they were, trapped in the snow with forty hours of warmth left.

Jesse turned on him. His fingers flexed again as though aching for a throat to throttle. "Why the hell did you save me?"

"It wasn't my idea. You—"

"You should of run me over. If Lynn's gone, I don't wanna be here, either."

"You might not be much longer."

"Why didn't you throw me out? Run me over?"

"Don't be an idiot."

"Probably eases your damn conscience to bail out indigents."

"I'm surprised you know a word that big." Will returned to his drawing, his finger poised to add something, anything, but what could he add?

"My mama read to me at bedtime. Did your nanny?"

"Maybe I *should* have run you over."

Not that he could have. When someone falls in front of your car, you don't think. You react. You slam on the breaks. Take evasive action. Tires squeal, adrenaline wracks your body, your mind goes as blank as a fresh sheet of paper. That's how it happened, followed by metal rending as Will's black Lincoln Navigator plowed into the side of a garbage truck, spewing fender shards and split trash bags into the street. Horns blared. Shouts filled the air. His door was jammed against the truck. He clambered across the passenger seat to get out, then he was standing over Jesse, a stranger at that moment, a nameless young black man in black jeans and a heavy black hoodie, hands clawing at the pavement, legs struggling to get under him.

Struck dumb, Will thought the worst. There he stood, a well-off white guy in a pricey black overcoat, his burgundy tie peeking out. Planted beside his monster SUV in which he'd all but run over some poor black kid, he shivered, part from fear, part from the late November cold. What would happen? He'd be sued, that's what. If he was lucky. If not, a mob would beat him, maybe kill him before police arrived. They were already encroaching, throngs of enraged people shouting, screaming, pouring from nearby buildings as though the whole damned city had witnessed the accident and was hell-bent on revenge.

"He fell!" Will cried. "He *fell*! Right in front of me!"

Jesse was blind to Will. Terror in his eyes, he all but crawled under the vehicle, seeking escape as though the mob was after him.

There were sirens, more sirens than Will had ever heard, far more than necessary for a traffic accident. The mob rushed by and around, an incoherent mass spreading in all directions along the sidewalks, through the streets, clambering over cars. But not to get at him. Something else had enraged them. They attacked each other, attacked themselves, howled like wounded animals. Shots echoed from stone and steel walls. Will sank to his knees and pressed against the side of his SUV. Wide-eyed, Jesse watched the unfolding riot from beneath the front bumper.

The buildings disgorged people running and screaming, stumbling and babbling. Sirens wailed nonstop. A police helicopter flashed by overhead. Gunshots popped along the street. Not ten yards away, a young man beat an old woman to the ground with an umbrella. Swallowing his fear, Will rose to stop the assault, but before he could take a step, a police officer shot the man in the arm. Blood pouring from his wound, the assailant attacked with greater ferocity. The officer dropped him with a head shot, only to be attacked from behind by a young woman wielding bare hands and teeth.

Jesse covered his head with his arms and wailed, "What the hell! What the hell!"

Hell it was. Will crouched frozen at its gates as people clawed their own faces, screamed at inanimate objects, hurled whatever came to hand. The dead and dying lay everywhere.

Go, some part of his overwhelmed brain urged. *Go before they get you!*

He clawed his way back into the Navigator through the passenger door. Before he could pull it shut, Jesse dove in. There was no time to argue. Will clambered into the driver's seat, locked the doors, started the engine. Metal scraped on metal as he backed away from the garbage truck. He slammed the gearshift into drive and floored the accelerator, then hit the brake as a man lunged in front of him. Falling onto the hood, the man attacked it with a shiny blunt instrument, knocking dent after dent into the black metal.

In a panic, Will floored the accelerator again. The attacker rolled up the windshield and tumbled off the side. Two more threw themselves at the hood. Will closed his eyes and ran them over, babbling, "I'm sorry! I'm sorry!" The Navigator bounced as though lofted by speed bump after speed bump.

"Fuck," Will muttered. He opened his eyes, tightened his grip on the wheel, drove on. More men and women threw themselves at the car right, left, and front as though they could stop it in their hands. He drove into and over them, eyes unblinking, soul sickened by the thumps and screams, but he couldn't stop.

He couldn't.

Cars crashed into storefronts, into each other, spun and rolled and blocked the way. Will dodged what he could, squeezed through the gaps, knocked into a few other vehicles when he couldn't avoid it. Somehow, he kept going, making for the one place that had to be safe. Home. He didn't know how he'd get there through this madness, but he had to try.

Jesse cringed and squeezed his eyes shut and gagged. And then he was pointing and all but wailing, "There! Over there! Let me out!"

"Are you *mad*?"

"Lynn works there! At the U.N. She's in there!"

Will kept going.

"Let me out! Please, please, Lynn's in there!"

Will didn't know who the hell Lynn was. He didn't know who Jesse was or what had happened to the city, but he wasn't stopping. Stopping meant death. He must have killed fifty people already—no, they killed themselves, hurling themselves at the Lincoln. It wasn't his fault. He had no choice, he couldn't stop, couldn't, not until he escaped, not until this madness was far, far behind.

But the madness had no edge, no containing wall. It seethed around them, everywhere, out to infinity.

That's how it started. Chaos swallowing the whole world, no edge to be found.

Strange. He hadn't realized until now, here at what may well be the frozen end of his life, but he'd been seeking that edge for three weeks, and only here was he approaching the one possible edge: death.

That insight led to another. He'd spoken in anger, yes, but also in truth. Even if they got out of this, they were dead. They'd been dead from the start. They just didn't know it. Maybe he *should* have run Jesse over. Maybe he *should* have spared him this past month, spared him this moment. It might have been kinder.

"No wonder it ended this way." Jesse tweaked his window-fog drawings, adding clothing as a child might. A triangle dress on the woman, rectangle shirt sleeves and pant legs on the man.

Will didn't question the statement. The end was the end, that was all. Why didn't change anything, so it couldn't matter.

Jesse told him anyway. "Two guys in a van waiting to die, and what do they do? Argue."

"I'm not arguing."

Choking on an acid laugh, Jessie continued to draw. A house. Trees. Flowers. Then in one savage motion, he swept them away with the palm of his hand. Outside, moonlight glittered on the snow.

Will peered into the night and discovered some measure of comfort in those sparkles. "It's not the end of the world," he said. And it wasn't. Stars, moon, mountains, snow, trees—all still there, all so normal, so natural, so peaceful. "Maybe the end of us, but maybe we had it coming. Think how quiet it will be once…"

It proved too desolate to utter.

"Once the arguments stop," Jesse suggested.

Ironically, Will couldn't argue.

Jesse leaned back, closed his eyes, half smiled. "Yeah, that's something to celebrate. No wars. No hatred. No greed."

Will felt a bit of light piercing the dark. "No politics, pollution, or noise."

Then they looked at each other, and their almost-smiles slipped. All but simultaneously, they said, "No music."

After a moment of silence, Will suggested, "Let's stop there."

Jesse twisted about and peered into the recesses of the van. With the shattered rear windows sealed by carboard and duct tape, the cargo slumbered in darkness. "Don't we have *anything* useful?"

Lots and lots, yes, but that wasn't the question. "Useful for what?"

"Staying warm. Staying alive. Getting out of here."

Some, sure. They'd brought everything from cabin at the foot of Devil's Peak, but they'd been unable to resupply before leaving the gas station, before parting company with Daffodil because winter was coming and she convinced them to run for the safety of the Sacramento Valley. And what had happened? Winter caught them anyway.

"We'll be okay," Will said. "There are houses nearby. Tomorrow, we'll try to reach them."

"Are they reachable?"

Who knew? "Maybe."

Jesse closed his eyes. "Yeah," he said with zero enthusiasm. "We been lucky so far. But luck can run out."

Will knew. It probably would, sooner or later. It sure had with Sarah.

How the hell had humanity fallen into this open grave?

3

REWIND.

New York. Will's ninth-floor condo in Brooklyn Heights. Sunset on the Monday after Thanksgiving. Will, leaning forward on the couch, still in his suit pants and striped shirt but minus coat and tie, hands on knees, mouth pinched in a tight line as though working a tough financial analysis.

The Monday after Thanksgiving. How damned ironic.

Will couldn't remember how they got here. He drove, that was all, drove over people living and dead, nudged and knocked aside smaller vehicles with his Navigator, somehow plowed across the Brooklyn Bridge, trailing mayhem. At least, he assumed so. How else could they have made it through? And now here they were, and here was no better.

The news played on his seventy-five-inch television. The device covered the wall, almost *was* the wall in fulfillment of a prophecy from *Fahrenheit 451*. But the content was something else, badly produced and directed, barely on air six hours after mayhem erupted. The unshaven anchor, trembling with stage fright, might have been pulled from the mail room to read the reports. His image slithered in and out of focus as he stammered through the words in a tremulous monotone.

"Police believe the unrest began inside the U.N. building. It probably spread into the streets and from there other buildings in the vin...the vin... the vicinity. Violence spreaded throughout the city since this morning with no signs of abetting. No, sorry, abating. Doctors at Mount Sinai Hospital say many of the dead show signs of an infection in..."

He looked like he was about to hurl on the camera.

"...in their brains. But the deceased all died of injuries sustained in the violence, not the disease. Doctors think the infection somehow affects brain chem...chemistry, radically altering behavior. Reports of similar riots have come in from other large cities across the country."

"That's the fifth time he said that," Jesse complained from the confines of Will's Harris leather power recliner. His eyes were shut and his head back, his cell phone clutched in his dangling left hand. He had ditched his hoodie, which hung forlorn on a dining room chair, revealing a black t-shirt.

Didn't the kid ever wear anything but black? "You're free to leave the room," Will said. "Or the condo. I don't know why I let you in here."

"You wouldn't leave a guy out *there*, would you?" Jesse gestured at the window.

If it came down to Will's life or Jesse's, he probably would. This wasn't a crime wave. It was a disease, and they'd been in the thick of it. It might be only a matter of time before one or the other turned homicidal. It might be in Will's interest to throw Jesse out. In Jesse's, too. He'd be safer finding his own place to hole up.

The anchor stumbled on: "Chicago, Atlanta, Philadelphia, Washington, D.C., Phoenix, Los Angeles, San Francisco, and Seattle all report similar incidents. The CDC says if this is a new disease, it must be extremely con... contagious, moreso than any known before."

"Lynn's not answering my calls or texts." Jesse lunged to his feet. "I gotta find her."

"She's probably dead." Will was only half listening. He spoke it like an automated phone message.

"She can't be." Jesse retrieved his hoodie.

"Everyone else is. Anyway, it's dark."

No response, just the sound of Jesse turning the doorknob.

Will motioned at the TV. "Do you *want* to die?"

"I gotta find her." The bottom of the door swished over the carpet.

"Great. I save you, then you throw your life away."

"*Save* me?" The door slammed. "You kidnapped me!"

"*You* dove into *my* car."

"More like a tank. You wouldn't stop for anything. Or anyone. Just rolled right over 'em." Jesse shuddered. "You killed everyone in your path. How do I know *you* ain't gone mad?"

"That was survival instinct. And yes, I saved your life. But hey, throw it away if you want."

"I could of found her if you'd let me out!"

Hell with it. Jesse could do whatever he wanted. Not that Will had any better ideas. They were both frightened and confused, that was all. The world had gone insane—literally—and neither of them knew what to do. There ought to be something you could do. You didn't lie down and die. You rose to the challenge. Rode out the storm. Devised solutions. Came through better, stronger, smarter.

You sound like a fucking motivational poster, he scolded himself. "Let's stay calm and make a plan." That was as much for his own benefit as Jesse's. "So we don't end up dead like everyone else."

"Who's we, *massa*?" Jesse all but spat the last word. "You want a plan? Make it your own damn self." He opened the door and stepped out.

Silence followed, broken only by the voice of the accidental news anchor. "Symptoms include confusion, depression, rage, hallucinations, hysteria..." Aside from that, a strange silence fell, like the world holding its breath. Will didn't realize why at first, but then he did. The door hadn't clicked shut.

He looked over his shoulder. Jesse was backing into the condo, one tiny step at a time. He eased the door shut and turned the deadbolt with equal caution.

"What?" Will asked.

Jesse set a finger to his lips and slipped from the foyer into the living room, where he perched on the edge of the recliner. "Someone's out there," he whispered. "With a gun."

"It's impossible to estimate the number of dead," the anchor read, "and the number of injured is far greater."

Something knocked against the door, just once, a dull thud that might have been accidental or intentional. And then nothing. Someone was prowling the halls, maybe looking for survivors. To help them? Or kill them? A flock of crows—it sure wasn't butterflies—took flight in Will's stomach. He slipped through the condo, closing every curtain, then returned to the couch. Silent, they waited.

Nothing happened.

Nothing happened for ten minutes.

Jesse drew a shaking breath. "What kind of plan?" he asked.

The thud sounded at the door three times that night, just once each time, each thud separated from the next by over an hour of silence. Will tossed and turned in his bed, leaving the couch to Jesse. He couldn't get the mayhem out of his head. People beating each other to death, people throwing themselves at the Navigator, the vehicle bouncing over their bodies. Jesse was right. He'd run them over like they were blades of grass.

No, not really. They'd killed themselves, hadn't they? Just as they had killed each other. He wouldn't have run them down if they hadn't dived in front of him, hadn't tried to attack a moving vehicle. They were dead anyway, driven mad by disease. That wasn't Will's fault.

But it was, in some measure. His foot was on the accelerator, his hands on the wheel. He'd killed them.

No! They were dead already!

But he'd run them over like trash blowing through the street...

Come morning, he looked like someone had punched him in the eyes. So did Jesse.

Will turned on the TV and found a different jittery anchor reading the news, reciting toneless words much the same as his predecessor's. He and Jesse watched, waited, peeked out windows, ate little, talked less. Will's mind had been erased. Everything he knew was gone, replaced by snapshots of insanity.

What had happened to the city?

How had it happened?

When would things return to normal?

He nearly laughed at that last query. There could be no normal, not anymore. People liked to say disasters changed everything. 9/11 changed everything. COVID changed everything. Everything was now "unprecedented" (no doubt the most overused word of the twenty-first century). But none of that had been this. This was the asteroid that wiped out the dinosaurs.

Had T-rex felt this way, watching dust envelope its world?

The day wore on. Their unseen companion rapped on the door every few hours. By evening, the list of affected cities recited by news anchors spanned the globe. Another night of fitful sleep came and went.

On the third day, every broadcast and cable channel went dead. Will found a smattering of confused, sporadic chatter on the radio but learned nothing from it. The interval between thuds on the door stretched until, about sunset, they ceased. Jesse got edgy. The intrusions had grown normal, expected, and their absence jarred him as much as their appearance. He prowled from window to window, nudging the curtains a finger width aside to peer out. He crept to the door and set an ear to it. Whenever Will told him to calm down, Jesse set a finger to his lips to sush him.

At a quarter to midnight, Will opened the refrigerator, gave its contents a cursory examination, and closed it again, none too gently.

"Quiet!" Jesse snapped from the living room.

Will opened it and slammed it.

"Hey!"

Open. Slam.

"That guy might still be out there!"

"Who cares?"

Jesse scurried into the kitchen, motioning for silence. "He'll hear us and kill us!"

So what? Anyway, he was likely dead. Either way, they had a bigger problem.

"Look at this." Will opened the refrigerator for Jesse's inspection. The yellowed light inside revealed their precarious state: half a jar of grape jelly, most of a stick of butter, a few slices of American cheese. "You're welcome to scrounge the cabinets. You won't find much more there." He slammed the door one last time. The shelves rattled. "Might as well get shot. At least that would be quick."

"Why don't you have food?"

"Because my housekeeper leapt to her death."

Jesse gaped at him.

"We don't all have housekeepers. I eat out a lot."

Jaw quivering, Jesse turned away from the cabinets. Will couldn't blame him. Who wants to gaze into their own grave? "What about that brilliant plan of yours?"

Will didn't have a brilliant plan, only one semi-rational idea and no clear way to execute it. "Leave New York," he said. "Take as much food as possible."

"That's *it*?"

"It's a start."

"Yeah? How do we get out without being killed? Where do we go? And how much can that Lincoln hold?"

"It'll hold enough. We'll go upstate, someplace rural. Fewer people, so it should be safer."

Jesse put up a hand for silence, listened, shook his head. "Now I'm hearing things," he muttered. "No, not that tank of yours. Too flashy. They'll come after us. Anyway, we need something bigger."

Will didn't know whether to laugh or choke. "Bigger than a Navigator? A semi, maybe?"

"A van."

"You want to steal a van."

"It ain't stealing. Not anymore"

"Is that one of your skills?"

Jesse grabbed a fistful of Will's shirt and yanked him off balance. "Keep it up, asshole."

Will pushed him away. "You couldn't take on a paraplegic."

Yanking open a drawer, Jesse snatched a steak knife and brandished it like Michael Meyers. "Try me." A wild gleam filled his eyes. His face drew taught.

"What the hell are you—"

Jesse swiped at him. Will stumbled back, barely avoiding the blade tip. He caught his balance just in time to dodge another lunge. Jesse circled. Will pivoted, and when the next strike came, he caught Jesse's arm and all but threw him face first into the counter. The knife clattered to the floor. Jesse dropped to his knees, gulping air, and sputtered.

"Had enough?" Will asked.

Jesse flopped over and sat with his back against the cabinets. He touched a hand to his forehead and winced. "Damn, that hurt." He checked his fingers for blood. Will wasn't sure how, but the kid hadn't been injured even to that extent. The knife had landed next to Jesse's foot. He kicked it away as though it was a venomous snake. "I could of killed you."

"Not damn likely." Will left him sitting there and retreated to the living room, where he nudged aside the curtain. Outside was nothing, just the darkened lines of buildings glowing in the streetlights and a gray sky speckled with yellowed clouds. An unnerving silence held the city in its grasp. He let the curtain fall.

Jesse shuffled up behind him. "Not your car," he insisted.

"Whatever. You want a van, we'll find a van. First thing in the morning. If we stay here much longer, one of us really will kill the other."

Jesse took a quick peek out. "I gotta find Lynn first."

"No."

"I just need an hour."

"No, damn it!"

"Yes, damn it! I'll just check a couple places."

How could hope still breathe while the city tore itself to pieces? They were more likely to be killed or contract the disease—if they hadn't already—than find Lynn. She was probably dead in the street. Or running mad through it. Would Jesse want to find her in either state? Best to assume the worst had already happened. It likely had.

Even so, Will found it hard to deny the desperation in Jesse's eyes and the pain in his voice. It mirrored his own on finding Sarah gone.

"Please, Will. Just an hour."

Will dropped onto the sofa, surrounded by his things: pricey furnishings, pricey art on the walls, pricey electronics, all worthless. He could carry none of it, and where he was going—wherever that was—only food, fuel, and shotgun shells had value. "Let's see what it's like in the morning. If it's safe, we'll look for her."

Jesse peeked out the window again. "We?"

He should have corrected himself, but he couldn't. "You need *someone* to watch your back."

Dropping the curtain, Jesse exhaled in relief. "Yeah," he said. "Thank you."

Red dawn yielded to blue morning. Will put on his overcoat and left his tie. They crept from his condo to the street, where they found a war-swept battlefield given over to the dead. A cool breeze whispered through the silent city. In the streets—

Will about threw up.

Corpses everywhere, battered and bloodied, shot and stabbed and beaten and run over, on the sidewalks, in the streets, in cars, under cars, pinned between cars, flopped through broken windows. An iron tang carried on the wind. Blood pooled like rusty rain along the curbs.

They couldn't drive through this. Even if he had the stomach for flattening the dead, too many wrecked and abandoned vehicles clogged the streets. Cars, SUVs, box trucks, everything turned at all angles, some on their sides, some on their backs, doors hanging open or ripped off, on the pavement, on the sidewalks, half buried in storefronts.

Will looked up at the building tops, at the sky, off into the distance so as not to see the carnage. "I guess we walk," he said. "Which way?"

Trembling at his side like a hiker cornered by a bear, Jesse didn't answer.

"Jesse?"

"Uh." Jesse fumbled in his jeans pocket for his cell phone. He woke it with his shaking fingers and launched the maps app. It took him a few minutes to tap out the address and get walking directions. "That way." He nodded. "About two hours."

Two hours! Hell.

Will led, weaving around the dead, doing his best to avoid them without looking directly at them. He'd gone half a block before he realized Jesse wasn't following. The younger man stood frozen, staring at a dead woman at his feet. Her neck was torqued at an odd angle, her arms flung outward as though she'd been trying to fly. Will couldn't see much else from that distance. He didn't want to see.

"Don't look at them," he called.

Jesse turned a catatonic gaze on him.

"Look at the path between them."

Swallowing, Jesse nodded and took a first slow step, then another. Will waited for him to catch up. "You want me to navigate?" he asked.

Jesse shook his head and took the lead. He set a halting pace, but after fifteen minutes gained a measure of confidence and moved more surely if not quite at speed.

The path from Brooklyn Heights to Jesse's Brownsville apartment was farther than Will had ever walked in one shot except maybe on a treadmill, made worse by their meandering course through the maze of demolition and death. This wasn't an old movie where apocalypse left the streets empty save a few abandoned cars and shreds of newspaper rattling by in the wind. Insanity had lodged in the city's throat and choked it to death. As they picked their way through, Will noticed the corpses had become playgrounds for ants and flies and other six-leggers he didn't care to identify even if he could.

Though horror was strewn everywhere, in some spots it was worse. At the intersection of Park Place and Kingston, in the shadow of an historic church, three police cars had fused in a head-on crash. They must have been playing chicken flat-out. Their front ends were welded into a smoldering mass. Glass shards and fractured metal had sprayed everywhere. The shrapnel had torn through people and storefronts. The smell of gasoline still permeated the air. The officers remained in their cars, half-pulverized.

In the aftermath, people had swarmed the twisted cop cars, where they beat and stabbed and tore at each other. Carnage overflowed the intersection. Blood ran down streets and sidewalks in all directions. It was a colorized version of the twisted, agonized figures from Picasso's *Guernica*.

Jesse stumbled along, that catatonic look overtaking him again. Will kept his gaze on the distance and followed. And on and on it went.

Two hours stretched to three before they arrived at their destination, a line of three-story brick apartment buildings fronted by trees of modest age, their leaves half fallen, the remainder painted gold, brown, and red. The cars parked along both sides of the street had been vandalized: windows cracked and smashed, tires slashed, dents knocked into their bodies with hammers. The dead scattered about might have been vandals or hapless passers-by. One middle-aged woman wrapped in a green bathrobe had her dead fingers curled about the handle of a bloodied claw hammer. Gunshot wounds peppered her back.

"Over here." Jesse indicated the entrance to one of the buildings. He led Will to the third floor, fumbled with the key, and convinced the deadbolt to turn.

While the apartment wasn't the dump Will had imagined, it was cramped, just a small living room sided by a smaller kitchen, a bedroom, and a bath barely large enough to turn around in. Particleboard furnishings. James Webb Space Telescope posters on the walls. Will studied the posters while Jesse checked each room.

"She ain't here," he said.

What a surprise.

"Her brother Andrew lives eight blocks south," Jesse said. He looked more than a little shell shocked, but at least the wheels were still turning in his head.

On second thought, that might not have been great. Will's legs ached and his stomach revolted at the thought of pounding the pavement again. "It's a long walk out. We should rest up for it, not spend the day on a snipe hunt."

"It's just eight blocks."

"It's an open mass grave."

"Stay if you want. I'm going."

A crash and a scream penetrated the walls. They both froze.

"Was that next door?" Will whispered.

Jesse shook his head.

Nothing further sounded. Whoever it was might be dead, but had they died by their own hand, or had someone helped them out the door? Will didn't want to stick around to find out. Neither did he want to go out on the streets again, but if Jesse could endure a few more blocks of horror, so could he. At least there would be two of them against whatever might be waiting. "I'll tag along," he said.

As quietly as possible, they left the apartment, descended the stairs, and slipped out among the dead once more. All eight blocks of it. They managed. It seemed less horrid this time, more natural, which Will found horrid in itself. This was probably how soldiers felt after a few battles. He'd never been in the military, so he wouldn't know, but here they were, and that's how it was.

Andrew's apartment proved larger than Jesse's and featured better-quality particleboard and a poster of a naked female pop star on the bedroom wall, her dark, air-brushed body turned to avoid an MA rating. Jesse ignored her. Will wondered if money, fame, and beauty had protected her. Of course not. Nobody seemed immune. Nobody but Jesse and himself, and they had survived—so far—by luck alone. As for Andrew, Lynn, or anyone else who might have been hiding under the beds or in the closets, no trace.

In the living room, Will looked out the window. They were on the third floor, overlooking the street. Below were wrecked vehicles and death, nothing more. He was about to turn away when he caught a hint of movement out of the corner of his eye. Squinting, he tried to bring whatever it was into focus. If it was anything.

Jesse shuffled in from the back and made for the apartment door. "Let's go," he mumbled.

"Hold on," Will said. It hadn't been his imagination. There it was again, someone raising their head from behind a blue Camry that had crashed into a bus stop shelter.

"We got more places to look."

"Hold *on!*"

The figure lifted something over the windshield and struck it several times, then threw the object away and ducked behind the car again.

"No time to waste. Lots more places to look." Jesse opened the door. "Her parents' place, friends, church, police station, hospital—"

"Damn it, someone's *out* there!" Will rushed the door, grabbed Jesse's arm and pulled him back into the apartment. "It's not safe. And what's the point, anyway, running all over the city looking for a dead woman?" He closed the door, quietly.

Jesse slumped against the wall and looked at his shoes.

"It's too late today. First thing in the morning, we're leaving."

"I can't." Sinking to the floor, Jesse covered his head in his arms and wept.

Madness. Not the madness that had sundered the world; the madness of grief. Will understood, but there was no time for it. "I'm leaving first thing tomorrow," he said. "You can do whatever the hell you want."

He returned to the living room and dropped onto the couch. Yeah, he'd leave. Over and over he'd said it, but the truth was, he didn't feel safe trying to make his way on his own. Jesse might not be the most useful partner, but he was better than nobody.

Jesse wiped his eyes with his fingers and looked up. "She might come home."

"Don't bet on it."

"Let's go back. Just in case."

Will pinched his eyes shut. They had a long walk out of the city ahead of them. They needed to rest. Hell, maybe he'd sleep for a few weeks first. Or maybe death would come for him and spare him the journey.

"How you getting out?" Jesse asked.

"The shortest way. Brooklyn Bridge, Holland Tunnel, Jersey."

"That'll be hell. Both the bridge and the tunnel."

What wouldn't be? "It's the shortest road through hell."

Jesse rose, shuffled to the window, peeked out. "Shorter from my place."

"Not by much."

"But some."

Who would've thought a guy from a loading dock could out-logic him? Will joined him at the window. If the windshield-smasher was still out there, he or she was well-hidden. Not that it mattered. They had to risk it sooner or later. "Fine. But Lynn's not coming back, and I'm leaving in the morning, with or without you."

Jesse didn't acknowledge that. The threat probably had no substance anymore.

They saw no one on the walk back to Jesse's apartment. No one living. But they weren't the only ones alive. Come evening, sounds infiltrated the building. Metal striking metal. Gunfire. The occasional scream. Jesse slept in his room, Will on the sofa, only "slept" wasn't quite the word. Each bang, each pop, each shout jarred Will awake, after which he wouldn't drift back to sleep for twenty minutes or more. Come dawn, he felt as refreshed as a corpse in the street. Jesse fared no better. He emerged from his room with eyelids sagging and mouth half open.

With no energy for domestic work, they made do with toaster pastries and coffee brewed from a pod. Jesse then packed crackers, dried fruit, more toaster pastries, jerky, and six bottles of water into a black backpack, then they began the long walk out of the city, again navigating by cell phone. Legs sore, minds numbed by the carnage and the buzzing of flies, they trudged northwest, making for the Brooklyn Bridge. The wind picked up, blowing heavy clouds overhead, but no rain fell. The city remained cloaked in shadow throughout the morning. Will's nerves tingled a warning, like they were being watched or followed. He kept looking over his shoulder, scanning the wreckage, half expecting the dead to rise in ambush. He nearly laughed at the thought. A Zombie apocalypse held no terror in the wake of a real one.

But there were no zombies, only the wind and the hum of insects.

Three and a half hours passed that way, longer than before, harder, like they were walking uphill. Three blocks from the Brooklyn Bridge, Jesse veered off course and entered a restaurant at the foot of a towering apartment building. Will didn't have the energy to object.

The lights were on. The sign in the front window announced the establishment open. The dining room had the ambiance of mass murder scene: dead customers and staff everywhere, knives protruding from arms and legs and backs and chests, a few handguns on the floor, blood everywhere. A cop had entered the melee, but he'd identified the wrong culprits. He'd shot up the drink station before turning the gun on himself and blowing out his brains. His ruin lay in a puddle of blood and coffee and juices.

Jesse trudged by him, not looking, and pushed through the swinging double doors into the kitchen. Will followed.

"That's strange," he said. The place looked freshly prepped for the health inspector. No death, no destruction, not even a splotch of grease on a counter.

"Looks like they wasn't even open," Jesse agreed. "Maybe they wasn't when…" He waved about.

"I suppose those Pop-Tarts wore off? That's why we're here?"

"Something like that."

Jesse rummaged for food in cabinets and the walk-in freezer, assembling ingredients for a brunch of eggs, bacon, and hash browns. Will didn't offer to help. He wasn't much of a cook. That had been Sarah's job. She liked cooking, he didn't. In fact, she never much wanted him invading her kitchen.

An hour and a half later, fueled and almost rested, they left their dirty dishes and cooking utensils and slipped out the back door. As they emerged, a metallic clang startled them, followed by the slap of shoes on concrete. There was a dumpster a few yards to their left. Someone must have been rummaging in the trash. Will moved to investigate, but Jesse caught his arm. "Don't," he pleaded. "Let's get out of here."

Yeah, that was a sound plan.

Soon they were on the Brooklyn Bridge, crossing via the pedestrian lanes, which were blocked only in one spot. There, a box truck had struck and tumbled over the barrier and come to rest almost on its side. They couldn't get around it, so they clambered over it, scaling the undercarriage and lowering themselves down the opposite side. Back on the walkway, Will inspected his clothing. He might have been wearing grease and filth instead of suit pants and overcoat. *At least I left the tie at home*, he grumbled to himself. Which was irrational. What use was an Armani label now?

They dragged themselves through Lower Manhattan, weaving west and north on any street not completely choked with wrecked vehicles and dead bodies. Not that any weren't. Some were just less so. At one point, they passed by an ironic scene: an ambulance partially crushed by cars that had struck on opposite sides. The paramedics had been dragged out and beaten to death with tire irons, which had been discarded beside their crushed skulls. The rear doors stood open, revealing a young woman strapped to a gurney. She looked so peaceful, she might have been sleeping. But her breath had left her. Will climbed in to check on her while Jesse waited with downcast eyes.

After what seemed a thousand years, they reached the entrance to the Holland Tunnel. Where the road dipped into the earth, a jumble of wrecked vehicles and mangled bodies clogged the entrance.

"Told you," Jesse muttered.

Will didn't care. He led the way, blazing a trail through and over the pileup, squeezing between vehicles, pushing doors shut to open a passage, clambering over corpses of metal, dodging corpses of flesh. Slicks of blood threaded through the pileup. Some of the bodies seemed locked in their death struggles, hands on each other's throats, guns palmed, fingers over the hilts of knives embedded in their victims.

The crush thickened as they approached the tunnel entrance until of a sudden it was behind them. Strings of lights ran overhead into the distance, illuminating the curving tiled walls that hugged the empty ribbon of asphalt.

"Weird," Jesse said.

Will agreed, until he realized why. "Once the tunnel was blocked, nobody could get in. Anyone inside must have made it through."

They hopped the guardrail onto the service walkway and hiked onward. The mile and a half tube wasn't completely empty. They passed a wrecked vehicle here, a mangled body there. Yet it was paradise compared to above ground. The only things slowing them were their own exhausted legs.

They emerged into the bright early afternoon sun in Newport, New Jersey. A few paces into the light deposited them back in a hell of wrecked vehicles and corpses. Still, it had one thing going for it. The buildings were spaced more widely and separated by parking lots, allowing them to skirt the worst of it. And maybe an end was finally in sight. In the distance, the road turned to expressway. Will couldn't be sure, but the wreckage might have thinned a bit up there.

"Look," Jesse said, pointing at a gas station.

Will froze, expecting to find someone alive, murderously deranged, or maybe just sane enough to kill interlopers. He saw nothing, only the gas station and a few cars. A body sprawled across the hood of one of them, a red stain on the asphalt below.

Jesse made for the gas station, picking his way through the chaos on the street.

"What?" Will called, but Jesse neither answered nor stopped. Whatever it was, it hadn't frightened him.

By the time Will caught up, Jesse had worked his way to the gas station's convenience store, where a battered gray Ram ProMaster cargo van sat, driver's door open. A middle-aged man from India or thereabouts was slumped over the steering wheel, a gunshot wound piercing his left temple.

"Key's in the ignition," Jesse said. "Don't even have to steal it."

"Technically, it *is* stealing.".

"From who? According to you, his next of kin is dead, too."

"Don't be a smartass." Will went to the passenger side and opened the door. He winced at the exit wound and the mess sprayed over the seat and window and...everything. "We can't ride in this. Not without cleaning it up."

"Good thing we got a store. They probably got cleaning supplies." Jesse went in to check.

Will didn't think that was a good idea. Who knew what was lying in ambush within? But no shouts or screams followed, so whatever. He retrieved the keys, went to the back of the van, and opened the doors. The cargo space was crammed full of stuff. Nonperishable foods, a pair of shotguns, ammunition, blankets, clothing, tools, rope, a camp stove and several cans of fuel. The driver must have been making his escape before someone blew a hole in his head. Someone mad, someone not together enough to take the vehicle or even the goods.

Jesse returned with an armful of paper towels and cleaning spray. He dumped them on the ground. "First," he said, "we gotta get him outta there."

"At least you thought it through," Will said. "I don't suppose you figured out how we're supposed to drive through this mess?" He motioned at the road.

"I got an idea about that, yeah."

"Great. You can drive." He doubted Jesse would make it over the first body. Will didn't relish the thought of bumping over corpses, either, but he'd done it before, so he could probably do it again. Although, then he'd been in a panic. Now he was…

Okay, not exactly calm. Numb, maybe. Unsure what was real. Maybe it wasn't real. Maybe this was a nightmare. Maybe he'd wake up. The dead driver managed, without answering, to deny it.

"Let's get it over with," Will said.

4

Wɪᴛʜ ᴛʜᴇ body of the van's previous owner lying in state on the asphalt behind the gas pumps, Will and Jesse cleaned and disinfected the vehicle's interior. They worked in silence, jaws tight, eyes not quite on what they were doing. When the job was done and the reddened cleaning supplies discarded in the trash bin, they leaned against the back of the van, staring at nothing.

Will considered inventorying the van's contents. The deceased seemed to have prepared well, but one never knew. They may as well raid the gas station store as needed before venturing into the unknown.

A squeal of tires interrupted that thought. A block down the road, a white SUV careened around the corner, overturned, and slammed into a utility pole. The pole broke, tearing down wires and igniting a shower of sparks. The traffic signals at the intersection went black.

Startled, Jesse knocked the back of his head against the van. Will scrambled to hide behind the vehicle, tripping over his own feet.

A minute passed. Two. Three. Nobody emerged from the wreck.

Hell with inventory, Will thought. *Just get out of here.* Except the disabled signals felt like a warning. How long would the power stay on? Generators required fuel. Lines and transformers and switches had to be maintained. Accidents happened, whether courtesy of people or nature. They'd need power to charge their cell phones, for navigation if nothing else. The van had USB ports, but what if they found themselves separated from it in a place with no power?

He ducked into the gas station's store and loaded up on lithium-ion power packs.

Jesse took the wheel and implemented his idea for worming through the chaos. It proved of limited utility. He made use of parking lots and connecting drives to avoid pileups on the streets, but once they got on the highway, there was no refusing whatever it served up.

Will, playing navigator, fiddled with maps on his phone. "We'll make for Pennsylvania," he said. "Maybe the Appalachians north of Harrisburg. That should be a low-population area." Or so he hoped. He was an urban creature with only suppositions about the rest of the world. "We'll be safe there."

"Why so far?"

"What?"

"We want to get back quick when this blows over."

"Blows over!"

"When the disease burns out. When folks crawl out of wherever they's hiding, and—"

"Did you see one living person in the whole damned city?" Will shoved his phone into a cup holder. They were heading west on Interstate 78 toward Allentown, their van a moth flitting toward the westering sun. They hadn't planned to go this way. It just happened. North, south, east, west, all seemed the same until Will started playing with maps.

Jesse squeezed the steering wheel as though to throttle it. "We sure as hell heard them. She's gotta be alive. You got family, too, don't you?"

That was a verbal dagger piercing Will's heart. He nearly took a swing at Jesse's jaw, but his rage sublimated into hopelessness. And then confusion. Where had *that* come from? He'd never hit anyone in his life. That scuffle in the kitchen didn't count. That was self-defense, not malice. And this—Jesse knew nothing of Will's family, nothing of Sarah, not even that she existed, let alone that she'd walked out seven months before. Will had no cause for anger. Not at Jesse. If anger it was. Would he know the difference between anger and madness?

"No," Will said. "Nobody."

Jesse bit his lip.

"Neither do you."

Their tires ate up the road.

Will watched the lane markings stream by. "Granted, we don't know how many survived. Not many, probably. And we don't know what's going to happen. All we can do is stay alive. That means keeping our distance. So keep driving. Let me know when you want me to take over."

"Sounds like you already did."

Jesse drove in silence for three hours, which suited Will. Past Allentown, through rolling farmland, toward Harrisburg. Most of it wasn't horrible. The rural Interstate was dotted with abandoned vehicles. The going was slower in populated areas, where Jesse was forced to weave through greater wreckage and carnage, but it wasn't like earlier. As they approached Harrisburg, he said, "Thank God we're almost away from this. North into the hills, you said. Which exit?"

Will fiddled with his phone. Now that it came to it, he wasn't sure he liked that plan. Maybe it wasn't the crush of New York City, but it wasn't the middle of nowhere. Anyone fleeing Harrisburg, York, Lancaster, even Philadelphia and Pittsburgh might have come this way. Then he questioned that thought. Paranoia? Madness? Good sense? He wished he knew how to tell.

"Change of plans," he said. "Keep going. I'll figure it out."

Jesse shot him a grimace, but on he drove, skirting the dead and the crashes and driverless trucks and once a pile of flaming debris in the middle of the road. The stench suggested tires with something more sinister in the mix. They held their breaths as they passed, gulping air at random intervals until it was behind them.

Picking his way through the map, Will directed Jesse north around the city via I-81, state route 11, and finally I-76, the Pennsylvania Turnpike. As they blew through the toll booth, Will felt a strange guilt. They had no transponder, no means of paying. The van's owner would be stuck with the bill.

No he won't, he told himself. *The guy's dead in Newport.*

Jesse must've thought something similar. "Big time crooks," he said. "Ain't we?"

Soon they were back in farm country with evening fading and dark hills edging the world. They passed into tree-shrouded Appalachian ridges and valleys, through the Blue Mountain and Kittatinny Mountain tunnels, and on and on for two hours until the sun was gone and all color washed from the world. Another two hours brought them to the Midway Service Plaza alongside the town of Bedford. The gas gauge had sunk to near-empty. Jesse pulled off without asking permission.

The wind came in gusts, rattling leaves, tumbling stray bits of paper across the warm asphalt in the glare of the rest stop's lights. Jesse parked where the food was, right at the entrance to the main building. The gas pumps waited beyond the end of the building.

"Shouldn't we be down there?" Will pointed.

"I'm hungry," Jesse said. "And I need the facilities."

"We have food in the back. You don't know what's inside." Will leaned into the windshield and scanned the surround. The parking lot slumbered in the dark, silent, all but vacant. A paltry few cars were scattered here and there. A semi had jackknifed at the far end of the plaza, taking out a diesel pump. Its trailer was burning, but the flames merely licked at the blackened undercarriage like nursing pups. The wreck must have happened some time ago.

Jesse's door creaked open, and he nearly tumbled from the seat. He stretched and motioned toward the building. "Be just a minute," he said. "Get gas if you want. I'll catch up with you."

"Don't," Will commanded.

Jesse did. He made for the door. The light flooding the inside poured out the windows, revealing fast food counters, vending machines, zero employees, zero customers. No one to serve you. No one to take your payment. With luck, no one to throttle you or split your skull. Jesse pushed open the door and passed through as though everything was back to normal.

"I thought you wanted to live," Will muttered. Taking the wheel, he drove to the gas pumps, where he swiped his credit card and filled the tank.

Now, this was strange. You could walk into a store and take whatever you wanted, but you had to pay for gas. Unless, maybe, you knew how to authorize the pump from the register, which Will didn't. Maybe Jesse did. A guy of his background might have worked a gas station or two. Not that it mattered. So long as the computers didn't crash, Will had enough on account to finance their escape. And nothing else to spend it on.

He watched the burning truck while the pump ran. Was this even safe? If not, he'd blow himself up, which would solve all his problems. Maybe that was an insane thought, too. He was having too many of those today. Best not to dwell on that. He finished fueling and washed the van's windows, and Jesse hadn't returned. After dropping the squeegee into the quarter-full fluid reservoir, he drove back to the main building, where he got out, leaned on the van, and waited.

An empty foam cup clattered through the parking lot, propelled by the wind. The pavement and highway beyond, awash in streetlight glow, stood empty save the shadows of a few abandoned cars, most with doors ajar. Something felt wrong. Jesse should have been back with his candy bars by now.

Nerves prickling, Will moved haltingly toward the storefront, gaze darting from cars to windows to the road, to the building, to the van. He paused at the store entrance and listened. Nothing. He pulled the door open a hair, listened again. Still nothing. He went in.

The place was a chaos of cups and trays and bags strewn about the floor and tables. Chairs were overturned, food scattered and stomped into oblivion. Smashed glass was sprayed about. A rotisserie lay sideways on the floor, bleeding cold hot dogs.

And actual blood, lots of it, streaked and smeared about the floor, the tables and chairs, the counters and trash containers. A leg protruded from behind one of the food counters. A dead woman was flopped across it. Will turned his head, but there were others, a dozen or more sprawled among the tables. Against his better judgement, he closed his eyes. The place was silent, cool, not yet tainted by the smell of death.

Then footsteps, slow and quiet. Frozen, he waited for the blow, knowing it didn't matter anymore. The end would come today, tomorrow, in a week. Might as well be now.

"Will?"

He opened his eyes to find Jesse before him, frowning. It felt like a year since his last breath. "Where the hell were you?"

"Restroom." Jesse pointed. "It's safe." He winced at the corpse on the counter. "I'll grab some food and wait outside."

Safe? Hell.

"Not the hot dogs," Will said. He availed himself of the facilities. Back at the van, he found Jesse staring at the darkened bulk of the mountains. The driver's door hung open. A pile of junk food occupied the driver's seat. Jerky. Bags of chips. Candy bars. A few bottles of soda.

"Let's go," Will said, but Jesse didn't move, and neither did he.

The wind swelled and subsided. Clouds were gathering.

"It's over," Jesse said. "It's really over." He swiped at his eyes.

What could Will say?

"How?" Jesse demanded, suddenly angry. "With no warning at all!"

"Life doesn't give you many warnings."

"This ain't life!" Jesse waved at the glowing windows that looked so alive despite the dead bodies beyond.

"Afraid so. You're born to die. Usually more than once. And when you're gone, you're gone, no reward, no punishment, no point, not even a cosmic joke."

"I don't believe that. I *can't* believe that."

"Believe what you like. Your beliefs don't change anything."

"And yours do?"

Will wasn't going down that road. "Get in. We should keep moving." He rounded to the passenger side and climbed in, but Jesse stood his ground and searched the dark for answers. "I said, get in."

"You my boss now?"

Somebody sure needed to be.

The wind grew steady. Will could see nothing in the sky but blotches of greater and lesser dark. Were those storm clouds gathering?

A mad rustling and a series of thumps signaled the food hitting the floor between the seats. The driver's door slammed shut. The engine grumbled to life. Jesse backed out of the parking space and accelerated toward the on-ramp. "How do you die more than once?"

"You know what I mean."

"Nope."

"You will, once you stop denying the obvious."

"Like what?"

Will felt like a teacher cramming knowledge down a willfully obtuse student's throat, only he didn't have the requisite patience. "Lynn's dead. Half of you has been obliterated. How can you not feel it?"

Jesse's fingers tightened on the wheel. "She ain't. No way."

"Dead, disappeared, abducted by aliens." Will looked out the side window, though there was nothing to see. "Walked out one day with no warning or explanation. It's all the same."

They drove for a mile in silence.

"Look," Jesse said, but nothing followed. Not for another mile. Then, "I'm sorry. I didn't know."

Obviously.

A few drops of rain splattered on the windshield.

"What was her name?" Jesse asked.

Will didn't care to remember, although he could hardly help it.

"How long's it been?"

"A day. A lifetime. I don't know."

"No warning at all? Didn't she—"

"Shut up and drive."

Jesse turned the wipers on as the rain grew insistent.

Will leaned back against the headrest and closed his eyes, but in the darkness he saw the dead woman on the counter, so he opened them again and watched water splatter on the windshield, listened to it hammer on the roof of the van.

Jesse turned up the wipers.

Will realized he still had the receipt from the gas pump in his right hand. He looked at the slick scrap but couldn't make out the printing in the darkness. "Did you ever work at a gas station?" he asked.

Jesse glanced at him. "That's a weird question."

"What's the weird answer?"

"No. And I never will. Not after that."

Will crunched the receipt and dropped it on the floor. "No," he agreed. "I don't guess you will."

Emerging from an underpass, Jesse stomped the brake. The van fishtailed on the wet road.

Will threw both hands against the dash and yelped, "What the hell!"

"There." Jesse pointed toward the side of the road. Will peered out the window, expecting to see a gun pointed at them or a bear rearing up or little green men with ray guns. All he saw was a one-lane road breaking off from the shoulder, tracking alongside the overpass. A no parking sign was posted beside the road.

Jesse backed up then drove up that road a hundred or so feet to a closed and locked barrier. A service entrance, probably, for maintenance or emergency vehicles. Not for them.

"What are you doing?" Will asked.

"I'm drifting off," Jesse said. "This is a good place to stop for the night."

"A good place to get attacked, you mean."

"C'mon, it's hidden by the overpass. I wouldn't of seen it if I wasn't looking to stop. Kill the lights, and we're invisible." He did so. Darkness enveloped them. "Right?"

Maybe. Probably. Not that Will was about to admit it. "Where's that jerky?"

Jesse rummaged through the pickings from the service plaza. "Here you go. *Bon appétit.*"

His fake French accent was terrible.

Jesse slept like someone had koshed him on the head with a brick. Will, not so much. The seat wasn't comfortable, no matter how he leaned it. The night cold seeped in. He heard noises that weren't there. At least twice, once around midnight and once at two thirty in the morning, a car swished by on the turnpike. He heard the rush and caught the vanishing red glow of the taillights.

Who were they, where they were going? Were they sane or disease-maddened? What was this sickness, anyway? Where had it come from, how many had it killed, how many had it spared? Had it taken his friends? Not that he had close friends, but colleagues. Workday friends. Suraj, Chloe, David, Nathan, Erasmo, Travis, Jenny, Joel...

Stop it.

Lynn? Sarah?

Stop, damn it!

He couldn't stop, not where Sarah was concerned. Why not? Did he care? Maybe. Probably. A bit. The first two months he'd spent deep in grief. The next three he'd tried to move on, tried to bury himself in his work. And then two months of denial, telling the world and himself that everything was fine, he was over it, he could be his own man again. All lies. The grief remained, prowling the dark recesses of his mind, waiting for this moment to spring, take him down, disembowel him, consume him.

He had but one defense: indifference. Whether above or below ground, mad or sane, she was dead to him.

I don't care, he lied and knew it to be a lie.

He must have slept at some point, because he opened his eyes to an orange sunrise bathing the mountain forest in blood tones.

Jesse wasn't in his seat. Alarmed, Will fumbled for the door latch, but before he got it open, Jesse climbed in behind the wheel.

"Where were you?" Will demanded.

"Where d'you think? Taking a leak."

Will threw himself back in his seat and huffed.

"Nobody's here. It's safe."

"You scared me."

"More'n New York? This is almost normal." Jesse picked some jerky out of his hoard and handed a pack to Will. "'Cept this. This ain't a normal breakfast."

Will took the offering, stuffed it in his pocket, and opened his door.

"Where you off to?" Jesse asked.

"Where d'you think?" he mocked. "It's my turn."

Will took the wheel for the next two hours, three, three and a half. The radio played only static. At every population center, he messed with the tuner and found nothing save the hiss of emptiness. Just west of Zanesville, Ohio he gave it another go. Still nothing.

"Quit playing with it," Jesse snapped. "I hate that noise."

"It's worth a try."

"Is not."

"Says the guy who thinks his girlfriend is still alive."

Jesse stabbed the power button, and the static ceased. "Says the guy who says we're alone. Quit playing with it. Why you always act like you're in charge?"

If Jesse quit whining, it'd be worth giving up on the radio. "Habit. I was a manager for ten years."

"And I'm just a dumb black kid."

"I didn't say that."

"You don't have to. It's in your eyes."

"What, you're a psychiatrist?"

"No, just a dumb black kid who works—worked—a loading dock. Admit it, that's what you think."

"Don't play the race card on me. That's nothing to do—"

"Damn straight it is," Jesse insisted. "You may not know it, but it's there."

Will's grip on the steering wheel tightened. Too bad he couldn't control the conversation as easily as the van.

"Score one for the dumb black kid."

"You're a thousand miles off."

"Go on, then. What *do* you see when you look at me?"

"Shut up."

"C'mon. You can't offend me, 'cause I already know."

"Got me all figured out, do you?"

"Pretty much."

Fine. The idiot deserved a shot of truth. "Young, inexperienced, no degree, probably not even a high school diploma, no goals, no ambition, no prospects. You'd have been on that loading dock your whole damn life, and that's if you were lucky. I'll bet you proposed to Lynn so she could support you."

"Wow," Jesse breathed in mock admiration. "Got black written all over me, don't I?"

"Don't be stupid."

"At least I ain't in denial."

"You think she's still alive!"

"And you think you're right about everything."

"Wasn't I?"

"Hardly. 'Cept one thing. I don't got a degree."

Close enough, Will figured. "I have an MBA."

"I got a telescope."

Will glanced at him. What the hell did that have to do with anything?

"Didn't even steal it. Saved up for it. Not that it's much, just a six-inch F8 Dobsonian, but better than nothing." Jesse grinned at the road. "Don't even know what that means, do you, Mr. MBA?" He slid down in the seat and looked at his fingers. His smile slid, too, and his voice took on a haunted quality. "Took it up on the roof sometimes, me and Lynn. Looked at the moon and planets and some double stars. Couldn't see much else with all the light pollution. Alberio's beautiful in a scope, though. Silver and gold. That was our favorite. I'd tell her it was us. A beautiful couple."

Will wouldn't have pegged him for a science buff. Or a poet. Or much of anything, really.

Jesse pulled himself up in the seat. "I was doing night classes. Computers. A few more years and I'd of been off that loading dock. Now..." He shook his head. "Don't count for much now. No more than your MBA."

That was a fair point. More than fair, now Will thought about it. "I guess that never did count for much. Just money." He laughed. "Gas money." He gazed ahead down the long, empty road stretching before them. "Her name was Sarah. I don't know why she left. One day she was there, the next..." He shrugged.

Jesse nodded. "Why never matters. Gone is gone."

They passed an exit sign. "I'm pulling off," Will said. "We're pretty far out here. It ought to be safe. Maybe we can find an empty house to adopt."

Jesse smirked. "Steal, you mean?"

"Whatever."

"Sign said Gratiot." Jesse pronounced it like *idiot* but with a long *a*. "Is that how you say it?"

"Looks French," Will told him. "Maybe Gray-schwa."

"You French?"

"No."

"You speak French?"

"No."

Another smirk. "Then how d'you know?"

That wasn't worth a response. Will guided the van down the exit ramp, past corn and soybean fields until they came to an isolated house with a small cluster of outbuildings: garage, barn, smaller structures whose purpose he couldn't guess. He pulled into the gravel drive. The van's tires crunched over the rock until they came to a halt beside the house. They studied the windows, the door, the tidy lawn, the drive curving by the other buildings. Nothing moved, not even a bird.

"Seems empty," Jesse said.

"Seems," Will agreed. "Only one way to find out."

Neither moved.

"We got guns back there," Jesse said. "Want one?"

Will figured Jesse probably knew guns better than he, but that would likely restart the argument. "I've never fired a gun in my life."

Jesse surprised him again. "Me, neither. I watched my daddy a few times. He was in the army before I was born, did some target shooting when I was little, 'til his arthritis got bad."

"You never learned?"

With a grunt, Jesse crawled into the back of the van. "Never cared for noise. Or violence. Saw too much of that." There was distance in his voice, the faint echo of a memory from afar. "Yeah, here we go. Gun, ammo. You're smart, you can figure it out."

He passed the weapon to Will and crawled back into his seat holding a box of shotgun shells as though they were poison. Will examined the gun and fiddled with the bolt. It opened with a click. "I suppose they go in here," he said. "Let's get out before we mess with it. I don't want to shoot out the windshield."

They climbed out and eased the doors shut to avoid making noise. Will examined the gun. How was he supposed to know what to do with it? Leaning it against the car, he got out his phone and searched for loading instructions. What he had, he discovered, was a pump action shotgun. Following the directions, he loaded up three shells and operated the pump to chamber the first. It wasn't difficult, although he wondered how fast he could get three shots off, if necessary. He ought to try it out, but not here, not now. Until they knew the house was empty, the need for quiet outweighed the need for target practice.

He motioned for the door.

Their footfalls crunched at double volume—or so Will felt—as they crossed the gravel drive to the concrete walk and mounted the wooden porch. They stopped before a white door with a square window bisected horizontally and vertically into four panes. A lace curtain on the inside veiled the glass. Within, they could see only shadows of indistinct furnishings. Nothing moved.

Will tested the doorknob, which turned easily. At his touch, the door creaked open. Jesse winced at the sound. Then they waited, breath held. Stillness prevailed. Gun barrel leading, Will stepped over the threshold.

He came into a living room with a wood stove, an old green couch, two matching easy chairs, and a CRT television. He stared at the unit, a relic of a lost world. But all TVs were now, with no faces left to fill their screens, no voices left to vibrate their speakers.

Jesse tapped Will's shoulder and pointed right, where a door framed in dark moldings opened on the kitchen. There, on a table draped with a white tablecloth, the remains of somebody's meal were spread: an open loaf of bread, a jar of peanut butter, a dish of grape jelly, a plate dotted with crumbs, a glass containing a splash of water.

They slipped into the kitchen like mice intent upon raiding it. Jesse touched the jelly dish. "My grandmother made jelly like this," he whispered. "The dish is cold."

Will nodded toward the back, where a doorway led to a lightless room. The only sound was their own breathing, yet shadows seemed to swirl in the dark. Both men lacked the courage to provoke them, so they trembled in place for some minutes. Then something did move.

Gathering a bit of light to itself, it advanced one halting step at a time until the form of a man materialized from the shadows and came without sound into the light of the kitchen. A grandfather, maybe a great-grandfather, he was short, bald, clad in tattered jeans and a filthy t-shirt. He held his wrinkled hands half up, palms out, while his mouth twitched without sound.

Will licked his lips. Jesse gulped.

"You with *them*?" the man asked.

"Them?" Jesse's voice quivered, though it was only one syllable.

"*Them*," the man repeated. Slow and deliberate, he pointed an unsteady finger at the window.

"We didn't see anyone," Will replied.

"No." The man squinted at the window. "You don't. They hide. In the barn. Behind the barn. In the fields. They wait for night."

"Infected people?" It seemed logical, but as soon as he'd said it, he realized logic had fled this place. The diseased didn't hide in the shadows. They raged in the streets.

"Worse. Lots worse."

"It's okay," Jesse said. "We got a gun."

"Gun's no good. Fire, that's the ticket. Burn them. Burn everything, down to the ground!" He slapped his hands together. They made a sharp crack.

Will shivered at the hatred in the man's voice.

Jesse backed a step and glanced at the door as though making sure it hadn't vanished. "That what you did?"

"Couldn't find the matches. Used to have boxes of them, hundreds of boxes, but they stole them. Snuck in in the dead of night and took every last one."

"Who are they?" Will asked. He let the gun barrel slide toward the man's chest, or as near as possible. Now that it came to it, he found it hard to draw a bead on a human being. But he had no choice. Something wasn't right, be it the old man's mind or demons lurking in the darkness behind him.

"Skulls." The old man shuddered. "Skull people, with black, empty sockets and boney fingers that grope for your neck and voices that whisper in your head, controlling you, making you do hideous, hideous things." He wrapped his arms about himself and shivered.

Jesse imitated the action and murmured, "Oh, hell."

"You're with them, aren't you?" the man said. His fear morphed into fury. "You're with them!"

Awash with adrenaline, Will couldn't hold the gun steady. "No, no, look at us. Look at us! We're just people!"

"Your eyes are on me! You're trying to hypnotize me!" With a terrified, terrifying scream, the man rushed Will. The gun discharged, blowing holes in the cabinetry. Wooden shrapnel flew everywhere. Glass shattered. Jesse screamed and dropped to the floor in a ball, hands covering his head. The man grabbed the barrel with both hands and tried to wrench it from Will's grasp. Will pulled the trigger again, but nothing happened. For a moment that seemed an eternity, he didn't understand. Both men fought for possession of the gun, locked in a futile tug-of-war, and then as though on autopilot Will remembered the forestock, slammed it back and forward, and squeezed the life from the trigger. Another explosion filled his ears, the room, the universe. The old man's eyes went wide with shock. His mouth hung open in horror, and he fell, blood pouring from his wounds.

Will dropped the gun. Stumbling backward, he fell to his knees.

"No," he moaned. "Oh, no. I...no...Jesse...I..."

Jesse uncurled like a flower opening in the sun. He sat gasping as though he'd run a marathon. He stared at the corpse and the pooling blood. "Oh my God," he breathed. "Oh my God, what did you do?"

Will put his hands on his knees and gulped mouthfuls of air.

"You killed him!"

"I know! I know, damn it, I *know*!" Will fought his way to his feet and forced himself to look on his handiwork. He felt like throwing up. Somehow, he didn't.

"What did you do?"

He didn't know. He only knew one thing, as he had known just one thing as he plowed through the New York madness in his Navigator. "I had to. You heard him. You saw him. I had no choice."

Grabbing at a chair, Jesse struggled into it and bent over, head in hands.

"You saw," Will repeated. And to himself he chanted, *No choice, no choice, no choice.* He might have said it a hundred times, a thousand, but did he believe it? Probably. Maybe. Who knew? Maybe it was an accident. He'd been scared. Hell, he was *still* scared. He lifted his hands and watched them shake.

"Yeah," Jesse said. "I saw." He stood and nudged the gun with his foot. "I saw. You did the right thing."

The affirmation didn't convince Will, but at least there would be no argument.

Jesse stared at the body, at the gun, at the body. He swallowed hard. "We can't leave him here. Not if we're going to stay."

"No." Will gazed about the antiquated kitchen. What would they need for body disposal? What did they have? He could think of only one thing. "Gloves."

"What?"

"He was infected. We should wear gloves. When we move him."

Jesse looked at his own hands, flexed his fingers, turned them over. "Sure," he said. "And hope it's not airborne."

Jesse could tell Will wasn't as in command as he let on, so he searched the outbuildings for what they needed. He found work gloves and shovels in the garage and behind the barn a neat mound of dirt marked with a makeshift wooden cross. On the cross, written in blue chalk, was a name: Martha. They buried the old man next to her.

Jesse insisted on a cross for him, too. That was proper, whether Will cared or not. Finding a small pile of splintered wood tucked into a dark corner of the barn, Jesse made the marker himself. The only thing missing was the deceased's name.

"It'll be in the house somewhere," he suggested.

"I'm not rummaging through his stuff." Will started for the house.

"We ain't done. We need a prayer."

"Your department, not mine."

Wouldn't hurt you to try, Jesse griped to himself, but that wasn't about to happen. Will had either lost his faith or never had any to begin with. Probably the second. People didn't much lose faith. Sometimes they mislaid it. That's what his grandpa used to say, anyway.

Jesse wracked his brain for suitable words, but they wouldn't come. Watching Will's retreating back, he fell into a dark pool of loneliness. For the first time, it sunk in. Everyone he'd ever known was gone, and here he was, alone beside a stranger's grave, just as the old man had been alone when he buried Martha.

Jesse closed his eyes, bowed his head, and folded his hands before him. "Grant him peace, Lord," he whispered. "It wasn't his fault." The appeal seemed insignificant, unnecessary even, but it was all he had. He trudged back to the house and the kitchen. Will wasn't there. Nor was the gun.

Jesse tensed. The house was as silent as death.

Until Will's head popped through the darkened doorway in back. "Come here," he said.

Heart in his throat, Jesse grabbed at a chair for support. "Don't *do* that!"

"Do what? Come here, look at this."

The room beyond proved little more than a storage area. Will led him through to a brighter, larger space, a bedroom with a four-poster and a couple of ornate chests of drawers. A full-length mirror hung in the middle of one wall, reflecting light from the single window opposite it. On the pale yellow walls, blue markings had been scratched around the window.

"Chalk," Will said. "Like on the grave marker."

Not quite. These weren't words.

Jesse didn't know what to make of them. Each one a letter slipping toward a picture, a picture sliding into a letter, they suggested wheels and arrows and bolts of lightning, a torrent of falling icicles, illegible scrawls in the margins of a book. They streamed out from the window and the mirror, spreading toward and meeting in the corners of the room.

"What do you think it means?" Will asked.

"It means I ain't sleeping in this room. I'll take the couch."

Jesse returned to the living room without Will, where he sat and listened to the unnatural quiet and wondered how long the old man and his wife Martha—she must have been his wife—had lived here. Where were the children? Had disease driven him mad, or had Martha's death? Or both?

On an end table beside the couch, beneath a gold lamp with a cream shade, a Bible rested. Jesse picked it up. As though handling an ancient text, he opened to the frontispiece, a sprawling oak marked with names. A family tree.

Matthew Buhler, father. Mary (Conrad) Buhler, mother. David Buhler, son, married to Martha Volker. Issuing from that union, three children, eight grandchildren, and two great-grandchildren crowded the page. Birth years were listed for everyone. David had been eighty-nine, Martha eighty-four.

Jesse cradled the Bible as tears ran down his cheeks.

"What's wrong?"

Will had come in, gun tucked under his arm, barrel pointed at the floor. *One kill*, Jesse thought, *and you already look like a pro.* He offered the Bible to Will.

Will studied the family tree without laying a hand on the book before claiming an easy chair at the side of the room. He leaned his head back, closed his eyes, and stretched his legs. He looked like hell.

Yeah, okay, he'd been through hell. They both had. "You probably did him a favor," Jesse said.

"If you're trying to make me feel better, don't bother."

"Just saying."

"Sure."

Jesse settled the Bible back on the end table, making sure he replaced it just as it had been. "His name was David."

"So I saw."

"He was a great-grandfather. Martha was his wife. She must have—"

"Shut up."

Jesse folded his arms over his chest and stared at nothing. It didn't seem right, refusing to acknowledge the couple, like they hadn't existed. But maybe that was how Will coped.

Will absently ran a finger over the gunstock. "This is life now. It'll happen again. And again. And again." Jaw set firm as though biting back a scream, he added, "We have to be ready."

How could anyone be ready for this? For monsters in men's skins? For gunning down old men and maybe young women whose tortured minds no longer knew friend from foe? For one of them to topple into madness and attack the other?

For the one with the gun to slip over the edge?

There was no ready. There was only this moment. Jesse pushed himself to his feet. "Is the chalk back there?"

"Chalk?"

"Yeah, the blue chalk."

"Why?"

"To put David's name on his cross."

Will said nothing.

Jesse went in search. After rummaging through drawers in the bedroom, he found the chalk and performed his final service for the deceased. When he returned, he found Will in the kitchen, dumping green beans from a can into a saucepan. That, canned corn, and wheat bread served as their lunch.

"I don't want to stay here, after all," Will said after the meal. "We should check our supplies, maybe load up on whatever is here. We'll move on in the morning."

"To where?"

"Anywhere but here."

Jesse had to admit, the place felt haunted. "Another farmhouse?"

"Maybe. But farther west. The farther west you go, the less people there are."

Jesse pushed his plate away. "'Cept in Chicago."

"Great, you know your geography. Ever been out of New York?"

"Course not. You?"

"A few times. Once even to Chicago."

Jesse figured he was supposed to laugh. He didn't.

5

MORNING. A thin line of deep blue in the east, a flotilla of altocumulus overhead, darkness hovering in the west. Jesse drove. As they approached Columbus, Will fiddled with the radio again, finding only static. From the farm, they had pilfered additional supplies, including canned and dried food and twine. They had run their clothes through the wash and now looked semi-presentable again, aside from the stubble on their faces. The Buhlers had owned a shotgun, but Will didn't see the need for three, so he left that. The shells he took.

Firearms were on his mind as they drew near the city. In particular, the possibility of having to use them. The loaded shotgun felt heavy lying across his lap. The road, median, and shoulders were strewn with cars and trucks and bodies. Jesse slowed to a crawl to weave among them. Will detected no sign of anyone living, but they might be out there. He could feel them watching, waiting. They were no more than ghosts haunting his imagination, yet somehow they had substance. His fingers tightened on the weapon. "We should practice," he said.

"Practice?"

"Shooting.

Jesse made a face. "If praying's my department, shooting can be yours."

"Shooting better be both our departments."

"Praying, too."

Will didn't see where that provided the protection of a firearm and good aim, but he kept his mouth shut. Sooner or later, Jesse would be forced to pick up a gun, and no amount of praying would change it.

For now, Jesse's mind was on the road, not firearms. He drove the grim slalom, faster when he could, slower when he must. The nearer the city drew, the more obstacles cluttered their path. The sky darkened in the distance. At first, he thought a storm was blowing up, but the cloud resolved into a column of black smoke ascending to heaven. It lofted on the wind, feathered into streamers, and dispersed. As they closed on it, a hell-red glare flickered at its base, throwing down shadows that danced on the road.

Jesse braked a quarter mile before the fire. "Whatever it is, it's in the road. Got a detour?"

Will pulled up the map on his phone. "Did we pass I-270?"

"A couple miles back. Is that someone moving?"

"Where?"

Jesse pointed. "Left of the fire."

Low shadows loped along the asphalt.

"Dogs," Will said.

"Too big for dogs."

The creatures moved among the dead and the wreckage, pausing over a body here, pushing at one there.

Will revised his identification. "Coyotes, maybe."

"What they doing?" As soon as Jesse said it, he realized what a stupid question it was.

"Turn around," Will said. "We'll go around the city."

The coyotes, noses down, began to feast.

Jesse pinched his eyes shut and shuddered.

"Drive," Will commanded.

Executing a U-turn, Jesse drove the wrong way back to I-270, where another U-turn deposited them on the exit ramp. While there was no fire here, the beltway proved equally cluttered, and other scavengers had come to breakfast. Turkey and black vultures. A fox here, an opossum there. Will tried not to look. Jesse kept his eyes on the jagged path through the carnage. But sometimes neither could help but see. When he finally hit a clear stretch of highway, what they'd just seen finally overwhelmed Jesse. He hit the brake, threw the gear into park, and fled the van for the shoulder. He doubled over, grabbed the guardrail, and retched.

When it stopped, his lungs sucked in the cool morning air like it was his first breath ever. With the blinding morning sun still on his right, he focused on the low buildings and greenery of Westerville. All was quiet save the whisper of wind and the symphony of morning birdsong, but the calm was illusion. In normal times, the place would have hummed with rush hour traffic. This silence bespoke tragedy, not peace. Still, he drank it up. If it was still possible to live anywhere anymore, he could see abandoning New York for this. Almost. The dead strewn about like spilled French fries and the scavengers feasting upon them resurrected the memory of his younger brother Martin lying in a pool of blood while gang member vultures picked through his meager possessions.

No. He mustn't dwell on that. Nothing could bring Martin back. Nothing could bring anyone back. He asked but one thing, just one, just the smallest of favors. *Please, God, please let Lynn be alive. Please bring us back together.*

He almost laughed at himself for stretching one favor into two. But really, it was just one. He had to see her, had to hold her again, else they would both be as good as dead.

He shoved his hands into his pockets and shuffled back to the van.

Will was waiting in the road in front of the grille, staring into the distant west. He might have been a statue of a once famous, now forgotten explorer frozen in bronze. Jesse silently joined him. Maybe Lewis and Clarke had looked like this. *Nah,* Jesse thought. *Neither of them was black.* Anyway, no unexplored lands waited beneath the gray clouds smeared on the horizon.

"You okay?" Will asked.

"Yeah."

"Want me to drive?"

"Nah."

Neither moved. A turkey vulture soared overhead. A dog barked in the distance.

"When I shot the old man…" Will shrugged.

"David," Jesse reminded him. "Buhler."

"David. It's not that I don't care. I wish I hadn't had to do it. I wish none of this had happened."

And I wish Martin had seen his eighteenth birthday, Jesse thought. *A lot of things happen that shouldn't. Damn, ol' Will was right about something, after all.*

The dog barked again, very close. The men turned. Near the side of the highway, a white and tan animal watched, tail down, head cocked. It whined, then yipped.

"What's that?" Jesse asked. "A beagle?"

"I don't know. I never owned a dog."

The dog took a few tentative steps, stopped, barked once.

"Doesn't look dangerous." Jesse bent over and held out his hand.

"Don't encourage it. Let's get going."

Will was probably right about this, too. The dog might be dangerous, rabid, even. Though, it didn't look it, didn't move, didn't do anything but whimper. Probably it was just hungry. Still, better safe than sorry.

Jesse got behind the wheel. Will had just taken his seat and was about to close his door when, in a blur of white, the animal bolted and made a leap worthy of Superman, landing in his lap. Startled, Will grunted and nearly pushed the dog out, but it flopped on him, whining, and hooked its front paws over his thigh. It looked up at him as though begging forgiveness for being so forward.

Jesse laughed. "Looks like you made a friend."

"I don't want a friend."

"Oh, c'mon, look at him. He's not dangerous. Let him stay."

"Not a good idea."

"It's fine. Scratch him behind the ears. Or her. Is he a he or a she?"

"How should I know? All I can see is the top side."

"Close your door."

"What about the dog?

Jesse rolled from his seat and rummaged in the back of the van. "We got some jerky left." Plastic rattled. "Yeah, here we go." Returning with a package, he ripped it open and offered a piece to the dog, which grabbed it and nearly swallowed it whole. "Here, you do the honors."

Will reluctantly took the package and fed the dog another piece. "He—she—whatever—can't live on this stuff."

"We'll find some dog food. Close your door."

"This isn't a good idea," Will repeated, but he closed the door, and Jesse drove.

The expressway remained an obstacle course, littered with the dead and their abandoned, crashed, and overturned vehicles. The dog ate half the package of jerky, then it fell asleep in Will's lap and refused to wake even when he leaned his forearms on it to steady his phone and study the map. Will directed Jesse northwest via U.S. 33 towards Marysville, Bellefontaine, and Wapakoneta.

"Where you taking us?" Jesse asked. "Most of Ohio's behind us now."

"I don't know. Indiana, maybe."

"You can't run forever."

He wasn't running. He was searching. But if he said so, it would spawn another argument. "True," he said. "Eventually I'll die."

That hadn't been the right thing to say, either. Jesse shot him one of those looks.

They passed through small-town and rural Ohio, where death sprawled in front yards and desolation lurked in the fields that had once fed the nation but now had none to tend them.

"Somebody must be out there," Jesse said two hours later as they left behind Willshire, Ohio, population four hundred last week, zero today, and entered Indiana farmland. "You'd think a town like that, somebody musta pulled through."

"Do the math," Will said. "Only two of us got out of New York City."

"Two you know of," Jesse objected.

Will refused to count anyone he couldn't verify. "Two out of twenty million. That's one one-hundred-thousandth of a percent. The whole of Ohio is probably lucky to have one guy left alive."

"I'm just saying, New York's crowded. Small towns got more space. People could of kept their distance. The disease might not of hit everyone."

The dog was awake now, lying on the floor between the men, poking its nose under the seats. Will absently reached down and scratched it behind the ears. So far, the animal had been the only one who came running when they drove by. Humans might not be so eager to make a stranger's acquaintance, of course, but if any had survived, they'd be longing to know they weren't alone. Which argued eradication.

Fields and farmhouses passed by, yielding no hints of life. Death dotted the roadside and yards. The dog climbed into Will's lap, looked out the window, and whined.

"Time for a break," Jesse suggested. The road had little shoulder, so he stopped on the pavement. When Will opened his door, the dog bolted into the grass and squatted.

"Girl," Jesse commented. "She needs a name."

She ran back and forth along the roadside, sniffing everything. Will had no talent for naming things. That was Sarah's gift. Sarah named everything: cars, condos, even his suits when they were first married. She called one Mr. President, because—she said—it looked like something a U.S. president might wear. Another became Uncle Wayne, after her used car salesman uncle.

The dog made another pass, still sniffing and rooting. Then she stopped, thrust her nose into a clump of weeds, and whined. She looked back at Will and whined again. He didn't care to risk finding out, but he supposed he'd better. He joined the dog in the grass and knelt to investigate.

She hadn't located a corpse. Not exactly. It was a doll, run through with a steak knife. The blade protruded from the doll's back, its hilt tight against the chest. "Good girl," he said. "Come on." Picking up the find, he withdrew the knife and dropped it on the ground. He returned to the van with the dog trotting by his side and handed the doll to Jesse. "More weirdness."

Jesse turned the doll over a few times, examining the wound. "Daphne," he suggested.

"Daphne?"

"The smart girl from *Scooby Doo*."

Will didn't see the resemblance. "I doubt it."

"Not the doll, the dog."

Daphne sat, wagged her tail, and licked her lips.

"Daphne works," Will said. "Let's get some treats for a job well done." He opened the passenger door and Daphne vaulted in.

Jesse tossed the doll away and got behind the wheel. They continued down the road, all three chewing on jerky sticks.

Decatur, Indiana was ablaze. Flames licked the sky while devouring the town's trees, homes, and businesses. Jesse saw it first, well before reaching the city, and asked Will for a detour.

Working his phone, Will directed Jesse down country roads to keep clear of the devastation. West of town, they took U.S. 224 into the heart of northern Indiana, flying through small towns, passing corn, soybean, and wheat fields at speed. They stopped for nothing and slowed only to avoid obstacles in the road. There were enough of those, particularly in the towns. Cars. Tractors. Dead animals. Dead people. "It's like some macabre video game," Jesse muttered.

Will grunted in disinterested agreement. Jesse figured he didn't play video games. Daphne alternately whimpered at the window and tucked herself into the space between the front seats, feigning sleep.

A silent forty minutes later, approaching Huntington, smoke and flame again greeted them. Will detoured Jesse around the town to U.S. 24. "We should make Peoria, Illinois, by sunset," he said.

"So much for Indiana," Jesse griped.

"If you're tired, I can drive."

"It ain't I'm tired. Anyway, I'd rather operate the vehicle than the weaponry."

The highway bypassed Andrews and Lagro, towns of barely one thousand souls and four hundred respectively, both ablaze. Likewise Wabash, where Will had to improvise a route. Daphne climbed into his lap and watched the town burn, nose twitching, ears flattened.

"I don't get it," Jesse said as they put the inferno behind them. "Why would only the Indiana towns burn?"

"Maybe pyromania only manifests if you live long enough."

It wasn't a joke, but Jesse couldn't help it. He laughed.

"I'm serious."

"I know. It's just..." He laughed again. "The world's gone mad, right? What else can you do?"

"Use your brain," Will suggested. "Maybe different strains of the disease cause different behavioral..." He looked down the road as though the word he wanted might be lying there among the scattered bodies and debris.

"Lunacy," Jesse suggested.

"Abnormalities."

"If you say so. To me, it's just insanity. Damn!" He slammed on the brakes. Tires squealed. The van fishtailed to a halt as a deer vaulted across the road, followed by another, another, another. A small herd of the animals poured through, oblivious to the van's presence.

Daphne jumped into Will's lap and growled until they were gone. Will craned his neck to watch as they crossed a field and vanished into a stand of woods. "Is that nature coming back?"

"Nah, places like this are up to their noses in deer. Maybe they go mad, too." Jesse continued down the road. "How d'you know a deer's insane?"

"Is that a joke?"

"Just a question. I got no answer. You?"

"No clue."

"Think about it, though. A world full of looney deer, squirrels, rabbits, cats, dogs." He glanced at Daphne, who was still in Will's lap, watching the fields pass by, nose twitching. Maybe that hadn't been a smart thing to say.

Will patted Daphne on the back. "Viruses jump from animals to people sometimes. Why not from people to animals?"

No, not at all smart. Daphne going for their throats while the van was in motion...damn, that was a scary image.

Halfway between Peru and Logansport, Will called for a halt as they crossed the Wabash River. Jesse stopped where the bridge deck abutted the asphalt. They climbed out. Daphne bounded after, then ran madly into the grass. She checked out a wire fence along the top of the riverbank, skittered onto the bridge and sniffed along the barrier overlooking the water, then returned to the grass and squatted. The men relieved themselves, too, taking widely separate positions along the line of trees, their backs to the farmhouse half a mile or more down the road as though someone might be watching.

After, Jesse wandered onto the bridge and leaned over the barrier, staring into the olive green water flowing by. Its gurgle accompanied the rustling of leaves in the trees lining the banks. He'd seen the East River and the Hudson, surrounded by the constant roar of the city, but they weren't like this. This was a river to sit by, barefoot, with a fishing pole in your hands and the sun overhead and no place you had to be for an entire day. It was a river to picnic beside with your girl and lie in the grass and make love and take a nap and watch the sun go down and the stars come out.

"We should go." Will had come up beside him. He leaned on the concrete, too, and stared into the water. What did this river mean to him? Did it remind him of good times with Sarah? Or did it conjure no memories, no hopes, no dreams of any kind? His face was a blank slate, revealing nothing.

Jesse felt tears running down his face. Embarrassed, he straightened and wiped them away. Daphne was at his feet, sitting very proper, watching as though expecting more treats. Having got his attention, she barked.

"I guess you're right," Jesse told her. "Tell Will it's time to go." To Will, he said, "The dog's in charge now, so we don't argue 'bout who gives the orders." As he started for the van, a glint of light in the distance caught his eye. Up the road, something approached. Fast. "Uh, Will?"

Will turned. Daphne ran toward the van, stopped when she realized they weren't following, and barked at them.

The object resolved itself into a red pickup racing toward them. Sunlight flashed from the windshield as the rush of its motion grew.

"Damn it," Will said. "I left the gun in the van."

"Maybe they won't stop," Jesse suggested.

"Or maybe they're a homicidal lunatic." Will motioned to the end of the bridge. "Come on, let's get off the road."

Jesse didn't think it was a good time to remind him Daphne was in charge. They trotted around the barrier and ducked behind. Daphne rejoined them. She sat beside them, nose twitching. Will scratched her behind the ears. "Good girl," he said. "Stay quiet, now."

The rush grew and passed them by, but then brakes squealed. Someone shouted words they couldn't resolve. Gunfire erupted, blasting holes in the sky or the trees or the concrete of the bridge. They couldn't tell which, but explosion after explosion sounded while they clapped their hands over their ears and squeezed their eyes shut. And then all fell quiet for a moment, before the truck roared to life and faded away.

Daphne ran onto the shoulder and barked at the retreating vehicle. Fortunately, she didn't draw it back. Shaking, Jesse crept to the road and peered out from behind the barrier. The world appeared as it had before, just the three of them. Emerging from hiding, Will growled something and rushed the van. He circled it, inspecting.

Jesse joined him. "Any damage?"

"The front driver's side tire is flat. A few holes on the side of the engine compartment."

Jesse looked it over, too, touching the bullet holes to assure himself they were real. They were. It wasn't a nightmare. "I hope you know how to change a tire," he said.

"Don't you?"

"Nope."

"I guess I can manage. Assuming we have a spare."

They opened the back doors, shoved supplies aside, and found the jack and lug wrench stowed in a compartment under the floor. But no tire, not inside. Will got on his knees and found it under the vehicle's chassis. It took some thought and experimentation to unstow the thing, but eventually they had it out, the front of the van jacked up, and the flat removed. Daphne lay on the road, watching the operation.

While Will placed the spare onto the wheel and hand-tightened the lug nuts, Jesse rubbed the back of his neck. "I don't get it," he said.

"Don't get what?"

"Crazy guy shooting the place up. Why isn't he dead already?"

"Maybe it doesn't kill you," Will said. He lowered the van until the tires touched the road, then he began tightening the nuts. "That's what they said on the news the first day. The dead were all killed in the fighting. Or had killed themselves."

"So he's the last survivor from some town or farm?"

"Maybe. Or maybe it affects different people differently. Some die fast and some slow."

Jesse kicked a stone out of the road. "Or maybe he caught it late."

"Maybe."

"Then maybe we ain't here 'cause we're immune. We could still catch it."

Will finished cranking down the van. He packed up the jack and slammed shut the doors, then wiped his hands together as though that would clean them. It didn't.

"The future," Jesse said, "don't look too good."

"It hasn't since the day we met. You think that's a coincidence?" Will looked around but didn't find whatever he wanted. "I'm going down to the river."

"Why?"

"To wash my hands." He trekked back to the bridge. Daphne leaped to her feet and trotted after him.

Jesse set his hands on his hips and watched them go. "Traitor," he muttered.

6

THEY REACHED the outskirts of Peoria shortly before sunset. On approach, the town appeared normal if dead. No flames. No smoke. The closer it grew, the more debris and bodies littered the road, but that felt commonplace now. Will wasn't sure if he should find comfort or terror in that. Either way, spare tires concerned him more. They no longer had one, which fact gnawed at him until he told Jesse they had to find one. Or two. Or three. Which meant locating a donor vehicle. Jesse agreed.

Before long, they spotted a Walmart off an exit. They made for it and cruised the parking lot. A strange scene, it put Will in mind of a Salvidor Dali painting, maybe *The Persistence of Memory*. Or rather, *The Disintegration of the Persistence of Memory*: the regularity of the lanes and lined parking spaces half filled with neatly parked vehicles; the confusion of wrecked cars, overturned shopping carts, spilled merchandise, and mangled bodies. Sprawled on top of a white Tesla Model S, the naked body of a young woman stared visionless into the sky. She might have wandered in from another of the master's paintings, *Dream Caused by the Flight of a Bee Around a Pomegranate a Second Before Awakening*. She was that beautiful, save the dried river of red spilling from her shoulder down the windshield.

"There," Jesse said, pointing to a white Ford Econoline. "Just our size." They stopped to investigate. The vehicle was locked. The owner must have been in the store when insanity struck. Will dug out the tire iron from the back of their ProMaster and smashed the Econoline's driver's window to gain entry.

Jesse stood watch, grinning like an idiot.

"What's so funny?" Will asked.

"White guy doing a smash and grab," he said.

"At least he's doing *something*. How about helping me?"

Jesse did, sort of. He shone a flashlight on the lug nuts while Will worked in the gathering dark and Daphne trotted around the parking lot, sniffing at tires and trash and bodies. Will called her back, but she hadn't quite gotten her name yet. Besides, her finds proved too interesting to rush. She might have been a detective, sifting evidence to solve the riddle of a mass murder.

It required time and care to ensure he didn't drop a Ford on his foot, but eventually Will boosted all four tires plus the spare and piled them in the back of the ProMaster. The Econoline now sat forlorn on bare wheels. Not that it was going anywhere.

"That should do it," Will told Jesse as he wiped his filthy hands on a wad of paper towels.

"Sure," Jesse agreed. "So long as we don't get shot at too much."

"We only lost one tire crossing three and a half states. The odds are on our side, I'd say."

"When's the last time odds were on our side? Oh yeah, before we met." Without waiting for a reply, Jesse hopped into the back of the van and rummaged for dinner.

Odds may not have been with them even back then. Will hadn't much been happy since Sarah left. And Jesse? Sure, he'd had Lynn, but look where they were living.

That was a pointless reflection. Where was Daphne? Ah, there she was, nosing around the next parking lane over. Will called her. She looked up as though wondering why he was bothering her, then resumed her business. Even the dog was ignoring him now. He called again and again, increasingly testy, until she gave up and trotted back to him. But once there, she took an interest in the van's rear passenger tire, sniffing it, a low rumble issuing from her throat.

"Come on, Daphne," Will insisted. "Into the van." He held the door open and motioned with a sweep of his arm. She growled at the tire again.

In the growing dark, Will couldn't see what had disturbed her. He didn't care to find out. "Let's go, Daphne!"

The growl became a snarl, and Daphne snapped at the tire.

Jesse thrust a bag of jerky out the door. "Wiggle this under her nose."

"I'm not getting anywhere near her nose. Her teeth are under it." But Will took the bag, opened it, and rattled it. "Come on, Daphne, treats."

Daphne looked up, tail wagging.

"Come on, let's go." He took out a stick of jerky and held it down for her. She trotted over, carefully took the stick in her mouth, and lowered her head to chew. Will climbed in and waited. Once the first treat was gone, Daphne leapt into the vehicle, sat very properly between the seats, and waited for more. Will fed her another stick. "What's our dinner?" he asked.

"Depends on if you want to fire up the stove. Spaghetti and a jar of roasted red pepper and garlic sauce, or canned chicken on semi-stale white."

"Whatever."

"I been driving all day. I ain't cooking."

"Chicken, then."

Daphne perked up, interested.

"We'd better raid the store for dog food." Jesse gave her a pat. Then he climbed in back, dug out a can opener, and slapped the sandwiches together.

Will felt like a waiter, doling out jerky on demand, but it diverted Daphne's attention from his sandwich. It was full dark by the time the three of them had eaten their fill. Jesse then pulled to the storefront and parked by the door.

"I'll go," Will said. "You and Daphne wait here." The dog didn't listen. She bounded out the moment he opened his door.

Jesse laughed. "She's still in charge," he said.

Will grabbed his gun and followed the leader, leaving Jesse to guard the van. The second gun slumbered in back, but Jesse wouldn't touch it even if he needed it. Will was going to have to break his fear somehow. Their lives might one day depend on Jesse's aim.

The store was unlocked and all the lights on. Inside, Will found a chaos of bodies, merchandise pulled from shelves and strewn about, worthless cash and coin flung up and down the checkout aisles. He did his best not to notice the bruised, lacerated, broken bodies or speculate on how they met their ends. The smell of death had begun to permeate the air. He gagged on it. By the time he and Daphne found the dog food aisle, he'd taught himself to breath through his mouth. Daphne whined as she inspected some of the victims.

He grabbed an empty, abandoned cart from the end of the dog food aisle, settled the gun in, and filled the basket with cans and several large bags of dry. He was eager to escape, until he contemplated his clothing. Filthy again, and a bit ragged. He detoured to the men's clothing section and tossed in jeans, button-down shirts, and a couple of coats, some in his size, some in what he guessed was Jesse's.

Shopping spree done, he zigzagged around the dead, making for the exit. Just before they got there, Daphne snarled. Will turned to find her growling at the body of an old man. The deceased was face-down on the floor, a power cord wrapped about his neck, his limbs sprawled at strange angles. Daphne's fur stood on end. Her tail was puffed up, her ears flattened as she threatened the deceased.

Will slapped his thigh to get her attention, which it didn't. "Daphne! Come on!"

Daphne lunged, bit into the man's shoe, and shook as though trying to pull his foot off.

"No, Daphne! No! Daphne!"

The dog snarled and shook and pulled, but the shoe wouldn't give. She pulled the body a few inches back before releasing it. Then she turned on Will, teeth bared.

Will yanked the cart between himself and the dog. "Daphne! Stop it!"

She inched forward, low, teeth bared, a rumble in her throat.

Backing through the door, the cart his only protection, Will called, "Jesse! Bring me the damn jerky!"

As if that would stop her. Daphne lunged at the cart. Grabbing it with her mouth, she dug in and tried to pull it from his hands. She was surprisingly strong for her size, but Will kept a grip and with effort hauled cart and animal through the door.

Jesse rushed to his side, rattling the bag of jerky. "Hey! Hey, Daphne! Here you go, girl!" He fumbled with the bag, pulled out a handful of jerky, and tossed it. The strips of meat clattered on the pavement.

Nose twitching, Daphne released the cart and fell on the treats, devouring them in short order. Then she looked at Jesse, whined, and wagged her tail.

Jesse tossed her another piece. "What the hell?" he muttered.

For just a moment, Will thought he might pass out. He leaned on the cart and took a few breaths to steady himself. "I don't know. She wasn't acting..."

Daphne finished the jerky and licked her lips.

"Normal." Will stared at the shotgun in the cart. He felt a bit of Jesse's loathing of the instrument, but he took it in hand, just in case.

"She's normal now," Jesse objected. "It don't come and go. You go crazy and stay crazy 'til you die."

"If you're human. But a dog?"

Daphne rounded the cart and sat at Will's feet, looking up and wagging her tail.

He looked at the dog and the gun and the dog, then extended his hand—he was still trembling—and scratched her behind the ears. "It's all the dead bodies. She's probably just rattled."

"Maybe."

It had to be. There was no other logical explanation.

"You don't want to shoot her," Jesse said.

Was that an observation or a plea? But no, he didn't. Not unless he had no choice, and right now she seemed as harmless as ever.

Jesse scanned the parking lot. Light rained down from LEDs on high. Nothing moved but an occasional bird skittering through the artificial glow. "Hell," he said. "Your call. I can't make it." He climbed in and waited, hands perched atop the wheel.

Gun in one hand and cart handle in the other, Will maneuvered the goods to the back of the van. Daphne watched. He set the gun aside and loaded the dog food into the back, then shoved the cart away. It clattered into the middle of the drive, blocking the opposite lane. Retrieving the weapon, Will opened the passenger door and waited while Daphne leapt into the front and settled between the seats, tail wagging. She seemed the same dog they had picked up that morning in Columbus, but was she?

"Where to?" Jesse asked.

"We should find someplace to stay for the night."

"'Cause the last place worked out so well?"

"Because I can't sleep in this seat."

Jesse put the van in gear. "Okay. You're in charge when Daphne's not. Tell me where to go."

"Go to hell," Will suggested.

"Already there," Jesse said.

They found a farm alongside Interstate 74 south of a town called Kickapoo, which Will thought amusing. He'd encountered the name in a Dr. Seuss book as a child, although he no longer remembered the context. To Jesse, it just sounded strange.

The farm looked promising from the outside. A dirt drive, devoid of vehicles, curved away from the road and passed between the house and the outbuildings. A rise shielded the house from view of the highway. White with black shutters, the well-maintained home had a comfortable feel. The front door stood open as though guests were expected, but none were in evidence, living or dead. Will kept his gun at the ready. He made Daphne stay in the van while he and Jesse slipped in for a look around.

The living room, dining room, and kitchen felt curiously urban, furnished in chrome and smoked glass with walls painted Bauhaus gray. Clean floors, clean table, all dishes stacked in the cabinets. Food filled the refrigerator and freezer. The milk hadn't spoiled. The veggies hadn't wilted. In another week, those commodities would be a memory for any-one lacking cows and a green thumb, but not yet. Somebody had stocked this kitchen recently. Odds were, they hadn't gone far.

"Hey," Jesse whispered. He had moved into the room beyond the kitchen.

"What?"

"Back here. Bedrooms. Someone's there."

Will joined him and took the lead, gun at the ready. A small sound broke the silence, the creak of a rocking chair and a murmur of conversation.

The kitchen led to a family room with a forty-inch TV on the wall, bookcases, and a card table spread with a half-finished mountain scene puzzle. A hall ran by, connecting the living room up front to the bedrooms in back. They crept down the hall, one halting step at a time, until they came to the first door.

Will paused, too nervous to peek in. He didn't need to.

"I have a gun," a woman said.

Will tightened his grip. "So do I."

"How sane are you?"

"Enough. You?"

"Enough."

Big help that was. Anyone who wasn't wouldn't know. "What happens now?" Will asked.

The woman said nothing for a moment. Naturally. If this hadn't been her house to start with, she'd made it hers. Interlopers could spell trouble, sane or no. "Wait in the living room," she said. "I'll come out in a minute. Don't shoot me."

"So long as you don't shoot me," Will promised.

"Fair enough."

They returned to the living room. "How do we know she'll keep her word?" Jesse asked.

"How do we know anything?"

In the van, Daphne began barking and wouldn't shut up. Will looked out the window. Nothing moved in the yard or on the road.

"You have a dog?" the woman asked. She entered with her gun aimed at the floor. She gave Jesse a quick examination before turning to Will, the one with the weapon, thus the one who had spoken, thus likely the man in charge.

Her skin was the color of coffee with a dollop of cream, her voice Midwestern, her body lean and strong. Will thought she might be about his own age. He hoped he wasn't gaping, but he might have been. Had she been Caucasian, she might have been Sarah. She inspired a pang of longing for his ex, that was for sure.

"In the car," he said.

"Shouldn't it be with you? For protection?"

"We aren't too sure about her," Jesse said in a curiously subdued tone. Will glanced at him. Damned if he wasn't gaping at her, too.

"Oh." The woman didn't notice Jesse's expression. She hadn't shifted her gaze from Will, probably since that's where the shotgun was. "What are your names?"

"I'm Will, this is Jesse. We're from New York."

"That's where it started, they said."

That must've been about all they'd said, given how fast the news had fallen silent back home.

She relaxed a little, but Will bet she could be quick on the draw if she wanted. "I'm Kaylee. This place is mine. You can sleep on the sofa tonight if you promise to leave first thing in the morning. I'll lock up the back. We won't see each other again. I'll know if you try to get in. I'm a light sleeper."

"Agreed," Will decided.

Jesse shuffled his feet and cleared his throat.

"What?" Will hoped he wasn't going to argue authority again.

Jesse nodded at Kaylee's gun. "What if she comes after us? When we're sleeping?"

Kaylee gave him a crooked smile. "You aren't *that* good looking, Jesse."

Jesse gaped at her. Then he laughed and put up his hands in surrender. "Okay, okay. It's been a strange week, ya know?"

She smiled in acknowledgment before withdrawing to the back. A door snicked shut.

"That is so weird," Jesse muttered.

"What?" Will sank onto the sofa, gun across his lap. Outside, Daphne continued to bark. She sounded frantic. Maybe she needed to relieve herself.

"Lynn used to say that. 'You aren't *that* good looking, Jesse.' One of her running jokes."

"Maybe she only loved you for your telescope."

"Har-dee-har."

"Go let Daphne out. She sounds desperate."

Jesse dropped into a chair. "You got the gun, you let her out."

"Why can't you ever—"

"Do as I'm told? 'Cause you don't own me. They outlawed that a few years back."

"It's always about race with you, isn't it? I never brought it up. I just asked you to do a little work for a change."

"Yeah, let's add lazy to my stereotyped profile. You got the gun, damn it, *you* deal with the psycho dog."

Will thrust the gun at him. "I'll be happy to give you a turn."

Jesse sank into the chair and looked away. He might have been on the verge of vomiting. "I don't want that thing."

"You can write down coward, too." Will stomped out, slamming the front door behind him. In the car, Daphne saw him coming and began jumping around in the driver's seat, yipping and whining. When he pulled open the door, she bounded out, rushed the grass, and took care of business before setting off at a run and making several wide circuits of the yard.

Watching her, Will thought she looked as normal as ever. Maybe the shopping cart incident had been triggered by the smell of death, after all. Or spilled bleach or detergent or who knew what else. Now in the fresh air, she ran and ran with no sign of slowing, rounding the house and returning to the van, tearing down the drive to the barn and back, until finally, tongue hanging out a mile and panting in great heaves, she sat at his feet and looked up, bright-eyed. He scratched her behind the ears.

The sun grew low in the west, and the dark arch of night rose in the east. Will was of two minds. He could lock Daphne in the car overnight, or he could risk bringing her inside. Kaylee said the dog should be with them for protection. Valid point. If nothing else, Daphne could alert them if their hostess proved a liar.

"Come on, girl," he said. They mounted the porch steps together.

"Are you nuts?" Jesse gasped when they came into the living room.

"She's okay," Will assured him.

Jesse didn't look assured.

"Let's get some sleep," Will said. "We have to be on our way at first light."

Jesse balled himself up in the chair, eyeing Daphne. Will turned out the lights, stretched out on the sofa, and placed the gun on the floor near to hand. Daphne jumped up next to him and settled in. Outside, crickets chirped and cicadas hummed.

"Why do guns scare you?" Will asked.

"Shouldn't they?"

Fair question. Will had never fired a gun until he killed the old man. He'd never had interest in, much less love of, weaponry. Whatever fondness he had for it now was born of desperation. Danger surrounded them. They needed protection. "I suppose," he decided.

In the darkness, Jesse shifted in the chair, a soft sound that reminded Will of Sarah turning in her sleep. Too many things summoned her memory of late.

"I grew up in a rough neighborhood," Jesse said. "My little brother Martin was shot to death."

Will couldn't even imagine that. For one thing, he was an only child. For another, nobody he knew had died of violence. Cancer, yes. A traffic accident, yes. But not gunshot wounds.

"Guns are the devil's toys," Jesse said.

"I'm sorry."

"Lots o' folks were."

"About what I said, I mean. You're not a coward. You're just..." Will didn't know the right word.

"Abused," Jesse suggested. "Most of us are. Black folk, white folk, all of us. Even you. Sarah did a number on you, right? We gotta be patient with each other, I guess. And ourselves."

"I guess. Maybe in the morning, we can start working on that."

"If Daphne don't rip our throats out before then."

Will scratched Daphne behind the ears. "She'll be okay." Maybe. He hoped. He'd grown rather attached to her.

Half an hour later, none of them had fallen asleep. Jesse tossed and turned in the chair. Will tried not to move for fear of pushing Daphne onto the floor, but she had draped herself across his legs, which were starting to go numb. He carefully extricated himself and sat. She perched beside him and gazed at him in the dark.

Jesse groaned. "Looks like a long night," he said. "I'm going out for a bit."

Will nudge aside the curtain and peered into the night. Pinprick lights dotted the sky. "Daphne and I'll go with you," he said. "You can teach me some star names."

"Really?"

"Why not?"

Jesse stood. "Why not," he agreed.

7

WILL WOKE to bacon frying in the kitchen and light growing in the window above the couch. He rolled away from the glow and buried his face in his arm to catch a few more minutes sleep, but a big, wet tongue slid over his cheek. He bolted upright. On the floor beside the sofa, Daphne wagged her tail and barked, happy he was finally conscious.

Startled awake, Jesse about fell from the chair on which he was curled. "What the hell," he mumbled.

Daphne whined and barked again.

"Yeah, all right," Will said. He stood and stretched the kinks from his back. In the kitchen, grease sizzled and popped. Creeping to the kitchen door, he found Sarah at the stove, already dressed in jeans and a white top, making breakfast as she often had on Sunday mornings.

He ran his gaze over her curves, at first drawn by the sight, then confused. Something was wrong. The woman *looked* like Sarah, sort of, but no, she was a touch too short, her hair a shade too dark. And what was with this kitchen? Too big, too...*old*. It wasn't theirs.

No, of course not. New York was a lifetime removed, Sarah twice a lifetime. How could she be here?

Jesse shuffled up behind and silently watched the woman, too, mouth knotted in puzzlement. Then Daphne slipped between them and advanced, wary, nose twitching. She stopped a muzzle-length behind the woman, who glanced down at her. Will's disorientation melted when he saw her profile. Of course. Kaylee.

Kaylee returned to her task. "I thought you didn't trust this dog."

"Daphne," Will said. "She seems okay."

"They do until they don't."

"Dogs?" Jesse asked.

"Same as people," Will said, thinking of David Buhler.

Kaylee transferred the bacon to a plate covered in paper towels. She fried it crispy, the way Will liked, the way Sarah always fried it. "Not quite," she said. "People go mad fast. Dogs can't seem to make up their minds." She set about scrambling eggs.

The aroma drew Jesse forward a step. "I thought you wanted us gone."

"Damn right I do. Right after breakfast."

A decent way to be evicted. Will motioned to the table in the corner. Jesse took a chair along the wall, Will in front of the window. They both had their eyes on her that way. She'd been true to her word, so Will didn't think she'd turn on them, but as she said, people went mad fast. Besides, he liked looking at her. She was a pleasant sight, even if she wasn't Sarah.

Daphne waited at Kaylee's feet, head cocked, eyes on the stove, licking her lips. Will about told Jesse to take her outside and feed her, but no, they should stick together, just in case. Even though Kaylee's gun wasn't in evidence, she had means of doing them in. Iron skillets, for one.

Speaking of guns, where was his? He must have left it in the living room. Will slipped out to retrieve it. Returning, he leaned it on the wall by his side. Kaylee was just taking the eggs off the stove and starting toast, her back still to him. Another moment of disorientation seized him, dropping him into New York with Sarah in the morning, everything happy and normal and comfortable except the hidden churning of her soul for something more, something different, something...

...he didn't know what. She'd never told him.

When he returned to the present, Kaylee was placing loaded plates before them. Returning to the stove, she filled two more. "Coffee maker is there," she said, pointing to the device. "Pods and tea bags are in the cabinet above. Sugar's on the table." She took a plate in each hand and with the confidence of a practiced waitress vanished into the back. Daphne

   Dale E. Lehman

whined. Claws clicking on the floor, she returned to Will's side and pleaded with soulful eyes. She licked her lips.

Will spoiled her with bits of bacon while he ate. Afterward, he took her out, leaving the gun with Jesse, just in case. He filled her food bowl and drew her a drink from an outside faucet. She ate nonstop, as though she hadn't been fed for a month. "Don't run off," Will told her. He returned to the table.

"We should get out of here," Jesse whispered.

"Why?"

"It's just…" Jesse shook his head. "You'll think I'm crazy."

"I already do. What's the problem?"

"Kaylee reminds me of Lynn."

Will would have laughed had he not confused her for Sarah. "How so?"

"Lighter skin, but same height, same…" He traced a feminine outline with his hands.

Maybe they were both going nuts. It wouldn't have surprised him. "Odd. She reminds me of Sarah."

Jesse raised an eyebrow.

"A younger, darker Sarah."

"Great," Jesse muttered.

Outside, Daphne barked. Will glanced out the window. Nothing stirred. "I don't know. She seems a decent sort. Maybe she'll let us stay. We could help out around the place." Whatever that meant. Neither of them knew the first thing about running a farm. Not that Kaylee was running it, either. This was just a place to hide, for all of them.

With a smirk, Jesse said, "Finally found a woman, huh?"

"Being practical. We're out of the way here. It should be safe enough. Plus, three sane people. Safety in numbers."

Jesse put a hand to his forehead. "God, it's happening already."

"What?"

"She's messing with our minds."

Will wasn't sure Jesse had much mind left to mess with. The trauma must have knocked loose what little sense he had.

"Not on purpose, but look at us. You see Sarah, I see Lynn. *That's* why you wanna stay. Me, too. But we can't. We'll end up fighting."

"We already fight."

"Over *her*, damn it!"

"For God's sake, Jesse."

"And she's hiding something. You didn't notice, did you?"

"Notice what?"

"She ain't alone. She took two plates back there."

Will sure had noticed, but preoccupied with Daphne, he hadn't given it any thought. "Maybe she has a kid," he suggested.

Before Jesse could reply, Kaylee returned with the plates, now empty, which she rinsed and stacked in the sink. That done, she faced the men, leaning against the counter, arms crossed. She gave them the sort of look Sarah used to give Will when he'd done something stupid. "Maybe," she said, "it's none of your business."

Outside, Daphne snarled. Will peered out the window again. The dog had planted herself in a defiant stance next to her food dish, eyes focused on something down the drive. As far as Will could tell, she was snarling at the gravel. Nothing moved, not even a squirrel or passing bird.

"Maybe not," he agreed. "Then again, maybe we should know who else is in the house."

"Not if you're leaving. Which you are."

"Then why feed us?"

She joined them at the table. Her movements were efficient and quick, her eyes wary. She didn't trust them any more than they trusted her, but she didn't fear them. Maybe she should have. Will had a gun by his side, and she had no defense against it. He couldn't help but admire her courage.

"If we lose our decency," she said, "civilization really will be dead."

"We were just thinking—"

"Don't. Take your dog and get off my land."

"What about decency?"

Kaylee raised an eyebrow. "Decent is one thing, stupid another."

Daphne continued to bark and snarl while Will and Kaylee locked eyes. Jesse leaned into the window, nearly pressing his nose to the glass. "Uh," he said. "About the dog..."

Will looked out again.

Now Daphne was snapping at chunks of gravel, picking up and tossing the larger ones, teeth bared, ears back.

"Take your gun," Kaylee said.

As if Will needed to be told. Weapon in hand, he eased the front door open and planted himself on the porch while Daphne savaged the rocks. The road and the drive were empty. A light breeze stirred the leaves. She continued to assault the gravel as though dismembering an intruder who had threatened her pups.

He should have brought the jerky into the house. Last time, that snapped her out of it. Without it, he didn't know what to do. He could wait until the madness—whatever it was—released her, but how long would that take? What if she hurt herself?

"Daphne!" he called. "It's okay, Daphne, nobody's there. Come on, Daphne, come on!"

Daphne turned, suddenly quiet but ears still back, teeth still bared. She growled a low, quiet warning.

"It's okay, Daphne. It's okay. Come on, we'll go inside now." Will tried to sound soothing, but his voice quavered.

She crept forward, still growling. Will waited on the edge of the porch, gun gripped in both hands but not aimed, speaking softly as though lulling a child to sleep. "Good girl, Daphne. Good girl. You know me. Be still, Daphne. Be still."

Jesse emerged onto the porch. "Hey, girl," he said. "Good girl. Good Daphne."

Daphne snarled at him, too, a little louder. She inched toward the porch until she came within a dog-length of the bottom step.

"Good girl, Daphne," Will cooed. "Good girl."

Daphne unleashed a barrage of savage barks. The men backed a step. Will shifted the gun but still didn't raise it. He couldn't. He couldn't aim it at her. Not her. He knew he should, knew it was inevitable, but he couldn't.

"Will?" Jesse said. He put a hand to the wall to steady himself.

Daphne stopped at the bottom step, snapped her jaws, snarled.

"You'd best...Will, you gotta—"

The dog lunged. Will swung the gun up but had no time to aim, couldn't find the trigger, couldn't do anything but block the attack with the weapon.

An explosion shocked Will into a stupor. He spun away, waiting for Daphne's fangs to lacerate his back, but nothing happened, nothing but a horrid silence like the end of the world. Even the wind held its breath.

He turned.

Daphne lay dead at his feet.

"Oh, God," Jesse muttered. "Oh, no. Oh, hell." He dropped to his knees and ran his hand through the fur on Daphne's back.

Will, too, sank to his knees. He cradled the animal's head in his lap and stared at the red dot between her eyes. For minutes, neither spoke, then Will heard a shuffle of feet behind him. Kaylee stepped to his side, rifle in hand, eyes distant, expression blank.

Jesse cried. Will only held back tears by force.

"I'm sorry," Kaylee said. "She would have killed you."

Yes, but so what? It would have been better if he'd died with her.

"I'll be inside," she said. "You can stay one more night."

Will buried his face in Daphne's while the porch boards vibrated and the door clicked shut.

They buried Daphne behind the barn. Jesse said words Will didn't hear, then returned to the house. Will wandered aimlessly among the out-buildings and yard and into the fields, eventually returning to the porch, where he sat and felt if not saw the sun ascend to the zenith. Jesse waited at the kitchen table, alone, thinking about Lynn and Sarah and Daphne and Kaylee and what the hell he was doing somewhere south of Kickapoo, Illinois of all the damn places in the country, if a country it still was.

Kaylee emerged at noon, made a ham sandwich on rye, and took it with a plastic bottle of water into the back. She returned fifteen minutes later and sat across from Jesse, examining her fingernails. "How long did he have Daphne?"

"Not even two days," Jesse said. "We picked her up in Columbus."

"Must've been love at first sight."

"It ain't funny."

"No, I mean it. You were fond of her, but Will…" She looked out the window. "He couldn't bear to shoot her. He would have died rather than put her down. I'm sorry. I really am. But I had to do it. You know that, right?"

"He killed a man the other day," Jesse said. To his own ears, his voice sounded a dozen miles off. "Crazy guy. No choice. Had to do it. He'd do it again. He'd kill you or me if he had to. But not Daphne."

"I get it." Kaylee rose. "Want anything to eat? I can heat up some soup."

"Nah."

She got out a pan and dumped a can of vegetable soup into it anyway.

"Who lives with you?" Jesse asked.

She rinsed out the can and put it in a recycling bin. Jesse thought that weird. Trash pickups were a thing of the past. Why bother? Why not toss it out in the field?

"Your kid?" he asked.

"No."

"Husband? Boyfriend?"

"No."

"I ain't no good at twenty questions."

She tossed a smile his way and stirred the pot. It was Lynn's smile. "I think he owns the farm."

"You don't know?"

She shook her head.

"You said it was your place."

"It is now."

Jesse propped his head up with his fist. She sure was good at evasion. Like Lynn could be when she wanted.

She smirked at him. "You can't quit, can you?"

"Just wanna know where I stand," he said. "The world's…" He wasn't sure what. Psychotic, probably.

"Changed," she supplied.

That was one way of putting it. "Who is he?"

"When I got here," she said, "I found a woman, a teenage boy, and two little girls shot dead in the yard. His family, I guess. He was…" She frowned at the soup. "What's the word? Blank stare, couldn't talk, didn't even know I was there."

"Catatonic," Jesse supplied.

"Catatonic. I don't know if it was the shock or the disease. I never saw anyone like that before."

"Did he snap out of it?"

"No. I settled him in a bedroom in the back. I talk to him and take care of him. He's able to eat, if I feed him, but that's about it. Without me, he'd soon be dead."

Was Kaylee noble or nuts? Jesse doubted he and Will would have taken the high road. Too risky. Besides, anyone in that state might be better off dead. "What if he's infected?" he asked. "You might catch it."

She finished heating the soup, ladled it into a trio of bowls, and brought them to the table. As before, she had the poise of a waitress balancing a full tray. Maybe that's what she had been last week. She set one bowl before Jesse, another at Will's place, and took the last for herself. "Does that scare you?" she asked.

"A little," he admitted. "It's crazy contagious."

"It sure is." She ate while Jesse ignored his soup in favor of her. Damn, she looked and talked and acted like Lynn. Or was he projecting his desires onto her? Why was he even thinking like this?

Will shuffled in about the time she finished, propped his gun against the wall, and dropped into the chair. He stared at his bowl of soup as though it had been beamed down from a starship. Kaylee rinsed her bowl and returned to the table. Fifteen minutes passed to the ticking of the clock on the wall.

Will pulled the bowl to himself and took up his spoon. "Thank you," he said. "For..." he jabbed his thumb at the door.

She nodded.

"I guess I—"

"I know. Dogs are family."

Setting the spoon down, he folded his hands on the table and stared at them. "You've seen them go mad from this thing before."

"A couple, yeah."

"Yours?"

Kaylee got up and rummaged in the cupboards. "Want anything else? I have stuff for sandwiches, cookies..." She shook her head as though it was too poor an offering.

"No, thanks."

Jesse tried to read Kaylee through the exchange. She seemed more of a mystery now than when they met her. She doled out information in droplets, never let them see her, never let them know her. Maintaining control had exhausted her. What was she afraid of?

She closed the cabinets. "I should go back for a bit, I guess."

"Back to your child?" Will asked.

She glanced at Jesse before replying, "Yeah."

"Boy or girl?"

With a quick smile, Kaylee left him to wonder.

"Strange," Will muttered.

Jesse didn't think it so strange. She knew Will could kill a man if not his dog. Given his current state of mind, who knew what he'd do if he learned the truth? "She's just protective," he said.

Will accepted that without question. "I'm grateful she's letting us stay another night, but you're right. We should leave tomorrow. And from now on, we keep to ourselves. No people, no dogs, no cats, no parakeets. Just us. That's the only safe way."

He was still playing boss-man, but Jesse didn't argue. He had a point. The fewer entanglements, the simpler life would be.

A coverlet of gray clouds muted the dawn. Kaylee rose early and had pancakes and sausages on the table by the time they staggered into the kitchen, dressed in some of the new clothing Will had picked up. He'd gotten Jesse's size right, or close enough that he couldn't tell the difference.

Soft rain pelted the window while they ate in silence. After, the men gathered up what little they had brought into the house, carried it down the steps and through the drizzle to their van. Their shoes scuffled on the wet gravel. Doors thunked shut, and the engine roared to life. Jesse U-turned behind the house and made for the road. The tires crunched along the broken surface.

Behind them, Kalyee stood on the porch, arms crossed against the morning cool. Will looked back just before they rounded the bend and passed from her sight. She raised a hand in farewell. He returned the gesture.

"I hope she'll be all right," he said.

Jesse said nothing. He pulled onto the road and made for the highway. Soon they were on I-74 west making for Galesburg and, if Will didn't change his mind, Davenport, Iowa. He'd had his fill of Illinois. So had Jesse. The van, full of supplies, felt empty.

"You did the leaving this time," Jesse said.

Will gazed over the passing fields. "She wasn't Sarah."

"She coulda been."

No. Maybe. Probably not. What difference did it make? Sarah would be dead, like most everyone. Even if not, she was long gone. Kaylee was a fluke, a coincidence, no part of Will's life save one moment when she rescued him from disaster. Anyway, she had a child, and he wasn't daddy material. He had no experience in that arena, was too old to learn the trade.

"She could have been Lynn, too," Will said. "Or so you said."

Jesse drew a long breath. The road disappeared beneath their tires. "She's a sign."

"Sign?"

"That Lynn's still alive. That she's still out there somewhere, waiting for me. I knew it the moment I saw Kaylee."

"A chance meeting, that's all."

No argument, but Jesse pinched his lips.

Will pulled up the map on his phone and studied it. The gray splash of Davenport looked large when stitched to Moline, Illinois by the blue thread of the Mississippi, but only the interstates and a handful of bridges crossed the river. They'd have to skirt the edge of the city. With luck, the highway would be passable. With luck, they could blow through without stopping.

"She didn't want us to go," Jesse said.

"Of course she did. She made that clear."

"She had no choice, is all." Jesse's expression was as serious as it ever got.

"Meaning?"

He told Will about the dead woman and children and the catatonic man in Kaylee's care. "Too dangerous to keep us around. We might of gotten sick. Or killed him to make sure we didn't."

Why had she told Jesse but not him? Why should she fear a man who couldn't shoot a dog?

It didn't matter. She was a memory now, like everyone else, like everything else.

"Or she might get sick and turn on us," Jesse added. "She knows but takes care of him anyway. Why risk that for a stranger?"

"Maybe she's immune." Will said it without believing it. People didn't have immunity to novel diseases, not until they built it up. At least, that's what he'd heard. Medicine had never been his field, or his interest. He was a glorified bean counter, a man who'd spent his whole life obsessing over financials, now thrust into a world where money counted for nothing.

"Maybe she's just a better person than we are," Jesse suggested.

Maybe. Probably. Will had enough guilt for ten people already, though. No point in magnifying it.

"When we get to Iowa..." Jesse bit his lip and looked ill.

"What about it?"

"It's wide-open spaces out there, right?"

Will shrugged. The map rather suggested it, but he'd never been to Iowa, himself.

"Best teach me to shoot."

"Oh. Okay."

Jesse forced a laugh. "Not that you're any expert."

Will wasn't, but he was at least two shots more experienced than Jesse. "Just one condition," he said.

"Name it."

"Don't throw up on me."

Jesse looked like he was ready to. "Not more than once," he promised.

8

ORE OF THE SAME.

They sailed through western Illinois farmland, bypassed Moline, and crossed the Mississippi River at Rapids City. The river ran blue-gray beneath the drab concrete bridge. Halfway over, jagged black streaks ran up the Jersey barrier as though a truck had slammed it, clawed over the top, and plunged into the water. As far as Will knew, that wasn't supposed to happen, not from a glancing blow at least. Yet there was no sign of the vehicle.

North of Davenport, the interstate took a country route most of the way, just kissing the fringes of the city on the northwest. Then it snaked among the fields and creeks until they hit Iowa City, where they stopped for gas at a Sinclair station with a small convenience store and a green, man-sized sauropod out front. Next door, a Mexican restaurant sat empty with a few cars and corpses in the parking lot. Across the street, an unmarked one-story office building of white stone and smoked glass perched atop a low hill. Flies buzzed thick in the decay-laden air.

Once the ProMaster was fueled, Will stood in the grass at the edge of the road, drinking in the deep quiet. Nothing broke the silence, not bird-song, not even a breeze. The Earth held its breath, and he held his, too, so as not to wake it. Jesse emerged from the store, tossed a small load of snacks into the van, and joined him in vigil.

Will considered the hill. The lawn still looked manicured. A scattering of trees rose from perfect circles of brown mulch. With all that dark glass, the office building provided plenty of targets to shatter.

"Wait here," he said. He retrieved the shotguns and a box of shells from the van and presented one of the weapons to Jesse. He then demonstrated loading and chambering a round and watched while Jesse fumbled through the procedure, hands quaking. Nodding to the building, Will said, "Let's see if we can blow out the windows." He set the gun to his shoulder and aimed.

Jesse did nothing. A sickly look had frozen on his face.

"What's wrong?" Will asked.

"What if someone's in there?"

"Like who?"

"Anyone."

Will lowered his weapon. Nobody would be. Everyone was dead. Most everyone. Okay, someone *could* be in there, but it was unlikely. "Don't worry about it," he said, as much to assure himself as Jesse.

Jesse drew a breath and raised his weapon. It shook with him. He forced air into his lungs and out again, in and out, in and out, as though through sheer will he could steady his hand. He couldn't. He closed his eyes and pulled the trigger. The explosion echoed off the gas station, the restaurant, the trees, the target building. He jumped and dropped the shotgun in the grass.

"Watch it!" Will snapped.

"Hell," Jesse muttered. Retrieving the gun, he pointed it skyward and eyed it as though it was the Eden serpent.

"Don't close your eyes when you fire," Will said. "And for God's sake, don't drop it. It might go off and hit one of us."

That alarmed Jesse more than the discharge had. "Can that happen?"

"Maybe. How the hell should I know?"

Jesse gave the weapon the evil eye once more. "Let's see you do it, Mr. Manager."

Will took aim, or tried to. Now that it came to it, it wasn't so easy. The barrel waggled all over, no matter how he tried to still it. As it zigged by the center window on the distant building, he held his breath and squeezed the trigger. The boom startled a flock of starlings from a nearby tree, but he saw no sign of impact. No broken glass, no spray of concrete powder from the wall.

"Zero points," Jesse said.

"At least the gun's still in my hands," Will countered. He took aim and fired again. And again. Nothing, nothing at all. He frowned at the unharmed building, chastising it for failing to take the hit.

"Wait," Jesse said. "Shotgun. The bullets spray out like that." He made a fist and opened his fingers.

"Shot," Will said.

"What?"

"Shot, not bullets. Like birdshot or buckshot."

"Great. You sound expert, no matter how you shoot. Let's aim for something closer." Jesse raised his gun, repeated his breathing ritual, and fired. The blast didn't startle him this time, and he kept his grip on the weapon. The shot kicked up grass and soil from the side of the hill. "Got it!"

"Is that where you were aiming?" Will asked.

"Close enough."

"Where were you aiming?"

Jesse waved at the hillside. "Around there."

"You need a specific target."

"Why?"

The question was too stupid to merit an answer. Will took aim and announced his target, a planting of low shrubs edging the road on the left. "Dead center," he added. He again fought the gun into rough alignment but couldn't hold the position. He stilled his mind, held his breath, waited for the heart of the shrubs to come into his sights.

The gun discharged. Grass and soil sprayed the air in front of his target.

"Close enough," Jesse said.

"Not if it's about to kill us."

"If a bush is about to kill us, I'll shoot *myself*."

Will turned on Jesse. "Why the hell do you think we're doing this?" He shook the gun. "This is to stay alive!"

Jesse took aim at the bushes and fired. A spray of leaves signaled the hit. Pleased with himself, he took another shot, or tried to. The trigger clicked, but the chamber was empty. He dug three more shells out of the box and reloaded while Will watched. "You could say, 'Nice shot,'" Jesse suggested.

"Nice shot." Will aimed and fired, this time winging the bushes. He reloaded while Jesse fired three times in succession, scoring leaves twice and grass once. They continued to trade off, and over the next half hour their aim improved—marginally—while the bushes took a mild beating. Finally, Will called a halt. "We should get moving," he said.

"Just when I was getting the hang of it," Jesse objected. He gathered the ammo and led the way.

"Now that you can almost shoot," Will said, "I'll take a turn driving."

They packed up the weapons and Will got behind the wheel. Jesse stopped beside the open passenger door, staring at nothing. "What's wrong?" Will asked.

Jesse shrugged. "Just..."

"Just what?"

"This is a nice place. Quiet. Maybe we could find an empty house, stay for a while."

"Quiet means nothing. The whole world's quiet. We're too close to the city here." Will turned the key. The engine growled to life. "Get in."

Jesse might have become stone. "We can't run forever."

"We aren't running."

"No? What you call it, then?"

Staying safe, Will wanted to say, *keeping our distance*. You couldn't stop. You couldn't rest. You had to stay alert, keep moving, watch and hide and slip through the shadows or the world would ambush you, drive you to the ground, devour you. It had stalked humans since the Paleolithic, and now it had them in its claws. It had slaughtered them almost to a person.

Jesse climbed in and slammed the door. "Go," he said.

"We'll stop soon," Will promised. "Just not here."

"Sure. When we drown in the Pacific."

"Whatever." Will put the van in gear and returned to the highway.

An hour of travel put them in Iowa City. Another hour and a half and they reached Des Moines, by which time it was just past noon. The flight through fields and around small towns had become curiously normal. Jesse had never set foot outside New York City before the world crashed and burned, and now he could barely remember the steel spires and crowds and smells and noise. He lowered the window to sniff earth and water and corn and wheat while the fields flew by. He closed it whenever they passed through a town or city, where decay hung heavy in the air. Cars, trucks, and bodies littered the urban expressways, forcing Will to slow and thread the needle through the carnage.

Once through Des Moines, fresh country air replaced the stench, and Jesse opened the window again. Half an hour later, just north of Earlham, Will took the exit. Coming down the cracked ramp, they spotted an isolated dirt parking area on the right, perched atop a rise off a dirt road. It was exposed to the highway and the road to the east. Stands of trees neighbored it north and west. It stood empty save a single vehicle, a dusty gray Dodge Ram.

Will eased into the lot and stopped twenty feet from the truck. Jesse held his shotgun across his lap, hoping he wouldn't need it. They sat for ten minutes, watching, waiting, but nothing stirred, not even a breeze. A turkey vulture wheeled in from beyond the woods and circled overhead before gliding south toward the town.

Looking for lunch, Jesse thought. He was hungry, too, or had been before the scavenger floated by. "What are we doing here?" he asked.

"Taking a break," Will said. He nodded at the Ram. "It looks abandoned, but keep your gun close, just in case." He retrieved his shotgun from the back and got out.

"Don't leave home without it," Jesse muttered. He opened the door and slid out. They reloaded and pocketed a few extra shells before closing the doors. The impact echoed off the trees. Otherwise, silence engulfed the land. Slinking toward the pickup, they watched for movement within, under, around. Nothing. Jesse held his breath as he approached the passenger door and looked through the window. Empty. He exhaled in relief.

Will inspected the bed, looked underneath, and scouted the grasses alongside the dirt parking lot. Tire tracks bespoke traffic that had come and gone, but that might have been days or weeks or years past. Now there was nothing save the two of them, their ProMaster, and this pickup.

Jesse tried the passenger door. It was locked. He circled to the other side and found the driver's door locked, too. "Someone left it here on purpose," he called to Will. "Maybe it's a park and ride. Maybe they took a bus somewhere."

Will raised a hand in acknowledgement.

"Maybe they ain't coming back," Jesse added to himself. Maybe he wasn't, either. Maybe he'd never see New York again. Or Lynn. Or anyone. Maybe he'd die out here and lie in a tire track until the vulture returned for him.

"Let's eat," Will said. "We can make Cheyenne by nightfall, I think."

"Cheyenne?"

"Wyoming."

"Now it's Wyoming?"

"Low population. We might find a safe place there."

"That where you been going all along?"

Will put his gun away and opened the back of the van. "Not consciously. It just occurred to me, though. I read somewhere that Wyoming has the lowest population density in the continental U.S." He motioned for Jesse to scrounge up some food.

Jesse didn't move, didn't look at Will, didn't look at anything. That vulture might have already perched on him and begun to feed. He scuffed the packed dirt with his foot and watched the dust float away. That was them, drifting on the wind, thinning out until nothing remained of them.

"Couple things," he said. "One, I ain't your kitchen staff. Two…" He sat heavily in the dirt and picked at it. "I'm sick of running."

Will leaned on the van and folded his arms over his chest. He looked everywhere but at Jesse.

"A farmhouse here's as good as Wyoming," Jesse said.

"It's just another eight hours or so."

"For what? What's the damn point?"

Will pushed off the van, eyes now fixed on the clear western sky. He floundered for words before saying, "It might be the last thing I ever do."

Jesse didn't see the point in making Wyoming the last thing you ever did, unless you'd been born there, maybe. He didn't even know what they'd find. Baked grasses? Dust? Horses running wild with nobody to tame them?

Will shrugged. "The only places I ever traveled to were financial centers. New York, Chicago, Boston, Philly, D.C., Atlanta. Even then, all I ever saw were airports and office buildings. I've never seen the west. Mountains. Tall mountains, I mean. So tall the snow never melts. Now that I think about it, I think that's where I've been going all along."

Jesse picked himself up and dusted himself off. "Ain't a horrible excuse, I guess." Effecting a truly poor John Wayne, he added, "I'll rustle us up some grub." He pointed a finger at Will. "But I still ain't your kitchen staff."

"I'll make dinner," Will promised. "But it might not be edible."

Climbing into the back of the van, Jesse rummaged through the supplies and settled on canned spaghetti. He brought out the camp stove, hooked up the fuel, and dumped the food into a pan to heat. He watched in silence while it gradually came to a simmer, then turned it off and served it on doubled paper plates with a side of plastic forks.

"This don't look sustainable to me," he commented as they sat cross-legged in the dirt and ate.

Will looked puzzled, which was a first as far as Jesse knew.

"Sustainable," Jesse explained. "Paper plates, plastic forks, canned food, propane. They don't grow from seed, you know."

"What counts as sustainable now? Camping skills, I guess. Roughing it. I never learned to make fire by banging rocks together. Did you?"

"Nope," Jesse admitted.

"You're suggesting we learn?"

"Just saying, if we can't loot what we need, we're screwed."

Will flicked a speck of dirt from his plate.

Low population could be both a blessing and a curse. "How many stores they have per square mile in Wyoming?" Jesse asked.

"I don't know, but if we're the only two people in the state, we should be good."

Jesse looked around for a trash can, but there wasn't any, so he tossed his empty plate and plastic fork to the side. So much for sustainable. But then, how much could a little litter hurt anymore? "If you don't decide to head for sunny California," he grumbled.

Will set his empty plate beside him. It looked surprisingly neat there. "Why would I?"

"You never seen the Pacific Ocean."

"You should've been a stand-up comic. Too bad the audiences are gone." Will rose and brushed off his pants. "Look at this. I'm filthy again. Good thing I picked up extra clothes."

"Yeah, at least we got something to wear while we scrub these on the rocks in the dry river. They got those in Wyoming, too, right?"

Will kicked his plate away. "Let's get going."

"Sure thing, boss."

Jesse started to get up, but Will shoved him to the ground. "I'm sick of that."

"Makes two of us."

"You don't have to tag along. Walk to the nearest town and steal your own van. Or show some initiative. You don't like what I'm doing? Suggest an alternative other than hunting for your dead girlfriend's twisted body." Will stalked to the van and climbed behind the wheel. He slammed the door and started the engine, then sat there, white fingers squeezing the life out of the steering wheel, going nowhere.

Jesse eyed him. At least this was ordinary anger. Familiar, oddly comforting. He could almost see once more the deranged mob in New York tearing each other to pieces. He shuddered, got into the van, closed the door as gently as possible. "Initiative," he said. "Okay, how about this. Let's go see them mountains."

"Is that what you want?"

"Me? No. I mean, sure, mountains would be cool. But what I want…" He leaned back and closed his eyes. "According to you, what I want don't exist no more."

"I could be wrong," Will finally admitted. "I'm just…" He started the engine and put the van in drive. "Playing the odds. Maybe she's alive. Kaylee was."

They returned to the Interstate on-ramp. As they got up to speed, Jesse laughed.

"Now what?" Will asked.

"Maybe Lynn'll turn up in Wyoming, too."

Will pinched his lips. It was hard to tell if he was angry or amused. Or both.

"If she does," Jesse added, "I'm definitely stealing my own van and taking her far away from you."

Will grimaced. Then he laughed, too. "That," he said, "is the first good idea you've had."

• • •

The long, silent drive across western Iowa yielded to a long, silent drive across Nebraska, save for Jesse messing with his phone and relaying directions to Will as they bypassed Omaha. They rejoined Interstate 80 a few miles before crossing the Platte River, where they stopped on the bridge for a break and spent twenty minutes staring into the waters flowing below. Low hills surrounded them. On the far bank, an American flag flapped in the breeze above a silent office building.

Will thought about Sarah, about the day they met, the day he proposed to her, their wedding day. She could always remember the details, but for him particulars had long since blended into a haze, like the colors fading behind the setting sun. He wondered if it might be the same for Jesse someday, or if his memory of someone he knew before Lynn had long since been consumed by the fog of the past.

"Was Lynn your first girlfriend?" he asked.

Jesse looked surprised. Probably it wasn't the question. Probably it was who had asked it. "More or less. Why?"

"More, or less?"

"I knew her in high school. Had a few classes with her, but we weren't together then. Didn't even talk much. There was this other girl, then. She had the hots for me." He leaned over the bridge and stared into the rippled water. "And half the other guys in the school. She was my first. Just one time, at her place when her dad was passed out from booze and her mom from work. She got what she wanted and trotted off to her next victim." He shrugged. "How 'bout you? Anyone before or after Sarah?"

"A girl in college," Will said. "She went to London after she graduated. Dinners with a few women since. Nothing that went anywhere."

"Not too broke up about it, huh?"

"Not really. Sarah made me feel alive. The others, they were just there."

"I got ya. Same with Lynn."

"Stupid, needing someone else to feel alive. Depending on them that much."

Jesse slapped the guard rail a few times, impatient for something. Will figured he didn't agree.

Feeling a need to explain, Will added, "Sooner or later, she dies or you die and one of you is left in living death. If I'd known that then—"

"Wouldn't of mattered," Jesse interrupted. "You'd of fallen in love just the same. It's destiny."

"Destiny," Will scoffed. "Random collisions in a flask of randomly-moving particles. Dumb luck, that was all, until another random collision carried her away again. Or was that destiny, too?"

"That was evil," Jesse said. "Destiny brings people together, but it don't make them do what they do."

Will believed in free will as little as he believed in destiny, but he was already tired of the disagreement. "We could save ourselves a lot of trouble by not forming attachments."

"Well sure. 'Cause then we wouldn't even be here."

When Jesse's logic turned irrefutable, it was doubly irritating. "If we weren't, nature wouldn't have to clean up our mess. Come on. Time to hit the road."

Jesse shuffled alongside Will to the van. "How come I don't ever get to say what time it is?"

"You want to?"

He grinned. "Nope."

"That's why." Will reclaimed the driver's seat.

"I don't think that's it," Jesse said as he climbed in and shut the door. "I think it's 'cause you have to be in charge all the time."

"Are we really going to do this again?"

Returning to his phone, Jesse traced road lines on the map. "What else is there to do?"

Will put the car in gear. "Go crazy," he suggested.

"Already done that. What else you got?"

"Get where we're going."

"Uh-huh. Where's that?"

The mountains. Maybe. Will didn't know. "I'll tell you when we get there," he said.

Jesse smirked and shook his head. "How come I don't ever get to say where we're going?"

"Because," Will snapped. "You wouldn't know it if you saw it."

Jesse leaned his head back and closed his eyes. "Probably not," he said. "Dumb black kid never did know nothin'."

It wasn't worth the breath. You couldn't convince someone who refused to listen. Will kept his eyes on the road. In the distance, a line of gray hills crossed the horizon. He hoped the mountains were near, but he had no clear idea where he was anymore, much less how far he was from his objective.

Whatever that was.

9

THE REST of the day vanished in a mental fog. They passed Lincoln, crossed the Platte once more and dogged its north bank, then recrossed as the afternoon wore on. The river split beyond the town of North Platte, where they followed the threads of the South Platte River up its long, shallow valley. The land morphed from green farms to golden brown grasslands. Bright circular fields watered by center pivot irrigation systems dotted the prairie. The sky felt lower, the puffs of cumulus closer. Jesse almost believed he could put a hand into the wind and, with a bit of a stretch, grab a fistful of cloud.

The sun dropped into their eyes. They passed by Ogallala. Gas stations, truck stops, fast food restaurants, and hotels clustered near the interchange. In the corner of the state where Colorado bumped into Nebraska, they passed over the river one last time and struck into grass-covered hills drying in the late autumn chill. High tension towers marched across the horizon, carrying power to nobody. They encountered an overturned truck in the median, its driver nowhere to be seen. Farther along, a pair of cars had collided and spun out beyond the shoulder. A vulture took flight from behind the fused vehicles.

Jesse didn't care to see what had drawn the bird's attention. This place creeped him out as it was. He'd come to an alien land with no buildings, no trees save a distant few scattered about. The land undulated around them. All was brown and gray, with only dollops of green and the blue, blue sky arching overhead, not a consistent blue but pale around the edges, grading toward cerulean at the zenith. Still, this emptiness offered something worth seeing. As the sun dipped to the horizon, it painted the edge of the world yellow and orange. When it sank from view, Jesse tugged Will's sleeve.

"Pull over," he said.

Will glanced at him. "Why?"

"I wanna see something."

"We need to make Cheyenne before it gets too late."

"I don't give a damn about Cheyenne. Pull over."

They were in the middle of nowhere, between Potter and Dix according the electronic map. Will stomped the brake and squealed to a halt in the travel lane.

Jesse ignored his fit of temper. "Come on," he said. Climbing out, he took up position at the back of the van to get a clear view of the eastern sky.

Will joined him. The only sound was the whisper of wind. "What am I looking at?" he asked.

"Earth's shadow. It's coming for us."

In the east, a dusky gray dome crawled up the sky, tinging it with night. No stars were yet visible, but as they watched, the darkness crept higher and higher.

"Earth's rotation carries us that way." Jesse pointed east. "Away from the sun."

Will watched the encroaching darkness. He tottered and leaned on the back of the van for support as though feeling the Earth move beneath him. "You can see it," he said. "I never realized the Earth turned that fast."

"A thousand miles an hour. A quarter mile every second."

"That makes the van seem slow."

"A tad, yeah."

Will shoved his hands in his pockets and stared into the void. "No wonder life goes by so fast. The planet whips you through twenty-four thousand miles every day."

"At the equator," Jesse said. "At our latitude, more like nineteen thousand. And that's nothing. The sun travels six trillion miles around the galactic center every year. Also nothing. It's made twenty o' those orbits in four and a half billion years."

"If you say so, professor."

Jesse laughed. "That's the nicest thing you've said."

Will cracked a smile. "So why did we stop? I assume you've seen this before."

"Not like this." Jesse swept his hand before him. "Look at that. End to end. The whole horizon. Back home, it's just darkness sneaking up on you. Here, it's got a shape."

"Great, now you've seen it. Let's go."

"Oh, come on, you were impressed."

"For a minute, yeah." He returned to the driver's seat. He grunted as he pulled himself up using the steering wheel. Once there, he neither closed the door nor spoke.

For the first time, Jesse realized his traveling companion, although hardly old, wasn't young. He got in and watched Will stare at nothing. "Want me to drive?" he asked.

Will shook his head.

"You need a break."

"I'm fine."

"You're not."

Will exhaled annoyance.

"We keep this up," Jesse said, "ain't neither of us seeing those mountains."

"I thought you didn't care."

He didn't, but maybe nothing he cared about existed anymore. "Lynn once said I'm too selfish," he said. "If all I got is her memory, I guess I should honor it. C'mon, let me drive."

"Fine." They exchanged places. Once situated, Will leaned back and closed his eyes. "Drive, already," he said.

Jesse drove.

Full dark overtook them, and Will fell asleep. Cheyenne was the plan, so Jesse kept going, although he had no idea what to do once he got there. To him, the name conjured ranchers clad in chaps and Stetsons packing six-shooters, riding horses through fields of tumbleweed. He guessed they had houses, but they must be spaced a dozen or more miles apart.

Dumb, Jesse, dumb, he scolded. Cheyenne might not be New York, but it *was* a city. Probably.

He didn't get that far, though. Darkness and silence conspired to lull him to sleep, too. After shaking himself to awareness three times in less than ten minutes, he decided it was time to stop. He took the next exit, intending to find a place to hide the van so he could sleep. Cheyenne was still fifteen miles over the horizon, but that was nothing. They would get there soon enough. This place would do, though it wasn't much more than a crossroads.

Except it was more. As he descended the ramp, a bubble of light down the road drew his attention. He made for it and found a small RV park where motor homes and trailers clustered along a dirt road encircling a restaurant and swimming pool. Exterior lights illuminated the facilities. Here and there, a vehicle's interior glowed yellow. Creeping about the circle, he scrutinized the place. Nothing moved. Lights notwithstanding, the buildings and vehicles looked deserted. No shadows slunk among them. Will would scold him for stopping here, but Jesse didn't care. They could sleep, and in the morning they could borrow the kitchen to cook a decent breakfast. Everything would be fine.

He parked in an empty lot and killed the engine and headlights. Just in case, he kept watch for a time, window cracked so he could listen. Nothing.

Just as he was starting to relax, Will stirred and yawned and asked, "Where are we?"

"Wyoming. Not quite Cheyenne."

Will straightened and blinked at the lights. "What the hell is this?"

"A place to sleep. Maybe eat, if you're hungry."

"What kind of place?"

"RV park."

"Damn it, Jesse, we shouldn't be here."

"Where should we be?"

Will took up his shotgun, loaded it, and stuffed extra shells into his pocket. "Not here. There are too many hiding places."

"But we're going in anyway, huh?" Jesse got his gun out of the back and followed suit.

"Only because you mentioned food."

They slipped out and closed the doors as quietly as possible. Even so, the impact sounded like an explosion. All around, crickets chirped in the night.

"Our dome light was a signal to anyone watching," Will said. "Keep your eyes open."

"I wasn't gonna stumble around with them closed."

They slipped toward the restaurant. Its windows glowed golden. Its door hung strangely ajar. Upon reaching the wooden porch, they saw why. A man's decomposing body sprawled on the planks, one leg thrust through the doorway, holding it open. The smell of decay filled the air. Will used the barrel of his shotgun to push the door open, and they slid past the deceased, careful not to step on him. Or it. It was a man no longer. Jesse thought of autumn leaves blanketing the park, beautiful in death, part of an eternal cycle of renewal. But it was too great a leap. This wasn't beautiful, wasn't a pile of leaves, and this autumn might descend into a winter never followed by spring.

Within, they found not a restaurant but a battlefield after an offensive. More than twenty dead littered the floors, tabletops, and chairs, all bearing gunshot and cutlery wounds. Knives and forks still protruded from some of the bodies. The carnage surrounded them, leaving no safe place to look. They picked their way to the kitchen, peered through the round windows, pushed open the double doors. More of the same greeted them.

"The health department won't like this," Will said.

Jesse covered his nose and mouth with his hand and mumbled, "Shut 'em down for sure."

Will motioned to the back. They escaped through the rear into the clean prairie air. Jesse shivered in the cooling night. "I guess it's the camp stove again," he said.

Setting a finger to his lips, Will motioned to a darkened trailer behind the restaurant. Jesse squinted at it, hearing and seeing nothing. He was about to say so when a faint squeal sounded, and the door of the trailer inched open. Will pointed his shotgun at a shadow silently spilling through the gap.

A floodlight snapped on, blinding them. Will's gun discharged. Jesse threw himself to the ground, rolled into an awkward sprawl, and tried to aim into the light, with nothing before him but the glare. Something skittered through the dirt, then the world fell silent.

"Damn it," Will muttered. "Damn it, where'd he go?"

Jesse caught a flicker in the corner of his eye. He turned toward it just as a car door slammed and the light went out. "He's in our van!"

"You have the keys, I hope?"

"Yeah." He patted his trouser pocket to check. "Yeah, I got 'em."

The light came on again, followed by clattering and crashing.

"Come on," Will commanded and took off at a run for the van. Jesse scrambled to his feet and followed, expecting to be knocked down by a gun blast at any moment. The attack never came. They reached the van to find a quarter of their food and equipment dumped on the ground but no sign of the vandal. Will kicked a can of corn out of the way. "Great. What was the point of that?"

"Crazy people don't need no point," Jesse said. "At least he didn't knife us in the back."

"Not yet," Will agreed. "But he will if he gets half a chance."

The floodlight on the RV snapped off.

"Start the van and turn on the headlights," Will instructed.

Jesse about complied but stopped halfway into the driver's seat. He slid out again. "Maybe not," he said.

"We need light."

"No, we need dark adaptation."

"What's that?"

"It's how we see in the dark. Our pupils dilate pretty quick, but after twenty minutes, chemical changes in our eyes let us see best in the dark. Problem is, you lose that in a second if you turn on a light, then it takes another twenty minutes to get it back. It's easier to see if it stays dark."

"All right, professor. Let there be dark. But keep your ears open."

They watched and listened and waited. The RV remained cloaked in night. Nothing moved, neither did any sound reach them. Half an hour later, Jesse flipped the dome light from auto to off, slipped out, and began gathering food cans, rope, maps, tools, everything. Will kept watch, gun at the ready. "I'm doin' all the work," Jesse whispered.

"Quiet."

The need for silence made the gathering take longer, but eventually everything was back inside, if in a jumbled mess. Jesse crept about the van, checking beneath it as well as beside it. "All done," he said.

"Inside, then," Will commanded.

Something struck the hood of the van with a bang. They both jumped. Will swung the gun in a wild arc, seeking a target. Jesse hit the ground as the barrel crossed his path. "Watch it!" he yelped.

Another bang sounded. Will skittered to the passenger side of the van and ducked down. "He's not shooting," he said. "He's throwing rocks."

"That supposed to make me feel better?"

"I'm just telling you."

Another bang. A rock rolled in front of Jesse's face.

"Let's get out of here," Will said. They bolted into the van and slammed the doors. Fumbling with the keys, Jesse started the vehicle, turned on the headlights, and jammed it into gear. Tires kicking up dirt and stones, he swerved around an abandoned car and made for the road. As the headlights splashed across the vehicle, they saw a head pop up from behind it. Jesse stared into the wild eyes of a girl, probably no more than fifteen. Her hair hung in matted tangles. Dirt streaked her cheeks. Head thrown back, she laughed as they passed by and flung one more rock, shouting words he couldn't decipher.

Jesse didn't realize he was shaking until they were back on the interstate. He braked and threw it into park and collapsed on the steering wheel, eyes pinched shut, still seeing the girl's face twisted in maniacal glee.

Will placed his shotgun on the floor between them and leaned back. "Damn," he muttered.

Jesse lifted his head. Beyond the windshield, the headlights splashed on the ground, revealing only empty pavement. "Did you see that?"

"I saw."

"What's it mean?"

Will gave no answer.

"How's she still alive?"

"Do I look like a doctor?" Will snapped. "I don't know anything about any of this!"

"She oughta be dead. She shoulda died days ago."

"Maybe nobody told her that."

Nobody told anybody anything. The disease had taken down half the world before anybody had a chance to tell anyone anything. But this was different. The girl had been infected but survived, survived the killing, escaped both murder and suicide despite her madness. Or had she only gone mad after, because of what she'd seen, because she'd survived?

Jesse blinked away the tears forming in his eyes. "Maybe we shoulda helped her."

"There's no helping her. She'll be dead soon enough."

"I mean we shoulda..." He couldn't say it. He looked away to the darkness on the other side of the highway.

          Dale E. Lehman

Will didn't answer right away. He flipped on the dome light, climbed in back, and began rummaging. "Only if she was about to hurt one of us," he said.

Rocks could hurt. But Jesse couldn't have killed her, either.

"If you show me how the stove works," Will said, "I'll heat up something for us."

In other circumstances, it would have been a small kindness. Now it seemed an offer of life itself. They clambered out, and shortly Will had a can of ravioli heating. Jesse wondered how often Will cooked for himself. Not often, if the state of his condo kitchen had been any indicator. How often had he dined out alone? This might be a step up for him. At least he had someone to share a meal with now.

They ate on the back of the van with their legs dangling over the road. Will stabbed a ravioli with his plastic fork and held it up for examination. "I wonder how many years we can live on this stuff. If the plague doesn't kill us, the food probably will." He picked up the can and read it by the van's dome light. "Enough sodium to choke a moose."

Jesse could almost see that. "Don't feed it to no moose, then."

Will grinned. The night grew colder. The wind stiffened.

"You think it's gonna be years?" Jesse asked. Though death had surrounded them for over a week, the possibility of extinction hadn't occurred to him until now. He assumed a light at the end of a tunnel— daylight, not the lamp of an oncoming train. Once the disease burned itself out, he figured cities and towns would recover. Despite Will's pessimism, he expected to find Lynn. Time would right itself, the world would heal, normal would return. Will had been right, though; that was fantasy.

Standing and stretching, Will gazed at the stars. Jesse looked, too. Dark pools of emptiness moved across the sky, clouds hidden in the dark. In New York, they would have glowed yellow and orange in the light pollution.

"No idea," Will said. "Maybe not, if enough people survived. If it's just us?"

Jesse still refused to countenance that. After all, they'd encountered a few survivors. Maybe they were like cockroaches. If you saw one, hundreds more were hiding in the walls. "How do we find out?" he asked.

"We don't. Not yet. For now, it's safest to keep our distance."

"We're plenty distant here."

"Mountains," Will reminded him. "I was looking at the maps. We can be in the Sierra Nevada in two days."

Two more days. Another thousand miles, probably. When the hell would they stop?

Will closed and packed the stove, gathered their trash and looked at it as though unsure what to do with it.

"Throw it in the dirt," Jesse suggested. "You just keep running, don't you?"

"I'm not running." He dropped the refuse at the side of the road.

"The Rockies are closer."

"You in a hurry?"

Jesse closed the back of the van. "I already gone farther than I planned."

"You're welcome to walk back." Will peered into the darkness that surrounded them on all sides. "I guess we're sleeping in the van tonight."

Sure, if they ran the engine all night to keep warm. The temperature was dropping fast and the wind picking up. Jesse wrapped his arms about himself for warmth. "If it is the end," he said, "maybe we should quit arguing."

Will motioned forward. Once they were inside, he took up his phone and studied the map again.

Jesse started the engine. The gas gauge hovered just above half. He supposed that would last through a night of idling. He twisted into the back, found a couple of blankets, and gave one to Will. Then he settled in with the other.

"We can stop around Salt Lake City tomorrow," Will said. "We'll reach Reno or farther the next day."

"Then what?"

Will arranged the blanket over himself. "Who knows?"

That summed up the trip so far. Probably the whole of life from now on. Not that life ever had been certain. Jesse learned that the day Martin died. Yet it all changed once he had Lynn and they made plans and could at least imagine a future. Good jobs, a place in a better neighborhood, raising a family in safety, growing old together.

All that gone the instant he dove into Will's Lincoln. He should have stayed. Worst case, he and Lynn could have died together. It was only a matter of time, anyway. Probably. In hindsight, he'd likely contracted the disease that morning. He'd felt the sudden rage, nearly throttled his boss. Pulling back from the edge was just dumb luck. He was carrying the bug. He had to be. He'd probably end up killing Will, if not by violence then by sneezing on him.

Will stirred. "Something wrong?"

"Nah. Just..." Jesse closed his eyes. "Regrets."

A long silence later, Will said, "Me, too."

Later, Jesse turned off the van to save gas. Sleep came, but neither quickly nor peacefully.

10

THE FOLLOWING day, they passed through a land folded and wrinkled, drying in the chill wind, flecked with grasses, sagebrush, and greasewood, all wrapped in blue sky. Will drove in the morning, Jesse in the afternoon. Both fiddled now and again with the radio but caught only static. They filled up the tank in a small town, loaded up on junk food and paper products, picked up some sweaters in anticipation of the winter, and argued about the path around Salt Lake City. According to the map, the only viable route detoured through Provo, which Jesse thought nearly as bad. "Let's blow straight through," he insisted. "How big can it be?"

Will let him win that dispute. Jesse had the wheel, after all, and maybe a point. The city didn't look that big on the map.

Mountains rose and fell alongside them until they passed Kimball Junction and climbed into the Wasatch Range east of the Great Salt Lake. Will lowered the window to breathe in the cool air, but it proved too cold for his tastes. So much for that. He powered the glass back up. On the peaks, a blanket of snow blazed in the sun as they passed through red stone road cuts. It sparkled in his eyes, but it was a short-lived revel, and soon they descended into the city. Jesse tried the radio one more time.

Shrouded in static, a voice mumbled incoherently.

"Hey," Jesse said, leaning forward as though that might bring clarity to the words. "Someone's there." He turned up the volume.

At the foot of the mountains, the interstate was choked with wrecked cars, overturned trucks, decaying bodies, flesh ripped by scavenging animals, a nightmare of destruction that grew too dense to negotiate. Jesse was forced to stop. His quaking hands gripped the wheel. "We gotta go back," he muttered. "We gotta go back."

But there was no way back. They'd probably find the same in Provo. Will almost told him to press on, but the kid looked like he might throw up at any second. "Take a break," Will said. "I'll drive."

Jesse put the vehicle in park. Like pieces in a sliding number puzzle, they exchanged places: Jesse to the back of the van, Will into the driver's seat, Jesse into the passenger seat. Will put the engine in gear and guided the van over the bodies in the road.

"What're you doing!" Jesse yelped.

"Close your eyes," Will said. "Don't think about it."

Jesse covered his eyes and whimpered. The van bumped along, crushing the dead under its wheels. Will stared straight ahead, always ahead, never down at what was passing beneath them, and in time reached the tangle of asphalt where I-80 joined I-15 north for a few miles before splitting and making for the lake.

The voice on the radio grew clearer. Soon they made out words and sentences, such as they were.

"The point is the bleach. You need the bleach to kill the germs, although you can't use too much because the smell attracts them. It's like how lions are attracted to the smell of blood, only this isn't red, it's totally clear, just like water. So you can disguise it in water bottles and they'll never know, until they drink it. And that's the thing, see, you don't know who they are, but you know who you are, so you just have to keep all that in mind. It's mostly about having enough food and water and, okay, nobody wants to think of this, but shovels. Shovels are multipurpose. You can dig potatoes, bury the kiddies, whack those aliens when they poke their ugly heads through the windows. Get a shovel, a pitchfork, what-ever, even an umbrella will do, plus it will keep the UV off you. They've poisoned the sunlight, you see. Oh yes, they're that clever, but we can be more clever..."

Will switched it off. "Good thing he's holed up in the radio sta-tion," he said.

Face still buried in his hands, Jesse mumbled agreement.

The road looked less like a war zone as they left the city and approached the water. They passed by marshes edging the lake. Chunks of mountain were scattered nearby. Jesse hazarded a peek and, finding the road nearly clear, dropped his hands.

"Sorry," he mumbled.

"It's all right," Will said. "That was worse than New York."

They skittered by the northern end of the Cedar Mountains, surrounded by dry grasses and scrub and bare soil. The world lay dead around them. Descending from the highlands half an hour later, they passed into the western salt flats, a brighter desolation.

Jesse cracked the window, shivered, put it back up. "How could you do it?" he asked. "Keep going like that?"

Will shrugged. "No choice." That seemed to be the theme of his life now.

Shaking his head, Jesse gazed into the whiteness stretching from the road to the horizon.

"When Sarah left," Will said, "I thought I'd die. Almost literally. I couldn't see ten seconds into the future. I didn't know what to do, didn't..." He brought the van to a halt and stared at nothing. "I don't know how I got through, really. I just kept putting one foot in front of the other. I did what I had to do to keep going. Eventually, the world didn't look quite so bleak."

"Like when Martin died," Jesse acknowledged. "'Cept this is different. This is everything, the whole world gone."

"The guy on the radio is still there."

"If you call that being there."

The sun touched the tops of the mountains to the west.

"Anyplace nearby we can stop for the night?" Will asked.

Jesse checked the map on his phone. "Town called Wendover, on the state line. They got a casino. Maybe we'll strike it rich."

Will put the car in gear. "I'm rich enough already."

"I ain't. Whoa, look at this. The Enola Gay's hangar is there."

"How appropriate. How far to town?"

Jesse cocked his head and fiddled with the image. "Thirty miles, just after the Bonneville Salt Flats."

"Great. In under an hour, we could be breaking the bank."

Wendover and its twin, West Wendover, stretched along the interstate from east to west, a four-mile strip of main street straddling the Utah-Nevada state line with a cluster of homes at either end. Desert yielded to greenery in only three places: lawns and trees surrounding the houses, the high school's athletic field, and a rambling golf course on the west side. Mountains loomed behind the town north and west. The casino and its associated hotel perched on the Nevada side of the state line, a complex of southwest stucco molded as American corporate.

The main street was strangely empty. No vehicles, no bodies, not even a stray dog loping by. Behind the wheel, Will risked a tour of the residential area. The silent houses yielded no sign of inhabitants current or former. A few cars sat forlorn in driveways, but if the plague had struck here, it must have vaporized its victims.

On edge, Jesse slumped in the passenger seat as dusk overtook the town. No lights came on to hold back the growing darkness. The place was simply empty. "Where is everyone?" he asked.

Will executed a U-turn in the middle of the street and made for the main road. "Maybe they all died in their houses," he suggested, which made it a sure bet neither man wanted to commandeer a house for the evening. They took their chances with the casino's hotel, logically the worse bet, but reason had fled the planet.

The hotel, too, sat abandoned. No bodies, no blood, nothing save the trappings of luxury and deserted luggage in the lobby. They wandered the first floor, peered into the pool, the gym, the business center, the meeting rooms. Nothing. Guest rooms were locked by key card, so they couldn't get in, but they heard no sounds suggesting habitation. They returned to the lobby, exhausted. Jesse flopped on a couch, Will in a chair.

Will didn't like it. "Something's wrong," he said. "There should at least be bodies."

"Nobody decaying in the streets is wrong?" Jesse asked. "What the hell's right, then?"

The sarcasm only darkened the mood. "You know what I mean."

"Yeah, okay. But maybe it's a gift."

"Hardly a gift," a new voice intruded.

Jesse scrambled up, arms and legs working almost at cross-purposes. Will was on his feet in an instant, shotgun trained on the intruder, who squatted behind the information counter. He had a gun of his own steadied on the desktop, pointed at Will's face. They stared each other down like gunfighters in an old western film, each waiting for the other to make a move.

"More like a war," the stranger added. "The sane against the mad. The sane won."

"Did they?" Will asked.

"A pyrrhic victory. Only one left standing."

"You're sure you're sane?"

"Sure enough."

"So where are the bodies?"

Jesse snagged his shotgun from the floor and eased onto the couch, hidden by its back. Not that the furniture would protect him for long if the other guy started shooting.

The stranger made a slight motion with the barrel of his weapon, as though pointing. "West, mostly. I'd appreciate it if you and your friend left town."

"In the morning. We need sleep."

"Oh, fine, I'll get you a room. Two queens or a king? Smoking or non? I'm afraid room service is closed."

Jesse choked back a laugh.

"Or maybe you'd prefer separate rooms."

"The lobby's fine," Will said.

At least no bullets had flown yet. Emboldened by the peaceful negotiation, the stranger straightened and set his gun aside. One good turn deserved another, so Will lowered his barrel, though he kept the weapon in hand.

"Are *you* sane?" the man asked. "What if I creep up in the night and murder you?"

Will must have been more tired than he realized. He hadn't considered that. Yet he had an answer. "I'm a light sleeper. You wouldn't get that far."

Slowly, the man slipped to the end of the counter and emerged from behind it, hands spread in a gesture of harmlessness. His words were another matter. "Don't count on it. I've killed men, women, and children in their sleep. I'm not proud of it, but I am damn good at it. Had to be, to stay alive."

"We ain't a threat," Jesse protested. "We'll stay just the one night."

The man didn't hear. Eyes fixed on Will, he continued to advance at a crawl, step by tiny step, his feet swishing against the carpet, voice hollow now, like a whisper of wind through a canyon. "It drives a man mad, fighting madness. The disease gets us all in time. The disease itself, or the horror of it. No difference, really, except the sick bear no guilt. They have no choice. We do, and we kill anyway." He stopped. He cocked his head. "If staying alive constitutes a choice. Maybe not. Maybe we can't help it."

"What's your name?" Will asked.

"A word to the wise, assuming you are. Don't get friendly. When you must take someone down, it's easier if they're a stranger. How many have you killed?"

"Enough," Will said. He didn't know the number. One with the shotgun, more than he cared to think about while plowing through the chaos of New York in his Navigator. Their faces flashed before his eyes, wild with rage.

"How do you pay that debt?" the man asked. "And you're not done racking up your bill. You can bet on that." He laughed and swept his hand about the place. "Might as well bet on it. You're in a casino."

"Self-defense isn't a crime," Will countered.

The man tapped his temple. "Someone in here says it is." He turned suddenly and strode back to the counter. He picked up his gun, held it upright. "Stay the night," he said. "If I kill you, it will only be in repayment of my own debt."

"How's that repayment?" Jesse yelped. "That's just adding murder to murder!"

The man looked over his shoulder. "It's stopping you from murdering." He vanished into the darkness of the hallway beyond.

Sounds woke Jesse a dozen times that night. Air moving through the ventilation system. The ping of a computer alerting no one to incoming spam. The twitter of a phone announcing a robocall. Footfalls that, when he bolted upright and peered into the gloom, proved phantasms.

Will gave the appearance of sleeping, but his dim form occasionally revealed the glint of eyes half-open. Neither would be in any shape to drive come morning.

At four A.M., the distant sound of gunshots startled Jesse awake. Before he knew it, he was sprawled on the floor behind the couch, shotgun in hand.

"It's nothing," Will said.

"That ain't nothing."

"Our host snuck out about an hour ago. I expect he's making his nightly cleanup rounds."

"He was here? In the lobby?"

"He just passed by on his way out. I had my eyes on him."

"Hell. Let's get out of here."

"No rush. Try to get some sleep."

"Ain't neither of us sleeping."

Will half sat. "He's probably shooting anything that moves. Best we stay put until he's done."

"You're giving the orders again, huh?"

Flopping back, Will sighed. "Only because I'm right."

"Like always." Jesse didn't know why he was arguing. Will had a point. This time, anyway. It must be his exhaustion griping.

"Not always." Will packed so much defeat into those two words that Jesse almost apologized. "Anyway," he continued, "there's no need to rush. Reno's only five hours off. After that, we'll be up in the Sierras. We'll find an isolated place to stay for a while."

Isolated sounded pretty good after all they'd seen. Part of him wanted to get back to New York and search for Lynn. He'd seen her in Kaylee, knew that somehow she had survived. But the city was a death-trap. If Lynn still lived, she too must have fled the shadow as it fell over the world. Where would she have gone? How could he search the whole country for her? Or Canada, if she ran north? Look how far he and Will and gone in the days since. Or the week. Or weeks.

"How long's it been?" he asked.

"I don't know. I stopped counting after we buried Daphne."

That dog had really gotten under Will's skin. Jesse figured she might have been the only thing he'd loved after Sarah.

"We'll need to make some plans," Will continued.

"For what?"

"Staying alive as long as possible."

"Why?"

Will had no answer, and Jesse didn't expect one. Will had repeatedly said the world was dead, but something inside his skull clung to life. They'd met a few sane people along the way and hadn't themselves succumbed to the plague, whatever it was. Maybe Will hadn't given up hope that civilization could recover, after all, that they could someday return to New York, that Jesse could find Lynn and Will could find...

...someone. Another Sarah, maybe, or at least another Daphne. Something, anything, to make it worth keeping on.

"Okay," Jesse said. "I'm with you."

He almost didn't hear Will's whispered thank you.

11

THEY LEFT not long after sunrise without seeing the other man, without seeing carnage in the streets, without finding any sign they weren't the only two people alive in this town. With Will at the wheel, they struck into Nevada's dry, wrinkled interior, passing desert and parched grassland, dry mountains and dry rivers, occasionally flitting by patches of green and catching the glint of snow on the upper slopes. Not far beyond West Wendover, they passed the scene of an accident—or had it been intentional?—where five cars had piled into each other and fused, the middle two having struck each other head-on. Although they tried not to look at the partially consumed bodies inside the wreckage, they caught glimpses of the horror.

"Damn," Jesse muttered.

"Tire tracks in the median," Will said. "At least one crossed and ran straight into the others."

"Maybe he died at the wheel. Went off the road."

"Or turned murderous. Or suicidal."

"Or both."

Will nodded. "Maybe."

"Don't you do that."

Will thought it strange that he didn't find it a strange comment. In other circumstances it might have been a joke. "I'll try not to."

Jesse chewed on a fingernail. "I been thinking. Could be a genetic factor in all this. Maybe the bug couldn't get its hooks into us."

"It's possible."

"So maybe it's safe for us to be around people."

"Safe?"

"Safer, anyway. If we can't catch the disease."

Will didn't bother pointing out they could still be shot, stabbed, strangled, or run down.

"It gives us more options, anyway," Jesse insisted. "If we don't gotta stay totally isolated."

"I'm not that optimistic. We've just been lucky so far. Plus, variants will emerge. They always do. That may be when our luck runs out."

Jesse continued gnawing on his nail.

"What we need," Will said, "is an epidemiologist who hasn't gone mad. Maybe he could tell us what's going on and how to stay safe."

"You know any?"

"Hardly."

"So much for that, then. What's your backup plan?"

"Hide in the mountains."

"I thought that was your main plan."

"It is."

Jesse smirked. "You need a refresher course in planning, Mr. Manager."

"Says the kid from the loading dock."

"The kid from the loading dock ain't making the plans. He just follows orders."

What a way to spend eternity, Will thought. *Stuck in this same pointless argument.* "Viruses don't go away. We adapt to them, but it takes time. This one hasn't given us time. It's trying to eradicate us."

"Ain't the first time something had it in for the planet," Jesse said. "End of the Permian, over ninety percent of all species died out, but life bounced back."

"You're a paleontologist, too?"

"Sure, I got a library card *and* the Internet. I can be whatever I want."

"So why are you still on that loading dock?"

"I ain't. I'm here in the desert philosophizing with you."

"Great. What's the meaning of life?"

Jesse looked out the side window. A quarter of a mile later, about when Will figured the question had been forgotten, Jesse resurrected it: "To live long enough to find meaning."

That was hopelessly circular, just like their running arguments. Maybe the meaning of life was to break out of the cycle. But no, not even that. There was no meaning. Life, the planet, the entire universe was a statistical fluke. That it existed signified nothing, and whatever meaning people fabricated died with them. Meaning had no objective reality and thus was fiction. But why bother voicing that? Jesse wouldn't listen. He never listened.

They wound through the arid landscape, catching occasional glints of salt flats in the distance. Jesse climbed in back and rummaged for breakfast bars and juice boxes. At half past ten, they reached Imlay, the barest of towns overlooked by snow-capped Star Peak to the south and tan ridges on every other horizon. Population less than two hundred, Will guessed. Before, anyway. Zero, now. Just as well. It felt desolate, its only trees those shading the handful of houses. The rest was sage and sand.

Beyond the exit to the town, the Interstate vaulted over one of the local roads. At the summit, Will slammed on the brakes and muttered, "Damn it."

Ahead, an overturned semi blocked the entire road and both shoulders. It sprawled in a straight line, perpendicular to the lanes as though tipped over on purpose to stop traffic.

"I guess we go back," Will said. "Take the exit and then the on-ramp on the other side."

Easing the vehicle back the way they came, Will watched in his side mirror. The way was clear, no vehicles in evidence, no people, no dogs, no vultures, no nothing. Reaching the exit ramp, he rolled down it toward the crossroads at the bottom. To the north, a simple white church bearing a great black cross on its side marked the edge of the town. A few cars stood in the parking lot, most with doors hanging open.

Jesse pointed. "Here comes the welcome wagon."

One of the vehicles, a powder blue sedan, pulled out of the parking lot and sped toward the bottom of the ramp, nearly tipping on one of the turns. It squealed to a halt, blocking the intersection. The driver's door flew open, and a woman sprang out. She stood, hands on hips, watching, waiting.

Will slowed to a halt twenty feet from the stop sign. "Get your gun," he ordered.

Jesse squinted at the woman. "She's awful pretty for a roadblock."

"Get your gun!"

"I'm getting it." Jesse reached back for the weapon and placed it across his lap.

"It's loaded, right?"

"No, it's just for decoration. Of course, it's loaded!"

The woman approached slow and easy, her dark hair fluttering in the breeze, her complexion Native American, her smile way too friendly for the circumstance. She hardly looked dangerous, so Will figured she was. She came alongside the van, rapped on the window, made a "roll it down" motion.

Will cracked the window enough to hear but not enough to allow her hand through.

"Where you boys headed?" she asked.

"Just passing through."

"Well, yeah. Nobody stops here. Hardly nobody lived here, even before. You're the first I've seen since it happened." She examined Will with some interest, then cocked her head and afforded Jesse the same. "Not a bad sight."

Nice try, Will thought.

"I'm all alone now," she added.

Jesse leaned toward the window. "Must'a been hard for you."

Don't talk to her. Not that Jesse was a mind reader.

"I hid in a closet for three days," she said. "Only came out 'cause I needed water and food."

She seemed as sane as anyone they'd met so far, but Will didn't care to play the odds. "I sympathize, but we need to be on our way."

"Where you so hot to get to? The world's dead. The week-old news on the Internet says so, anyway. Come back to my place. I could use the company, and I'm a damn good cook. Been raiding everyone's kitchens. Got plenty to share."

"I wouldn't mind a decent meal," Jesse said.

"Quiet," Will ordered. To the woman, he said, "That's very kind, but…"

"Oh, come on. I been alone here for God knows how many days."

Will about rolled up the window, but Jesse whispered, "Have a heart."

"I suppose this one reminds you of Lynn, too?"

"C,mon, Will. She ain't gone mad. Anyway, we got the guns."

Her car was blocking their way. He could drive around it, leave her standing there, but Jesse would never let him hear the end of it. "Aren't you afraid of us?" Will asked her.

"Hell, no. If you were gonna kill me, I'd be dead already. You can't rob me, 'cause I got a town full of stuff. Take whatever you need. And if you got a mind to lay me, I consent, so no problem there. That covers it, right?"

Will looked away. Jesse frowned at the floor mat.

The woman laughed. "Did I embarrass you? Sorry. Pretend I didn't say that. Let me give you a decent meal, at least."

Her logic, anyway, was sound. "All right," Will decided. "Lead on."

The woman bounced on her toes before starting for her car. Two steps later, she hurried back to his window. "I'm Anita, by the way. What're your names?"

"I'm Will, that's Jesse."

"Hi, Will, hi Jesse." She practically skipped to her car. She pulled around and made for the town with them following. Will considered abandoning her anyway, but Jesse did read his mind that time and gave him a "don't you dare" look.

She led them on a short drive down Main Street past the church and an elementary school, then right on California Street and, two blocks later, left on Unita. The journey ended at a blocky little house with peeling paint and a porch full of junk. Anita parked on the street. Will pulled up behind her. She motioned to the men and led them in without remarking on their shotguns. A small living room occupied the front of the house, with a kitchen behind and more rooms beyond, presumably the bedrooms. The furniture was threadbare and mismatched, but the heat was running and kept the place comfortable.

"Come sit in the kitchen," Anita said. "I'll whip you up something. Pancakes and sausage good?"

"Sounds great," Jesse said as she set to work.

"So long as the meat isn't spoiled," Will added. "Anything fresh is probably going bad."

Anita smiled at him over her shoulder. "I got freezers full of stuff all over town. It'll last a while."

It must be nice owning everything by default.

"I gave the food situation lots of thought," she went on. "Can't live without food and water, right? The water's still running, so that's no problem. Not yet. Food, well, we only have so much on the shelves in this little burg, so I checked out nearby towns. Nobody's alive, but they left a lot behind. I spent a couple days stashing as much as I could into freezers."

"How many towns are nearby?" Will asked.

"Winnemuca's thirty-five miles east, Lovelock's forty miles west. That's about it. Every other is just a crossroads. Lovelock's a thousand people and Winnemuca's seven thousand. Used to be, anyway. Now that I think of it, I should move to Winnemuca. It'd be a lot more convenient. Don't suppose you'd care to go with me?" She looked at the men with hope in her eyes.

Will didn't know about Jesse, but he had no plans to go anywhere with her.

She shrugged and continued the meal prep.

"You live with anyone?" Jesse asked. "Before, I mean?"

"Yeah, I had a boyfriend. Jimmy. He got himself killed the first night. Good riddance. Bastard used to get sloshed and beat me up, 'til I learned how to stay out of his way."

Jesse looked horrified. "Why didn't you leave?"

"Needed his money. Food's not free. Besides, he wasn't always bad to me. Even when he was, I didn't have nowhere to go. Now I got three whole towns to myself. I wouldn't mind sharing."

She was working overtime to convince them. Will couldn't blame her for wanting company. At least he and Jesse had each other for companionship, even if they spent half their time in ludicrous disputes.

She finished cooking and brought them each a plate and a cup of coffee, serving herself last. The pancakes were laced with cinnamon, and the sausage tasted like it had just come from the butcher shop. It was the best meal Will had eaten in a long time. Jesse praised Anita's culinary skills three times in the first two bites.

"What about you boys?" she asked. "Where you from? Where you going?"

"Came from New York," Jesse said. "Will has a hankering to see the California mountains."

"New York!" Anita set down her fork and gaped at them. "I read that was a war zone!"

"Pretty much," Will said. "We were lucky to get away."

"What's in the mountains?"

"Nothing. That's why we're going. It's safest to stay away from people."

"So why're you traveling together?"

Will wondered if she was teasing him.

"We haven't killed each other yet," Jesse said. "So we're probably safe."

"That makes three of us. Why not stay with me?" She waved a hand in a great circle. "Seriously. You can't get more isolated than this."

Jesse drained his coffee cup and pushed away his empty plate. He stretched and yawned and said, "I wouldn't mind staying for a nap."

She nodded toward the rear door. "Beds are back there. Take your pick."

"We shouldn't, really," Will said, but he, too, felt a bit drowsy. Odd. Food didn't usually have that effect on him. Not this early in the day, anyway. It must've been the lack of sleep the previous night. Bad timing, though. They shouldn't let their guard down.

Anita grinned at Jesse. "If you get lucky, you'll pick my bed."

"Oh," Jesse said. He folded his arms on the table and settled his head in them. "I got a girl back home."

"I'm not particular about that," she said. "What about you, Will? You got a girl?"

"No." Will closed his eyes. They didn't want to open again. "Not anymore. She left." He felt like flopping on the table, too, but he couldn't, not with Jesse falling asleep. One of them had to stay awake.

One of them had to.

"Oh, that's sad, Will. I'm sorry."

Why should she be? It wasn't her fault. Will folded his arms on the table and leaned into them.

"I can be your girl now. For both of you. You guys wanna have sex before?"

No. He wanted… He wanted… No. What had she meant? "Be… fore…what?"

"Before you die."

Will groped for the shotgun. He couldn't find it. Maybe his hand wasn't moving. He couldn't tell. His eyes wouldn't open. He couldn't fight off the encroaching dark.

Sleep forced itself upon him. He couldn't fight it.

He couldn't find the gun.

Damn.

Light and sound, maybe from a dream, pulled Will to the edge of wakefulness. He resented it, wanted it to go away. He wanted to sleep, to dream, to be left alone, but the growing light and congealing sounds wouldn't release him. They drew him relentlessly on, as though he was being pulled by a chain collared at his neck.

Except he wasn't moving, not physically. He was flat on his back and bound somehow, unable to sit, unable to stretch forth his hands. Whenever he tried, something cut into his flesh.

"Hi there, handsome."

He knew that voice from somewhere. Squinting into the light, he saw a face, Anita's face, smiling down from heaven. No, not heaven. The ceiling. Not that, either. She came into focus, standing over him.

"Don't fight it," she said. "Hold still for a bit. You, too, Jesse."

They lay side by side, handcuffed and lashed to a bed. Not gagged. No need for that. Nobody could hear them. The whole town was just the three of them.

"When the killing started," Anita said, and her voice sounded far away although she hovered over them, "it scared the hell out of me. The first hour was pure terror. But then I thought, hey, this is a blessing in disguise. Know why? 'Cause most of the pricks out there deserved it."

Will's head felt like a bowl of oatmeal, but it wasn't hard to guess at least one prick's name. "Jimmy," he said.

"First in line," Anita agreed. "Easy, too. Knife in the back." She made a stabbing motion. "It felt so good, I decided I'd cross off a few other wastes of space. For a small town, we had more'n our share. Everyone was killing everyone anyway. Nobody cared. I took out five guys and two girls. The others took out the rest. Then I settled in to enjoy the peace and quiet. But that was no good, 'cause, well, once I got a taste of killing, I wanted more."

Jesse groaned.

"The other towns," Will guessed. "They weren't totally deserted."

"Hey, you're smart! I killed three in Lovelock, two girls, one guy. Hunting was better in Winnemuca. I got eleven there. Six and five. And then nothing, leaving me hungry again. Until who should come along but Will and Jesse." She bent over and stroked Will's cheek. "Damn, you boys turn me on."

"This ain't fair," Jesse mumbled. "We come too far for this."

Anita reached over Will and ran a finger over Jesse's lips. "I know, babe. But that's how it is."

Will strained against the ropes, but she'd tied them too well. He couldn't move, couldn't see a way out unless he could talk her down, but how do you reason with a psycho? He had but one shot. A poor one, but he had to take it. "What happens once you're done with us? You'll be alone again."

"Yeah, that's no fair, either, is it? I been thinking about it. If someone showed up, should I kill them straight away? Keep them around for a while? Always comes back to the same thing. Once they're dead, I'm alone with my cravings." She went to the window, looked out, ran a finger over the glass. "All I can do is hope someone else comes along."

"They won't," Will said. "We've come twenty-five hundred miles and seen only five people, counting you. Two had gone mad, and two weren't going anywhere. The three of us are probably the only ones left in Nevada."

She neither spoke nor moved for a long time. The twitter of a bird filtered through the glass. Shadows moved with the rustling of leaves.

"Hell, woman," Jesse said. "What'd you put in that coffee? My head's throbbing like a hammer hit it."

Anita grinned at him. "Good stuff, huh? Drugs come easy these days. Don't even need insurance no more. I don't remember the name. Couldn't say it if I did. But I guess it works. You've been out for five hours."

"Five hours!"

Will wondered why she hadn't killed them already. Maybe she *was* that conflicted. "If you're going to keep us alive," he said, "you'll have to let us eat."

"And go to the bathroom," Jesse added. He squirmed a bit.

She laughed. "Hadn't thought of that, but okay, come on." She rounded the bed, undid some of the rope, and hauled Jesse up. He couldn't provide much help with wrists still cuffed and arms bound tight against his sides, yet she made it look easy. "Don't get any ideas. If I push you over, you won't get up. March." She pointed out the door. Jesse grumbled something but did as he was told. She followed him out of the room.

Not long after, the toilet flushed, and presently they returned, Jesse still in the lead, hands and arms still bound. She helped him sit on the edge of the bed.

"Back in a flash," she said, and hurried off to somewhere.

"That was embarrassing," Jesse mumbled.

Will didn't doubt it. She wouldn't have given him use of his hands, which meant she had to help. "I suppose she had no shame."

Jesse shook his head.

"Just think of her as a nurse."

"A nurse who wants to kill us."

Footsteps approached. Anita returned with two glasses of iced tea, each with a straw. She set one on each of the nightstands, then undid the ropes binding Will to the bed and pulled him up. "Your turn, I suppose?"

She might've made a good nurse had she not been homicidal. "I guess."

She pulled him to his feet, directed him to the bathroom, undid his pants, and held his penis until he was done. She shook it off before tucking him away and pulling his clothes back into place. "Your buddy's bigger," she quipped.

"That's racist," he said. Maybe Jesse was projecting thoughts into his head.

"Not if it's true," she said. "Maybe that's why he's got a girlfriend. Dead girlfriend, anyway."

Will neither confirmed nor denied.

"Don't think I'm stupid," Anita scolded as she steered him out of the bathroom. "She'd be with him."

"He still hopes. He's irrational like that."

"I never did a black man. Maybe I should, before I kill him. What d'you think?"

"He might be willing, if you agreed *not* to kill him."

"I could kill you and keep him around for pleasure."

"Or keep us both."

Anita stopped him in the hall, turned him around, looked into his eyes. Her face was impossible to read. "Then who do I kill? I need *someone*."

Either she was a damn good actress, or she really wanted his opinion. "Either way," he said, "you end up in the same place. Nobody left to kill. Maybe it's time to give it up. You can always shoot prairie dogs, or whatever you have around here."

"Not the same," she said. Reaching the bedroom, she steered him to the bed, pushed him down, and went to Jesse's side to give him a drink of his tea. "I want to shove a knife in *your* hearts and watch you bleed out. I can't give it up. Not cold turkey."

She returned to Will and gave him a drink. The cold liquid soothed his throat. "It's not like you can phase it out slowly," he said. "Cold turkey is the only way."

"Hmm." She eyed Will as though calculating his worth. "Maybe not. I could cut you up a little, maybe a couple times a week. I wonder if that would give me the same rush?"

Will felt his blood freeze. Jesse struggled against the restraints.

Anita ran a finger along Will's cheek, down his neck, over his chest, circled his heart a few times. "Yeah," she said. "If it doesn't, I can always kill you later."

Jesse rolled his head to face her. "Your conversations always go like this?"

"I haven't had any conversations lately."

"Just shoot us and get it over with."

"I don't keep guns here," Anita said. "Never much liked them."

That made as much sense as anything else about her.

"Not even yours." She waved at the window. "I stashed them in one of my other houses."

"Fine," Jesse snapped. "Kill us some other way, then."

"Maybe." Anita touched a finger to her lips and gave both men a searching look. "Nah, what the hell. Let's take my idea for a spin, see how it goes. Hang on a sec. Gotta get my knife."

12

THE FIRST cut stung like hell as she slowly raked the knife across Jesse's left cheek. The second, crossing the right side of his abdomen, hurt worse. Overwhelmed by the pain of those slices, Jesse almost didn't feel the third as she slid the blade across his left thigh. He didn't scream, but a sound he'd never made before was bottled up in his throat. His whole body grew rigid as he strained against the unyielding ropes, the strands of which cut into his flesh. He felt warm blood running down his skin from the wounds. Panic seized him. He must be bleeding to death.

"Wow," Anita breathed. She ran her left palm over Jesse's arms, chest, and thighs, pressing against his muscles, feeling the tension in them. Then she leaned in and kissed him on the lips. "Hot damn, it *is* better than killing you. I can't wait to try Will. Better bandage you up first, though. Don't want too much of a mess, do we?"

Along with a kitchen knife, she'd brought a bag of medical supplies. "I loaded up when I was in Winnemuca," she explained. "Grabbed some of everything. I could mummify the both of you." She laughed and set to work. Before long, she had the wounds dressed. Jesse couldn't quite see the bandages, so he couldn't gauge how much damage she'd done, but his flesh continued to throb.

Anita noticed him trying to look. "It's not bad," she promised. "Just a few nicks. You probably did more damage when you skinned your knees."

She went to Will's side, set the supplies on the floor, and raised the knife. "Your turn, babe."

Will grunted at the first cut and winced at the second. By the third, he'd turned to stone, silent and immobile. When she probed his rigid body with her fingers, the result must have been disappointing. "Come on," she purred. "Gimme a reaction."

Will obliged, with sarcasm. "Ouch."

"Ouch?"

"Ouch."

"It's our first time, so I'll cut you some slack. Pun intended. But I'll expect more next time. Don't you dare disappoint me." She set the knife on the nightstand and bandaged him up. "Before I get ambitious, I gotta do some research. Don't want to hit a big artery. I'm not very good at anatomy. Internal anatomy, I mean. I know your outsides, don't I?" Retrieving the knife, she left the room.

Once she was gone, Jesse whispered, "We gotta get out of here."

"How? She's having too much fun to let us walk."

"How's she expect to keep us here? We're like invalids. She'll spend all day taking care of us. When she's not slicing us up."

Will offered no answer. Jesse would have found that funny if the situation weren't so horrific. He wrestled with the ropes for a time, to no avail.

"If she gets tired of taking care of us," Will said, "we're dead."

"I'd rather I be dead than tortured every day."

Will gave the ceiling a puzzled frown. "Why hasn't she killed us already?"

"'Cause she found a better idea."

"But it doesn't work that way. She's still got a brain."

"A warped brain." Will had a point, though. The disease turned its victims into unthinking killing machines. Whatever she was, Anita wasn't that. Insanity hadn't been high on Jesse's reading list, but based on the people they'd encountered, there were several variations on the theme. In New York, yes, mindless rage had overtaken the population. David Buhler, the Gratiot, Ohio farmer, had been different. Crazy, but possessed of some manner of reason. The girl in the Cheyenne trailer park? Maybe crazy, maybe not, but not blinded by rage. The guy on the radio in Salt Lake City? Off his rocker, yet talking instead of murdering.

"They's different kinds of madness," he said.

Will pondered that. "Right. It affects different people differently."

"Or different diseases. Or variants, like you said."

Will didn't respond at once. Jesse didn't see how such speculation could help. So what if Anita was serial-killer crazy instead of berserker crazy? She'd kill them either way, only now she planned on slicing them up a bit at a time until they went mad, too.

They heard her footfalls approaching.

"Follow my lead," Will whispered.

Sure, Jesse thought. *Like always.*

Anita slipped into the room. "Got it figured out," she said. "The trick is, don't cut too deep. You don't cut too deep, you won't hit anything important."

"You're sure?" Will asked.

Don't encourage her! Jesse wanted to scream.

"Yep. Internet still works, and it says so. Amazing what you can find out there."

Jesse didn't care to trust his fate to psychos armed with Internet knowledge. But he kept his mouth shut until he knew which way Will was taking this.

"We've been talking," Will said. "Could you teach us to do it?"

Anita cocked her head like a dog receiving an unfamiliar command. "Cut people up?"

"Yeah."

"Why?"

"Might be fun."

She circled the bed to lean over Jesse. Her warm breath washed his face. "Your partner's gone nuts."

It was at least a lead to follow. "You said it's fun," Jesse objected.

"Maybe I'm nuts, too."

Best not to comment on that.

Anita ran her tongue over Jesse's lips, then looked at Will. "Who do we work on? Didn't think of that, did you?"

"Sure, there's nobody left here," Will admitted. "But—"

"There's you," she pointed out.

How could they get around that? She wouldn't make them partners in her lunacy.

Will remained undeterred. "We can take you places."

"Hell, Will, I go places myself. I got a driver's license and everything."

"I mean, we know where the people are. We've been across the country."

Okay, that was a point. Jesse jumped on it. "Right. We ain't just talking two or three towns. We been through dozens."

Anita sat beside Will and stroked his hair. "You said you only saw five, counting me."

"I did," Will said. "But we also saw things, signs that maybe other people were hiding."

Anita studied his eyes while she thought about it. "You really want to do this, huh?"

"Absolutely."

"How do I know you won't try to kill me the minute I cut you loose?"

Her hand slid down the side of his face, over his shoulder, across his chest. Jesse thought she was looking at him with more than a little interest. Was that part of her madness? Homicidal one minute, horny the next? Will would hate him for playing that hunch, but what had they to lose?

"Why d'you think we followed you?" he said. "You're the first woman we seen in a while."

Choking back a laugh, Anita gaped at Jesse. "Seriously?"

No way. "Hell, yeah. You know how long it's been?"

She leaned over Will and licked his lips. "That's the deal, is it?"

Will nodded, but he looked somewhere between frightened and irate.

"Hmm. I don't trust you. Let's test this theory." Anita whipped off her shirt and tossed it aside, undid her bra and dropped it on the floor. "Who's first?" she asked.

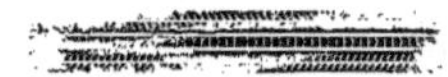

For a woman so far off the planet, Anita had a knack for detailed planning. And procurement. And construction.

Jesse and Will were still handcuffed but no longer tied down. Anita granted them limited range of movement via lengths of chain padlocked tight about their waists and secured to a ground anchor bolted to the kitchen floor. They could neither slip out nor pull up the anchor. Their restraints gave them the run of the kitchen and the bathroom next door, but no further. She removed all breakables and sharp implements from the kitchen, leaving them paper plates and cups, plastic utensils, and whatever food came in boxes and bags.

She also confiscated their car keys. "If you want 'em," she said with a devilish grin, "they're somewhere in town."

The town was full of hiding places.

Jesse thought if she got close enough, one of them—preferably Will—could throttle her with the chains, but she didn't untie them until they were secured. Once ready to undo the ropes, she marched them to the edge of the kitchen for the procedure, where the chain offered too little slack to use as a weapon. With them facing away from her, she cut them loose. If they made a move against her, she had the knife.

Then she left without saying where she was going or when she'd return. Her car rumbled down the deserted street until distance consumed the sound.

They sat at the circular kitchen table, staring at the faux wood surface as though it might offer escape. Jesse wasn't sure Will could manage even that much thought. But at least they weren't bound hand and foot, awaiting the kiss of a knife.

"I can't believe she fell for it," he said, as though he'd scored a point.

"Fell for what?"

"Neither of us exactly performed."

Will said nothing.

"She acted like—"

"I know what she acted like. I had a very clear view."

They both had. "Sorry," Jesse mumbled.

Will looked up. "For what, volunteering us to be raped?"

"I didn't think—"

"Shut up. Don't *ever* mention it again."

So much for that discussion. Jesse rose, dragged his chains to the refrigerator, and looked inside. It promised slightly more than Will's had in New York: a carton of cheap orange juice, half a dozen eggs, two and a half sticks of butter, and a package of American cheese slices. How fresh was this stuff by now? Jesse closed the door and returned to his chair.

"She's finding us a victim," Will said. "When she does, it'll be our job to cut them up."

Jesse knew. It set his stomach on edge.

"We can't win this. I shouldn't have tried to talk her out of killing us." Will shook his head. "That one's on me."

"Don't blame yourself," Jesse said. "Nobody wants to die."

"Maybe not, but I was the idiot this time."

"We ain't idiots. The dice just rolled bad."

"Then we need different dice."

For sure, but different dice wouldn't come easy. For one thing, Anita was too smart to leave anything useful lying around.

"Listen," Will said. "When she comes back..." A sickly look overtook him.

Jesse didn't need to hear the rest. He got it. They'd have but two choices, both nightmares. "I can't torture anyone," he said. "Can you?"

"Probably not."

"But you'd give it a go, huh?"

Will nodded, then shook his head, then shoved his chair back and clanked to the stove. "Is this gas or electric? Electric. Damn."

Pity. Gassing themselves might have been an elegant solution, under the circumstances, although that couldn't have been Will's idea. Whatever he was, he wasn't a quitter. Jesse watched him fiddle with the controls.

"Doesn't work," Will grumbled. "She must have unplugged it. Or threw the breaker." He tried to wrestle the appliance out from the wall, but with his hands still in the cuffs, he couldn't manage it. Jesse joined the effort, and they scooted it far enough for Will to inspect the connection. "Plugged in," he said. "Must be the breaker."

They rummaged through cabinets and drawers, hoping to find something, anything, that could be weaponized or help them escape, but Anita hadn't left much, useful or otherwise. Giving up, they returned to the table and sank into a silence made deeper by the lack of sound from beyond. No wind. No birds. Nothing.

Half an hour passed that way.

Will looked up. "Suppose we don't cooperate," he suggested.

Jesse had no idea what not cooperating looked like in this situation.

"We don't come when she calls. We stay at the table. She can't come for us." He rattled his chain. "This becomes a weapon when it's loose."

"She's got our guns," Jesse pointed out. "Anyway, the food'll run out sometime."

"But it might get her riled up. People make mistakes when they're angry."

Jesse conceded that, but it didn't much tip the odds in their favor. Anita was a nightmare within a nightmare from which they couldn't wake. "You think she'll find someone?" he asked.

"She thinks so. She wouldn't have gone otherwise."

Jesse folded his arms on the table and buried his face in them. "How the hell did this happen?" He didn't expect an answer. He wasn't disappointed.

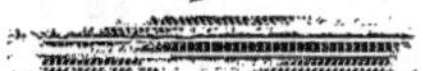

Anita returned a day and a half later, a successful hunter with her bagged quarry, leading a frightened young woman bound by handcuffs and ropes. Her stringy dark hair in disarray and her face streaked with dirt, the woman looked malnourished. Her wild blue eyes took in everything but comprehended nothing. Her quivering lips spilled a soundless, nonstop plea for mercy.

Stopping in the kitchen doorway with her prize, Anita beamed at the men. "Miss me?" she asked.

Jesse felt so weak, he might not have eaten or slept in a month. He and Will had managed occasional naps at the table, but they always woke with sore necks and arms tingling from lack of blood. They hadn't bothered with food. Jesse hadn't felt hungry since Anita drugged them. He couldn't muster any emotion at Anita's return, neither fear nor relief nor anything in between.

"Say hi to Daffodil," Anita said, pushing the girl forward. "Daffodil's from way down in Fallon. She's a nurse at the hospital, and she's lonely. I figure a couple big, strong men oughta suit her." She nudged Daffodil into the kitchen. "Come and get it."

Will rattled his chain like Marley's ghost. "I'm tired of dragging this around," he said. He sounded like a kid whining about vegetables. "Bring her here."

Anita smirked. "Don't get cute. You're on probation. Get your ass over here."

Will didn't budge. Jesse figured this would end badly no matter what they did. Having no bright ideas of his own, he followed Will's lead. As usual.

"Fine," Anita said. "I'll play with her myself. You can watch. After, I'll shoot the both of you."

Daffodil wailed until Anita slapped her. "Put a sock in it, girl." The prisoner quieted, her mouth moving in a silent scream while tears drenched her cheeks and dripped from her jawline.

Trembling, Jesse pushed himself to his feet. "Wait," he said, motivated by Daffodil's fear and a half-formed notion born of desperation. "I'll get her."

Will grabbed for Jesse's arm to stop him, but Jesse evaded his grasp. Approaching the kitchen door, he reached for Daffodil. The chain yanked taught. Anita pushed the terrified woman into his waiting arms. Wrapping her in a gentle if unsteady embrace, he escorted her to the table and sat her in his chair. While he did so, Anita slipped away and returned with the knife she had used on the men. She tossed it carelessly into the middle of the kitchen. It clattered on the linoleum, setting Jesse's teeth on edge. He scooped it up and placed it on the table.

Will looked away as though expecting the worst, but Jesse felt a bit bolder. He'd accomplished two things. First, he'd gotten Daffodil away from Anita. Second, he now had a weapon. He undid the ropes binding Daffodil's arms to her sides. He could do nothing about the handcuffs, but at least she had a touch more freedom of movement. Another plus. Maybe.

When Will realized Jesse was up to something, he watched the operation with a puzzled frown. Maybe he wasn't quite sure what was happening, or maybe he got it but didn't want to let on.

"I wouldn't of done that," Anita said. "That girl's stronger than she looks. It'll take you both to hold her down."

Jesse whispered to Daffodil, "Don't fight us. We won't hurt you." The girl's desperate eyes revealed no hint of understanding. She stared at the knife as though it might attack of its own accord. Like a terrified rabbit, she wouldn't move unless one of them took up the blade, and then she'd be nonstop struggle. He stroked her hair and whispered, "It's okay, you're safe. It's okay."

Unable to hear Jesse's words, Anita misread his actions. "Oh yeah, I like that. Do it."

"Do what?"

"Fuck her first."

Daffodil whimpered.

Feigning more courage than he felt, Jesse looked Anita in the eyes. "We ain't doing that."

"C'mon, I wanna watch."

"No."

"Who's got the guns, Jesse?"

"So use 'em. We shoulda been dead days ago."

Anita's eyes took on a demonic cast. Jesse found it hard to return her glare, but he did his best until she spat, "Fine," and rushed off. A moment later, the front door banged shut.

"Where's she going now?" Will asked.

An adrenaline rush overtook Jesse. "For the guns. She don't keep 'em here. Quick. Fridge."

For once, Will asked no questions. He and Jesse pulled the refrigerator away from the wall and unplugged it, then Jesse pointed the way, and they shoved the unit into the doorway, blocking it. Daffodil remained in her chair, quivering, probably comprehending nothing.

"We got one thing going for us," Jesse told Will. "Daffodil ain't chained up. She could slip out and grab a hacksaw or bolt cutters."

Will frowned at the woman. "Are you kidding? Her brain's fried."

Taking a shuddering breath, Daffodil rose on trembling legs. "I'll manage," she said. She picked up the knife and gave the blade a terrified scrutiny, then scurried out the back door, fumbling with the knob on her way out. The handcuffs slowed her only a moment.

"How about that," Will said. He ran a hand over the refrigerator. "I'm not sure these things stop bullets."

"One of 'em saved Indiana Jones from a nuclear blast," Jesse said. "Anyway, they block doorways. Anita won't move it with both of us pushing back."

"What if she's shooting?"

"Fine, let's get the stove, too."

Again, no argument. They wrestled the stove into place behind the refrigerator and sank to the floor with their backs against it. The wall clock ticked on.

Half an hour passed with no sound of Anita's return, no sign of Daffodil, nothing. Jesse wondered if they'd sit behind this stove until they starved to death. An ironic thought, that, but after another half hour, he was sure that was their destiny.

"Hell," Will said. "We're idiots. What's to stop Anita from coming in the back door?"

Jesse closed his eyes and knocked the back of his head on the stove. "Damn it. I never even thought of that."

"We're dead."

"Unless Daffodil gets back real soon."

"She's dead, too. She won't get out of those cuffs by herself."

Jesse found it hard to be alarmed by the prospect. Like he'd told Anita, they should have died long ago. Even Daffodil would've fallen victim to Anita's insanity sooner or later. The three of them had enjoyed more luck than the rest of the world.

The back door banged open.

"Here it comes," Will whispered.

"Let's hope it's quick," Jesse whispered back.

Anita barged in, a handgun gripped carelessly at her side. "Don't know why you bothered," she said. She glanced around the kitchen. "Where'd you hide our plaything?"

Before the men could answer, Anita sucked in a sharp breath, face contorted with shock. A pair of manacled hands slid over her head and caught her throat in a chokehold. She dropped the gun and grasped at her assailant, but with the chain cutting into her flesh, she could do nothing. Her feet slipped out in front of her. She crashed backwards to the floor atop her attacker, still held in a death grip, flailing like a trapped animal, unable to make any sound.

Jesse could almost feel his own throat being lacerated and crushed. He kicked back as though trying to melt into the stove's door. Anita flailed on and on while, terrified, Jesse himself almost couldn't breathe.

Anita's body went limp. For a moment, the silence of deep space permeated the house. Air seeped back into Jesse's lungs. With a thump, Anita's body fell to the side, coming to rest face down. A tide of blood rose from beneath the corpse.

"Oh my God," Daffodil gasped. She sat gulping air and staring at her handiwork. "Oh my God. I killed her. Oh my God."

Jesse couldn't move.

Will rose, shaking all over. "It's okay," he said, although he sounded as rattled as her. "You saved us."

"I stabbed her. In the back. I…" She raised her bloodied hands, showed them to herself, showed them to Will and Jesse. "I…"

"It's okay," Will repeated. "She was insane. She would have killed us all. You did what you had to do."

"I'm a nurse! I'm supposed to help people, not kill them!"

"You helped. You helped us."

Daffodil stared at her hands, then wiped them on her jeans. Groping for the countertop, she struggled to her feet. Her gaze swept over Anita's body, then Will, then Jesse, who was still pressed against the stove.

She looked at the handcuffs binding her wrists.

"Who the hell are you guys?"

Jesse at last managed to untense enough to pull himself to his feet. "That's a long story," he said.

13

WILL PRESSED his hands to the kitchen table and tugged the handcuff chain taught. Positioning the hacksaw, Jesse cut slow and deliberate while Daffodil watched. Anita's body lay on the floor behind them where she had died.

"Sheds and garages all over," Daffodil said. "Most were already busted open, but it took time to find that saw. I couldn't move too fast. I didn't want to fall and not get up."

Her foresight impressed Will, given that terror had possessed her not long before.

"I had to keep an eye out, too. She could've been anywhere. But I didn't see her 'til I got back."

The chain snapped. Jesse pushed the saw to Will and positioned his own cuffs. Will went to work.

"When I stabbed her..." Daffodil's expression morphed into horror, as though she was once more Anita's captive. "I never felt anything like that. I stick people with needles all the time. I even assist with minor surgeries. But this..." She licked her lips and studied her fingers. "It felt horrible."

"I know what you mean," Will said. "I killed a man a few days ago."

"With a knife?"

"Gun."

"Not the same. With a knife, you feel it. The resistance. The warm blood spurting on you."

True, but it had felt horrid all the same.

Saw whined on metal until the chain snapped. Will then cut the chains confining Jesse and himself to the kitchen. Finally, he motioned Daffodil into position and cut the chain on her cuffs.

"Why're you still alive?" Jesse asked her. "And sane?"

"I hid," she said. "I was on duty when it happened. I hid in a storage closet for two days. After that..." She rose and stood over Anita's body and dribbled tears onto the dark tangles of the deceased's hair.

The men watched her. Jesse's mouth moved as though silently offering words of comfort.

Will set aside the saw. "We're free to move about the world again, but I don't care to wear these bracelets the rest of my life. Anita must have a key somewhere in the house. Let's look for it."

They divided the rooms between them and searched in silence. Jesse struck gold; he found the key in a nightstand in one of the bedrooms, along with the keys to the ProMaster. Two problems simultaneously solved. Cuffs off, they stepped from the house into the late afternoon sun. The day was cold, the sky blue, the breeze light. The nightmare receded.

"What happens now?" Daffodil asked.

"We need our guns," Will said. "Or replacements."

"We oughta bury Anita," Jesse suggested.

Will shook his head. "No point. The whole town's dead, and we aren't staying."

"It's the decent thing to do."

"She wasn't decent."

"We are."

Daffodil refrained from comment, didn't even signal her thoughts. But when Will had no answer, she said, "I'll help."

Will sighed. "Fine."

"After that?" she asked.

"We leave."

"Where do we go?"

"Wherever you want." Will swept his hand about. "Plenty of vehicles."

"Can I go with you?"

Will shook his head. Every time they took up with a stranger, something bad happened.

"But Will," Jesse objected. "After what she's been through? You can't be that heartless."

"Remember how safe Anita seemed?" Will reminded him. "Or the last passenger we picked up?"

"Daffodil saved our lives. And she ain't a dog."

"Let's focus on the problem at hand. First, we need guns." Will searched the trees and the sky as though one might fall on him.

Daffodil gaped at Jesse. "A *dog*?"

"Yeah, we found a stray dog. She seemed okay, but then she attacked us. We had to put her down."

Not exactly the story, but Will didn't care to relive it just to set the record straight.

"A dog," she muttered. "You're comparing me to a dog."

"No," Will snapped. "But we don't know if you're safe, and you don't know if we're safe. I'd rather not kill you three days from now. Or be killed by you."

"Not gonna happen," she said.

"You don't know that."

"I do so."

"How?"

"We haven't developed symptoms." She looked like a teacher scolding a dull student.

"We might," Will insisted.

"Not likely. Once this thing goes to work, it works fast. It took down everyone in just a few days."

"Why not us?" Jesse asked.

Daffodil shrugged. "We fought it off. Some people store up antibodies and T-cells more readily than others. They have a stronger reserve, so they fight off infections better. That's why some people don't catch colds as easily as others. We must be the lucky ones."

"Lucky ain't the word," Jesse said. "Not if it means living like this."

"Point is," Daffodil told him, "We're most likely safe."

"Most likely isn't good enough," Will objected.

"It is for driving," Jesse countered. "You'd never drive nowhere if you gotta be certain nothing would go wrong."

Will huffed at the clouds.

"Please," Daffodil whispered. "Please don't leave me alone."

"I'll fix a spot for you in the van," Jesse said.

She touched his arm in thanks. Then she looked puzzled. "Who are you guys, again?" she asked.

They spent one more day in Imlay restocking and searching for weapons and ammunition. In the end, they settled on a trio of Winchester model 70 rifles because Daffodil endorsed them. Will wasn't sure he wanted to know how she would know, but as they pulled out of town, Jesse asked. Will was driving, Daffodil in the front passenger seat, Jesse cross-legged on the floor in the middle behind the seats.

"Lots of folks have them around here," she said. "There's good hunting on public lands."

"You a hunter?" Jesse asked. "Or your husband?"

"No husband." She nibbled on a fingernail. "Living or dead."

"Boyfriend?"

She grinned at him. "You hitting on me, Jesse?"

"Just wondering." He sounded embarrassed.

She stared out the side window. "I wasn't after a relationship. Not yet. But when I wanted some fun, I knew where to get it." She chewed on her fingernail again. "I figured I had lots of time to find the right partner. How was I to know the world wouldn't last that long?" She pivoted and threw her arm over the back of the seat. "What about you?"

Jesse's silence proved an eloquent answer. Daffodil reached for his hand. He allowed her to take it for a moment. "What about you, Will?"

"No." Let her interpret that how she would.

"And here we are," she said. "Going where, by the by?"

"The mountains," Will said.

She looked at the dry land passing by. "We have mountains are here." Which they did, albeit sparse and mostly distant.

"The Sierra Nevada."

She gaped at him. "Why?"

"I want to see them."

Daffodil nibbled on her fingernail again. "They're pretty and all. But bad idea."

"Why?" Jesse asked.

Will didn't care.

Daffodil bit her lip. "You boys aren't from around here, are you?"

They passed from baked land into baked mountains sculpted from brown sand. An hour and a half on, they crossed a ribbon of greenery hugging the Truckee River. Fiddling with his cell phone, Jesse said, "Bad news."

"What?" Will asked.

"Can't get around Reno. Gotta go through it."

"There must be some way around."

"Don't look like it. We're looking at a mess whether we loop around north or south or cut straight through."

Daffodil turned. "Let me see."

Jesse showed her the map.

She pondered it for a moment, moving it with her finger. "Leave the interstate at Fernley. Head south to U.S. 50 and take that to Carson City. You'll have to go through, but it's smaller than Reno. From there, north around Lake Tahoe back to I-80 at Truckee."

"Adds about an hour to the trip," Jesse objected.

"You in a hurry?"

"The boss is. He hasn't even seen those mountains, and he's in love with them."

"I can wait an hour," Will grumbled.

Settling back, Daffodil examined her fingernails. "Waiting's a form of gambling," she said.

"How so?" Jesse asked.

She changed the subject. "I never thought I'd get out of Fallon. Lived there my whole life, except when I was in college."

"What school?"

"Nevada State in Henderson." She smiled at Jesse's ignorance of local geography. "Suburb of Las Vegas."

"Sounds fun."

"Only if you have money."

"What's it like?"

She waved at the thirsty land. "Like this, but less green and more people."

"Same number of people now," Will said.

Daffodil turned her attention to her fingernails again. "There must be people somewhere. We can't be the only ones who survived."

"One here, one there," Will said. "Not enough to matter."

She didn't look up, didn't answer, might not even have heard. But then she turned to Jesse. "Is that what you think?"

Before Jesse could answer, Will snapped, "It doesn't matter what he thinks. That's how it is."

"I wasn't asking *you*."

Just when I had our dynamic figured out, Jesse thought. "I dunno," he said. "We been clear across the country and sure haven't seen many. One here, one there. Two one time, but one of 'em wasn't in any shape to say hi."

She stared down the empty road. "Anita said she was gathering survivors. That's why I went with her."

"That was one sick woman," Jesse said.

"Not like the others, though."

"So maybe she wasn't infected," Will said. "Maybe she just went nuts. Either way, she's better off dead. Let's forget her."

"What's your problem, anyway?" Daffodil demanded.

Will shot her an annoyed glance.

"Same as us," Jesse told her. "He deals with it his way, I deal with it mine. Makes what's left of life interesting."

"Interesting, huh?" Daffodil studied Will's profile. "Who did he lose?"

"He's not my spokesman," Will said.

"Yeah? So who did you lose?"

"My losses came before all this."

She returned her attention to Jesse and raised an inquisitive eyebrow.

"My fiancée," Jesse said. "Lynn. Maybe." He waited for Will's rebuke, but it never came. "How 'bout you?"

"You name 'em, I lost 'em. Parents, grandparents, brother, sister, friends, lovers." She choked down a sob. "It's like hell conquered heaven in five minutes. How does that happen?"

Jesse figured Daffodil should know better than Will and himself. She was the nurse. But he speculated anyway. "The bug must've spread like wildfire."

"Yes and no," she said. "It's got to be airborne to have spread so far, so it enters through the lungs. But the brain is the site of action. When the site of action isn't the site of infection, there's usually a long incubation period. It could have taken its time getting around. But why did the symptoms appear almost everywhere at once? That's the weird part." She chewed on a nail while she thought.

"Not quite all at once," Will said. "Two or three days, you said."

"Yeah, but that's crazy fast."

She dropped her hand and gaped at nothing.

"What?" Jesse asked.

"Damn. You think…"

Jesse couldn't even guess what he was supposed to think.

Daffodil turned to him.

"What?" he repeated.

"Maybe it was engineered to act that way."

Will glanced at her. "Engineered?"

"Just a guess," she said. "But yeah. Maybe it's not a disease after all. Maybe…"

When she didn't finish, Will supplied the rest. "Maybe," he said, "it's a weapon."

14

CARSON CITY presented few obstacles. The roads ran clear save scattered vehicles, abandoned or wrecked. As they swung south on I-580, Will at last set eyes on his goal: the sharp-ridged mountains of the Sierra Nevada in the near distance, capped with white. Beyond the city, they picked up state route 28 and made for the shore of Lake Tahoe. Surrounded by bare rock and pine forest, they caught glimpses of the lake and soon came alongside it. Its waters rippled in the wind, bluer than the sky, edged by snowy peaks. Reaching Crystal Bay on the north, the road swept out from the shore and carried them through Incline Village, where buildings hid as though embarrassed behind stands of tall pine.

Another day, it might have been paradise. Not today. Today, the streets were a jumble of smashed vehicles, decaying human corpses picked apart by scavengers, and a scattering of the damned shambling aimlessly through the devastation, filthy clothing torn to shreds, sunken eyes vacant. Jesse thought it a vision of hell made worse by the heaven of its backdrop.

Will maneuvered the van through wreckage and carnage. The sight sickened Daffodil, so Jesse helped her into the back and assumed the passenger seat himself. He settled one of the guns in his lap just in case, but the living paid them no mind, if minds they had. Daffodil buried her face in her hands and shook. Jesse watched survivors meander across the road. "Why ain't they dead?" he wondered.

"They will be soon enough," Will replied.

Concealed behind her fingers, Daffodil spoke with surprising steadiness. "People don't die of this disease. They kill each other, or themselves. These aren't doing that."

"Different variant?" Jesse suggested.

"Maybe," she replied. "Tell me when we're through it."

"You okay?"

"No."

Jesse settled the gun between the seats. "Want me to come back there with you?"

"No room."

"I can make room."

She shook her head.

Jesse still didn't know what to make of Daffodil. Her strength and weakness seemed locked in struggle, each gaining supremacy in turn, only to yield it back. Maybe that was her form of madness. Maybe she hadn't escaped infection, after all. Maybe none of them had.

"You hid in a closet?" Jesse asked.

Daffodil nodded behind her hands. "Two days."

"How'd you know you could come out?"

"I didn't. I just had to. You need food and water eventually."

That much was true.

"When the noises stopped," she added, "I took a chance."

Jesse recalled the knocking on the doors while they holed up in Will's apartment in New York. "Scary times," he said.

"Yeah."

"You said you had a brother and sister. Younger or older?"

She spread her fingers just enough to peek at Jesse. "Older sister, younger brother."

"I had a younger brother once."

"What happened to him?"

"Gang killed him."

She sucked in a breath. "I'm sorry."

Jesse turned back to the windshield. The roads were clearing, fewer smashed vehicles, fewer dead bodies, fewer living shambling through the chaos. "I feel like them," he said.

Will's grip on the wheel eased as they reached a clear stretch of road. "Which?" he asked. "The living or the dead?"

"I only saw dead. Just some were walking, is all."

The road came alongside the Lake again. Its crystalline waters mocked what remained of the human world.

"You can come out, now," Jesse told Daffodil.

She dropped her hands and gazed at the lake and the sky and the mountains for a time. Then she borrowed Jesse's phone and studied it. At first, Jesse wondered where she'd left her own, but that was dumb. When Anita kidnapped her, she'd lost everything but the clothes she was wearing.

"Crystal Bay is next," she said. "Then we're in California. Take state route 267 north from Kings Beach. That'll put you on I-80 again."

"Then what?" Will asked.

"Then Truckee. Then Donner Pass."

Jesse shivered as a cold wind blew through his mind. "Donner Pass?"

Daffodil waggled her hand. "Close enough," she said.

The road remained clear until they got to Truckee, where dead-eyed people enacted a play like that in Crystal Bay. Having crossed a seven-thousand-foot ridge, they dipped back to just under six thousand, rejoined I-80, and made west out of town. Along the north shore of Donner Lake, they rose again to seven and beyond.

Daffodil chewed her nails and stared out the window at the pine slopes, the remains of last season's snows, the white-capped peaks. "Everything's Donner up here," she said, half to herself. "Donner Lake, Donner Peak, Donner Pass Road, Donner Ski Ranch, Donner State Snopark. Why do we always turn tragedy into entertainment?"

Will didn't know. Things flowed downhill, that was all.

He drove on through Soda Springs. At Kingvale, he pulled off the interstate for gas at a two-pump station with a two-floor building, blue on top, white on the bottom. Pines lined the mountainside behind. An undulating ridge rode the far shoulder of the Interstate. They'd driven nearly six hours from Imlay, what with the morning's detour and the chaos in the towns along the way.

Will peeled himself from the driver's seat, thunked open the gas cover, and started fueling. Exhausted, he leaned against the van and breathed in the cold mountain air. On the upper floor of the building, a white banner proclaimed "OPEN" in giant red letters.

Jesse and Daffodil climbed out, too. "Pizza place next door," Jesse said.

Will had seen it when they drove into the station. Another two-story structure, it might once have been a fun place to stop for lunch. Overlooking the scenery, outdoor tables with umbrellas furled and tied waited on a second-floor deck for customers who would no longer visit. But he had no desire to case either the store or the restaurant. Nothing good could be inside. He waited for the pump to shut off, told the machine to forget the receipt, and recapped the filler tube. By then, Jesse and Daffodil had cupped their hands against the pizza joint's big window, shielding their eyes as they peered inside. Will didn't want to know what they saw. He made for the back edge of the parking lot and wandered into the trees. He clambered over a small boulder and skirted a patch of lingering snow and, once hidden from view, relieved himself.

So here he was. On a mountainside. Not much of a slope, but a mountainside. Mission accomplished. It was time to stop running, as Jesse would say. Put a bit of distance between himself and this town, find an isolated house, hunker down to wait until…

Until what?

Death, he supposed. The world wasn't coming back online. Too few people remained, and those who did were either stunned out of their minds or incapable of surviving once the power died and the gas in the underground tanks staled. All he could do was hang onto whatever life remained as age siphoned it away, little by little.

"Will!" Jesse called. "Where'd you go?"

Here he was, but the mountains had failed to deliver on whatever his imagination had promised. He'd run out of plans. He'd find a place and stay until he wore out the world's welcome.

He picked his way back down to the parking lot.

"Don't run off like that," Jesse said. "'Specially not with the keys."

"Nice to know where your priorities are." Will tossed the keys to Jesse. "We're almost home. You take it from here. I'll navigate."

"Where's home?" Daffodil asked.

"I'll let you know when I see it."

"Listen," she said. "We should keep going, down to the valley. Sacramento can't be more than an hour and a half."

No more running. No more plans. Will shook his head.

"Why not?"

"It's too risky."

Her twisted mouth said she didn't buy that, but she offered another alternative. "Let's stay here, then."

Will ignored her and climbed into the passenger seat.

"No use arguing with him," Jesse told her. "Believe me. I been doing it for two weeks."

Daffodil crossed her arms. "I'm serious. We should stay."

Will took up his phone and fiddled with the maps. "There's a road south to someplace called Devil's Peak. Looks to be no more than two miles off the interstate. We'll try that. If it doesn't work out, we'll find somewhere else."

She stared at him as though he'd grown antlers.

"What?" he asked.

"Seriously? You want to go to someplace called Devil's Peak?"

"I doubt Satan is in residence."

Daffodil gave up. She clambered into the van and tucked herself into the back. "Not yet," she muttered. "But just wait."

Jesse got behind the wheel and drove south on Donner Pass Road. Will instructed him to take the next left, which he did. And then hit the brakes. The pavement had ended abruptly. Beyond, a dirt road led under the interstate into the pines. In the distance, a patch of snow sprawled across the road. "You sure about this?" Jesse asked.

"Go," Will snapped.

Jesse went, but he clearly didn't like it. As they bumped down the road, Daffodil leaned forward. "Looks like a road where Satan would live, doesn't it?"

The van cut through the snow, which proved thankfully thin. For the most part, the road was dry, the dirt well-packed and reasonably smooth. Jesse picked up the speed once he got the hang of it, although he slowed to cross the white patches. Three quarters of a mile on, they bumped over a railway. After another half mile, the road ended at a crossroad. Will directed Jesse left. Farther still, that road ended in another crossroad, and again Will sent them left. Behind scattered trees, a ridge dogged them on the right. The slope ran down to a small lake on their left. Ahead, the bulk of a mountain peeked at them from behind the ridge.

"That must be the devil's place," Daffodil said.

The forest thickened as they climbed, and the mountain came into full view ahead, towering over the treetops, its dark rock liberally splashed with snow. The summit was a sharp point. Will liked it; it was exactly how he imagined a mountain should look, and right in their backyard. Now all they needed was a house.

Tucked into the woods, they found it. Running south, the road crossed the western foot of the mountain. There, a dirt track rose from the road to a clearing, and in the clearing a house perched on the side of a low ridge that rose to the base of the mountain's north slope.

Will studied the structure. It was small, wood-sided to give the impression of a log cabin, wrapped by an empty porch guarded by a wooden rail. The door stood dead center in the façade with a window flanking it on each side. The roof, pitched alpine steep, rose high over them, Devil's Peak in miniature. They were off the grid here for sure. No power lines, no other houses to be seen in this wilderness. Well water, probably. Septic or outhouse? The former, with luck. Only one way to find out.

Jesse stopped, killed the engine, and stared at the cabin door as though dreading what lurked within.

Will climbed out. "Bring the guns," he said and clomped up the wooden steps to the porch.

15

"LOOKS LIKE SNOW," Daffodil said, closing the door behind her.

Jesse sampled the canned beef and vegetable soup he was heating on the propane stove. Not quite hot enough. He dialed the flame up. "Snows every third day here," he said.

They'd been in the cabin for twelve days, Daffodil in one bedroom, Jesse in the other, and Will by his own choice sleeping on the small sofa in what they'd taken to calling the front room, a mashup of living room and kitchen. Over those twelve days, snow had blanketed the land four times, although never more than an inch at a time. Some of the powder sublimated in the sunlight each day. Some blew off in the wind. It maintained a depth of four inches in shaded patches beneath the trees. On open ground, mere dots remained, speckling swaths of bare granite that glinted in the sun.

"It'll do that," Daffodil said. "We're on the windward side of a seven-thousand-foot range. Thank God it's not Christmas yet."

Seated at a tiny wooden table by a window in the back, Will rummaged through piles of stuff brought in from the van. Over the past few days, they had emptied the vehicle and stacked everything in a corner, separating food from medical supplies from miscellany. Aside from that crude organization, it remained a chaotic stockpile from which they pulled items at need. Yesterday, Will began an inventory, recording everything on his cell phone. At least the device was still good for that; he couldn't get a signal out here, even though he could keep it charged thanks to electricity from a propane generator. "What's Christmas got to do with it?" he asked, not looking up from his work.

"The heaviest snows usually come end of December, beginning of January. But you never know. The Donners got trapped a month earlier. We should've stayed at the gas station."

Jesse wished she'd stop bringing that up. Now he knew how Will felt about his pining for Lynn. *We should've stayed* fell from her lips with far greater frequency than flakes fell from the sky, nearly always coupled with mention of the Donner tragedy. "Let's keep some optimism," he suggested. "This ain't a bad place. Quiet, warm, killer view."

"Killer. You got that right." Daffodil plopped in a chair at the table opposite Will and craned her neck. "Tallying food?"

"That's done. I'm working on medical supplies now."

"How much food we got?"

"Enough."

"Enough for what?"

He raised his head, said nothing, resumed his work.

Jesse sampled the soup one more time. Just right. He ladled three bowls and brought two to the table. Then he plopped the beef onto plates and served that. "*Bon appetite*," he said with no trace of French accent. Retrieving his own bowl and plate, he joined his companions. Daffodil made to stare Will down, but Will refused to join the battle.

"We should be good for a while, right, Will?" Jesse asked. "We restocked along the way."

"Restocked junk food," Will muttered.

Daffodil sampled the soup. "What's a while? Three, four months?"

"One, anyway." Jesse blew on a spoonful and carefully sipped.

"One's no good."

Will pulled his bowl close and stirred it. "You didn't have to tag along."

"You didn't have to bring us up here. I told you it was a bad idea. More than once."

Jesse put up his hands like a referee pushing a pair of boxers apart. "Can we give it a rest?"

Will ate as though demonstrating his inner calm. Daffodil smirked and mimicked him, spoonful for spoonful.

"Why's the gas station better, anyway?" Jesse asked.

"Maybe," Daffodil said between slurps, "because it has supplies and electricity and freezers."

"We have everything we need," Will said. "Well water, two full propane tanks, even indoor plumbing and a septic system."

"And one month of food," Daffodil said, deadpan. "To face down months and months of winter. That's why the gas station's better. Between the store, the restaurant, and what you guys brought, we might not have starved."

"It's only two miles," Jesse objected. "We can make supply runs."

"That van won't make two inches in hip-deep snow."

"You're welcome to walk," Will grumbled. "We're staying."

"What's so great about here, anyway? Besides the killer view."

"It's isolated. Nobody will blunder in. We're safe here."

"Snowed in and starving isn't safe." She shoved her bowl aside. Soup slopped over the table and onto the floor. She stomped out, slamming the door behind her.

Will continued eating as though she'd never been there. Jesse swore he felt a cold wind testing the door and windows. Big New York snows seldom topped two feet. Even when they shut the city down, it soon reopened. Stock a week's provisions, and you'd make it no problem. Here? If Daffodil was right, they could be cut off from the world for twelve times that long. Time enough to kill them without a mountain of provisions.

"Maybe she's got a point," he said.

Will looked up. "Don't start."

"But—"

"What do you think I'm doing?"

Inventorying, of course. So what? Jesse shrugged.

"I'm not stupid. I'm planning. Once I have a handle on what we've got, I'll figure out what we need. We'll stock up before the snow sets in. One or two trips should be enough."

"Why didn't you tell her?"

He lifted another spoonful to his mouth. "She doesn't listen."

Appetite gone, Jesse pushed his bowl away. "Sounds like someone else I know. You two might make an ideal couple." He went to find Daffodil, half expecting Will to order him back. But only silence followed in his wake.

Outside, the air had indeed acquired a greater chill. The sky glowed deep blue in the east, while slate clouds flowed in from the west. A rush of wind sounded in the trees, reminding Jesse of traffic flowing down a busy street. Daffodil stood on the porch, leaning on the rail, gazing at the snow-flecked mountains to the west. The cabin was perched on the edge of an undulating bowl two miles wide and four long. Whichever way they turned, peaks ringed them.

Jesse leaned on the rail beside her. Scattered bird chatter flowed from the trees in waves.

"He's wrong," Daffodil said.

"He does his best."

"We can't stay here forever. Or even for long."

"He's making plans. We'll lay in supplies."

"I know he thinks so." She pointed at the encroaching clouds. "See that?"

They'd be hard to miss.

"What if that's the first big snow?"

It could be, but how was Jesse to know? How was Daffodil to know, for that matter? His weather app had stopped providing forecasts within a couple of days of the outbreak. It used human-analyzed forecasts from the National Weather Service. Jesse never trusted apps that based forecasts on models only. He'd read they could be significantly less accurate, so he had never downloaded one, and now it was too late. No signal.

Then again, maybe Daffodil did know. This wasn't Vegas, but she was more native to the area than Will or himself. "Is it?" he asked.

"How the hell should I know? I'm just a nurse."

"That's more'n I ever was," Jesse said. "I just unloaded trucks."

"Doesn't mean you should do everything Will says."

"I don't. But we got this far mostly 'cause of him. I almost trust him."

Daffodil laughed. "That's a compliment?"

He'd meant it as a statement of fact, but he had to admit, it sounded lame. He laughed with her.

Her blue eyes lifted to the sky. The clouds invaded them. "I want to stay with you guys," she said in a muted tone. "I won't survive on my own. But yes, I'm afraid of that." She poked a finger at the encroaching weather. "We should get down to the valley while we can."

"Cities and towns ain't safe. Even farmhouses ain't." Jesse shivered at the memory of the incident in Gratiot, Ohio.

"Neither is starving."

As if in agreement, the staccato call of a Steller's jay erupted from the forest. Jesse wondered if it was a sign. "What will you do?" he asked.

She watched the clouds in silence.

It was after midnight before Will packed it in. Jesse and Daffodil had retired to their respective rooms, leaving him to sort and catalogue at the table at the rear of the front room. He hadn't quite finished when he gave up, stood for a stretch, and turned out the lights. A darkness deeper than any he'd known engulfed him. He stood for a few moments in blackness, waiting for his eyes to adapt. They never quite did, but back at that RV park near Cheyenne, Jesse had said dark adaptation took twenty minutes.

Hell with it. Hands stretched before him, Will shuffled toward the couch. He bumped into it and almost fell face-down on it, catching his balance at the last moment. He sat. Random thoughts and memories drifted through his mind, flashing by like shooting stars. Sarah. New York. Jesse. Gratiot. Sarah. Daphne. Kaylee. The RV park. Sarah. Earth's shadow crawling up the sky. Anita. Daffodil. Sarah.

When the mental meteor shower faded, one bright trail remained, oddly not Sarah.

Daffodil.

Why her?

Maybe because he didn't understand her. Why was she tagging along? They weren't set on her preferred course, so what did she want? She was young, maybe not as young as Jesse but full of energy and opinions and more strength than one might guess. As much as Will hated to admit it, she could be an asset. Maybe, someday, she could be more than that. Jesse had a fragment of hope, however irrational, that Lynn was still alive, but what did Will have? Nothing, that's what. Whatever Sarah's fate, he had nothing.

And then Daffodil came along.

Where had *that* come from? Will pushed the thought aside. He was exhausted, that was all. He needed sleep. Yet he couldn't bring himself to lie down. Instead, he fumbled his way to the door and stepped out onto the porch. The mountain night gathered him into its frigid embrace. He hugged himself to keep warm and looked up to the sky, wishing for stars. Instead, he saw only blackness, and from that blackness frozen specks descended, brushed his face, melted into cold droplets. So much for that. He went back in and settled down for the night. Sleep took him quickly.

A bang startled him awake. He jerked upright and searched the room for the source of the noise. Gray light seeped in through the curtained windows, making ghosts of the furniture and kitchen appliances. Another bang sounded, not from within the cabin but from without. He nudged the curtain aside just enough to peer out. A thin layer of snow covered the rock and soil sloping down to the road. The pines were dusted with the stuff. The ProMaster, too. One more bang echoed through the trees as a fist-sized rock ricocheted from the side of the van and bounced through the snow.

"What the hell was that?" Jesse complained, emerging from his room.

Will motioned him to silence. Someone must be out there. A moment later, Daffodil joined them, and they all peeked through the curtains, Will center, Jesse left, Daffodil right.

Will spotted the interloper first. "There," he whispered. "Maybe ten, fifteen paces, back in that cluster of pines left of the drive."

As they watched, a shadow moved beneath the trees. It stooped to pick up something, then waited. Another a rock sailed through the air and struck the van's taillight, shattering the red lens. The shadow bellowed words muddied by distance.

"They think we're in there?" Jesse wondered.

"No," Daffodil said. "They're trying to kill the van."

Will didn't see where it mattered. Either way, he'd been wrong. He hadn't expected anyone would wander into someplace so remote, but here someone was—someone disease-maddened. "Guns," he said. Another rock hurled toward the van. It struck one of the rear windows. Glass shattered, peppering the snow with shards. In the trees, the shadow laughed and whooped and danced about, then another rock flew, and the other window fractured.

"Damn it," Will muttered. "Come on."

They retrieved the guns from the back, made sure they were loaded, and crept out the back door. Keeping close to the wall, they circled the cabin, Will and Daffodil on the left, Jesse on the right. Hidden around the front corners, they took aim, but the shadow no longer slid through the trees. At first, Will couldn't find it anywhere, neither by the van nor in the drive or among the pines, but then Daffodil said, "On the ground by the rear wheel."

A human figure lay crumpled there, not moving, maybe not even breathing.

Will watched it for a long time. Jesse, at the other end of the house, gestured to ask what was going on. Will tentatively motioned him over. "I thought you said the disease doesn't kill," Will said to Daffodil.

She shrugged and tilted her gun upright. "Let's find out."

Jesse joined them, and together they approached the figure. When they got close, they found a man of maybe thirty, dark hair matted and tangled, a two-week growth of beard, vacant eyes turned to the overcast sky. He sprawled like a rag doll that had been tossed aside, arms and legs at unnatural angles. His wrists had both been slashed with shards of broken glass, which had also sliced his fingertips and now rested beside his cupped hands. Blood mixed with snow in a ghastly rivulet trickling down the drive toward the road.

"Wasn't the disease," Jesse said. He took a shuddering breath. "At least we didn't have to shoot him."

Will side-stepped body and blood to inspect the rear windows. Smashed to hell, splintered glass had sprayed the snow and the van's interior. Since they'd removed everything earlier, cleaning up wouldn't be horrible, but they'd have to cover the gaping holes before driving to keep warmth in and exhaust out. He looked up at the unrelenting clouds and revised the thought: before it snowed again.

Daffodil came alongside Will and inspected the damage. "Cardboard and blankets," she suggested.

"And duct tape," Will added. "That's supposed to be good for everything, right?"

"My dad always swore by it."

He waited for her to state the obvious, but to her credit she said nothing.

Jesse wore the expression of a bewildered child. "What now?"

Daffodil remained silent.

"We'd better leave," Will said. "Pack up and get out of here before the snow gets worse. We'll pick up more supplies at the gas station and make for lower ground."

Daffodil shoved her hands in her jeans pockets and stared at her feet.

"I'd say we bury him." Jesse's voice was as distant as his expression. "But the ground's almost solid rock."

Will was glad of that, anyway. He made for the cabin to see what they had to cover the window. Behind him, Daffodil told Jesse, "I like a man who admits when he's wrong."

"Pleasant surprise, huh?" Jesse said.

Will felt a flush of warmth, whether from embarrassment or pleasure. He wasn't sure which, but it felt good.

16

ANOTHER SURPRISE waited at the gas station. As Will pulled into the parking lot, a filthy gray pickup that hadn't been there before sat empty at the back of the lot. He pointed it out as he stopped at the pumps. Seated in the back of the van, Jesse muttered, "Damn," He handed guns to Daffodil and Will and took one for himself.

They waited in silence for several minutes. When a shadow crossed the glass of the convenience store door, Daffodil asked, "Just one, you think?"

"If we're lucky," Will said. "But they've seen us."

Jesse leaned to the window for a look. "How d'you know?"

"How could they not? Let's give them some space." Putting the van in gear, Will circled to the restaurant and parked near its door. The building's darkened windows yielded no sign of movement within. "Cross your fingers," he said and opened the door.

Daffodil touched his arm. "Hey. If they know how to shoot…"

A fair point, but no shots had been fired yet. He hoped that meant something. He slid out and waited, gun pointed at the ground.

When no attack came, Daffodil and Jesse joined Will. A cold breeze chilled their faces. The gas station door opened. The shadow emerged and transformed into a woman bundled against the cold, a ski cap on her head, blonde locks spilling out and fluttering in wind. She held a rifle crosswise before her as she advanced, step by slow step. She halted halfway to the restaurant.

Jesse swallowed and glanced at Will. Daffodil shifted her rifle as though afraid she might drop it. Will remained as still as the granite mountains.

"Who the hell are you?" the woman called.

"Just passing through," Will told her. "We need gas, then we'll be on our way."

"Forget it. We were here first."

Will didn't argue. Possession had become the sum of the law, and they hadn't staked a claim when they passed through before.

"We won't take anything else," Daffodil said.

"Pump it somewhere else," a voice behind them said. A lanky young man had hobbled out of the restaurant. He also wore a heavy coat. He carried no weapon as such but used a cane for support on his right side. The cane had a price tag stuck just below the curved grip. His golden hair had the same hue as the woman's, and his lopsided grin morphed into a grimace as he took another step with his right leg. His jeans bulged a bit around his right calf.

"How'd you get hurt?" Daffodil asked.

"Never you mind," the woman called. "And you keep your mouth shut, Jared."

Jared laughed. "Chill, Mom. They won't hurt us." He halted and gave Daffodil a leisurely inspection. Will didn't like the way he looked at her. It was too like a predator sizing up its prey. "What's your name?"

"Daffodil. What's your mom's?"

"Carolyn, but you best call her ma'am." He grinned.

Carolyn approached, gun aimed away, maybe because her son was in the line of fire, maybe because the interlopers had made no threatening moves. Whatever the case, she didn't look pleased. "Don't act like your father," she snapped. "You don't need more trouble."

Jared's gaze, fixed on Daffodil, said he could handle a shot of trouble.

"I just want to help," Daffodil objected. "I'm a nurse."

"He's fine," Carolyn snapped. "He took a little fall and got banged up a bit,"

"Looks like more than a bit. I'll be happy to look at it."

"I'll bet. Get in your van and get the hell out of here."

Jared shifted his weight and winced again. "Mom—"

"Shut up." Carolyn's gun edged upward.

"Sprain or open wound?" Daffodil asked Jared.

"Bit of both," Jared told her.

"When did it happen?"

"Four days ago. I slipped on some loose rock."

"Did you clean it good? You don't want it infected."

He glanced at his mother, who pinched her lips and shook her head in disgust. "Wouldn't hurt to have her check, Mom."

Carolyn's stare could have frozen a polar bear, but Jared didn't as much as blink. "Fine," she said. "But I'll be watching. Inside." She motioned to the restaurant with the muzzle of her gun. "And you two." She turned her arctic stare on Will and Jesse. "Fill up and come right back here. I used to hunt with my ex-husband. I can hit my target."

Will didn't doubt it. He nodded and waited until Carolyn, Jared, and Daffodil vanished into the restaurant. Then he said, "I shouldn't have let her go in there alone."

"Like you could stop her," Jesse said. "They ain't crazy, at least."

"That Jared, though."

Jesse smirked. "Feeling protective, are we?"

He wasn't about to rise to that bait. "Come on," he told Jesse. "The sooner we're out of here, the better."

They drove to the pumps, filled the tank, and returned to the restaurant as instructed. They waited in the vehicle to avoid giving Carolyn reason for suspicion. They'd be in trouble if she decided she didn't like their faces.

Fifteen minutes passed before Daffodil emerged. She came straight to Will's window. He lowered it and asked, "Are we good to go?"

It took her a moment to answer. When she did, she tried to sound nonchalant, but Will sensed tension in her. "I'm staying," she said.

Jesse craned his neck to see her better. "What? Why?"

"His leg's infected. Not too horrible, but he needs care. I can't leave him like that."

Will looked up at the lowering clouds. Off to the west, they seemed to descend and kiss the land. "Carolyn won't like us staying," he said.

"She's letting me stay. She wants you guys gone." Stepping back, Daffodil shrugged. "So, go. Get to the valley while you can."

"I'm not leaving you here. Not with them."

"Go. You didn't want me tagging along anyway."

Will felt like she'd punched him in the gut.

"Hey," Jesse said. "I did."

A smile touched her lips. "I know." To Will, she said, "I'll look for you once Jared's better."

That took the edge off the sting, but it couldn't deaden it, not completely. Because how could she hope to find them?

Will started the van. "Don't let your guard down," he warned. "Jared wants more than a nurse."

She laughed. "I'll handle him."

Will raised the window, put the van in gear, and made for the highway, jaw locked tight, hands quivering on the wheel. In the mirror, he saw Daffodil raise a hand in a tentative farewell, then she dropped it and watched until the road carried them from each other's sight.

A mile down the road, Jesse muttered, "Damn."

"What?" Will asked.

"You got no luck with women, do you?"

"Shut up," Will whispered.

Part 2:

Resurrection

17

Forty minutes later, the weather had ambushed and surrounded them. What began as a few stray snowflakes became a crystalline deluge, transforming the mountains from pine paradise to frozen desert in minutes. Will coaxed the van through the deepening powder until the tires spun without effect, and eventually the ProMaster settled at the bottom of a small dip in the road, from whence it refused to budge.

Wind buffeted them. The wipers kept the windshield clear save compacted ice about the edges, but they could see nothing through the snowy fog streaming by. They broke out shovels and tried to dig out the tires, but the sea of white swelled and buried them again and again until, fingers and toes numb, the men gave up and retreated to the warmth within.

An hour passed. Two. Three. Darkness fell. The clouds blew away to the east and the stars winked on, brilliant cold fires in a frigid heaven. Jesse said, "God grants you one day to relive," and Will denied it, and they argued and stopped arguing and talked of New York and argued some more and gave up, for what was the point anymore? They had crossed a dead continent to escape death and now, here, they faced it without benefit of disease or insanity or guns or anything but the most impersonal force in the universe, a force that wasn't a force at all, only an absence, an emptiness, a nothingness: the cold.

They countered it the only way they could that night: with silence, another absence. In the still dark, each retreated into his own skull, and eventually sleep took them.

They woke to golden morning light spilling over their shoulders, whiteness blazing all about them, snow-laden pines standing guard to either side. They breakfasted on warm apple juice from individual serving bottles and cold toaster pastries.

Will fiddled with his phone and by some miracle found a modest signal. He logged into the app store, scrounged up an automated weather app, and installed it. It didn't serve up any information, so he tried again, and again. On the fourth try, he landed one that gave a forecast. The temperature here, it said, had dropped into the single digits overnight and wouldn't rise above fifteen for the next three days. He stared at the numbers, willing them to change.

"What?" Jesse asked.

Will showed him the forecast.

"You got a plan B, then?"

How could there be a plan B? They had to find shelter before the gas ran out. He pulled up the map, turned on the satellite imagery, and waited for it to load. It took so long, he could almost believe the electromagnetic waves had frozen right out of the atmosphere. But then a happy sight greeted his eyes.

"There are houses nearby," he said. "South side of the highway. We just have to get to them. Look." He showed Jesse the map.

"How far is that?"

"A mile, mile and a half at the most."

"Twenty, thirty minute walk in good conditions," Jesse said. "Won't be fun, but doable."

No, not fun at all in these temperatures. "We'll start once it warms up a bit. Maybe about eleven o'clock."

Jesse nodded. "Hell of a choice," he said.

"What's that?"

"Die in here, die out there, or get really lucky. We shoulda stayed at the casino."

Except that had been occupied, and the owner would have killed them if they lingered. Anyway, should-haves counted for nothing. "This is the hand we've been dealt," Will said. "We have to play it."

"Go fish," Jesse said. He climbed into the back and rummaged for expedition clothing.

Problem was, they didn't have such clothing. Not really. They'd picked up a few items along the way, including coats and baseball caps, but hardly arctic gear. Now they had to improvise, which meant layers. Doubled shirts. Doubled cotton socks. (Why hadn't they looked for wool?) Doubled driving gloves, which almost didn't go on. Doubled jeans were out of the question, and as for footwear, they hadn't thought to nab boots. Hiking through several feet of snow never entered their minds.

Once they were suited up as best as possible, Jesse flexed his fingers. "Can't hardly move," he said. "I'm suing you if I get frostbite."

Will smirked. For the first time, he realized Jesse's barbs weren't always barbs. The guy just had that kind of sense of humor. "Good luck finding a lawyer," he said. "Or a judge. But listen, if we get turned around, or if for any reason it looks like we won't make it to the houses, we follow our tracks back here. We can warm up and try again."

"Got it," Jesse said, though he didn't sound too sure.

"You okay?"

"As okay as I gotta be."

Will turned off the engine. "Don't lock the door. I'm leaving the key here. If we get separated, the first one back can get the heat going. Let's go."

They trekked into winter, over the pine-covered median, and across the eastbound lanes. Even that short distance took longer than expected. The snow was loose packed, turning every step into a struggle as they sank to mid-calf. Jesse was winded before they reached the trees along the far edge of the highway. They paused there to catch their breaths, then trudged into the woods, picking their way around the trunks, occasionally tripping over buried obstructions. The snow was so deep, they might have been snagging the tops of bushes.

They reached the fence separating the highway from the rest of the world. Tips of fence posts peeked from the snow, but the men's footsteps sank enough to catch on the topmost wires. They had to high-step over them. Will tripped and landed face-down in the powder. He struggled to his feet and brushed himself off as Jesse came alongside him. They should have picked up some ski masks, he thought, or scarves, or something. And proper socks and boots. His face burned from the cold. He could barely feel his feet.

Onward, slightly downslope, slipping and sliding, sinking to their knees, falling, getting up. They broke from the trees to find a snow-laden road parallelling the Interstate. Beyond it, more trees. Will tried to pull his phone from his coat pocket but couldn't get a grip on it with the doubled gloves. Muttering a curse, he removed them. The phone was cold, but not freezing, because his pocket had trapped some of his body heat. He fumbled with it, got the map to display, and oriented it. Then, shoving it back into his pocket and stuffing his hand back into the gloves, he pointed.

They shuffled off in that direction.

Time dragged. Will's face stung, his fingers throbbed, his feet—he couldn't feel his feet at all. He told Jesse.

"Can't feel mine, either," Jesse said. "We're close, though, right?"

Will didn't know. He could check the phone again, but he didn't want to. He didn't want to pull off his gloves, not so much because of the cold, but because it was just too much effort. For that matter, so was walking. Each step took a lifetime, drained away half his energy. He stopped.

Jesse nearly ran into him. "What's wrong?" he asked.

Will couldn't even summon an answer. He sank to his knees. He sat in the snow in the road and couldn't say a thing, couldn't get up, wanted nothing more than to sleep. He was so tired, he might not have slept for a year.

Jesse grabbed and shook him, but without much enthusiasm. "Hey," he said. "C'mon, get up."

"In a minute," Will said. "Need...rest."

"Me, too. But...hold on. I think I see..."

Will never heard what Jesse saw. Or maybe he did and it didn't register. He didn't care. He closed his eyes and told himself he'd just take a short nap, and then he could find out. It couldn't be that important.

He thought he heard footsteps crunching through the snow, slow, deliberate, fading into the distance.

Just a short nap. That's all he wanted. Just a short nap.

Sunlight splashed over Will's closed eyelids. He turned from it, threw an arm over his face, grumbled at it for all the good that did. He turned and reached for Sarah. She wasn't there. She must have risen already, must have opened the curtains to rouse him, and gone to make breakfast. She hated waking him with a touch or a shake or by calling his name. She always let the light do her dirty work.

He sat, rubbed his eyes, squinted out the window. The snow-laded trees sparkled in the morning light. It took him a moment to realize that wasn't right. Sarah was long gone. Their bedroom window overlooked buildings, not a forest. This wasn't his condo, wasn't even New York. Where was he?

It *was* a bedroom, though. He was buried under a pile of blankets in a room that could have been any bedroom, done up in blues and greens, with bed, dresser, nightstand, mountain scenes on the walls. Will pushed the blanket off and swung his shaking legs off the bed. They trembled as though the minor exertion had been too much for them.

The van. He and Jesse had been trapped in the snow in the van in the California mountains. They had ventured into the cold in search of shelter. He didn't remember finding it, but now they were here in somebody's house.

No, not they. He. Jesse wasn't here, not in this room, anyway.

He remembered something else. Footsteps. Footsteps receding. Had Jesse left him? Wandered into the wilderness? Gotten lost? Died?

The bedroom door creaked open. Startled, Will sprang to his feet and stumbled into the wall. He leaned on it, barely keeping his balance.

A face not Jesse's leaned in. The newcomer—a gray-headed man with an unkempt beard and worry lines burned into his forehead—squinted. He had an Asian face. Not pure Asian, though. Eastern and western genes mingled in him. "Not dead, huh?" he said. "Good. I'll make you some cocoa."

The door shut.

"Wait," Will called too late. He slunk to the door using walls and furniture for balance. He listened, cracked the door, listened some more. The house lay as silent as the snow.

Whoever his host was, he didn't seem dangerous, but the possibility triggered another realization: Will's gun was still in the van, wherever the van was. They had carried nothing but themselves and their phones.

Nudging the door further, he peeked up and down the hall. Finding it empty, he crept out. A closed door across the hall might be another bedroom. Maybe Jesse was there. To the right, an open door revealed a bathroom. The hall ended in a living room with a kitchen on the left. Sounds of shuffling and clanking emanated from there. Will peeked around the corner and found the old man at work, bent over a saucepan on the stove, stirring, a box of powdered milk close by on the counter.

The fellow turned, a canister of cocoa in hand. Startled, he nearly dropped it. "God, don't do that! I thought you were a ghost. Come in, sit at the table. It's almost ready." Raising the container, he studied the instructions on the back. "I think it's safe. I don't think they know about chocolate. Not yet."

Will felt a shiver of fear. "Who?"

"Aliens. They poisoned the coffee, so I threw it out."

"Aliens?"

The man nodded and stirred.

"Is Jesse here?" Will didn't care to engage the fellow, but he had to find his companion and get out before anything nasty happened.

"Who?"

"The guy traveling with me."

"Oh, him. He's in the room across from yours. Still asleep, last I looked, but not dead. You two had me worried. Dumb place to be, out in the arctic wastes." He turned off the stove and poured the contents of the pan into three mugs waiting on the counter. "Not literally arctic, but it sure feels like it today. Well, don't just stand there, sit down, sit down." He carried two mugs to the table and retrieved the third for himself. He sat on the far side of the table and motioned Will to sit across from him.

Will obliged but didn't touch the mug. He studied the man's face for some sign of impending violence. He found nothing but a befuddled smile.

"Go on, drink it. You nearly froze to death, you know."

Will lifted the mug and took a sip. It tasted fine, so far as he could tell. "How did you find us?"

"Your friend knocked on my door, if you can call it knocking. He barely managed to tell me about you. After that, he was useless." The man took a hearty gulp of his drink. "At least he passed out on the porch. You were down the road. Took some effort to get you up here, I'll tell you that."

"Thank you. I guess we're lucky you were here."

"Lucky I found you before *them*."

A small cough caught their attention. Jesse stood in the kitchen doorway, biting his lip.

"Oh good," the old man said. "Sit, have some cocoa."

Jesse looked at Will, worried.

"It's okay," Will said, not sure it was, but at least now they had their host outnumbered.

His eyes twitching from Will to the old man and back, Jesse shuffled in and sat. "Who're you?" he asked.

The other drank his cocoa, his gaze fixed on Jesse's mug.

Jesse picked it up and took a cautious sip.

"Call me Spike."

Jesse and Will set down their mugs in unison. "Seriously?" Jesse asked.

Spike looked embarrassed. "It's a nickname. A dumb nickname, but after all these years, I'm kind of used to it. Legally, I'm Ike. My great-grandfather's name. Dad wanted to keep it in the family."

"So why Spike?"

"Drink your cocoa."

Jesse and Will drank, then Will gave him their names. "Was this your house before?"

Spike shook his head. "I buried the owners out back." He examined the chrome appliances and yellow striped wallpaper. "They had a nice place, so I stayed."

"You found them dead."

"Yep. Aliens, probably. They're all over." He squeezed his eyes shut and shook his head as though to dislodge an obstruction. "Sorry. You want to know if I killed them. No. I never killed anyone. They were dead when I got here."

"Aliens," Jesse said and nodded as though he understood.

Spike blinked at him. "What?"

"You said aliens killed them."

Leaning back, Spike shrugged. "I'm an old man," he said. "Sometimes I talk crazy. Don't listen to it."

Will had never heard of dementia producing aliens. This sounded more like David Buhler in Gratiot, Ohio, or the guy on the radio in Salt Lake City, except it wasn't constant. Maybe Spike's illness hadn't advanced that far. Yet. "We'll need to find the van," he told Jesse. "All our stuff is in it." Particularly the weapons.

Spike laughed. "You'll never manage that."

"It's not far," Will insisted.

"Forget it. Everything you need is here. So long as the power doesn't go out, we're set for the winter."

They weren't about to be taken prisoner again. Will stood and motioned Jesse up. Jesse, less than enthused, joined him.

"You almost died when you *weren't* carrying anything," Spike snapped. "And I'm not rescuing you again. Once was tough enough."

"We'll manage," Will said. "Worst case, there must be other houses nearby." He turned to go.

"I said, everything you need is here. Hint, hint."

Jesse put a hand on Will's shoulder to stop him. "What's that mean?" he asked.

Spike stared at Jesse like a teacher awaiting an answer.

"You got our guns, don't you?"

"I didn't know if you were wackos," Spike said. It wasn't exactly an answer, but maybe it was.

"No, wait." Jesse put his hands to the sides of his face as though holding his brains in. "We almost died getting up here. How'd *you* get down and back?"

"How do you think?"

Will knew the answer. "By following our tracks."

"Plus, when I go out, I wear proper clothing. Unlike you."

Will returned to the table. "You think we're wackos?"

"Not so far."

"Then we can have our guns back."

"Nope."

"Why not?"

Spike gave him a disappointed look. "Wrong question."

Jesse sat and folded his hands on the table. He frowned at them. "Are *you* wacko?"

"Right question. Answer: sometimes. I'd rather not die for it."

Will couldn't fault his reasoning, at least when it didn't involve aliens. "Are you dangerous?"

"Good follow-up question. I don't think so. At least, I don't remember doing anyone harm. I said I never killed anyone. More accurately, I don't remember killing anyone. But I don't always remember everything I do."

Will pondered that. As they travelled westward, they'd encountered variations on the disease, a national cocktail of psychotic violence, but nothing like this. Spike's madness not only came and went, it had an intelligence. He'd analyzed himself, drawn conclusions. How was that possible?

"That ain't a comfort," Jesse said.

Spike stirred his cocoa, spoon clanking on the side of the mug.

"Why would you want us to stay?" Will asked. "We might be dangerous, even if we're not infected."

"You're the first sane people I've seen since this started."

"You're lonely," Jesse said.

"I'm fine being alone." The words carried no conviction.

"Then what?"

Spike took a drink, set the mug down, rotated it and studied the design on the sides.

"Out with it," Will demanded.

The old man didn't look up, and his answer was the barest of whispers. "I just want to help," he said.

For the next four days, Spike limited his help to providing food and shelter and slinking off when his mind descended into psychosis. At least, Will figured it was psychosis. He remembered something from an introductory psychology course he'd taken his freshman year at college. "Neurotics," the professor had explained, "build castles in the sky. Psychotics live in them." Which Spike did. Aliens proved a recurring theme. He took to soaping the windows to prevent little green men from spying on them, pushed furniture against the doors to keep them from getting in. Black pepper apparently had anti-ET properties, too; he added it to everything he cooked, until Jesse forcibly took over chef's duties.

Spike allowed it, but warned, "Don't forget the pepper."

Jesse promised he wouldn't, but he lied, and their host didn't notice.

A few times in the middle of the night, Spike donned a heavy parka and boots and slipped out, tramping through the snow behind the house, doing who knew what. He would be out an hour or more before returning, seemingly unaffected by the cold, which according to a thermometer mounted outside the kitchen window regularly dipped into the low twenties or upper teens in the dark. Some nights, wind ripped through the trees. The wind chill must have been far lower. But come morning, he would appear at the breakfast table unscathed, as though he'd spent the whole night tucked in a warm bed.

His episodes afforded Will and Jesse time to search the house for their guns and any other supplies Spike might have retrieved from the van, but they found nothing. Closets, basement, and attic yielded only the former owners' belongings. Nothing but dust hid beneath beds or behind the furnishings. Will began to wonder if Spike had lied to them. Maybe he'd never visited the van at all.

Although daytime temperatures struggled upward and melted the top few centimeters of snow, white still blanketed the mountains on the fifth day when over a breakfast of cereal and powdered milk, Spike—eyes fixed on his bowl and spoon—said, "Happy New Year. We're going out today."

Will put down his spoon. He'd lost count of the days. If this was January first, then New York had been a bit over a month ago. Thirty-five days. Not long, really, yet an entire lifetime. "Out?" he asked.

"Out."

"Where?"

Spike shoveled a dripping spoonful into his mouth.

"You said we shouldn't leave," Jesse objected.

"It's not leaving," Spike said. "It's just going out."

"Into the cold."

Spike stared at Jesse as though he'd spoken Pawnee.

"Why?" Will demanded.

Spike exhaled irritation. Beyond the window behind him, dots of snow pirouetted beneath slate clouds.

"We aren't chasing aliens," Will added.

"I didn't say aliens."

"You didn't say anything."

Spike poked his thumb in Will's direction and asked Jesse, "Is he always this stubborn?"

Jesse laughed. "He can't help it. He's a bigshot New York financial manager."

"New York." Spike shuddered. "They say it started there."

"Apparently," Will said.

"They say is a liar." He eyed Will as though trying to read his personal history from his face. "What was it like?"

"Mayhem."

"What kind of mayhem?"

An odd question. Spike must have seen the same things they had, if on a smaller scale. "What do you think?"

Spike shrugged. "I heard of various manifestations. Pyromania was the oddest. I never understood that one."

Jesse gaped at him. "You understood murder? Suicide?"

"Sure. Those at least made sense." He pushed himself to his feet, looking a thousand years old. "Come on. It's New Year's Day. A fresh start. Let's not waste time."

It looked to Will like any other day recently, but this guy had been short a bag of marbles since they met. Best to keep an eye on him. Will followed and motioned Jesse to join them. Jaw set in irritation, Jesse fell in line.

At the coat closet by the front door, Spike rummaged up parkas for the three of them, and boots and thick gloves and wool scarves. The fits weren't perfect, but at least they wouldn't so readily succumb to exposure this time. Once outfitted, Spike led them into the cold, locking the door as though burglars were lurking behind the drifts. He meandered the unbroken expanse of snow marking the road as it snaked up a rise and down, then more steeply upward, cresting a low ridge. Through breaks in the pines, they caught sight of a wider river of white, the eastbound lanes of the Interstate, winding through the mountains below.

They slogged for fifteen, twenty minutes, cold nipping at them, legs aching, with no word helpful or otherwise from Spike. Coming around a pine-rimmed bend, they found a cluster of small buildings huddled at the bottom of a gentle down slope. Spike put up a hand to halt them.

"There," he said, pointing.

Will saw nothing special. This might have been any middle-of-nowhere crossroads off the interstate offering gas and food and, maybe, lodging.

"What is it?" Jesse asked.

Spike turned to him. "What *is* it? Can't you tell?" He hugged himself and spun around, muttering unintelligible words.

"Here come the aliens," Jesse whispered to Will.

The aliens were everywhere. The mountains, the snow piled to a depth Will couldn't fathom, the pine spires spearing the deep blue of the morning sky, the cries of unfamiliar birds, even the buildings below, their doors all but buried, their silence, the human absence. And something else. A shape skittering between the shadows, slipping around corners, dashing across the white roads. Not an animal. Upright. Bipedal. Human.

"Did you ever use those guns?" Spike asked.

Jesse shivered in the cold. Will watched the shape melt into the shade of a building.

Spike turned, red-faced. "I asked you a question!"

"You aren't my mother," Will snapped.

Spike might have pulled his hair out if he hadn't been wearing a hood. He rushed the trees, snatched a fallen branch, and charged Will, wielding it like a club. Will threw up his arms to block the blow, but Spike stopped dead, branch raised high. He was shaking, but not from rage. From horror.

The look passed as quickly as it had come. "Damn it," he muttered. He threw the makeshift weapon aside. "Sorry. Bit of IED. Don't worry, I always get it under control before... you know."

"IED?" Jesse asked. "I thought that was bombs, not sticks."

"A mental illness. Intermittent Explosive Disorder."

"You're joking."

"Look it up. The internet still works." Spike kicked at the branch. "I never could hurt anyone. I almost failed high school biology because I refused to dissect anything." He laughed. "I've had a strange career. But to the point. Did you ever use your guns?"

Will thought he might use it on Spike if he had it now. He nodded warily.

"Kill anyone?"

"Once."

"That's once more than me." He pointed to the buildings, where the shape was scampering along the road. "I need you to kill that one."

Will and Jesse looked at the shape, at each other, at Spike.

"What's he done?" Jesse asked.

"She. Nothing. Yet."

"Then why should we kill her?" Will demanded.

"Because," Spike said. "I can't."

18

Happy New Year. Fresh start. Kill someone for me.

Sure, that made sense. As much sense as anything about Spike or the world in general now.

Will watched the figure scamper about town. It might've been a woman, but from their distance, who could tell? Male or female, Will saw no threat. In perpetual motion, she—if Spike was right—rushed from building to building, never entering, never even trying the doors, just running about the outsides, touching the walls, striking into the street, burying herself in the shadows only to emerge again at a trot. Probably infected, but at this rate she'd burn herself out before doing anyone harm. Maybe Spike pitied her, wanted to euthanize her. He just wanted to help, that's what he'd said. That had to be it.

"You have our guns," Will reminded him.

"No guns," he said. "Find some other way."

"Like what?"

"How should I know? You're the killer, not me."

"I shot a man once, in self-defense." No point in mentioning his vehicular homicide record. "This is different."

Jesse stomped his feet in the snow. "It's cold. Let's go back."

Spike exhaled a cloud of steam. "We came here to do a job."

"*We* didn't," Jesse pointed out.

They sure hadn't. Will started back, following their tracks in the snow. Jesse fell in line behind him. Spike grumbled at his boots until his guests had a hundred-foot lead, then he rushed to catch up. Puffing, he came alongside them. "Please. You've got to do this."

"Give me a good reason and a gun."

Jesse grabbed Will's arm. "You can't just shoot her!"

"Not without a damn good reason."

"No guns," Spike snapped. "And the reason is because I said so." He tromped onward as though not caring if they followed or froze.

They followed.

Spike must have some justification, even if he didn't care to utter it. Maybe a different tactic would pry it out of him. "Who is she?" Will asked.

Spike didn't look back. "Hell if I know."

"What's she done?"

They crunched through the snow in silence. A slight wind stirred the pines. A few puffs of cumulus floated by.

Fine, Will decided. *He'll get nothing from me, either.*

They reached the house, stomped the snow from their boots, shook off their coats. Spike sank into an easy chair and closed his eyes. Jesse perched on the edge of the couch and puzzled over their host. Will started for his room but pulled up short when Spike cleared his throat. Will waited, not expecting more than another plea.

"She showed up two days before you," Spike said. "Or that's when I first saw her. I don't know where she came from. She's been meandering this way, little by little. I don't want her too close."

Will returned to the living room and sat on the opposite end of the couch from Jesse. "Why not?"

"She's nuts."

"So are you."

Spike grunted.

"Some of the time," Jesse added. "You said so yourself."

"We aren't talking about me." He studied his neatly-trimmed fingernails. "First time I saw her, she was beating the hell out of a dead dog with a shovel." He shuddered. "So you tell me. Do we let her find us?"

"How would you handle it if we weren't here?" Will asked, but he knew the answer. Spike already said he couldn't kill her, mad or no, dangerous or no. He'd slink into the shadows, hide, maybe wander the snow-laden slopes until he found another place to hole up or died of exposure. Then again, who knew? Back to the wall, a gun in his hand, Spike just might pull the trigger. That's how Will had done it. In that moment, everything changed. You didn't really know what power lurked within until desperation forced it into the open, and then you couldn't ever tuck it away again. You might wrestle it into submission, but it was always there, waiting, peering over your shoulder, begging to be released.

Spike rose and wandered to the kitchen. Clinks and clanks and the dull thud of a cabinet door closing was Will's only answer.

"I promise I won't use the gun on you," he called. *So long as you don't try to murder us*, he added in silence.

When Spike returned, he had a mug of coffee in hand. He stared at Will narrow-eyed while he sipped.

"I won't, either," Jesse added.

"Question," Spike said. He took another drink before asking it. "Either of you know how to find food in the wild?"

What the hell did that have to do with anything? And of course they didn't. They were city folk.

"I've been researching that," Spike continued. "Sooner or later, we'll need to start foraging. And hunting. And butchering."

"Why?" Jesse asked.

"The stores aren't being stocked, are they? And they won't be, not given the..." He took another drink. "I about said mortality rate, but that's not it."

"I ain't butchering nothing."

Spike gave Jesse a searching look. "Then you'll be a vegetarian."

"If you want us to hunt—" Will began.

"No! No guns! Snares. Maybe bows and arrows, maybe spears. Best to start with small game, don't you think?"

Will figured he could shoot Spike just as well with a bow as a gun, except for one thing. "You know how to make those?"

"Of course not. That's what the research is for."

None of which connected at all with the lady with the shovel. Which may have been a blessing. Let Spike forget about her for now. They could deal with her if she tried to break into the house. If she never did, the problem would dissolve. Meanwhile, there ought to be enough canned goods to last a lifetime. Once the snow melted, they'd have no trouble restocking.

"Why bother?" Jesse said. "This has to end sometime."

"It only ends one way," Spike said. He put his head in his hands. "They get us. We run out of pepper, and they get us."

Around noon, Jesse slipped out back and shuffled by the kitchen window to the corner, where he couldn't be seen from inside. Spike was busy making himself a lunch of canned tuna mixed with mayo and ample pepper. Will had retreated to his room, probably to escape his host for a bit, the same reason Jesse was out here in the cold, watching the sun sparkle on the face of the snow. Behind the house, a gentle slope rose some five hundred feet to a dense cluster of pine. The forest scent drifted on the breeze.

What the hell were they doing here, twenty-seven hundred miles from home in the middle of nowhere, holed up with a madman? A semi-madman, anyway. A brainy semi-madman, although Jesse sensed Spike was hiding much of his intelligence. Maybe he wasn't so mad, after all. Maybe he was faking madness as a cover for...what?

Nah, that was stupid. Spike couldn't be *that* good of an actor.

Still. Where had Spike come from? Why had he called his career strange? Why had he bothered saving Will and Jesse? ("I just want to help," he'd said, but *why?*) Why did he think the disease hadn't started in New York, why did murder and suicide make sense but not arson? Why did he believe long-term survival meant going primitive?

Spike wasn't just another victim. Jesse didn't know what he was, but there was something unique about him. They needed to find out what, for their safety if nothing else. Although, they couldn't flat out ask him. Will's questions never got straight answers.

Maybe a different approach. Maybe they could trick him into answering unasked questions. Play dumb. Or smart. Or dummies who thought they were smart.

Jesse kicked at the snow and sent a fine spray of powder glittering on the wind. Trick him? That was a joke. Will didn't have a tenth that much subtlety. Nor did he, although he fancied himself a bit more tactful. Sometimes.

Ah, what the hell, it didn't matter. They were stuck here until the van could roll again. At least Spike wasn't trying to murder them.

Not yet.

He kicked at the snow one more time and trudged back inside. Stomping his boots clean, he peeled them off and put his shoes back on. As he came into the kitchen, Spike—seated now at the table, munching on his tuna and pepper sandwich—peered at him, suspicious.

"What?" Jesse said.

Spike put down the sandwich and brushed the crumbs from his fingers. "What were you doing out there?"

"Needed some fresh air."

Spike looked out the window. "The air's fine in here. You talk to anyone out there?"

Jesse laughed. "Ain't nobody to talk to. Most everyone's dead, remember?"

"Except *them*."

Right. Aliens. "I didn't see none of them."

"That's exactly what you'd say if they took you over."

"C'mon."

Spike eased himself up and shuffled around the table. Keeping his eyes on Jesse, he slid to the counter and opened a drawer from which he pulled a carving knife. "Prove it."

Jesse froze. Where the hell was Will? Where the hell were the guns?

"Prove it!"

How could he do that? How could he defend himself? Desperate for a weapon, he swept his gaze over stove, refrigerator, drawers, cabinets, the table with the remains of Spike's lunch. The empty tuna can. The pepper shaker.

Wait, pepper. A psychological weapon, maybe.

"Calm down," he said, although it sounded desperate to his ears. "Gimme a tuna and pepper sandwich, and I'll show you."

Spike slumped against the counter. Discovering the knife in his hand, he stared at it as though he'd found himself holding a lizard. He dropped it on the counter and returned to his chair, which he sank into it like a man twice his age. "Sorry," he muttered.

Will poked his head into the kitchen. "What's the noise about?"

"About damn time," Jesse grumbled under his breath. He plopped into the chair opposite Spike. "What the hell was that?" So much for subtlety. He'd have more luck asking the snow to blow off to Kansas.

Their host toyed with his sandwich, nudging it one way, then the other, as though trying to perfectly center it on the plate. Just when Jesse was about to snatch the damn thing from him, he shoved the plate across the table. It came to rest hanging over the edge.

"Out with it, already," Jesse snapped.

"A war," Spike said. He tapped his temple. "Up here." He cradled his head in his hands and closed his eyes.

Dancing around the truth again. Jesse'd had enough of that. "You got the disease, don't you? Sooner or later, you're gonna kill someone."

Will leaned against the wall, arms crossed over his chest, watching the exchange, oddly quiet. He might have been a spectator at a tennis match.

Spike exhaled as though releasing his last breath. "I won't kill anyone."

"Maybe you're only half nuts now, but once you've gone all the way—"

"No!" Spike jerked upright as though rigor mortis had suddenly gripped him. He slammed a fist on the table. The plate rattled and slipped a bit closer to the tipping point. "You know *nothing* about it! You're not a biologist or psychologist or even a fucking lab assistant!" He threw himself across the table, snatched up the plate, and flung it against the wall. The sandwich flew apart and splattered everywhere. The ceramic shattered, its fragments chattering as they hit the floor. "Violence is *not* associated with mental disease!"

Jesse about hit the ceiling. His chair tipped over and slammed to the floor as he skittered to the wall, where he cowered next to Will.

Will hadn't budged. Solid as the granite mountains, he remained in place, arms folded, eyes dull. "You could've fooled me," he said.

Spike ran his hands through his hair and arched his back, eyes turned heavenward. He took a few deep breaths. "Appearances can be deceiving," he said.

Crossing to the table, Will snagged a napkin from the holder and cleaned sandwich fragments from the seat of his usual chair. Then he sat and fixed Spike with a look that suggested he might fire him. "Undeceive us."

Spike didn't look at him, but he waved a languid hand at Jesse. "Come back, I won't hurt you."

"Don't throw no more peppered tuna," Jesse grumped.

Once Jesse was settled, Spike twined his fingers and studied them. "Where to begin? With the violence, I guess. Most mental illnesses aren't associated with an increased tendency to violence. Violence is more strongly linked to drug use, childhood abuse, and environmental factors. If you grow up surrounded by violence, you're more likely to become violent yourself."

"Or get killed," Jesse muttered, once more seeing Martin's lifeless body sprawled on the ground.

"Of course," Spike said. "My point is, mental disease doesn't change that picture significantly."

"Then what would you call all this?" Will waved a hand at the whole world. "Blind rage, murder, suicide, arson. That woman you wanted us to kill. You said she was nuts. You said she beat a dead dog."

"Nuts isn't a clinical term."

"So what is that, clinically? Sanity?"

"It's something very specific. Only a few mental conditions are linked to significantly increased violence, and then only sometimes. Extreme paranoia is one."

"I guess that covers aliens," Jesse said.

Spike narrowed his eyes but didn't argue it. "Another is command hallucinations."

"Which are?" Will asked.

"Auditory hallucinations instructing a person to do something. The commands aren't always dangerous or violent, but they can be. We don't fully understand where they come from. They can be associated with conditions on the schizophrenia spectrum or PTSD, but sometimes they occur in people with no discernable disorder."

Jesse felt a growing unease during the exchange. The "we" clinched it. "You're a psychologist, aren't you? You know what happened. Maybe you're even involved."

Spike pushed back from the table and tottered to the sink. He got a dishrag, wetted it, wrung it out, and returned to the table to wipe it down.

Jesse wanted to throttle him. He must have looked it, for Will put a hand on his shoulder.

Spike stopped wiping and leaned on the table, his eyes focused on nothing. "The human brain is the most complex structure in the universe," he said. "It's hard to kill. Damage it or throw its chemistry out of whack, and it keeps on ticking. But it may not tick in time with the rest of the world. Abnormal thoughts and behaviors can result. Often they make it difficult for a person to get through the day. Sometimes they interfere with one's ability to function in society. And sometimes they lead to suicidal thoughts and behaviors. Violence toward others is less common."

He looked up, first at Will, then at Jesse. "I need you to understand that. Violence isn't the norm. It wasn't the focus of..."

He returned to the sink and dropped the dishrag into it. Then he did nothing, neither rinsed it nor turned around nor spoke. He just stood there staring into the basin.

"What was the focus?" Will asked, as though the sentence had been completed. Jesse figured they both knew the unspoken words.

"There was a hypothesis," Spike continued. "An idea about how to get an unbalanced brain ticking in time again. It had potential. Not a panacea, not even a cure for a specific condition. More a bottle into which we could pour useful concoctions for delivery to the brain." He finally picked up the dishcloth and rinsed it out, then threw it down again. The metallic thump seemed to echo through the house.

"What sort of bottle?" Will asked.

Jesse wished he hadn't asked that. It might be better not to know. Except he already knew. He could see it as clearly as if it was happening here, now, on this very table. "Bottles break," he said. "The disease spilled out."

"Not a disease," Spike said, still not facing them. "The stuff in the bottle wasn't a disease."

"But the bottle was," Will guessed. "A genetically engineered microorganism designed to deliver medications to the brain. Across the—what's it called—the blood brain barrier?"

Spike nodded.

"The models looked good," Spike said. "But all we had were models. We hadn't even gotten to animal trials. We'd only prepared a few strains to test their secretions. And then..." He turned around and leaned back against the counter. Tears were dribbling down his face. He shrugged, shook his head, wiped away the moisture. "Do you know," he said, "I never saw my family again? I was trapped in that damn lab for five months."

Jesse shivered. Five months. Five months during which whatever this was had spread unchecked. And then...what?

"Where was this?" Will asked.

"Stanford. That's where it started. It didn't start in New York. It started out there." He waved vaguely westward. "They tried to contain it. They kept us locked up, but it was already out. When the killing started..." With a shudder, Spike groped for a chair and managed to sit without dumping himself on the floor. "I locked myself in an empty office and didn't come out for four days. And then I was alone. I didn't know what to do, didn't know where to go. I went home, went to find my wife and children and grandchildren. I never found them. Any of them."

Which explained everything and nothing. "Why didn't you go nuts?" Jesse asked. "Yeah, I know, that ain't a technical term."

"I *am* nuts," Spike replied. "But it's different with me."

"Why?"

"We had one bottle, but a dozen recipes to pour into it. We hadn't produced them all, only five. Once they got out into the world, each strain spread along a unique path. Different regions were hit by different strains, or combinations of strains. But in the lab, they intermixed about equally. I have a coinfection of all five strains. You'd think that would make it worse, but no. To put it simply, they're playing a game of keep-away with my brain, which sends me flying first this direction, then that."

"So sometimes you're in balance," Will said. "Sometimes you slip out of balance, but it doesn't last."

"Exactly."

"Are there others like you?"

Spike gazed out the window as though searching for his family. "Maybe. Maybe more than we realize."

Was that good or bad? Jesse wasn't sure. It might spell more survivors, but maybe the threat they posed was different, more dangerous in the long term.

With a heavy sigh, Spike turned back to the table. "We'd better break out the pepper," he said. "Shadows are on the move. They'll have us surrounded by nightfall."

19

SNOW FELL that night, another five inches by the looks of it. The storm cleared off by the time Will woke. From his room, he studied the world beyond the window, wondering if even the ProMaster's roof still peeked above the powder, wondering where Spike had stashed their guns (if he had), wondering what role the man had played in civilization's demise. The guy just wanted to help—that's what he'd said. Was that charity or guilt?

This disease, this not-quite-a-disease, whatever the hell it was...

Technicalities be damned. To Will, it was a disease.

Spike's fault or not, he'd been involved in the agent's creation. He deserved his special form of madness, delusional one minute, lucid the next, knowing some moments of his psychosis, not recalling others. Still, what must it be like, knowing you had destroyed the world (if he had), knowing you had the blood of your entire species on your hands (if he did)? Maybe it was no different than what any other person in the world felt. Everyone trashed the planet in some way. Sometimes it was inevitable. What did physicists call that? Entropy? But often it was just hunger and greed, and people chose to remain blind to the consequences.

We care nothing for anything but our own safety and comfort, Will mused. *We feed on the world and each other to secure our self-interest, and we cut our own throats in the process.*

Hell, look at New York. Given the choice, Will would have run over Jesse as readily as anyone throwing themselves in his path. Or Sarah, what about her? What had she wanted so badly that she could destroy Will without as much as a goodbye?

Or was that the consequence of his own nearsightedness?

The thought left him as cold as the mountain air. He replayed their life together. Their meeting at an industry conference, their growing acquaintance over dinners and walks in Central Park and visits to museums and their first tentative night together. The days had never seemed as warm, the sun never as bright. They lost themselves in each other. Eight months later they were married, and a year later they were still lost, and then another year passed and another and somehow they were still lost but not in each other anymore. In work and personal finances and buying stuff, having stuff, trying to meet the world's expectations and fill their own cravings and the needs of a future that, when it came, wouldn't be anything like they dreamed or feared.

Then the moment was gone, a moment they hadn't lived in for eight years, because they became so lost in themselves that they could no longer stay lost in each other. And who's fault was that?

Like he had to ask.

But what did it matter now?

A gentle rapping sounded on his door. "Will?" Jesse called. "You awake?"

Probably more than he had been in years. Not that it changed anything. "Yeah, I'll be right out."

"Be quick. We got trouble."

He went straightaway to the living room, where Spike was cowering behind an easy chair as though hiding from an irate grizzly.

"Outside," Jesse said.

Spike motioned them down and hissed, "Quiet!"

Outside the picture window, across the road among the trees, a figure skittered through the snow, wielding a long-handled axe, swinging it randomly at branches and trunks, doing little damage but far too enthusiastic for comfort.

"It's her," Spike said. "She's found us."

Will edged along the back of the room, moving slow in case he was visible from outside. It did look like the figure they had seen in the town, but she—maybe; he still couldn't tell the gender—was so bundled up that neither form nor face could be seen. She continued attacking the pines to no good effect, oblivious to all else.

"She doesn't know we're here," Will decided. "She'll move on soon enough."

"Kill her," Spike pleaded. "Before she breaks down the door."

"She's nowhere near the door."

"Please. Please stop her."

Jesse licked his lips and watched the woman flail the axe about. Bits of ponderosa bark flew here, a spray of snow there. "You really want that?" he asked. "You really wanna see her dead?"

Spike buried his face in the back of the easy chair. His fingers clawed at the fabric. "I don't want to be hacked to pieces."

Will wasn't about to kill someone who didn't pose an immediate threat, but this might be his best opportunity to rearm himself. "Where are the guns?" he asked. "Let me have one, and if she tries to get in, I'll stop her."

"No."

"I won't use it on you."

"You might."

"I won't. You saved our lives. You gave us shelter."

"Yeah," Jesse said, keeping an eye on the intruder. "We owe you."

Spike flopped with his back to the chair and shook his head. He feared them, it seemed, as much as he feared the crazy lady.

Outside, the woman had moved just beyond the house, still playing lumberjack to little effect. Will thought he heard her voice pierce the air now and again, but he could discern no words.

His window of opportunity almost slammed shut, he tried one more time. "What if she breaks in when we're all asleep? A gun might be all that stands between us and that axe."

Not that it was a cogent argument. In that circumstance, he'd be dead before he cleared the cobwebs from his brain. He'd never even lay hand on the gun much less aim it with an axe buried in his chest.

"Pepper," Spike mumbled. "Yes, pepper. On a blade. A knife. How do we make it stick, though? It has to stick. And then throw it." He made a vague tossing motion. "Throw it, it goes in, the pepper is absorbed into the tissue. Yes, that would do it."

"She's gone," Jesse said. "For now."

Will risked approaching the window. The woman had passed fifty or so feet through the trees, still hacking at them with her axe, still scoring few hits. Didn't she ever tire?

"Away from the window, you fool!" Spike had clawed his way up the back of the chair and now stood on bent knees, eyes wide with terror.

"It's all right," Will told him, but he left the window just the same. He planted himself before the easy chair and looked down on Spike, not sure whether to pity or loath him.

Jesse retreated to the couch and sank into it. He ran his hands through his hair. "Don't look like she cares about us."

Spike hauled himself to his feet and squared his shoulders. "She wouldn't. Not until she sees us. Not until a voice whispers in her skull, telling her we must die."

"Is that what happens?" Will asked.

"That's one thing that happens. There are others. Delusions, hallucinations, psychosis, severe depression leading to suicidal acts. And, of course, my personal favorite: IED. I do so love flying into a rage for no apparent reason." He circled the chair, waved Will back, and sat. "You have no symptoms whatsoever, do you?"

"Not as far as I know."

Spike turned an empty gaze on Jesse. "You?"

"When it first started, I about strangled my boss. But not since."

Spike cocked his head and gazed at Jesse like a puzzled owl.

"I take it that makes no sense to you," Will said.

Before Spike could answer, the picture window shattered like a stack of china plates splintering on a stone floor.

Dale E. Lehman

She flailed the axe, a berserker dismembering what remained of the window until it became an alien maw bristling with crystal fangs. Then, with an almost impossible leap, she was in their midst, swinging for their necks. Spike tumbled from the chair and threw himself behind it, curled into a keening ball, helpless, useless, dead if she made it to him. Jesse bolted for the front door, Will for the kitchen. But instead of fleeing, they each faced their attacker, shaking with fear and adrenaline. Weapons, they needed weapons, what could they use for *weapons*?

Pausing as though not sure who to kill first, the woman raised the axe over her head and let out a scream. She charged Will. Will stood his ground until the last second, then threw himself aside as the axe sliced through the space he'd vacated. He snatched up a cushion from the sofa, not that it would do much good as a shield. The woman turned on him, axe already in motion for his skull. He dropped to a crouch just in time. As the axe arced by, he lunged, pillow leading, and hit her midsection. The force of the impact knocked her from her feet. She crashed to the floor, Will on top, but somehow she kept both hands on the axe handle and would have brought the head down on his spine had not Jesse swept in with a table lamp and smashed it in her face.

She howled with rage and dropped the axe. Her arms flailed and her fingers clawed at the air. Jesse kicked her in the head again, again, again, screaming right back until his scream morphed into words.

"Leave him alone you bastards!" he bellowed. "Leave Martin alone!"

Disoriented, Will rolled onto his back and struggled to sit. "Jesse," he said. "Jesse."

Jesse sank to his knees, hands covering his face, sobs wracking his body.

The air hung heavy and cold in the room. Tracers of snow drifted in through the window and settled on the furniture and carpet. Spike rose like a specter from behind the easy chair and surveyed the damage. Pushing himself to his feet, he came to Jesse's side and looked down on the body of the intruder. He folded his hands before him, clicked his tongue, and slipped off to the kitchen.

"I couldn't stop," Jesse mumbled.

Will got to his feet and studied the body. Scores of bleeding cuts crossed her face. Blood seeped from the scalp beneath her hair. Her throat was crushed. Jesse must have stomped her neck.

He extended a hand to his traveling companion. "Come on," he said. "Let's see what Spike is up to."

Accepting the hand up, Jesse rose with the stiffness of a man four times his age. "I couldn't stop," he said, gaze fixed on the destruction he'd wreaked.

"It's all right," Will said, echoing Jesse's words from a month before. "You had no choice." Placing his hand on Jesse's shoulder, he steered his partner into the kitchen.

Spike was busy making three cups of cocoa. He settled the drinks on the table and motioned Will and Jesse to sit. He took his customary place by the window. "A bit chilly," he said. "Isn't it?"

"Sure," Will said. "You're minus a window." He sipped the hot drink.

"Good point. Thank you, by the way."

"For what?"

"Killing her."

Jesse shuddered.

"Self-defense," Will said.

"All's well that ends well," Spike added.

Not damn likely. How could this *ever* end well?

Spike took a long pull on his cocoa, then contemplated the steam rising from the mug. "Now that we're in the clear, we can start."

Will drained his mug and carried it to the sink. He rinsed down the last swirls of chocolate. They looked oddly like blood. Hadn't Hitchcock used chocolate syrup for blood in the shower scene in *Psycho*?

Jesse drew a deep breath. "Start what?"

"Survival practice."

"We been surviving for weeks, old man. We don't need no practice."

"You've been living off civilization's leftovers. You can't do that forever."

"Why not?"

"Things fall apart. Servers crash. The power grid fails. Who's left to fix them? We need to learn to make tools, to hunt, to gather. I've been printing everything that might help. I have a whole library. It's safe to go out again, so it's time to start learning."

"What about them aliens?" Jesse asked.

Spike took another drink and ignored him.

"You'll know when they're around," Will told Jesse.

Rising, Spike waved a hand toward the living room. "Come on, I'll show you."

He led them past the dead woman. Will hoped Jesse wouldn't want to bury her, not with six or eight or whatever the hell it was feet of snow on the ground and frozen rock beneath. Still, they had to get her out of the house. They'd have to board up the window, too, and clean up the broken glass. Quite the to-do list.

Spike, though, had his mind on other things. He steamed down the hall, past their bedrooms, and into a back room at the far end of the house. Will and Jesse followed. This room was furnished as a hunting lodge office, with wood paneling and photos of deer, bear and other shootable creatures on the walls. By the back window, looking onto the snowy slopes beyond, a computer station waited. A red light shone at the base of the monitor. A laser printer sat on an end table to the side. Piles of printouts were stacked all about the floor and on every available chair, some mounds a foot tall, some three feet or more, some neatly arranged, some spilling sideways in paper landslides.

Will and Jesse took in the white mass. It might have been snow drifted in through an open window. Will was used to pouring over financial data and opaque annual reports, but this dwarfed anything in his experience.

"It's all arranged by topic," Spike said as though showing off a collection of rare books. "Everything we'll need." He picked up a sheaf of papers from a chair and riffled through it, suddenly less than confident. "Unless I forgot something."

Will grabbed a handful of printouts and leafed through the sheets. It was everything you never wanted to know about building shelters: lean-tos, teepees, huts, snow caves, and more. Why would they need any of that? The house wasn't about to collapse anytime soon.

Jesse, too, had started in on a pile, but quickly replaced the printouts. "I ain't a butcher. One of you can do that."

"The specialists are dead," Spike said absently. "Or soon will be. It's time for generalists."

Will returned his pile and picked up another. Herbal cures. "So you think we're back in the stone age now."

"I don't know." Sinking to his knees, Spike dropped his papers on the floor and cradled his head in his hands. He began to rock back and forth, his face a mask of pain. His lips moved but no sound emerged. He was a reed flapping in the breeze, a branch tossed about by the wind until whatever force pushing on his mind stopped. Then he rose and faced the window, put his hand to the glass, drew invisible circles on it with his index finger.

He pivoted and stabbed a finger at Jesse. "It's your fault."

Jesse stiffened. "Me?"

"You went outside. You let them know we're here."

"C'mon, I told you. Nobody was out there."

"You caused it. You fix it. Get out there and kill them."

Will stepped between them. "Breathe," he said. "It's the disease again."

"Don't you side with him!" Spike grabbed a handful of papers and threw them at Will. The sheets fluttered harmlessly about the floor.

"It's okay," Jesse said. "I'll kill 'em. Can I have a gun?"

Spike waved a hand in denial. "If you're one of them, you'll use it on us. Get the hell out there. Now!"

Nice try, Will thought.

With a shrug, Jesse left. Will listened to his footsteps recede. The back door slammed. When Spike took up a post by the window, Will dared approach and watch over his shoulder. Jesse tromped into the snow. Fifteen feet behind the house, he pressed snowballs with his bare hands and chucked them with malice into the distance, where they silently splattered in the sea of white. He fought the invisible intruders for ten minutes before stopping, rubbing his hands together, and burying them in his armpits.

Spike looked puzzled. "What the hell is he doing?" he asked.

"What you told him to do," Will replied.

"Damn it, don't you two know better than to listen to me? Get him back in here before he gets frostbite."

Will rapped on the window and motioned Jesse in. Not listening to Spike sounded like a great idea.

"What do we do with the body?" Will asked once they were together again in the office, surrounded by piles of paper that might tell them how to stay alive but said nothing about disposing of the dead in the mountain winter.

"Snow's too deep for a proper funeral," Jesse said.

"Sky burial," Spike suggested.

Will didn't know what that meant. Nor did Jesse, given his expression.

"A Tibetan Buddhist practice," Spike explained. "The body is put out for the vultures and other scavengers."

Jesse shuddered. "That's horrid."

"On the contrary. It's considered a kindness in their culture. It's also the easiest thing to do, given our circumstances."

"Not in my backyard."

"It's not your backyard."

"Sure as hell ain't yours."

Spike poked Jesse in the chest. "It's more mine than yours."

"Only 'cause you stole it first."

Will pushed them apart and planted himself between them. "Nobody owns anything anymore. The body's got to go, and Spike's probably right. It's either leave her out in the open or bury her in the snow. What's the difference?"

Jesse turned away. He looked like he might be sick. Will couldn't blame him. He'd done the killing this time. Burying the deceased might have lessened his guilt.

"I'll help," Spike offered. "Let's get it over with."

After using black plastic trash bags to wrap the body, Will and Spike packed themselves into parkas, boots, and gloves and dragged her into the cold, leaving Jesse with a broom and dustpan so he could start glass shard removal. They hauled their load down the slope and across the road, then into the stand of pines beyond, leaving a scar in the snow. They dragged her downhill until they could no longer see the house. They were panting by then. Will thought his lungs might freeze.

"Good enough," Spike decreed, dropping his end. "Your friend won't be disturbed by her here. Let's be environmentally friendly and take the plastic back."

Will couldn't tell if Spike was serious or making a bad joke. The environment seemed pretty well done with humanity. But they unwrapped the corpse, opened one bag and stuffed the rest in, and tied it shut.

"That hill looks steeper now we have to go up it," Will said.

"Always does," Spike agreed.

They slogged their way back up, pausing every ten paces to catch their breath. When they reached the road, they rested once more. Will studied the house. "We need to board up that window," he said.

Spike set his gloved fists to his hips. "Waste of time. We'll commandeer another house. Not much needs to be moved, just my library and the food supply."

Moving didn't sound easier than making repairs, especially not since they'd be lugging everything on foot. "All we need is some plywood, nails, and a hammer."

"Don't argue!" Spike scooped up a handful of snow and flung it in Will's face.

Sputtering, Will swiped away the frigid moisture, grabbed the front of Spike's coat and about punched him in the gut.

Spike's legs went limp, and he dropped to his knees. He raised his face to the sky and let out a long, piercing moan.

Will released him. What the hell was this, now? Despair? Anguish? Another form of madness wracking his diseased brain?

Hanging his head, Spike fell silent. He poked a finger into the snow and scratched out a circle, then another, then another. "It's odd," he murmured so quietly that Will had to bend down to hear. "I've lived my whole life for myself. And this is its sum. Not even zero. Negative. Massively negative." His head tilted up once more, but this time he studied Will's face before turning his attention down the snow-choked road. "When I found you and Jesse in a hypothermic stupor, I almost left you there."

Will would have, had their places been reversed. Jesse wouldn't have let him, but that would've been his first impulse. "Why didn't you?"

"My life. It's like your lost van full of stuff. Trash, all of it. The parties, the Caribbean cruises, the drinks and the food and the women. I realized it when I saw all your stuff packed in there, stuck in the snow, doing nobody any good at all. From the minute we're born, we're marching toward the grave, and when we get there, everything we picked up along the way turns to dust. All that remains is the good we've done for others." Spike slapped the snow a few times. Puffs of powder drifted off. He pushed himself to his feet. "I don't know how much time I have left," he said, "but I want to leave behind more than trash." He trudged uphill, toward the house, his boots excavating a trail in the snow.

Will followed.

"I say we move," Spike called over his shoulder. "Today. If you insist on boarding up the window, I guess I'll help, but I don't know where we're going to find the materials."

20

WILL TOLD Jesse of Spike's plan for the broken window—to swap out the whole house—and he agreed, but not because of the lack of plywood. He didn't want to stay in a place where he'd killed someone. Will understood that, anyway, so the three of them spent the remainder of the day packing the survival library, nonperishable foods, and other necessities. They found a hoard of cardboard boxes in the attic and dumped the contents without ceremony to free the containers. It was all junk anyway, mostly old clothing, books, and trinkets that must have meant something to somebody once upon a time, but no more.

Only once the packing was done and the boxes piled in the living room did Jesse render a negative assessment of the operation: "I ain't busting my ass hauling that through hip-deep snow."

"You won't have to," Spike assured him. "The former residents were skiers. We'll rig a sled using skis. It'll be like dragging feathers."

"A million bucks says you're wrong."

"Where would you get a million dollars?"

Jessed pointed at Will. "I'll borrow it from the rich guy."

"Don't count on it," Will said. "I'm saving it for gas, once the snow melts."

Spike looked puzzled, as though he couldn't fathom the snow ever melting. "Garage," he said. "Everything we'll need is there."

There, they found an old wooden palette against the back wall. Four pairs of skis and accompanying poles were hanging on the side wall, alongside a peg board overstuffed with tools. Spike rummaged through the cabinets on the opposite wall and found a drill and machine screws. "Who has mechanical skills?" he asked.

Will shook his head. His handyman experience was limited to hanging pictures and calling the plumber.

Jesse waggled his hand.

"Good enough," Spike said. He turned the tools and materials over to Jesse with instructions to drill through the skis and mount them on the underside of the pallet. Jesse was less than enthusiastic, but he did a creditable job. Spike found some twine and fashioned a pair of pulls from it.

Once done, they opened the garage door and settled the makeshift sled on the mounded snow. They piled the boxes onto it. It worked, to a point. Once too much weight was added, the sled sank into the powder. Will halted the loading operation and tried to pull the cargo. He made it three steps before giving up. They lightened the load by degrees until he was comfortable with it, but it would mean two trips.

All they needed now was an unlocked house. What point in leaving a house with a broken window only to smash in another or kick open a door? Then again, how many houses must have been left unlocked when their maddened owners rampaged out? Probably a lot.

Spike decided it was time for cocoa and retreated to the kitchen to make some, pilfering a container of chocolate powder from the packed supplies. Not that hot drink would help that much. The temperature indoors had nearly equalized with the outside, even with the furnace running nonstop. Jesse followed after whispering to Will, "I got zero faith in this project."

Will decided to leave them to themselves and go house hunting. The cocoa wouldn't run out before he got back. He went westward down to the road along a mostly level stretch. Houses dotted the uphill side of the white lane, spaced widely, surrounded by pines, marked by snowed-under drives. Sometimes the snow had mounded over a vehicle. The clouds had begun to break up, revealing blue cracks in the gray ceiling. Golden crepuscular rays poured through. He could hear Sarah exclaim, "Look! Creation!" Such sights reminded her of artwork in old children's religion books depicting the newly-created world. Will thought creation stories childish indeed, but he had to admit, from an aesthetic viewpoint the designation fit.

He reached the first house, slogged through the snow to the front door, and tried it. Locked. He blazed a trail around back, where he found another door. Also locked. So much for a short trip. He moved on to the second house, where he repeated his investigation. Also locked.

The third house presented a different obstacle. A gloved hand protruded from the snow in the front yard. Will gave it a wide berth, but at the door he came upon a hooded head leaning against the frame. Long, black hair spilled from the hood, obscuring the face. The rest of the body was buried in the snow. The woman—he presumed it was a woman—might have sat down at the door and waited for the cold to kill her.

Forget about going in that way. Will detoured to the back of the house where a short flight of snowed-under stairs rose to a snowed-under deck. He mounted the steps and broke a trail to a sliding glass door. He gave it a tentative tug. It slid open without trouble.

Just his luck. The first open house had a corpse guarding the front entrance. He thought about continuing down the road, but cold and hunger gnawed on him. He had no taste for another bout of hypothermia. Closing the door, he headed back.

On his return, he found Spike and Jesse still at the kitchen table, huddled in their coats, their hands wrapped around fresh mugs of cocoa. "What is that, your fourth?" he asked.

"Third," Jesse said. "Find anything good?"

"Sort of." He related the details. Jesse shuddered. Spike just stared into his drink. "We can move the bodies across the road," Will continued, "like we did with—"

"We remember," Jesse snapped. "When does this end? All the bodies, all the burials. Or non-burials."

"I never looked up decomposition rates," Spike told his cocoa. "I could, if you want."

"Damn! What's with you?" Jesse sprang to his feet and searched the cabinets with no purpose but to forget about death.

"Point is," Will said, "it's a nearby house. We can go in the back way. We should haul everything down there before it gets dark. At least we won't have to sleep in the cold tonight. The bodies can wait until tomorrow."

"The white guy has the plan, as always," Jesse grumped. "Fine. Let's get it over with."

The move proved as unpalatable as the conversation. Even with a partial load, the makeshift sled persisted in sinking so far into the snow that it took all three of them hauling on the ropes to move it. Forty minutes later, they arrived at the deck behind their new home. They stared up the stairs, exhausted, overheated, soaked in sweat beneath their coats. Will's boot prints, left from his earlier reconnaissance, ascended to the sliding glass door.

Jesse hefted a box. "I guess I go first. 'Cause I'm the guy from the loading dock." He tromped up the steps.

Will half wished he'd cut that out, half found it oddly comforting that he wouldn't. He grabbed another box and followed.

Spike shoved his hands in his pockets and glowered at the remaining cartons. "Which one's got the pepper?" he asked. "Take that in first. Just in case."

Who knew? "Maybe that one on the end," Will said. With luck, the old man would snap out of it once indoors.

Cradling the indicated box in his arms, Spike mounted the steps.

The glass door opened onto a roomy kitchen with chrome appliances and a curious light fixture dangling from the ceiling. A white cylinder riddled with holes and covered in a multicolored material, it could hardly be potent enough to illuminate the table, much less the room. But when Jesse deposited his load on the table and found the switch, the thing proved surprisingly bright. White light gushed like a fountain from its top and bottom, while red, yellow, green, blue, and purple polka dots sprayed over

     Dale E. Lehman

walls and cabinets. It lent the room an oddly psychedelic feel. Maybe the designer was an old hippie.

After more back-and-forths than Will cared to count, half their worldly possessions were spread about the table and floor. He was loath to leave the warmth of the house, but he wanted the job done. They could rest later. "Back for round two," he said. Jesse grudgingly followed him out, but Spike parked himself in a chair at the table and grumbled to himself.

"Come on," Will urged. "We need to finish before dark."

Spike grimaced.

"What's wrong now?"

"You're trying to kill me."

"Wonderful," Jesse muttered. "We ain't aliens. I promise."

Spike shook his head and refused to look at them.

"We won't kill you," Will said. "We need your help." Not that reason had any power right now, but he didn't know what else to say.

"I'm staying right here," Spike said. "I know what you're up to."

Jesse threw up his hands. "Fine. Let's go." He descended the steps without waiting for Will to agree.

Being down a man ought to have made the work harder, but the trail of packed snow they'd blazed on the first trip compensated for the loss, and they were able to drag the laden sled with less effort this time. They didn't talk until they returned. Then, at the bottom of the deck stairs, Jesse nodded up at the glass door. "He's a problem," he said.

"At least he's not violent."

"Almost was, a couple times."

"If it came to that," Will said, "I could take him."

"Not if he knifes you in the back when you ain't looking."

"So, we don't turn our backs on him."

Jesse picked up a box. "Let's get this done. I just wish we had our guns."

Will did too, but where had Spike hidden them? Or had he never truly confiscated them? Will and Jesse had made repeated searches up until yesterday with no luck. In fact, now that he thought about it, nothing from the van had ever appeared at the house. Spike probably lied about taking them, although the way he spoke of being affected upon seeing the van's contents, he must have been there.

Whatever. It was too late to do anything about it. The ProMaster was their past. Picking up a box, Will nodded onward, and they went inside.

When they got there, Spike was still at the table, but smiling now, smiling like a doting father who had returned from a long trip to find his young daughter waiting for him.

And there beside him sat the daughter—not his daughter but somebody's—smiling back.

She was young, maybe thirteen or fourteen, no longer a child but not yet a woman, wearing tattered jeans and a white sweater. She startled when the door slid open, stared wide-eyed at Jesse, wider-eyed at Will. Those eyes were brown, her skin the color of turned soil, her hair black and just brushing her shoulder. Mexican, Will thought. South-of-the-border, at any rate.

"It's okay," Spike said softly. "They're good fellows. They're with me."

She exhaled in relief.

"This is Adalina," he told his companions. "She was hiding upstairs when we barged in. It's her house."

Will and Jesse put down their boxes. Jesse pulled the door shut to keep out the cold. "You here all alone?" he asked.

Adalina nodded.

"It's okay," Spike assured her again. "That's Jesse. This is Will. You can talk to them."

She looked skeptical.

Will pulled out a chair and sat. "We're sorry if we scared you. We thought the house was empty."

"Almost," she said.

The bodies in the snow must have been her parents. Will had no idea how to talk to a child about such tragedy. Probably nobody truly did.

"Have you had enough to eat?" Jesse asked.

She nodded again. "There's lots of food, if you know where to look. And I'm a good cook. Mama taught me…" A stricken look crossed her face. She put her hands over her face and cried for a moment. "I'm sorry," she whimpered.

"It's okay," Spike said once more. Will was starting to think the words were stuck somewhere in his brain. "We've all lost family. We understand."

"They ran outside and wouldn't come back. They stayed out there all night and it snowed and snowed and they just wouldn't come back. I called to them, I begged them, but they wouldn't." Adalina looked down at the table and squeezed her eyes shut.

Jesse reached across the table as though to take her hand but hesitated at the last moment. "Cry if you have to," he said. "We all done our share of it. It's natural. And good."

"No." She rose, opened the refrigerator, and stared into the empty interior. The perishables had all perished by now. "I cried for two weeks straight. That's enough."

Spike joined her at the refrigerator. The light within seemed oddly warm as it spilled from the cold. "Can we stay with you? If you let us stay, we'll help you."

Adalina shrugged and closed the refrigerator. "So long as you don't go crazy, too."

"We won't. Everyone who might already has."

Will nearly pointed out that Spike's crazy came and went, but it wasn't a great time for such revelations. Adalina needed stability, and they needed shelter. It was too late in the day to look for another place. "We should bring in the rest of the stuff," he said to Jesse.

Jesse eyed the back of Spike's head. In a whisper, he said, "You sure it's okay leaving..." He nodded toward the old man and the girl.

How could they be sure? Either way, they had to bring everything in. Will went out to retrieve a box. Jesse waited until he was back before taking a turn himself, and alternating trips they did the work, making sure Adalina was never left alone with Spike. They needn't have worried. Spike maintained his fatherly—or grandfatherly—attention on their young host as the two of them wandered the kitchen, the living room, the dining room, and back to the kitchen, talking in hushed tones. Whatever passed between them remained between them, but Adalina showed no uneasiness and Spike seemed more normal than he ever had. Maybe the girl had a stabilizing influence on him?

By the time the work was done, the long mountain shadows had engulfed the house as darkness stole over the eastern sky. Adalina began to putter around the kitchen, pulling together foods from the freezer and the cabinets, microwaving away ice from the frozens, mixing things on the stove. Jesse hovered nearby, watching her with interest and nodding his approval. When all was done, she'd made a skillet of ground beef, rice, and corn with sweet spices and a hot pepper sauce kick, served with a side of canned *refritos.*

"No cheese," she lamented. "It went moldy."

"We can live without it," Will assured her. His first bite of her creation astonished him. It tasted as good as anything he'd ever had at a restaurant. Maybe that was hunger talking, but he didn't think so. The young lady had talent. "It's delicious," he told her.

"Amazing," Jesse agreed.

Adalina blushed and smiled at her plate.

"Now that we know who the chef is," Spike said, winking at her, "we need a plan for procurement. Tomorrow we should start working on snares and basic hunting weapons."

"Or you could just tell us where the guns are," Will said.

"Forget the guns. They're history."

228

Dale E. Lehman

"What does that mean?"

Spike ate as though Will wasn't even there.

"It means," Jesse said, "we ain't never seeing them again. He's tossed them somewhere. Or never had them at all. Ain't that so?"

With a shrug, Spike declined to answer that, as well.

Will silently cursed the man's paranoia. Guns could mean the difference between life and death. They offered protection and a means of obtaining food. But Jesse was right. They were long gone.

Adalina didn't seem to be listening. She ate in silence as though alone. But when the conversation didn't pick up again, she ventured into the void. "Papá has guns," she said.

Spike dropped his fork. It clanked on his plate.

"Good," Will said. "Where does he keep them?"

She led them upstairs, where three bedrooms and a bathroom huddled around a short hallway. One room was hers. Another had been her parents'. The third was a game room, with a bookcase full of board games, a big table, and sports posters on the walls. In a corner, a glass-fronted cabinet displayed a set of firearms. Adalina led them to the weapons and pointed from left to right. "Those are papá's and mamá's rifles. Twenty-twos. This one's a twelve-gauge shotgun, that one's a twenty gauge. The one on the right is my twenty-two. I'm a good shot, even standing." She beamed as though being presented a blue ribbon.

Jesse kept his distance from the cabinet. "They taught you to shoot?" he asked, his voice quavering.

"Yep! They even took me hunting sometimes."

Will found it ironic that a young teen girl had more survival skills than the rest of them. But maybe that was the world now. Everything had been turned on its head. "What about ammunition?" he asked.

"In the drawers." She pointed to the bottom of the cabinet, where two long, narrow drawers with barely-there handles were secreted. The drawers and the glass doors to the gun compartment had locks.

Will tugged at one of the doors. Locked. "You know where the key is, I suppose?"

Adalina bit her lip. Spike exhaled in relief.

"We'll help you look for it," Will said. "Maybe your dad had it in his room?"

She shook her head.

Will didn't press the matter. He'd find it. How many hiding places could there be? "We don't need it immediately," he said, in part so she didn't feel she'd let him down, in part to keep Spike from blowing a gasket. Who knew what the old man might do in his paranoia to keep the firearms out of reach?

Adalina ran a finger over one of the locks. "I know where it is," she whispered. "On papá's keyring."

Spike put a hand on her shoulder. "Quiet, child. Don't tell us. We don't need to know. Guns are trouble."

"They sure are," Jesse agreed. "But we might need 'em anyway."

"You don't. We don't. We're starting over. We'll make what we need for hunting but not for killing each other."

Spike couldn't possibly be that naïve, could he? Any weapon capable of killing an animal could kill a human being. Besides, the demise of most of humanity had rendered the world no less dangerous. That very morning, they'd nearly been killed by a psychotic, or had Spike blanked that from his memory?

Still, best not to agitate him. His moods swings hadn't proven dangerous yet, but they would frighten Adalina. Will could talk to her about the keys later when Spike was asleep.

But she told him of her own accord. "His keyring is...it's...if you want it, you'll have to..." She sobbed, got herself under control, and finished in a rush. "It's in his pocket."

21

WILL WAS sick of dealing with corpses, but he'd do what he must. Jesse looked ill just thinking about it. Spike dropped to the floor and sat cross-legged, staring at nothing, while Adalina went to the piles of games and fidgeted with the boxes, straightening them, pulling them out a bit, pushing them back a bit. When the men said nothing, she walked out, muttering, "I'm hungry. Anyone want peanut butter crackers?"

Spike turned his head to make sure she was gone. "You don't want to do this," he said, quietly so she wouldn't overhear.

"It's not a matter of wanting," Will told him. "I promise, we won't shoot you."

"He's frozen. God knows how long he's been out there, but he's probably frozen solid. You won't be able to get those keys without taking an ice pick or a hammer to him."

Jesse cringed. "I ain't chipping no bits off him."

"It's a key in his pocket," Will snapped, "not his spleen."

"Whatever. I ain't doing it."

Spike got to his feet. "Moreover," he said, "our focus should be on long-term survival skills. What good are guns once the ammo runs out?"

The country was drowning in gun shops. How the hell hard could it be to replenish the ammo? Why were they stuck in this Ferris wheel of an argument? "I'll get the keys," Will said. "You two keep Adalina occupied. She doesn't need to see that.".

"Me, neither," Jesse said. "Maybe the kid plays blackjack."

"Don't lose your life's savings to her. You never know when a penny will come in handy." Will didn't wait for a reply. He passed through the kitchen, where Adalina was spreading peanut butter onto a plate of saltines as though preparing *hors d'oeuvres* for a five-star restaurant. On the way, he grabbed his coat from the chair. Pulling it on, he slipped out back without a sound.

He sailed through their tracks in the snow to the front of the house. The air was still, the blue mountain sky streaked with cirrus clouds. Silence engulfed him. Coming upon the gloved hand, he paused. An odd feeling stole over him, a feeling that the hand belonged not to a dead man but a living creature lying in wait for him, biding its time until he drew close, and then it would snatch him, pull him under, suffocate him.

Madness. This wasn't an ice zombie. It was a corpse, one of hundreds of millions gradually returning to the earth, just slower thanks to the natural deep freeze. Will knelt and began digging. He worked his way down, exposing the forearm, the elbow, the upper arm, the shoulder. This was the right arm. Adalina's father had died on his back, facing the sky, reaching up maybe for heaven, for God, for something. Probably he was Catholic, being from Mexico. Will had in the back of his head that over three-quarters of Mexicans were Catholic. He didn't know why he'd stashed away that statistic or where it had come from, only that it had taken up residence in his brain. He kept digging.

Soon he had a trench around the man's right side and located his trouser pocket. If he was right-handed, which seemed likely because he'd been reaching up with his right hand, his keys would be there. The material was stiff from the cold but pliable enough to yield when Will slid his hand in. The pocket, though, was empty.

Maybe his coat pocket, then. Will cleared more snow and tried again. Inside the coat pocket, his fingers touched cold metal and extracted the keys. He stuffed them into his own pocket and reburied the body, mounding snow over the hand so it wouldn't be visible to Adalina if she looked out the window.

The sun was dipping behind a ridge to the west by the time he finished. It must have taken longer than he realized. No matter. The job was done. Spike might grumble, but Will and Jesse would have weapons again, protection against intruders, easy means of hunting.

Now all they had to do was learn to hit a target at more than point blank range. They had never quite mastered that.

The following days felt stranger to Jesse than any that had gone before, which was saying something. Not that life had been normal since New York imploded, but along the way they'd settled into a pattern of sorts: running blind; bickering without purpose; random encounters with crazies and normals; and of late Spike's on-again, off-again madness.

Adalina's presence altered the shape of their shared existence. Spike hadn't had an episode since they found her. Now he spent large portions of his days sitting with her, conversing in hushed tones, listening to her, walking with her through the snow behind the house where the bodies of her parents couldn't darken her thoughts. She seemed to enjoy his company, as though he was her grandfather or a beloved uncle. Jesse never heard enough to know what they said, but whatever it was seemed to buoy them both.

When he wasn't with Adalina, Spike focused on survival skills. He required Jesse and Will's presence several times each day for tutoring. Together, they worked on tools and weapons, traps and snares. Few of their efforts turned out like the pictures in Spike's printouts, but—he insisted time and again—they'd get there with practice.

Will had a different practice on his mind: target practice. With annoying regularity, he marched Jesse into the snow to perfect their ability to kill with firearms. Will had scrounged up a pack of construction paper in the game room and from it made targets, which he impaled on nails driven into trees on the far side of the road. They shot parallel to the road so as not to hit the house. Some days they spent four hours shooting, and while Jesse still hated guns, he had to admit, he was getting good at decimating that paper. He just hoped he never needed to turn a weapon on a deer or even a rabbit, much less a human being. One death by his hand was one more than he could take.

But for all their work with weaponry stone age and modern, they hadn't gone hunting. Not even Adalina suggested it, and she was the one with actual experience. Fact was, they didn't need to hunt. Not yet. Her parents had kept two garage freezers well-stocked with beef and poultry and venison and vegetables. "In case relatives dropped by," Adalina explained. "We have a big family." So there was no shortage of protein and plant matter. Will inventoried it not long after their arrival and figured it would about last the four of them through the winter.

Beyond that, Jesse supposed they'd find plenty in grocery store freezers once the snow melted and they acquired new wheels. Life was secure enough for now.

Until the power went out.

It happened in the middle of the eleventh night after they met Adalina. Jesse noticed it first, waking in the dark to a chill permeating his room. Curled into a ball under the blankets, he felt the cold nipping at his nose and ears and feet. For a time, he listened for the low hum of the heating system and heard only a rush of wind in the trees outside. Rolling out of bed, he put a hand by the vent. Nothing. He flipped on the bedside light but remained immersed in darkness.

He dressed and fumbled his way to the door, crept down the darkened hallway to the stairs, and, gripping the railing, probed for the steps with his feet. It felt like an hour before he was planted securely on the first floor. A bit of light filtered in from outside, moonlight reflected off the snowpack. It illuminated the house just enough to guide him through the kitchen to the family room. He opened the curtains to get as much light as possible, then stacked a few chunks of wood in the fireplace grate. Kneeling before the pile, he used a fire starter and a butane lighter to coax a few tentative flames to life. He then rocked back and waited for the fire to build. A few minutes later, he was warming his chilled fingers in the flickering light.

What next? The heat wouldn't reach far beyond this room. Not that Jesse had any experience of fireplaces. In fact, this was the first time he'd ever lit a fire. But whatever warmth built up here would drift into the kitchen, only to be stalled by the falling temperatures as the rest of the house reached thermal equilibrium with the mountain air. To stay warm, they'd have to live and sleep in this room. That would be a trip.

Maybe it was just a circuit breaker? No, they wouldn't be that lucky. A tree had fallen on a power line, or some component in the grid had failed, or the whole damn power plant had gone belly up. Why had Will insisted on coming here? To the mountains, of all places? Why had Jesse let him? They should've gone south, out of winter's reach. That wouldn't have solved everything, no, but at least freezing to death would've been off the table. For the two of them, anyway. Spike and Adalina wouldn't have been so lucky.

The quiet sound of footsteps on the carpet broke his descent into paranoia. Jesse jumped, half expecting to find the crazy lady with her axe resurrected and intent upon round two.

It was just Will. He looked undead in the light of the fire, drained of life and maybe hope. He said nothing, just stood there watching the flames, hands stuffed in his pockets.

"Power's out," Jesse told him.

"I know."

"At least we got heat."

Will nodded.

"We should bring Adalina and Spike in here, so they don't get hypo-thermia."

Approaching the fire, Will took his hands from his pockets, warmed them for a moment, then dropped into a nearby easy chair. "That's a big word for this time of night."

Maybe. At least he hadn't said it was a big word for Jesse. "Get warm. I'll bring them." He returned to the cold of the kitchen, mounted the stairs with a bit less trepidation than on the descent, and went to Spike's room. He rapped on the door. "Hey, Spike. It's Jesse." He knocked again, a bit louder. "Wake up, old man. We got a problem."

From the other side of the door, a faint grunt sounded. Half a minute later, the door whined open and Spike poked his head out, although it was little more than a shadow in the darkness. "What's wrong?" He sounded like he had a mouth full of peanut butter.

"Power's out," Jesse said. "We got a fire going downstairs."

"Is that why it's so cold. Okay." The door closed.

Leaving Spike to make himself presentable, Jesse moved on to Adalina's room, knocked, called her name, did it again and again until the door opened and the girl stepped out. "It's cold," she said, hugging herself.

"Power's out," Jessed repeated. "We got a fire going downstairs. Come on down and get warm."

"Okay." She, too, closed her door.

By this time, Spike had reappeared and was making his way downstairs. Jesse followed, and Adalina appeared a moment later. The family room had warmed almost too much, but Jesse didn't mind. Will was still in the easy chair, eyes closed. Spike took the other, and Adalina flopped on the sofa, wrapped in a rose-colored robe. It appeared rose in the firelight, anyway. There was enough room at the other end of the sofa for Jesse, so he sat there. He almost asked if there were flashlights in the house, but it didn't matter. That could wait until morning. They didn't need light to sleep.

Problem was, he couldn't sleep, not anymore. Questions flitted through his mind like mosquitos intent upon his blood. How long would the firewood last? How long would the food last? What about the water, the sewers, all of life's support systems, the gadgets you never gave a thought to until they stopped working? How fast could they master the art of primitive living? Could they do it at all? Aside from Adalina, none of them had ever killed their own dinner. Had even she ever done the butchering?

The unknowns chased him through the night until, exhausted, he must have slipped into some manner of sleep, from which he awoke when the sun infiltrated the house and poked him in the eye. He slapped a hand over his face to block it. Something clanked in the kitchen.

"Come and get it," Will said.

Jesse sat forward and blinked at him. "Get what?

"Breakfast burritos. Adalina's favorite, I guess."

"Not even close," Adalina called from the kitchen. "They're just easy to make. Or were, when the microwave worked."

The freezer must have stayed cold enough so far. But how was she cooking? Before Jesse could ask, Will faded back into the kitchen.

Jesse stretched and shuffled after him. He all but fell into a chair at the table while Will and Adalina prepped the meal. One of them had found a camp stove much like the model Jesse had used when they still had the van. Adalina was heating the burritos in a pan over the flames. It made sense. Adalina's parents had been hunters. They were probably campers, too. Will had a pan of hot water which he poured into mugs and added packets of cocoa mix.

"Where's Spike?" Jesse asked.

"Checking the circuit breakers," Will said.

"Ain't the breakers."

"How do you know?"

"'Cause that'd be too easy."

Will finished his job and ferried the mugs to the table while Adalina slipped the hot burritos onto plates. About the time they had everything presented for consumption, Spike returned. "Wasn't the breakers," he said.

"Of course not," Will quipped. "That would be too easy."

Jesse smirked. "You owe me royalties for that."

Spike took a seat at the table and gave his burrito a suspicious examination. "We can check nearby houses, but probably the whole area's dead. What's this?"

"Fast food," Jesse said.

Taking up his fork, Spike picked at it. "Not sustainable."

"It'll sustain you for a while," Will told him. "Honestly, I think we have bigger problems than food, even without a working freezer. We have plenty of nonperishables and can raid nearby houses. But that fireplace won't warm more than the one or two rooms, and the wood supply is limited."

"We have trees," Spike said.

"Which we have to cut down without killing ourselves or smashing the house."

"It's in the printouts."

Will gave Jesse a skeptical look.

"And water," Jesse said. "How long does that run with the power out?"

Spike took a tentative taste of the burrito as though he hadn't been listening. His expression said he found it subpar.

"That's in the printouts, too." Will added a healthy dose of sarcasm to his delivery.

"Melt snow, for God's sake." Spike pushed his plate away and picked up his mug. "Boil it to make sure it's safe. People lived a hundred thousand years without indoor plumbing, you know."

"I didn't," Jesse objected. Nor did he care to think about it.

Cradling his head in his hands, Spike squeezed his eyes shut. Adalina, who had been ferrying food from camp stove to table, leaned over and whispered something to him. Under the influence of her voice, he unbent a bit and drew a deep breath. "I'm fine," he said.

She patted his shoulder and sat down to eat. Noticing Will and Jesse's puzzled looks, she nodded at Spike. "It's okay. He just gets worked up sometimes."

Will poked his burrito with his fork, then cut off a piece. "We know," he said.

Adalina, it turned out, had all kinds of skills. Despite her youth, she knew how to handle an axe as well as a gun, and since they were burning firewood nonstop, she felt an urge to show Jesse how it was done. The pair bundled up and went out to hack apart a small tree at the rear of the property that had been felled by Adalina's father before the world ended. She gave Jesse a basic lesson in handling an axe and demonstrated the necessary techniques, then watched and corrected him as he made cuts at alternating angles.

Jesse was puffing after a dozen swings. "Didn't your dad have a chainsaw?" he complained.

"Yeah."

"So why don't we use that?"

She shrugged. "I'm not allowed to. Anyway, he ran out of gas last time he mowed the lawn."

It figured. Jesse buried the axe in the wood and paused to catch his breath. "You know about Spike's…" He caught himself before he said disease.

"Yeah. He went crazy on me a time or two." She said it so calmly, she might have been saying he sneezed.

"Doesn't that scare you?"

"It was a bit freaky the first time, but he won't hurt me. Besides, when I tell him to calm down, he does."

Jesse had noticed that, but it made no sense. Why would madness listen to reason?

Adalina took up the axe and continued where Jesse had left off. She soon completed the cut and tossed the freed chunk of wood to the side. She handed the tool to him, maintaining a grip on it until he said, "Thank you," to signal he had control of it.

She watched Jesse go to work. "He says he's got more than one infection. They fight in his brain, but it doesn't hurt. It just makes him a little crazy sometimes."

"A little, yeah." Damn, this was hard work. Jesse hadn't thought of himself as sedentary, but city life must've made him soft. His muscles were aching already.

"Most people went totally bonkers," Adalina said. "Papá and Mamá..." She bit her lip.

Jesse wanted to tell her not to think about it. Or to let it out. He didn't know which would be worse.

"They were watching TV one minute, and the next they were running around in the snow and screaming and..." She kicked at the snow, spraying a cloud of white. "I guess they went bonkers, too."

Jesse buried the axe in the wood again. "I'm sorry," he said.

"That's what Spike said." She tugged the axe from the wood, took up position, and started cutting. Then she paused and frowned at Jesse. "You said it like you feel bad for me. He said it like it was his fault."

"He's carrying a load of guilt."

"Why?"

"Oh..." A dangerous question, probably too dangerous to answer. "It's probably the disease talking."

Adalina shrugged and continued the work.

They took turns swinging the axe until the tree had been reduced to a pile of firewood. Then they made a dozen trips from the work site, lugging the lumber in their arms and stacking it by the back of the house.

"I think he's hiding something," Adalina said as she brushed snow from her gloves.

Jesse didn't know whether to shiver or be amused. Uncanny insight? Youth straining for maturity? "Why do you think that?"

"I don't know. It just feels like he's hurt real bad inside. I gotta put the axe away." She plowed her way to it, retrieved it, and took it into the shed.

Jesse wondered if she wasn't right. Spike had told them about his work, but maybe he hadn't told them everything. Or maybe not everything he'd told them had been true. Probably it didn't matter. The damage was done and nothing could undo it. Besides, Spike had paid for whatever sins he'd committed.

Adalina returned and grabbed Jesse's gloved hand. "Come on," she said. "Let's get some cocoa."

22

T HE WATER supply didn't fail at once, which Spike said meant a water tower somewhere still provided sufficient pressure to keep it flowing. Yet the flow looked weaker than it should, and over time it ebbed further, so they took to melting snow and boiling water in a stockpot each day. The survival manual, as they started calling Spike's printouts, contained instructions on making and maintaining a pit toilet, but the mountain winter had other ideas. With the snowpack growing thicker by the week, it proved difficult to clear the ground, dig a hole, and keep it clear for use. They had no materials for building a structure, and with the nearest home improvement store twenty-five, thirty miles distant, they weren't about to hike there and back anytime soon. So they adopted a tree-shrouded corner of a former neighbor's property that now belonged to Mother Nature. She'd probably understand.

That was the worst part, aside from not being able to properly wash clothing or bodies, which was only bad for the first week. After that, they grew used to the smell of each other and didn't much notice it. As for food, they had plenty of powdered and canned edibles, and a manual can opener. Spike's insistence on learning the fine arts of hunting and butchering notwithstanding, none of them attempted it. Not even him. The fireplace kept them warm enough and chopping wood kept them fit enough, although most of the house grew too cold for comfort. The kitchen, next door to the family room, remained tolerable most of the time.

Will, though, felt increasingly edgy. Beauty beyond imagination embraced him in this land, yet he couldn't allow himself to be seduced. He could at most steal a kiss from the mountains before moving on. Their quartet couldn't stay much longer here, huddled in one room. Given a vehicle and a clear expressway, the Sacramento Valley was but fifty minutes away. In good weather, they might even walk that far in two or three days. But under these conditions? They'd be dead before they made the ten-mile mark. By all rights, they should have been dead already, but they'd gotten lucky over and over, if luck it was. How long could their fortune hold? No, they needed to escape these mountains, and soon.

But how?

He brought it up the third night after the power failure as they ate a makeshift stew of canned chicken, canned corn, and canned green beans washed down with snow melt.

Spike supplied a one-word answer: "Impossible."

Jesse elaborated on that. "I ain't marching off to die in the snow. Best we stick it out here."

"I don't think we'll last," Will said. "How long until the snow melts from the roads?"

Adalina slurped up some of her stew. "Maybe May," she said. "Maybe June. We get the most snow in March. It doesn't melt much until April." She gave the fireplace a thoughtful look as the wood sparked and popped. "If we had a plow, we could get down sooner."

Alas, they didn't. "Then we're stuck walking in the cold," Will said. "And it's a long walk." No, worse than that. With the power out, they'd be walking blind. Their cell phone batteries were dead, their spare power packs buried with the van in the snow. Maps had become a thing of the past.

But Adalina perked up. "Maybe not. Maybe we *can* walk."

Spike slapped his hand on the arm of the sofa. "No, young lady, we can't! They're out there waiting for us! They're hiding in every tree, don't you see that? The instant we set foot outside, we're dead!"

She put a gentle hand on his shoulder. "They won't catch us. You're smarter than them."

He sucked in a breath and squeezed his eyes shut. "Yes. Right. They don't know me. I know them." Opening his eyes again, he frowned at Will.

"Traipsing dozens of miles through the cold without knowing which way we're pointed…" He shook his head and picked up his bowl. "I'm not doing that."

The crazy bastard had a point.

"But that's just it," Adalina said. "We don't have to go miles, only a few houses down."

Jesse frowned at her. "You think the power's on there?"

She laughed. "No! We go a few houses down and stay overnight. Then a few more the next day. And a few more the next. We'll get to the valley, just not all at once."

The kid was a genius. Will pointed his spoon at her in acknowledgement. "Why didn't we think of that?"

"Might I point out," Spike said, "that we won't know how far it is to the next house. Out here, some houses occur in small clusters. Others could be miles apart."

But they had the makings of a plan, and Will wasn't about to be cowed. "We won't march blind. We'll do reconnaissance. Two of us, Jesse and I if nobody else—"

"Me!" Jesse objected.

"For safety."

"Whose?"

"Short walks to find the next house. We won't go far enough to freeze to death."

"You're nuts," Spike insisted.

Adalina touched his shoulder again. "It's worth a try," she told him, and somehow when he looked into her eyes, his objections evaporated.

"All right," he said. "For you. But they—" He gestured at Will and Jesse. "—they do the recon."

"Agreed," Will said.

Miffed, Jesse returned his attention to his meal.

The next day, Will and Jesse made their first expedition. January was just tilting toward February now, the snow deep and getting deeper, the cold bitter, the wind worse. They layered on clothing and ventured into the frigid morning feeling like yeti, probably looking the part, too, as westward they trekked down the road.

Widely-spaced houses edged their path, each buried in the woods back from the road. Without anyone to keep pavement clean—assuming these homes even had paved drives and walks—snow had piled and drifted around the structures until they poked above the undulating white like rocks. The only guide to the road's location Will and Jesse had was the lack of trees. The snow cut a canyon through the pines in great arcs, bending one way and then the other, rising and falling. Their dark tracks marked the way they had come until the wind erased them. Otherwise, no sign of human presence could be seen.

They had gained endurance since New York, but walking in this environment still taxed them. The snow clawed at their feet. The wind shoved them one way, then the other. Their legs ached on ascents, while descents tested their balance. Average walking speed, Will knew, was three miles per hour. They'd be lucky to make one today.

Not that they knew the time. They might have walked half an hour or half a day. Increasingly, they stopped to catch their breath until Jesse, puffing, waved at the trees. "Ain't seen a house for a while," he said around breaths. "Maybe it's time to turn back."

Will squinted in the general direction of the sun. It hadn't climbed that high yet, but what did that mean? "You're the astronomer," he said. "What time is it?"

"Uh." Jesse pointed at the sun, lowered his arm to the eastern horizon, raised it again. Then he dropped it and shrugged. "Damn mountains get in the way, but I guess it must be after ten by now. Earth turns fifteen degrees every hour. In winter, the sun stays low in the south, but it's moved maybe forty-five degrees since rising."

"Which means we've been walking over an hour. If we go much longer, we'll be too tired to make it back."

"Ain't gonna argue with that."

They reversed course. Upon reaching the last house they'd passed, they clomped up a snow lane to the pale green structure. It was much smaller than Adalina's home, narrow across the front with a door on the left and a curtained window on the right. The door was a quarter buried behind a drift. Stairs might be interred there, too, but the snow held as they mounted to the door. They kicked away the powder until the door was clear.

Before Will could open it, Jesse said, "Knock. Just in case."

They'd been surprised several times before, so Will knocked and called, "Hello!" The door remained shut, the house silent. No gunfire erupted.

Will turned the knob and the door opened without complaint. A bit of snow fell through the opening onto a paisley throw rug. They entered with caution, not knowing what they might find. The air within was nearly as cold as outside, but at least here they were out of the wind. Closing the door, Will called one more time, just in case. The house replied with silence.

"Let's check the place out," he said. "No telling what's in here."

"Great," Jesse mumbled.

"Better to find out now than when Adalina's with us."

"Yeah, yeah. Let's get it over with."

The front of the place had a living room right, a kitchen left, and almost no place to eat other than a worn couch facing a wall-mounted TV, a monster of a thing, probably seventy-five inches, much like the one Will had abandoned in New York. A hall led into darkness on the back side of the living room. Jesse, squaring his shoulders and flexing his fingers like a gunslinger preparing for a duel, marched into the back. Will wasn't sure whether to laugh or cringe.

The living room presented nothing of note—no bodies living or dead. He turned his attention to the kitchen. A small cabinet on wheels serving as an island afforded any corpses their only hiding place. But the air was too clean, so he expected nothing. He looked anyway and was proven wrong. A thin tabby cat lay there on its side, dead. He crouched beside it and pushed on the animal's front leg. Rigid. Will didn't know about cats, but from what he recalled, in people rigor mortis set in a few hours after death and lasted maybe a day. The poor critter must not have been dead too long. Given how thin it looked, it likely starved to death.

A strange world people had created, where animals couldn't survive on their own. Or maybe it could have, had it been able to open the door.

He returned to the hall. "Anything?" he called.

Jesse didn't answer.

"Jesse?" Will crept onward, peeking through first door he passed (a dark and disheveled bedroom with clothes strewn about and an unmade double bed awaiting someone who would never return), then the second (a miniscule bathroom, even darker, with towels scattered on the floor and in the sink), then the third (a room piled with junk in no discernable order). Brighter than the other rooms, the latter gathered light through two windows, one to the side, one to the back. Jesse's silhouette was outlined by light streaming through the back window. He was as still as the cat in the kitchen.

"Jesse?" Will repeated.

Jesse took a step back and nearly tripped over something on the floor. Will started for him, but Jesse waved him back. "Don't," he said.

"What's wrong?"

Turning in slow motion, Jesse tottered as though about to pass out.

Will grabbed his shoulders to steady him. "Is someone out there?"

Jesse blinked at him. "Sort of." When Will tried to get past him, he pushed him back, though not with much force. "I mean it. Don't."

Patience running out, Will snapped, "What the hell is out there?"

"War zone. Body parts all over. We can't bring Adalina here."

The shock in Jesse's eyes killed Will's desire to see. "All right, let's go. Maybe the next house will be safe."

Jesse hardly looked relieved, but he led the way out and west. Not quite a tenth of a mile later, they arrived at their second option, a faux log cabin flanked by a pair of junipers reaching for the sky, both just taller than the ridge of the roof. The front door stood visibly open.

"Now what?" Will wondered aloud.

Jesse shivered, but not from the cold.

Nothing seemed amiss. Snow undulated about the structure and spilled through the open door. Inside, they found a cozy living room, aside from it being the same temperature as outdoors, furnished in mountain chic, everything perfect, as though staged for an open house. They searched together this time, neither willing to tackle the job alone. The kitchen was in order, the three bedrooms and one bathroom pristine, the fireplace laid for a fire that had never been lit. Beyond the windows, the mountain winter spread in all its glory, unsullied by carnage. They couldn't have asked for better, aside from the power outage.

"I'll take it," Jesse said. "What's the asking price?"

"Dirt cheap," Will replied. "Let's get Spike and Adalina here before they freeze."

"Let's do it."

Will inspected the fireplace again. "Let's start a fire. Warm the place up before they get here."

"And leave it burning?"

"It's fine. There's a screen."

"A warm house is one thing. A pile of ashes is another."

Under normal circumstances, Jesse would have been right, but normal had fled the planet weeks ago. With the world an open-air asylum, they had to improvise. Will got the lighter and ignited the firestarters, which soon caught the wood. Heat began to fill the room.

Jesse appealed to heaven with his eyes, then went into the kitchen and rummaged. He returned within a few minutes. "We got enough nonperishables for a while," he said.

"Spike will want his cocoa and pepper," Will quipped.

Once warmed, they set out again, careful not to lock the door behind them. Then the long trudge back to Adalina's house. Adalina had scrounged up some backpacks. She and Spike already had them loaded with spare clothing, key portions of Spike's survival papers, food items, and bottles of water. She insisted on lugging the camp stove with them, so Will volunteered to carry it. There was fuel, too, three and a half cans, which they stuffed into plastic bags. Will took a can and a half, Jesse two cans.

An hour and a half later, they arrived at their new temporary home, cold, exhausted, and hungry. The house hadn't burned down, but it had grown comfortably warm, a major plus. Between that and the camp stove, which enabled them to boil water and mix up some boxed mac and cheese with reconstituted powdered milk, all that remained was exhaustion. Sleep proved deep and peaceful.

The morning, Will thought not long before he drifted off, might be another matter.

And it was.

A crash jarred Will from slumber. He sprang up, wide-eyed and shaking, almost before he knew he was awake. Jesse tumbled off the sofa where he'd been sleeping and scrambled to his feet, muttering, "What the hell?"

Somewhere a young girl screamed. More crashes, sounds of glass shattering and metal striking metal, screams mixed in, all muddled into an avant-garde symphony.

Adalina!

Will bolted for the kitchen. As he skidded to a halt on the tile floor, he found Spike throwing glassware, pots and pans, boxes and cans of food, silverware, cutlery, anything he could snatch from the cabinets, throwing it without aim all about the place while Adalina, curled into a ball under the kitchen table, cried and screamed and begged him to stop.

"*Spike!*" Will bellowed.

Spike turned on him, rage-red, teeth bared, and hurled a cereal box at him.

Will batted it aside. "Stop, damn it! Stop!"

Jesse edged into the kitchen behind Will. Hiding behind him, he said in shaky tones, "Hey, man, chill. Ain't no aliens here."

"*Aliens?*" Spike roared. "Why the hell are you always blaming aliens?"

"Wasn't me brought 'em up," Jesse informed him. Aside from the jitters, he might have been having an academic exchange.

Sucking in breaths as though only minutes of air remained to them and he wanted to get his fair share, Spike yanked a can of green beans from a cupboard and cocked his arm to throw it. Then his anger morphed into puzzlement and finally disgust. "Aliens," he growled. "You're such an idiot." He set the can on the counter. Confusion overtook him. "What happened?"

Adalina uncurled and crawled out, eyes wide, body shaking.

Spike about choked when he saw her. "Oh my God," he mumbled. "Oh my God. Adalina, did I hurt you?" He sank to his knees and reached to help her up.

She sniffed. "I'm okay." She accepted his hand. They helped each other to their feet.

"I'm sorry," Spike told her. "I'm so, so sorry. I can't do this anymore. I can't…" He dropped her hand, covered his face, turned away. "Leave me. Go, get down to the valley. Leave me here."

He had a point. He hadn't proven dangerous before—not too dangerous, anyway—but this was something new, maybe a worsening of his condition. Will couldn't trust him anymore, not when Adalina might get hurt. Yet the man *had* saved their lives. Will turned to Jesse, unspoken questions flooding his mind in a jumbled torrent.

If Jesse had any thoughts, he kept them to himself. Fine time for him to decide not to assert himself.

"Don't be silly," Adalina said. "We won't leave you behind. We're going together, like we planned."

Spike took her hand again and squeezed her fingers. "I can't control it. It comes and goes as it will. I could've hurt you."

"You didn't." She laughed a nervous little laugh. "You scared the crap out of me, but you didn't hurt me." She pulled her hand away and surveyed the destruction: broken glass, pots and pans and knives strewn about, cans of food on their sides, boxes of cereal and powders and pasta, and a bag of flour that had split open and coated everything in faux snow. "Come on," she said. "Let's clean up."

23

THE WEATHER turned ugly that night, with wind rushing through the trees like a bullet train, jet streams of horizontal snow, thuds on the roof that could have been hail or falling branches. None of them slept well.

They had sufficient wood stacked by the fireplace to last the night, but come morning, the storm hadn't subsided and the fuel supply dwindled. They wouldn't be venturing out in this for whatever wood was racked under the snow. Or to chop down a tree. Or look for an axe. Or do much of anything, including reconnoitering westward.

Spike found a blanket in one of the other rooms, wrapped himself in it, and brooded on the floor in a corner. Adalina sat by his side and whispered confidence in his ear, but he was having none of it. He might have gone deaf, judging by his lack of reaction. Eventually she gave up and returned to the fireplace with Will and Jesse. "I don't like it," she said in a whisper, glancing over her shoulder at the older man.

"It's probably just another of his mood swings," Will said. "He'll come out of it."

Jesse stood. "Better'n trashing the place," he said. He nodded toward the back of the house. "I'm gonna find blankets for the rest of us."

Will watched him go. "I wonder how long this weather will last."

Adalina opened the mesh screen and jabbed at the logs with the poker. Sparks swirled in the hearth. "They don't usually last more than a day," she said. "But you never know."

A day. The fire would be out by noon. They had the camp stove and fuel for a couple more days. Would hot drinks and blankets carry them through until they could bring in more wood? Maybe they could break down some furniture.

"You know the weather well," he commented.

"I want to be a meteorologist," Adalina said. "I'll be the first one in my family with a Ph.D." She slumped. "If any colleges are left."

In the corner, Spike groaned and picked himself up. "Colleges," he muttered. "Students. Damn students." He shuffled to the fireplace and dumped himself on the floor next to Adalina.

"What's wrong with students?" she asked him.

"Plenty. The women, especially. Young women always were my downfall. Her, especially. I never should have trusted her. Biggest mistake of my life. Biggest mistake in history."

That was some hyperbole. Spike's insanity seemed to be taking a new tack.

"Who?" Adalina asked.

"Jun."

"June?"

"Jun. Chinese name. Lai Jun.

"That's a funny name."

Spike eyed her as though sizing up a threat. Then he laughed. "Damn funny name. You don't think much about names, do you? When you meet a John Smith, you don't think, ah, he had a metalworker for an ancestor."

Adalina glanced at Will as though he might know what Spike was talking about. But of course he didn't. It was just Spike's addled brain, one more manifestation of a disease that, according to him, wasn't a disease.

Jesse returned with a pile of blankets and dropped them on the floor. "Help yourself," he said. "Feeling better, old man?"

Spike ignored him. "Lai signifies trust or reliance. Jun means truth. So you see: Lai Jun, a truthful young woman from a trustworthy family. Good name. Or good cover. Or tragic irony. Maybe all three."

Will waved off his ramblings. Adalina pursed her lips. Jesse sat beside Will and wrapped himself in a blanket. "Oh boy," he muttered.

"But who *was* she?" Adalina asked.

"A graduate student," Spike said. He clasped his head in his hands and squeezed his eyes shut. "She…" His features contorted as though he'd been knifed in the gut. "They…"

"Not again," Jesse said. "Steady, man. Breathe."

Spike wasn't just breathing, he was gasping. "Hide yourselves! They're coming! They're using the storm as a cloak! Hide! Quick!" He flung himself forward, scrambled about the floor on all fours looking for a hiding place, around chairs, behind the sofa, but everywhere was too exposed. In a panic, he grabbed one of the blankets and threw it over his head.

At least he wasn't whipping glassware about. Will waited for the madness to pass. They all did. Spike remained motionless under the blanket, managing to impersonate a rock for two, three, four minutes. And then he lifted the blanket, squinted at Will and Jesse and Adalina in turn, and sighed. "Did it again, didn't I?"

"We're used to it," Jesse said.

"You're better off without me."

"Don't start, old man."

Adalina leaned toward Spike, eyes wide. "We're sticking together. We need you."

Spike laughed bitterly.

Will had to admit he agreed with Spike, at least in principle. But the others wouldn't countenance leaving him behind, so best to put that discussion out of its misery. "I thought you wanted to help," he said, none too gently. "How does bailing on us help?"

"How does injuring or killing you help?"

"You haven't killed anyone yet. Or so you said. Were you lying?"

Jesse gaped at Will. "Hey, now."

Will stuck to his plan. "You could have let us die, but you didn't. Why? So you could butcher us at leisure?"

Spike balled his fists. An angry fire flickered in his narrowed eyes.

"You lied about wanting to help, anyway," Will went on. "You haven't done a damn thing. You begged us to take care of *your* problems while you kept our guns from us. You fought us every step of the way. It ends here. Start pulling your weight, or we *will* leave you behind."

Spike steamed to his stash of printouts, grabbed a handful, and shoved them in Will's face. "What about this! Who's teaching you to survive!" He threw them to the floor.

"Hey!" Adalina all but shrieked. "Just stop, okay? We're in this together. We're going together!"

"Damn right we are," Spike said. He kicked at the papers but missed. "If I *do* end up killing you, it's *his* damn fault." He jabbed a finger at Will.

How about that. Reverse psychology worked. "Deal," Will said. "Now we just need decent weather."

Spike stomped off.

"Where you going?" Jessed asked.

"Out," Spike snapped. "To find wood. And to get away from *him*."

In the silence that followed, Will figured both Jesse and Adalina were mentally punishing him for riding roughshod over Spike, but he didn't care. Let them think what they would. Sometimes you had to slap a person to get them to do the right thing. He only hoped he wouldn't have to repeat it. Pummeling Spike could be dangerous.

They sat together in isolation for some twenty minutes before the back door banged shut and Spike clomped in with an armful of split wood, not enough to last the day but sufficient to pump some heat back into the place. He dumped it on the floor before the fireplace and sneered at Will. "Don't ever again say I never did anything for you," he groused.

Will gave him a mock salute.

The snow stopped and the sky cleared overnight. Next morning, a brilliant sun rose over the mountains to the east. Brilliant, not warm. After a breakfast of instant oatmeal made with water heated on the camp stove,

Will and Jesse bundled up and set off on another trek, leaving deep tracks in the fresh powder. It looked like another foot had accumulated, which didn't make the going any easier. But their legs had learned the necessary technique and carried them better now.

As they passed the first house, the one they'd cased last journey, Jesse kept his eyes ahead. Will squinted into the trees, but he had no clear line of sight. Whatever had frightened his partner remained hidden.

A couple tenths of a mile on, the road took a bend to the left. They passed only trees, no houses, no manmade anything. The road ran from nowhere to nowhere, with nothing in between, nothing but snow and ponderosa, although once they found a sign poking its head above the powder at a fork in the buried lane.

Jesse brushed it off with a gloved hand. "No parking," he said.

Will laughed.

They trudged on, taking the fork to the right, which they judged more nearly westward. Another tenth of a mile brought them to a great lime-green shed half buried in the snow, four bay doors across the front, transmission towers and other structures behind, and another sign peeking above the snow.

"It better not say no parking," Jesse groused, "'cause I'm parking it for a bit."

Will cleared the sign. "No snowmobiles or motor vehicles allowed on airport November first through May first."

"Good thing you didn't bring your snowmobile," Jesse said.

The road ended beyond the shed, but a treeless lane led back from there. They followed it and found themselves at the edge of a vast stretch of snow, wide, straight as a ruler, stretching half a mile or more end to end.

"Must be the runway," Will said. Which did nothing for them. They had neither a plane nor the ability to fly it, even had it been high summer. "Maybe one of the buildings could serve as a shelter. We can't go much farther today."

"So long as they got powdered food," Jesse said. "Don't hold your breath, though."

They returned to the green shed. In each gap between the bay doors, a red, white, and blue shield proclaimed, "U.S. Property. No trespassing. Above, a security camera looked down, along with another warning: "Restricted area. Monitored by video camera." Just in case someone couldn't figure that out. Although it wasn't, not anymore. The power would be out here, too.

Behind the shed, several more buildings clustered. They investigated them all and found one accessible via an open door where snow had drifted into the interior. They plowed through the drift and entered a small office complex with a collection of ancient metal desks, beat-up office chairs, outdated computer terminals, and filing cabinets. The air within felt colder than outside, but there was a small break room with a coffee station stocked with instant coffee, tea bags, sugar, and nondairy creamer.

"At least there's that," Jesse quipped.

"Not comfortable and not well-stocked," Will mused. "But we could stay a night and press on."

"Yeah? And how far to the next comfortable stop?"

"Not too far, with any luck."

"It's the middle of nowhere, Will. Could be twenty miles. We might be stuck here."

"Then we can thank Spike for his survival manual."

"Great." Jesse sat in one of the office chairs. "Gimme a minute to catch my breath, then we can deliver the good news."

Will tried light switches and played with a computer, but the power was indeed out. If only they had a working Internet connection. He could have determined where they were and found a safe route to where they wanted to be. As it was, they were wandering blind, maybe into a wilderness with no shelter, no supplies, no means of life save Spike's printed instructions. What they had of them. They'd left a lot behind at Adalina's house. Still, they hadn't gone too far. Worst case, they could double back to her place, where at least they'd have a room with a fireplace and plenty of wood waiting to be cut and burned.

He found himself wishing for his New York condo, his work, his colleagues, his unfaithful wife. Yes, even her. Anything but this.

"I don't suppose you're ready yet," he said.

Jesse raised an eyebrow. "I guess. Let's hit the road. Or whatever."

Between the return trip, convincing Spike to leave the comforts of a cold house for the comforts of a cold, shabby office, packing, and finally hoofing it through the snow back to the airport, the rest of the day vanished. Along the way, Spike griped about anything he could. Adalina whispered confidence, which failed to soften his mood but maybe kept him from spiraling into madness. Will couldn't be sure. The old man seemed more stable in her presence, but why? Diseases didn't respond to positive vibes, did they?

He whispered the question to Jesse, who promptly redirected it to the resident expert. Will wished he'd kept his mouth shut.

They were halfway to the airport by then. Spike kicked at the snow as though it had attacked him. "Who knows?" he grumbled. "Like I said, the human brain is the most complex structure in the universe. It's a tangled web of wires and chemicals, inputs and logic and feedback, genetics and environment and God knows what else. Its own output affects its functioning."

"So why were you messing with it?" Jesse asked.

"We had controls in place, okay? We knew what we were doing."

"And yet, here we are."

"Enough," Will whispered. He hadn't meant his question to be voiced aloud, for this very reason.

"This isn't my fault!" Spike all but screamed.

"I get it was an accident," Jesse said. "But ain't nothing foolproof."

"It *should* have been foolproof! But who could have suspected Lai Jun?"

Adalina took Spike's arm. "It doesn't matter," she cooed. "It's done. Let's just keep going."

Spike shot Jesse a murderous look but said nothing.

Whoever Lai Jun was—real or figment of Spike's tortured imagination, living or dead—Will figured she made a convenient scapegoat. If she kept Spike from going full-on psycho, she could have all the blame and more. "Lai Jun," he said and shook his head. "Damn her."

"Damn her to hell," Spike muttered.

They crunched along the snowy road.

Jesse smirked. "You don't even know who the bitch is," he told Will.

"Drop it," Will snapped.

In mid-stride, Spike scooped up a handful of snow, packed it into a ball, and threw it with surprising strength at a pine trunk. It splattered, sticking to the tree in an irregular white splotch. "Nobody knew her," he said. "As it turned out."

They spent a miserable night at the airport, huddled under blankets they'd brought with them. They had a box of matches and a couple of butane lighters and a forest full of wood, but they couldn't start a fire inside for fear of burning the place down while they slept. They built a fire outside before darkness fell, melted snow for water, made a dinner of instant oatmeal supplemented by a can of white meat chicken. An odd combination, but it gave them sustenance and warmth and wasn't nearly as bad as Will expected. Even so, it offered only temporary respite.

Come morning, the cold had reinvaded their bones. Borderline lethargic, they moved slow and stiff while rekindling the fire. Once going, they warmed themselves beside it, made hot cocoa and more oatmeal, and restored some semblance of life to their chilled bodies.

"We can't spend another night this way," Spike said. "We were nearly hypothermic. We need a warm shelter. We could build one. I have the plans."

"I thought we was getting out of the mountains," Jesse objected. "You're talking about staying."

"We can survive perfectly well here if we follow the directions."

"We'll be dead before we figure them out."

Will agreed with Jesse, but before he could voice his opinion, Adalina asked, "How long does it take to build one?"

"Not long, I'm sure," Spike told her. "Well, let me look." His cold fingers extracted a sheaf of papers from his backpack and fumbled through them. "Here we are." He traced lines of text as though reading Braille. "Four hours, for this plan."

Assuming they knew what they were doing to begin with. Which they didn't. But the information gave Will an idea that might satisfy all parties. "We press on," he said, "together this time. If we don't find shelter in, say, three hours, we stop and build it."

Jesse looked skeptical, but Adalina chirped, "Sounds like a plan."

Spike frowned at her, at the sky, at the trees surrounding them. "Two hours," he said. "So we aren't worn out before we start the work."

Like any of them could tell time anymore. "Agreed," Will said. "Let's get on our way."

With a cloudless blue sky and zero wind, the air felt warmer today. The exertion of blazing a trail helped. Now and again, they heard swishing and rattling among the trees, but they never saw a thing. Mule deer, maybe, or squirrels. Will hoped it was nothing more dangerous. An hour into the trek, he almost asked Spike to show them how to hunt whatever was making that noise, but the old man wouldn't have been amused, so he kept his mouth shut.

And then, before the next hour was up, they happened on a house. Not just a house. "A damn mansion," Jesse said.

It rose above them at the top of a snow tributary descending the rise: a broad, gray roof capping something big. It was hard to gauge its true size, but it sure looked three or even four times the size of Adalina's house.

Spike didn't wait. He powered upslope.

Will and Jesse exchanged a glance before taking off after him, trailing Adalina.

"Hold on," Will called after him. "We don't know what's up there."

"We know one thing," Spike said over his shoulder. "They have heat."

"How do we know that?" Jesse asked.

"No snow on the roof. Heat's escaping from inside."

Jesse turned to Will. "Does that happen?"

"How should I know? I lived in a New York condo. I never saw the roof."

"It happens," Spike called back, "if the insulation is shoddy."

That didn't sound promising. Still, being a scientist infected with a designer disease, Spike must be smart. Or mad. Or both. The only way to find out was to follow. It was a bit of a climb up the curving, sloped path. Will was feeling the exertion by the time they reached the house. Jesse was panting. Adalina steamed along like she was going downhill.

The house proved not quite as large as it appeared from below, but it still made Adalina's place look crowded. The snowy driveway ended in a three-car garage. The front door was a double with etched sidelights, each featuring a tall pine tree. Arriving first, Spike tried the door. Unlocked. He gave it a tentative push, opened it just a sliver, peeked through. Silent, breath held, he didn't move for a long moment.

"Well?" Will prompted.

"It's warm inside, but dark. I can't see a thing."

"You want me to go first?"

Spike set his hand to the door and shoved. It swung open, hit an unseen stop, and bounced partway back.

"That's a no," Jesse said.

"I got that," Will replied.

Crossing the threshold, Spike crept into the foyer, still blocking the door so the others couldn't follow or see what awaited them. He might not have been breathing, so still was he. And then he vanished into the darkness. Will followed, with Jesse and Adalina right behind. They crowded into the foyer, and Jesse silently shut the door.

A coat closet with mirrored doors flanked them on the right, a staircase up on the left. A short hall ran into darkness before them. Spike's form crept through the hall, but before Will could follow, he paused and raised a warning hand.

"What?" Will demanded.

"Keep Adalina back," Spike ordered.

Which suggested they'd picked the wrong house again, working heat or no. "Stay with her," Will told Jesse.

Before Jesse could object, Will moved down the hall and came into a large kitchen with a picture window overlooking the slopes beyond. It might have been a nice place to dine once, but now it looked like the aftermath of an earthquake: cabinet doors ajar, refrigerator caught open by an upside-down ketchup bottle bleeding red onto the stone floor, food and pans and broken ceramic dishes everywhere. And amid the mess, two bodies, a short, balding man and a much younger redheaded woman. The place stank with decay. Oddly, a note was taped to the picture window. Will couldn't read it from his distance, but he could tell it was handwritten in blue ink.

Spike had covered his nose and mouth with his hand. "This complicates things," he said.

"That's one way of putting it," Will replied. "I wonder if there were others." He slipped around Spike, retrieved the note from the window, read it three times in silence. "Listen to this. 'If you find this before the roads are closed, follow the freeway west to Newcastle. Some of us are gathering there. If you're snowed in, feel free to stay as long as you can. The propane should last a month and a half if you're careful. Good luck.'"

Spike took the note and read it for himself, then dropped it on the table. "Thoughtful of them. I wonder how long ago they wrote it." He nodded at the corpses. "And if that was them."

"Who knows? The front door was unlocked. Anyone could have wandered in. We'd better search the rest of the house, then dispose of the bodies. Or find a different place to sleep."

Spike's face scrunched with displeasure. "I don't want to touch them."

"You've touched worse." Will tapped the side of his head.

The old man gave him a dull look.

"We'll wrap them in something," Will added.

They returned to the foyer, where Adalina was trying to coax Jesse into letting her venture down the hallway. "You've seen enough death," Will told her.

She crossed her arms over her chest. "I think I can handle it."

"*I* almost can't handle it," Jesse said.

"Then *you* stay here."

Will laughed. He wasn't sure why.

"We're checking the rest of the house," Spike announced as though he'd been in charge all along. "Will and I that way," he directed, pointing toward the kitchen. "You two upstairs. Let's hope we don't find more bodies."

The search took less than twenty minutes and uncovered no more amiss than they'd already found. The house had hardwood floors throughout, generously adorned with throw and area rugs, some of them Persian carpets. With Jesse's help, Will liberated two of the big rugs from the furniture and brought them to the kitchen. Around holding their breath and averting their eyes, he and Jesse wrangled the decaying corpses onto the carpets and rolled them up without touching the remains. The nearest exit was off a game room adjoining the kitchen. They dragged their horrid loads out and into a stand of trees not far from the house, there to be forgotten. Returning, they located a broom, trash bags, bleach and a bucket and mop. They disinfected the spot where the bodies had lain, swept up broken glass, piled pots and pans on the counters, restored everything to as much order as possible.

When all was done, Jesse leaned heavily on the counter. "I never wanna do that again," he said.

Retrieving the note from the table, Will reread it before handing it to Jesse.

Jesse studied it, then set it aside. "Where the hell is Newcastle?"

Will shrugged. "Probably just a place picked out of a hat."

"You wanna go?"

Will didn't know, but if it was out of the mountains, out of the winter, a place where survival came easier, then it was worth a shot. But if people were congregating there, wouldn't it just be more of the same?

Spike materialized from the darkened hall with Adalina at his side. "Yes," he said.

Jesse stared at him. Will didn't know whether to agree or object. In the silence, Adalina fixed a questioning look on each of them in turn. Sighing, Jesse retrieved the note and handed it to her. "Might as well," he said.

She read, licked her lips, handed it back. "Some of us are gathering there," she quoted. "People had time to talk about what was happening and work out a plan."

"Excellent," Spike said. "You're way ahead of these two." He waved a hand at Will and Jesse.

Jesse looked at the note again. "Hold on. How'd that happen?"

Spike shuffled to the table and sat in the nearest chair. He covered his face with his hands and shook his head. "Damn her."

"Who?" Adalina asked.

"Lai Jun."

"Here we go again," Jesse muttered.

Dropping his hands, Spike shot him an annoyed look. "I'm not hallucinating. I'm angry. Jun was here on a student visa from China. She was smart. Too damned smart to be what she claimed, but none of us caught on. We were too thrilled to have her working with us."

It wasn't hard to guess. Everyone knew of China's greed for western science and technology and the lengths to which it would go to obtain military and trade secrets. "She bottled the results of your work and slipped them out of the lab," Will said.

"She tried," Spike acknowledged. "Security stopped her before she got out the door, but not before she broke containment. When she realized she was in trouble, she panicked. She tried to destroy the evidence."

"What's that to do with folks having time to work out a plan?" Jesse asked.

Spike raised an eyebrow. "Nothing."

"You got any idea how hard it is to talk to you?"

"My wife frequently told me." Spike closed his eyes and put a hand to his forehead. "A late phase of our research involved mechanisms for timed release of the active agents. We hadn't figured it out, not entirely. The batch Jun stole was a sort of prototype. We knew release would be delayed. We didn't know by how long. Not very precisely, anyway. We were trying to coordinate the effect to create a sort of chain reaction."

"A chain reaction," Will said. "Like in a nuclear weapon."

Spike's glare suggested he might start throwing things again. "To achieve maximum therapeutic efficiency, not to blow up the world."

"Blew it up anyway," Jesse said.

Taking his head in his hands, Spike went on. "There were so many questions, still. How mutation would affect the timeline. How it would affect the agents themselves. It was stupid to remove those organisms from the facility, but suddenly they were out. They were out in the world for months, then they exploded everywhere, all at once. So now we know the timeline, and the effectiveness of the chain reaction process."

Jesse lost his patience. "What the hell does that have to do with what happened *here*?"

"Nothing! Nothing has anything to do with anything anymore!"

Adalina hurried to Spike's side. She put a hand on his shoulder and purred, "It's okay. None of this is your fault."

"I shouldn't have trusted her. I shouldn't have…"

"You can't know everything."

Spike drew a long breath. "Come on, Jesse. What happened is simple. Some people fought off the infection. But so what? They were surrounded by people who didn't. They died in the violence. Here, though, people were scattered. If you don't manifest symptoms and you're sufficiently isolated, you don't get killed. Survivors have time to contact each other and devise plans."

"And go to this Newcastle," Jesse said. "Wherever that is."

"Exactly. Newcastle might be a safe community, populated by the resistant. If nothing else, it's not under ten feet of snow. We absolutely should go."

Will mistrusted Spike's judgement, but he couldn't find any holes in the argument. A group would have a better chance of survival than the four of them, if nobody went homicidal. A big if, but as they needed to get out of the mountains anyway, it might be worth the risk.

"All right," he said. "Newcastle or bust."

24

BUT THEY didn't leave at once. Not even close. The house proved well-provisioned with nonperishables, the propane tank wasn't empty, although it was getting there, and there was no shortage of snow for water or wood for the fireplace. They had the means of cooking and heating and were starting to get comfortable.

Spike went into a wildly accelerated manic-depressive cycle, running hot and cold over the course of about ten hours. When he was down, he hid in one of the bedrooms and refused to show his face. His up moments found him tinkering with designs for traps, spears, and fire-making techniques. In the middle of the third day, he went outside, poked sticks into the snow, and marked their shadows with other sticks. When the suspense got to Will, he traipsed into the cold and asked.

"It's a compass," Spike said.

Pointing, Will said, "West is that way. Where the sun sets."

Spike gave him a tight-lipped smile.

"Am I wrong?"

"Not completely."

"Then what's the point of this?"

"I want to find true north."

Will figured that should be easy enough. Jesse could point out Polaris on any reasonably clear night. He mentioned that useful fact.

Spike wasn't impressed. "That only works at night. And Polaris is seven tenths of a degree off true north."

Will gave up and returned to the warmth. That night after Adalina had retired to her bedroom and Spike slunk off in another depressive phase, Will mentioned the sticks to Jesse.

"It's a form of sundial," Jesse said. "It works. 'Course, so does looking at the stars. North is that way." He pointed toward the back of the house.

Will knew that much from watching the sun rise and set. "Why does he care?"

Jesse shrugged. "We're on the south side of the freeway. If we go north, we oughta find it."

"Wonderful," Will said deadpan. "But since there aren't any houses on the interstate, why should we care?"

"I dunno. The man did say Newcastle is right down the freeway."

"The man is nuts."

Flashing a crooked smile, Jesse nodded. "But he knows how to find north."

Nuts, maybe, but Spike had an idea. Or said he did. On the morning of their fifth day in the house, he laid it out. "I recall passing a highway maintenance facility along I-80," he told them. "We should be near it."

"If it's anything like the last government facility we borrowed," Will said, "I'll take a pass."

They were having a breakfast of oatmeal with brown sugar and tea without sweeteners, hydrated with snow melt and heated in the fireplace. It wasn't half bad. Adalina was on her second bowl.

Spike finished his bowl and pushed it away, giving it a scowl no doubt meant for Will. "We aren't staying there."

Jesse wrapped his hands around his mug. "What they got, then?"

"We'll find out when we get there."

The old man wore on Will's patience more than any of his firm's clients ever had, and he'd had a few he would have gladly murdered. Figuratively, he reminded himself, figuratively. Used to be, saying such things was a sign of irritation, not madness. Just thinking the word made him question his sanity now. "You're after something," he said. "What?"

Crossing his arms on the table before him, Spike said nothing.

"A way out," Adalina suggested. She shoveled more oatmeal into her mouth. Hers must have been extra good. She'd put a double dose of brown sugar on it.

Spike's lips turned up in a slight smile, but he offered no other acknowledgement and no explanation.

"Do they have a snow cat?" she speculated. "Like in *The Shining*?"

Jesse laughed. "You old enough to know that movie?"

"Are *you*?" Will asked.

"I like scary movies," Adalina said. "My dad and I watch..." She choked back the remaining words. Her mouth quivered for a moment, then she loaded up her spoon and forced down another mouthful.

"Not a snow cat." Spike's voice was quiet now, soothing. "But something just as good, maybe. Want to come with me? Find out?"

She nodded without enthusiasm.

Will couldn't say no after that, and Jesse couldn't say anything at all. They finished breakfast, cleaned up, and packed for the journey. Spike insisted they take everything with them. Clearly, he didn't anticipate a return or at least hoped whatever they found would carry them to their next port of call. Will had no idea how far they were from the valley, nor how long it would take to reach it, nor where they would find another resting place as comfortable as this. But moving on had always been the plan.

They trudged into winter once more, Spike in the lead, Adalina at his side, Will and Jesse following. Spike backtracked eastward without telling them why. In a short time, he found a lane of white striking generally north, one they must have passed on the way in, although Will had no memory of it. Spike led them down it as it meandered through the trees, rising and falling with the land. At length, it descended to the great cascade of snow that was the interstate. This time there was no sign of the bordering fence. It was completely submerged. Below, nestled between the eastbound and westbound lanes, stood a collection of buildings, half hidden by pines.

Spike pointed. "That's it," he said. They crossed the highway and cut through the trees to reach them. All told, they couldn't have walked much more than half a mile, but already Will was cold and tired and hoping they wouldn't be forced to return.

The buildings had a scattered feel, like boulders of varying size deposited at random by the whim of nature. There were a dozen of them, some with great blue bay doors, others with people doors and windows, all half buried in snow. Two of the buildings rose to two-story height. Upon a flagpole, a battered American flag fluttered in the wind, with California's bear flag beneath.

There were vehicles, too, or what must have been vehicles beneath mounds of white. Here and there, a glint of glass or a flash of gold paint broke through, exposed by the wind. Still other mounds of snow, too long to contain vehicles, too small to be buildings, edged the area. When Jesse asked what they were, Spike said, "Gasoline and diesel and propane tanks, I'd guess." A couple flanked a small building before which stood a canopy not unlike a gas station's.

Inspiration struck. "You're looking for snowplows," Will said.

Spike pointed at him in acknowledgement.

"This where they keep them?" Jesse asked.

"I don't know, but if so, we can plow our way to Newcastle."

"How long will that take?" Will asked.

"Half an hour if the roads are clear."

Jesse waved around. "In case you didn't notice, they ain't."

"I noticed. I'm just saying, it's not that far. Thirty, forty miles. Even if we can't break ten miles per hour, it's only half a day. A day, worst case. And the snow will thin out before we get there. You have any idea what the annual snowfall in Newcastle is?"

Will and Jesse exchanged a glance. Of course they didn't know. They'd never even heard of the place.

Adalina raised her hand and waved it in an "Oh! Oh! Oh!" gesture.

"Young lady?" Spike asked.

"Zero!"

"Exactly right." He gave her a pat on the head. She winced in embarrassment.

Will decided maybe the lunatic wasn't entirely crazy, after all. They'd have heat and reach safety by nightfall, assuming they could all fit in a plow, get it started, and push through the snowpack without falling off a cliff.

Some of the bay doors were open. Even with the piled and drifted snow, they had access to the vehicles and equipment within. And the bodies. The dead were scattered around the facility. Despite their state of decay, Will thought most of them bore wounds from instruments both blunt and sharp. Possible weapons had been abandoned near several corpses, some bearing rusty stains. When they came upon the first body at the feathered edge of a snowbank that had drifted into the building, Spike tried to steer Adalina way, but she pushed by him and stood over the deceased, studying, taking in every detail, her mouth twisted, her nose wrinkled to ward off the stench. When she turned away, her expression was hard.

"Are you okay?" Spike asked.

She shrugged.

"You don't have to look. You shouldn't look."

"It's not the first time." She pointed down the length of the building. "There's a plow."

Four bays down, the truck awaited, backed into the bay, an enormous blade pointing toward the exit, a wing blade of smaller proportions hanging off the side. The blades and the cab were painted orange, the truck bed silver. Jesse trotted ahead. By the time the others got there, he was already climbing the steps to the cab.

"Door's unlocked!" He pulled the door open. "Key's in the—oh hell." He backed down, hand over his mouth.

"Another corpse," Will whispered to Spike. "Has to be."

Adalina heard anyway. She tossed her hands in the air and sighed. "I'll look for another one," she said.

Behind the first truck sat a pickup equipped with an amber light bar, hood open. Tools lay scattered on the concrete, as though they'd been thrown, and in their midst, an empty oil pan lay tipped on its side, a black slick spreading from it like a river delta. Trickles of dried oil vanished under the truck.

Perfect. A maintenance shed. The vehicles here probably all had problems, or had parts removed and not yet replaced, and Will had zero mechanical know-how. Jesse never hinted that he'd worked on cars, and Spike...it was probably best to keep him away from anything that might be wielded for destruction.

Beyond the pickup, a yellow loader awaited service, its scoop just kissing the floor. The body of a dark-skinned man reposed within the scoop as though asleep, save the unnatural angle of the head. Adalina had already passed the vehicle from behind, so maybe she hadn't seen that corpse. "Over here!" she called.

Will, Jesse, and Spike rounded the loader, and there it was, a second plow truck. They paused and examined it. A booted foot protruded from beneath, just in front of the rear tire. Aside from that, the only chaos here was a toolchest tipped over, vomiting silver sockets and a mishmash of other tools.

Jesse nudged Will. "Your turn," he said.

Drawing a breath, Will tugged on the handle and threw the door wide. The cab contained nothing but a confusing array of electronics—monitors, switches, joy sticks, and a keyboard, all mounted in the center. What did they do with this thing, launch nuclear missiles? He climbed up and slid into the passenger seat. The key was in the ignition, as Jesse had reported with the other truck, but thankfully no death lingered here, just a hint of stale tobacco smoke.

"It's safe," he called to the others. Unable to climb over the electronics, he circled to the driver's side. No bodies here, but a smear of red ran from the door all the way to the back of the truck and down the rear tire. Maybe that had been the life pouring from the unfortunate under the vehicle. Will opened the door and took the driver's seat. He turned the key, and the vehicle rumbled to life. The fuel gauge read a hair over half. They could fill up before they took to the road, assuming they could all fit in here. And figure out how the damned thing worked.

Will toyed with the controls while Jesse called out what was happening. Soon he knew how to manipulate the front plow, the wing, and the underbody blade. Then he put the vehicle in gear and eased out of the bay into the snow, cutting a path through it. He made a circuit around the lot, then another, then another, gradually coming to terms with the beast. It wasn't that hard, although likely he wouldn't win any contracts for the job. Not that anyone was left to offer one. At any rate, he was glad no moving vehicles were near him.

His self-directed training took most of an hour, after which he cautiously cleared a path to the fueling station. Jesse found snow shovels in the shed and recruited Spike and Adalina to help him clear the pumps. They fueled up the truck and were ready to go, except for one thing.

They couldn't, in fact, all fit in the cab, not with any degree of comfort and not without Adalina perched on one of the men's laps, which none of them cared to suggest. Nor did she.

"We'll take two vehicles," Will said. "I'll drive the plow. Jesse can follow in one of the pickups. Spike with me, Adalina with Jesse."

"Another executive decision," Jesse said, but with a grin. They sure didn't want Spike behind either wheel.

So situated, they took to the road once more, just shy of a month after their last run had ended in a blizzard. Sun and snow notwithstanding, Will wasn't sure the world looked much brighter. Then, death had stalked them, all but ready to spring. Now they had a fighting chance at life, but what sort of life? Spike thought more people might have survived in low population areas. How many would that be, and would they have the skills to rebuild a collapsed civilization? If one out of ten had survived, that made—what?—thirty or so million in the United States, seven or eight hundred million worldwide? Humanity had blasted itself back to—when? The late 1700's?

Still. Thirty million sounded like enough to get something done. If they were the right thirty million.

Will drove slow, fifteen miles per hour, getting the feel of the road, keeping to the center of the whiteness that undulated before him with the rise and fall of the land. He wanted to move faster, wanted to escape the mountain winter, but he didn't care to plummet over a precipice. The weather, at least, cooperated: clear skies, light wind. No traffic.

No traffic. He laughed.

Spike stared at him. "What?" he asked.

"Nothing."

"Must be something."

"Dumb joke. Forget it."

"If you insist." Spike leaned back and closed his eyes. "Tell me when we're there."

The first hour wore away in white monotony. It ended with a screech of metal tearing into metal. Will hit the brakes, although the truck had lost most of its momentum before his foot jammed the pedal.

Spike bolted upright. They peered into the snow, but it was impossible to tell what they'd struck. Whatever it was, the plow blade concealed it.

Will threw the truck into park and tugged on his gloves. "Wait here," he ordered as he clambered out into the snow.

Behind in the cleared lane, Jesse had parked and was trotting forward to join Will, calling, "What happened?"

"Don't know," Will said. Together, they slogged through the snow to find out.

The blade had scooped up another vehicle, a white SUV that had been buried in the snow. Tipped on its side either by the collision or whatever accident had killed it, it was sandwiched between the plow and a great mound of snow that had piled up as the truck pushed it forward. Will hoped it was an abandoned vehicle. If not, if someone had been trapped within, they were long dead. No point in looking.

They were on an uphill climb, curving around the bulk of a mountain split open to let the road pass. The cliff had been sliced into terraces. The snow clung to the stone where it could. Where it couldn't, mica and quartz sparkled in the sun. On the left, the snow yielded to open air as the mountainside descended into a deep valley.

"I guess I'll push it out of the way," Will said. "Just enough to get past it."

"Need me to direct?" Jesse offered.

"Sure. Just stay back. If I do the wrong thing, I don't want to push you off the cliff."

"Kind of you." Jesse laughed, but it was a nervous laugh, as though the probability of disaster was too high for comfort.

Will returned to the truck's cab. Jesse took up position well to the left, where he could wave his arms at Will without being run over.

"Now what?" Spike asked.

"An SUV buried in the snow," Will told him. "I'm pushing it out of the way.

"Tell me when it's over."

Will declined to comment on that vote of no confidence. He put the truck in gear and began the operation—a slow, ear-splitting operation that set his teeth on edge, but with Jesse waiving directions he maneuvered the SUV to the side of the road, backed up, and they got underway again. But now he found himself driving slower, expecting at any moment to strike another unseen object, maybe one too heavy to move, maybe one capable of wrecking the truck, overturning it, sending it careening into a rock wall or over the edge to destruction.

That didn't happen, thankfully, and another hour later the snow had thinned to less than a foot as they began the descent into the Sacramento Valley. Soon they left the mountain winter behind.

And found themselves once more in hell.

25

RUNNING ON clear roads, Will got up to speed, or as much speed as was comfortable: forty-five. The uphills and downhills felt longer and gentler, the land alongside the road close to eye level. The pines shared space with more broadleaf trees. A few vehicles had spun out or overturned here and there, but the travel lanes remained clear. Houses and businesses peeked out from the trees beyond the highway. More vehicles cluttered the road. Spike pointed toward an overpass beyond which the rising road curved out of view, and said, "What the hell is *that*?"

In the oncoming lanes, a tangle of trucks and cars and campers seemed to have fallen out of the sky in a heap. Animals prowled the on-road junkyard, some on four legs, some feathered, all too distant to identify. A few looked too big not to be dangerous as they circled the dead vehicles and strayed across both sides of the Interstate, reclaiming land that had once been theirs and, it seemed, would be again.

Will slowed. Animal carcasses littered both sides of the highway around the pileup, which resolved into a massive accident. Dozens, maybe more than a hundred vehicles had streamed down the on-ramp, colliding with a similar number already making east. Nobody had yielded, nobody had slowed. Cars and SUVs and semis and campers and motorcycles plowed into, over, and under each other as though half of northern California had stampeded this way.

They passed by the wreckage and decay. Live animals skittered out of Will's path. The dead ones he ran over. Odd, wasn't it, how you could get used to doing that, how you hardly noticed it after a while?

Spike exhaled as though he'd been holding his breath. "Let's hope we don't see that again."

He shouldn't have said it.

Up the rise they soared, around the bend, and down again, and now dead metal lay strewn about the highway in both directions, forcing Will to slow to a crawl. He skirted obstructions when he could, pushed them out of the way with the plow blade when he couldn't. He checked his mirrors every few seconds to make sure Jesse and Adalina were still following. They were, at a distance, no doubt understanding that Will had to break the trail.

Then they were in Auburn, awash in stores and homes and businesses, more and more wrecks still, and finally they came to a halt before a massive pileup that engulfed the whole highway. Bones and half-eaten, half-decayed body parts were strewn throughout the wreckage, most probably left by animals after their feasts. Spike slid down in his seat, moaning, and covered his head with his arms. Will put the truck in park. He searched for a way through. There wasn't any.

"I have to talk to Jesse," he said. "Will you be okay here?"

Buried under his limbs, Spike nodded.

Will took the keys in case Spike went nuts again. Jesse was already on his way to consult. He winced at the roadblock. "What do we do?" he asked.

"If we had a working cell phone, we could find a route around."

"We might." Jesse pulled his phone from his coat pocket. "There was a USB cable in the truck. I got mine partway charged." He fiddled with the device. "Zero bars, though" he said. "Maybe negative bars."

"That's impossible."

"I'm joking."

"Not much of a joke."

"No sense of humor, that's your problem." Jesse licked his lips and stole a glance at the chaos blocking their way. "Okay, here's another not-funny joke. We do it by dead reckoning."

He was right, that wasn't funny, but Will let out a choked laugh anyway.

Jesse smirked. "We turn around, take that last exit, and, I dunno, guess."

"We don't even know where Newcastle is, direction-wise."

"I guess that's the dead part."

Problem was, they had no choice. They couldn't go forward, so back it had to be, onto the roads of Auburn, which could be more of this. It wasn't New York, but from what Will could see from here, it wasn't a crossroads.

"All right," he decided. "Maybe Spike or Adalina can guide us."

Jesse eyed him. "You trust Spike with that?"

"God only knows."

"Suddenly you're religious."

"It's an expression."

"Uh-huh. Since we gotta turn 'round anyway, I'll take the lead and Adalina can navigate."

"If she can. She's not old enough to have a driver's license. You learn your way around by doing it."

"Fine. Once we're lost, you take the lead." Jesse gave a mock salute and returned to the pickup.

Will climbed back into the plow truck. Now he just had to get it turned around.

Jesse wanted to drive faster than Will, but when he tried, the plow fell behind, forcing him to slow. Will was doing that on purpose—wasn't he?—just to irritate Jesse. Okay, no, probably not. Probably he was scared to push the truck harder. Jesse had never driven anything that big, and why would have anyone of Will's background? That Navigator must've been the biggest vehicle he'd ever commanded.

Snail's pace notwithstanding, they made it to the exit across from the eastbound pileup. Animals scattered before them. Jesse did his best to weave around the dead ones but hit a few anyway. He cringed every time. So did Adalina, but she didn't speak a word until they reached the end of the on-ramp, which Jesse figured would be easier for Will than U-turning the plow to catch the off-ramp.

At the end of the ramp, Jesse stopped and looked both ways. The road wasn't clear, but it wasn't totally blocked. A few cars had rammed each other. Others were abandoned with open doors. The scavengers must have dealt with the bodies already.

"Any idea how to get through town?" he asked.

Adalina pointed to an intersection immediately left, where a small parking lot of twenty spaces harbored half as many vehicles nestled between the road and the ramp. "Get on that road. It follows the expressway."

"How far?"

She shrugged.

Jesse considered the parking lot. It seemed a good time to trade in the plow for something more manageable, not to mention eliminating the need for a convoy. Problem was, would any of them have keys? They must have been parked there before the outbreak. None of them looked to have been abandoned in a moment of madness.

He turned left on Bell Road—according to the signs—and left again onto Bowman. He pulled up enough to allow Will room to make the turn, then stopped. "Wait here," he told Adalina.

Jesse and Will got out and looked over the parked vehicles, thinking the same thing. Cars, pickups, a couple SUV's, and something Jeepish, although it probably wasn't. Some parked head-in, some backed in. White and blue and black and red and gray, all doors shut. No signs of panic or madness.

"Nah," Jesse said.

Will turned to the vehicles abandoned on Bell Road. "We'd need something undamaged and clean," he said. "No..."

"Contamination," Jesse suggested.

"Right. Let's look."

A door thunked shut, startling them, but it was only Spike. Rounding the front of the truck, he approached, slow and stiff. "What the hell are you doing?" he asked.

"Car shopping," Will told him. "Wait here with Adalina."

Spike grumbled something but shuffled to the pickup.

Jesse and Will walked to Bell Road and split up, Will taking the northbound lane and Jesse the southbound. More than a bit jittery, Jesse bypassed any vehicle that had suffered damage or was too small for the four of them. He looked in every potentially suitable car that had been left with doors open. Most bore stains and stank of decay, but on the overpass above the Interstate, he found one that might have come fresh from the dealer. It was a powder blue Cadillac Escalade. *Just Will's style*, he joked to himself.

The keys were in the ignition.

"This feels weird," Will said. For the first mile, they encountered only scattered wrecks. Paralleling the Interstate, they outflanked the blockade, passed a strip mall with palm trees, then an orchard, then a school, making good time now that Will wasn't in charge of a truck.

"What's weird?" Jesse asked. He was once again riding shotgun, with Spike and Adalina in the second row of seats.

"Driving a symbol of luxury again, with the world turned to ash. I needed it back then, or thought I did. To prove I was somebody. The world had to die before I realized what a pointless conceit that was."

Jesse waved it off. "We all got wants. My Aunt Clara used to say that. 'We all got wants, Jesse, just don't let 'em get the better of you.'"

"What did you want?"

Jesse looked out the side window.

"I wanted a Nobel Prize," Spike said. "Or failing that, a decent steak."

Great. Pepper would enter into it before long. Will adjusted his grip on the wheel.

"You know how hard it is to find a decent steak in Stanford?"

"No idea," Jesse said. "Never been there. But if you ain't got any bigger regret than that, you're doing fine."

"I've got plenty," Spike said, though maybe more to himself than Jesse. "Plenty."

Adalina remained silent throughout. She probably couldn't imagine adult regrets. Not yet.

Bowman Road ended at an intersection. Straight ahead was an on-ramp to the Interstate, but Will didn't think it prudent to go that way, not in the middle of a city that had tried to empty itself all at once. The ramp, in any case, was littered with wrecked vehicles. Not impassable, but not a pleasant drive. To the right, the road bent westward, which suggested it might continue to follow the freeway. Will chose that path without consulting the others. They all looked too deep in thought to question him.

Will wasn't sure of the name of this road, but yes, it ran as he had hoped, leading through denser population areas with homes, churches, schools, restaurants, and hotels. The aftermath of the outbreak was more liberally strewn about here. Cars and trucks, decaying bodies, scavengers scouring neighborhoods.

In due course, the road ended at a T-intersection, confronting him with another choice. Left seemed to return to the Interstate, so he turned right, and in a few hundred feet they were passing a cemetery. He brought the Escalade to a halt at the entrance and gazed down the drive at the green lawn, the trees arching over the monuments, the absolute peace of the place. Strange. The spot where people had once corralled death was the one place it hadn't touched.

"What?" Jesse asked.

Will turned his attention back to the road and drove on. Beyond the cemetery, Nevada Street crossed their path. Nevada made him think of Daffodil. And Anita, but mostly Daffodil, who had saved him—them—only to abandon him—them. What would she have made of Spike? Of Adalina? Of all that had happened since they parted ways?

He turned left, hoping to get closer to the highway. That brought him to an on-ramp, and he stopped again. There weren't too many good choices here. His other options were an overpass to the opposite side of the expressway and a route that climbed a small hill and bent out of view.

He opted for the hill and found himself stuck in a residential area of average homes with no obvious way out, so he retraced his path to the freeway. Although he had to weave around a clutter of wrecks and abandoned vehicles, it wasn't so awful as he feared. Most of the destruction obstructed the eastbound lanes. Most everyone had been fleeing to the mountains.

Less than fifteen minutes later, they reached their destination: Newcastle. It was smaller than they expected.

26

SMALL. Maybe a tenth the size of Auburn. Maybe a twentieth. Will didn't know, only that from the Interstate, Newcastle didn't look to be much there. But once you took the exit and got past the "Welcome to Newcastle" sign mounted on a pair of stone pillars underhung by signs for churches, the Lion's Club, and the Boy Scouts, then you found houses hidden in the trees, and old buildings, and streets climbing hills, and cars parked on the streets with powerlines strung everywhere. The town felt like it didn't care to be seen by outsiders, but now that you'd found it, sure, spend a bit of your money at a restaurant or the antiques store or whatever else took your fancy.

So this is where survivors had planned to gather. But had they? It sure didn't look it. Where could they be hiding among the homes and shops?

Will toured the streets as though seeking garage sales or open houses. Some of the dwellings looked pretty good: on the large side, well-maintained, solar panels on the roofs, stone steps and walks surrounded by manicured shrubs and hedges. Others were older, with peeling paint and shingles that looked ready to blow away in the next stiff wind. Here and there, an American flag fluttered in the breeze.

Did such a nation exist anymore?

Will was so focused on the houses, looking for signs of habitation, that he didn't notice the most obvious thing about the town.

Jesse mentioned it. "No bodies. Cars parked everywhere, but like they was never used. What happened here?"

"It's been cleaned up," Adalina suggested. "The people who came here must have done it."

Spike grunted. "Then where are they hiding?"

A great question, but no answer surfaced.

They came across a railroad cutting across Newcastle's northern edge. Diverging from the tracks, Taylor Road seemed to be the northern-most main drag. He followed that about half a mile and came to Newcastle Cemetery. A beige stone building with a red tile roof sat near the gated entrance. Possibly it was a funeral parlor. The lawn just behind the building adjacent to the road caught Will's eye. Rectangular mounds of brown earth all but covered the area.

He slowed to a halt and pointed. "Fresh graves. A lot of them. But no headstones."

"People cleaned up," Adalina repeated.

"Then they must be here." Will U-turned and followed Taylor to the tracks. The road tunneled beneath, leading to a side of town they hadn't explored yet. It turned out to be mostly industrial, hosting masonry, excavating, solar, and other businesses. Tucked among them to serve workers who no longer existed were a bar and a deli. An upholstery place separated them. Between the three, considerable parking space could be found. And it had been. Thirty or more vehicles were neatly arrayed there.

"That looks busy," Jesse commented. "Wanna have a look?" He suggested it, but with a tremor in his voice. Maybe he was hoping Will would say no.

In fact, Will wanted to say no. Even a sane gathering might shoot interlopers. But they needed to find out. "Let's leave the guns," he suggested. "They might not be well-received."

"We?" Jesse asked.

"Two people acting reasonable are probably sane."

"Just so's you don't start arguing again."

"Non-argumentative mode on," Will said. "Let's go."

Leaving Spike and Adalina to watch and wait, they approached the bar, mounted the three concrete steps to the concrete porch, and paused at the door. There were voices inside. Will drew a long breath and nudged the door open.

The voices stopped.

Will and Jesse stood in the doorway, peering into a darkness that gradually lifted as their eyes adjusted to the dim interior. Nobody said a word. Nobody moved. The place was packed with people, probably exceeding maximum occupancy, but who would issue the citation? Everyone in town was already here. Men. Women. Children. Everyone.

"Sorry to interrupt," Will said. "We found a note telling us to come here. To Newcastle."

"Where'd you find this note?" a woman asked. She had a raspy voice, like she had smoked too much in her life, or maybe she was just growing old. Will couldn't tell who had spoken.

"In a house up in the mountains," he said. "We took shelter there."

"That's where you're from? The mountains?"

Will thought mentioning New York City imprudent, but he didn't want to lie. Being caught in a lie might have harsh consequences. "We've been on the road since..." He motioned at the world behind him.

"Since it happened," Jesse finished for him.

The crowd parted to make room for the woman to come forward. She was short, gray, limping a bit, but her eyes skewered the newcomers. Had she carried a ruler, she might have been a teacher from a bygone era come to rap Will's knuckles for some misdemeanor.

"Names," she demanded.

"I'm Will, this is Jesse."

"Full names."

"William James Bancroft III," Will said going excessively formal in his irritation. He wagged his thumb at Jesse. "Jesse Markakis. I don't know his middle name."

Jesse opened his mouth, looked at Will, looked at the woman, closed his mouth.

The woman's eyes narrowed, but she wasn't squinting at Will. She was looking beyond him, to the Escalade. "Fancy wheels. Bought or stolen?"

"Commandeered," Will said.

"Uh huh. Who's in it?"

"An old man named Spike and a young girl named Adalina."

"Why are they still out there?

The interrogation had grown old. "Who are you?" Will asked.

"Mary Stevenson. I'm the mayor of Newcastle. Just elected, in fact." She swept her hand at the gathering behind her. "Welcome to town. Quick orientation. We have a few rules."

Will took the temperature of the room. Lukewarm, at best. Everyone was watching him, watching Jesse, waiting for them to do something irrational. He could guess the first rule.

Not that he had to. Mary spelled it out. "Rule number one. If you even look like you're about to go nuts, we'll kill you."

Jesse glanced at the Escalade , then at Will. There was no need to say it: Spike could be in trouble. They'd have to keep him away from others until they figured out how to break it to these people without them morphing into a lynch mob.

"Rule number two," the Mayor went on. "Everyone pulls their weight. Remember Captain John Smith?"

Will did, but Jesse beat him to the punch. "'He that will not work shall not eat,'" he said. "My dad quoted that if any of us complained 'bout doing chores."

"Good man," Mary said with a lopsided grin.

The rest of the rules could wait. Will was more concerned about their immediate future. "Where do we stay?"

"You'll be assigned housing. We have plenty. Cleaning it up is your responsibility, but we'll help if you need repairs. We have a couple of carpenters, an electrician, a plumber. All kinds of expertise here. Speaking of which, how do you fit in?"

Probably not at all, either of them. Will wasn't sure how to break that news.

Jesse shuffled his feet and looked away. "I worked a loading dock," he said. "I was training in computers, though."

Mary nodded and eyed Will.

"I was a financial manager."

A murmur ran through the crowd, mixed with muted laughter.

Looking over her shoulder, Mary snapped, "We can't all be tradesmen." To Will, she said, "There's no work for number crunchers, but we could use a decent manager. Things need organizing. A lot of things."

She took a step toward Jesse and eyed him like an appraiser figuring the worth of an uncut diamond. "Computer guy, huh? You must be smart. You could do whatever you wanted, I'll bet."

Jesse looked like he'd gagged on something. "'Cept what I want probably ain't what you need."

"No problem. You can try on something we do need." Turning back to Will, she asked, "What about your friends out there in the Caddy? The old man and the girl?"

"The old man is a..." Will wasn't sure of Spike's specialty and wasn't about to reveal what he'd been involved with. Not specifically. "...a scientist. Medical research."

Another wave of talk washed through the gathering, tense but brimming with curiosity. Mary kept her stone face on.

"I don't know the girl's interests. She's still young, but she's smart. And willing to help."

"Good qualities," the Mayor said. "And we could use a doctor."

Will doubted anyone would want Spike practicing medicine on them, not once they found out about his condition. But that would be a problem for another day. For now, it seemed they'd been accepted into the community, albeit on probation.

Three days jetted by in a blur of activity. They were assigned a house on the east side of the Interstate, a large thing sided in dark wood, perched on a hill. The end of a row of houses atop the rise, it was first of the group to be occupied. It wasn't a bad place, with a garage on the ground level, most of the living space on the second, and a porch hanging off the front above the garage. A two-flight staircase rose from the driveway to the porch. Beyond the back porch and fenced yard, which ascended partway up the hill, stood nothing but trees.

The interior was clean and well-furnished, offering four bedrooms, two full baths, an ample kitchen and dining room, living room, and laundry room. Unlike up in the mountains, Newcastle still had electricity and running water, although Will had overheard some debate about how long they would last.

Keeping the public utilities functioning would have to be a top priority, assuming it was possible. Will could state it, but he had no clue how to address it. He'd already been pulled into meetings with Mayor Stevenson and several others on the subject. Jesse, being the new resident computer expert, was included. The others were a civil engineer, one of the electricians, and a plumber. The result of the three-hour talkathon felt odd to Will. The plan was to ensure stability of the electric supply by creating a solar farm from panels commandeered around the area. Once electricity was assured, the water and sewer systems would be reasonably stable. At least the pumps would have power.

So long as nothing sprung a leak, anyway. Will had the feeling none of them really knew what they were talking about. Educated guesswork, maybe, but someday the infrastructure would fail, and nobody would be able to fix it. And then what?

One day at a time, though. For now, life was better than it had been since the outbreak. They weren't running, weren't surrounded by death, didn't dread contact with others. That was all he could reasonably ask for.

And then somebody got sick, and someone pounded on their door, begging for the doctor.

Doctor Spike.

"I haven't practiced medicine in three decades," Spike objected. Seated next to the driver, he grimaced as the car bounced through a pothole.

In the back seat, Will silently demanded that the old man keep calm and shut up and above all not go psycho on them.

The driver, a twenty-something stick figure of a man named Benny, looked ready to expire from fright. "You're the only doctor we got," he all but yelped. "Only one. You gotta help her."

Thus far, Benny hadn't offered any details, nor had Spike tried to elicit them. Rather, the new town doctor was trying to worm out of the job. "I don't have any equipment," he objected. "Or medications."

"There's a dentist's office," Benny said.

"Dentist! What the hell am I doing, pulling a tooth?"

Will put a hand on Spike's shoulder. "Take it easy. We'll figure it out and get whatever you need."

Spike half-turned. "I can't possibly diagnose, much less treat, anyone. I want to go back."

"Can't," Benny said, gripping the wheel tighter. "Mayor Stevenson said to bring you."

"Mayor, or dictator?"

"Relax," Will said. "Remember rule number one."

Spike folded his arms over his chest and looked out the side window. "Maybe I deserve to be shot," he said. "Lai Jun certainly—"

Will cut him off. "You're not her."

Benny glanced back. "Who?"

"Nobody. Someone Spike worked with before all this."

They arrived at a small yellow house amid the main residential area, a corner property surrounded by shrubs. A palm towered overhead. There was no garage, only a gravel parking pad. Benny led Spike and Will inside. They threaded through a small living room crowded with well-worn furniture, then a small kitchen with a two-person table. A short hall led to a pair of bedrooms. In the first, a young woman lay blanketed on an old four-poster bed. She looked to be sleeping. By her side, a sixtyish man sat in an eightyish wooden chair, his arm under the blanket so he could hold her hand.

Spike paused in the doorway. Will nudged him into the room. He crept to the bedside and set a hand to the woman's forehead, then jerked it back. "Do you have a thermometer?"

The man in the chair nodded. "One-oh-four point two, an hour ago."

Pulling the blanket slowly down, Spike set his ear to the woman's chest. "I need a stethoscope," he grumbled. After a moment, he raised his head and asked Benny, who was standing by the door, wringing his hands, "Got any paper towels?"

Benny nodded.

"Get me the cardboard tube from a roll."

"What for?"

"Just do it, will you?"

Jumping at Spike's tone, he rushed out.

"Who are you people?" Spike asked the old man.

"Bedside manner, Doc," Will chided.

"Damn the niceties. Who are you people?"

"Fred Waller," the old man said. "This is my daughter Jean. Benny's my son."

"Any mental symptoms?"

Fred shook his head absently.

Benny lurched back into the room, fumbling to unroll a mass of paper towels and free the tub within.

"We had a farm," Fred continued. "Pretty isolated. Kept to ourselves. My wife went to town that morning. Never came back."

Spike put a hand to his forehead and looked away just as Benny held out the tube. Will took it and placed it in Spike's hand. The "doctor" stared at it for a moment as though he'd found himself holding a mouse. Then he shook himself and used the tube to listen to the patient's heart and lungs. "Any coughing, wheezing, difficulty breathing?"

"Not that I noticed," Fred said.

Spike tossed the tube on the floor and covered up the woman. "Probably an infection, but not respiratory. All I can do is give her antibiotics. If we can find any. Is she allergic to any medications?"

Fred shook his head.

"Where's the nearest pharmacy?"

"Auburn."

Damn. That was the last place they wanted to go.

"There's a dentist's in town," Benny said.

Spike closed his eyes and muttered something.

Someone would have to brave Auburn. Will didn't trust Benny's state of mind, and Fred wasn't going anywhere. Could they spare the time to find someone else? Probably not. Jean's fever almost justified an emergency room visit, if only one existed anymore. There was only one logical choice.

"I'll go," Will decided. "But I'll need directions."

"Up I-80," Fred said. "Then route 49 north about half a mile. You'll see the pharmacy on the right."

It popped into Will's memory. They'd passed by it on their convoluted trek through the town. If all went well, he could get there and back in half an hour, forty-five minutes. With luck, Spike wouldn't go bonkers before then. But he had an idea about that. He needed to retrieve the Escalade anyway. He'd have Benny bring Jesse and Adalina here to keep an eye on Spike.

"Tell me what you need," he told Spike.

Jesse wasn't sure about exposing himself and Adalina to the sick girl's disease, but he had to concede Will's point. They couldn't let Spike go crazy, not in front of others. So the two of them hung out in the hallway. Jean slept between fits of moaning, Fred clung to her hand as though trying to pull her from a river before she drowned, and Spike muttered to himself while staring out the window at the trees.

Twenty minutes into their vigil, Spike turned, wide-eyed, and said, "Did you see that?" He pointed a trembling finger out the window.

Fred looked up. "What?"

"Out there."

"Damn," Jesse muttered. Aliens, no doubt. That was the last thing they needed.

Adalina hurried to Spike's side before Jesse could object. She clung to his arm and looked out the window with him. "Let's go check the back door," she whispered. She tugged at his arm.

"It's not safe for you," he whispered back.

Fred rose and came around the bed to look. "I don't see nothing," he said.

Adalina tugged again, and this time Spike followed her out of the room, to the kitchen, and into the back part of the house where a sliding door opened onto a deck. Jesse followed, telling Fred to stay with his daughter.

They peered into the back yard together. There was nothing but a breeze and sparrows in the trees.

"We have pepper here, I hope," Spike said.

"Tons," Adalina assured him.

He nodded and put a hand to his forehead. "If it's an infection, she'll be okay once we have the antibiotic. But what if it's not? I don't have the means to run tests to narrow it down." He dropped his hand and looked confused. "What are we doing out here?"

With luck, he could handle the truth. "You had an alien moment," Jesse told him.

"Damn. I can't hide this forever. I need to talk to that woman, that mayor."

"They'll kill you, man."

"No more than I deserve."

"Don't be so down on yourself," Adalina said. "You can help people. You said you wanted to help, right?"

Spike regarded her for a moment. "I did."

"So think about helping, and you'll be fine."

Jesse doubted optimism made much difference in Spike's condition, but he kept his mouth shut. Adalina's presence did have some positive effect. Maybe she reminded him of his own daughter or granddaughter?

Spike stared out the window a moment longer, then turned. "I'd better check on the patient."

They followed him back to the bedroom where he did nothing but direct a sad gaze at Jean. Fred watched in silence as though trying to figure out if he knew Spike from somewhere. Eventually, Spike muttered, "Where the hell is Will, anyway?" and wandered off, maybe up front to await the arrival of the medication. Adalina tailed him, leaving Jesse alone with Fred and his sleeping daughter.

"What was that about?" Fred asked.

A queasy sensation settled in Jesse's gut. "What was what about?"

"He saw something outside."

Jesse shrugged. "Nothing. Nothing was out there."

"But he saw something."

"Just shadows."

Fred narrowed his eyes. "Is he right in the head?"

Right now he was, so Jesse said, "Oh, sure. Just a bit jumpy. Everyone is, I guess."

The ensuing silence frightened Jesse more than the question. You could deny accusations. You could turn aside questions. But how did you fight silence?

After what seemed an hour but wasn't more than a few minutes, Fred turned his eyes on his daughter again. "I don't guess you'd keep him under your roof if anything was wrong."

"Sure wouldn't," Jesse lied.

27

WILL HAD no trouble retracing his steps, finding the drug store, grabbing Spike's orders from the pharmacy, and returning to Newcastle. Over the next three days, Jean's condition improved. The fever subsided and her strength returned. The success earned Spike a reputation about town, a reputation he refused to embrace, but whenever someone was hurt or ill, they called him in. Fortunately, those were rare cases, only a handful as winter groped toward springtime. With further trips to the drug store, they built up a small stockpile of medical supplies: wraps and bandages, over-the-counter medications, some of the more useful prescription meds, thermometers, stethoscopes, blood pressure cuffs.

Spike never went anywhere without Will, Jesse, and Adalina. He seemed more secure surrounded by them, and probably his mental state was less fragile in their company. In Adalina's, particularly. She was his life preserver.

Jesse apprenticed himself to one of the civil engineers and began learning about the electric grid, solar power, and the water supply. With a few others, they spent much of their time building, or attempting to build, a power system for the town that didn't rely on the region's dams, power plants, and distribution systems. They could do nothing should any of that fail, and there were increasing signs that something was failing somewhere. Power flickers. Brown-outs. Spike's continued insistence on learning to do without technology sat well with nobody except one older fellow who had built himself a life off the grid deep in the mountains and now spent most of his days grumbling that he ought to go back.

Will found himself helping Mayor Mary Stevenson organize and direct the public utility efforts, plus the ongoing cleanup of the town, trash disposal, and the settlement of newcomers. People occasionally drifted in, some by accident, some directed by notes like the one that brought Will and his party here. Newcastle was growing, albeit with the speed of an advancing glacier, and Mary speculated that their town wasn't the only one. Humanity, she assured everyone, was coming back online.

But the disease, or whatever it was—Spike refused to acknowledge it as such—might still be out there, plotting a resurgence. And it was in fact already here, in this town, though none but four of them knew it.

Not yet.

Late in February, the temperature leapt from its typical sixtyish to the upper seventies. On the third day of the heat wave, Spike was summoned to a little gray house with a picket fence. His entourage in tow, he was escorted in by a middle-aged Japanese fellow who seemed unable to get a complete sentence out. Leading them from the car to the front door, he'd stumbled through something less than a greeting and far less than an explanation: "It's...thank you for...this way, this way...I'm so...I didn't know, I couldn't think what..."

"What's your name?" Will asked as they passed into a small living room furnished largely in dark wood.

"Dan," he said, "Dan Uchida. My...she's...ah, she's not *legally* my wife, but..." He led them to a cramped bedroom. A mattress and springs were stuffed into a metal frame, and a cluttered dresser took up most of the side wall. On the bed, on top of the sheets, a young woman lay, sweat beaded on her face, her lips pinched in pain.

"What happened?" Spike asked.

"She fell. Her ankle..." Dan pointed to the woman's left leg.

Will doubted it much mattered how or where she fell. She'd either sprained or broken it. "What's her name?" he asked, since Dan hadn't managed to find that, either.

Clasping his hands before his chest, Dan whispered, "Jin. Please help her."

Spike had been examining the ankle without touching it. Swollen and bruised, it nevertheless appeared straight and didn't seem to much alarm him. But the name did. His head snapped up. "Jun?" he demanded.

"Jin," Dan corrected.

Spike bit his lip and scowled at the woman's face. "Lai Jun? No, it can't be."

Damn. He was going to flip out on them. Will moved to Spike's side and put a hand on his shoulder. "Not Jun," he said. "Jin. This is Jin...what's her last name, Dan?"

"Ashikawa. She's...not legally, but...she's..."

"Your wife?"

"We met after...after...and we decided..."

"I get it, thanks." Will nodded to Spike. "She's Japanese, not Chinese."

Spike blinked at him, then shook his head and studied the injured ankle again. "Without an x-ray, I can't tell, but probably a sprain. Moderately severe. It should be iced fifteen minutes on, fifteen minutes off. I'll wrap it and we'll get her some pain meds." He scrutinized her face again and shuddered. "She sure looks like Lai Jun. Or maybe not. Maybe just a bit."

Adalina came to Spike's side and took his hand. "It's okay," she whispered. "Let's get what you need to fix her leg."

"No, how could Jun be here?" Spike asked nobody. "She died, I'm sure she died. She didn't get out. She couldn't have. She was quarantined, too. We all were, and then..."

Dan stared at Spike as though he was a ghoul. "This is my wife," he snapped. "Jin. My *wife*." And then his mental fog cleared, and he registered the one key word Spike had uttered. "What do you mean, quarantined?"

"Nothing," Will said, but he knew that wouldn't work. It was something, all right.

"Why were you quarantined?"

"Easy, friend," Jesse said. "Spike's just rattled, like the rest of us. He lost family, too. Jun was..." He shifted under the weight of the lie he was about to utter. "Jun was his girlfriend. When you said Jin, he heard—"

Spike whirled and shoved Jesse into the wall. Jesse stumbled and nearly toppled. "Jun was *not* my girlfriend! She was a student, just another student! Whoever said I slept with her was lying! The demon spread those lies, didn't he? He hates me. He's the one that recruited them, the aliens, those fucking *aliens*, to have me killed! They never stop. They never give up. They'll hound me until I'm *dead*!" Shoving Dan aside, he rushed from the room. The front door slammed a moment later.

Dan blinked at Will, at Jesse, at nothing. "Oh my God," he whispered. "Oh my God. We've been in the same room with him. We've all been breathing the same air as him."

"I'll get him," Jesse said. "You deal with this."

Will fished the car key out of his pocket and tossed it to Jesse. Jesse snagged it from the air and hurried out.

"Wait!" Adalina called and took off after Jesse. Will tried to stop her, but she was too quick. He hoped Jesse could keep her out of harm's way. There was no telling what Spike might do in his current state.

Staring after her, Dan made a fist and gnawed on it.

"It's all right," Will told him. "The guy's a little unstable sometimes, but he's not full-blown crazy, and he isn't contagious." Which could have been wrong for all he knew. He and Jesse and Adalina had spent enough time with Spike without getting sick, but maybe they had fought it off, like Daffodil had suggested. "Right now, we need to take care of your wife. I'll get her something for the pain. Do you have ice? Fold some in a towel and apply it to the swelling. I can try to wrap her ankle, if Spike doesn't get back soon."

"Someone needs to...to take care of *him*."

"We'll take care of him."

"You'll kill him?"

"That's not what I meant."

"But—"

Will started for the door. "Please, get the ice. Help your wife. I'll get her something for the pain. Do you have a car? If so, I can be back in fifteen minutes at most. Otherwise, I'll have to walk."

Dan nodded and dug a set of keys out of his pocket. He separated the car key and handed it over. "In the garage," he said.

Will nodded his thanks and left. Leaving Dan and Jin alone probably wasn't a good idea, but he had no choice. The medical supplies were all at his house. He just hoped word of Spike's meltdown didn't circulate in his absence.

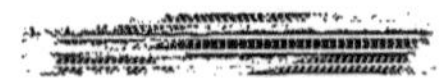

By the time Jesse got through the front door, Spike had disappeared. There was no telling which way he'd gone. They were on a dead-end street, but maybe he'd cut through the yards. No, not likely. They were all fenced here, so he must be sticking to the streets. Driving would be the best way to find him.

Jesse was just climbing into the Navigator when Adalina flew out the front door, crying, "Wait!"

"Stay here," he told her.

"No! You might need me!"

"Look, girl—"

"I'm coming with you."

Ah, hell. He started the engine as she climbed in and buckled up. "Keep your eyes open," he told her.

Jesse toured up the street, turned left, wandered around, retraced his route, explored the roads nearest the Interstate. Nothing. Spike might have slipped into a backyard and holed up there. If so, they might never find him, at least not before nightfall. On the plus side, that meant Adalina wouldn't get hurt should Spike turn violent.

But someone might.

They continued to search, passing down every street in the town twice, seeing nothing but houses and trees and shrubs and the occasional resident. Whenever they spotted someone, Jesse pulled over and asked if they'd seen Spike. Nobody had. Which might have been for the best, because if they had, and a gun was near to hand, they might have killed him.

The sun lowered in the west, and still they hadn't found him.

"We oughta go home," Jesse told Adalina. "Maybe he'll find his way back."

She chewed on a nail. "What if he's hurt?"

"Can't help him if we can't find him. And we looked everywhere."

She closed her eyes. Beneath the lids, her eyeballs flickered about as though she was looking for something. When she opened them, she looked surprised. "Not everywhere," she said.

By nightfall, Will had done all he could to help Jin. The pain had eased following a healthy dose of ibuprofen, and the combination of icing and wrapping had lessened the swelling. She wouldn't be walking on that leg for a while, but Will scrounged up a walker from an unoccupied house with a wheelchair ramp. That would give her some mobility.

Dan seemed less on edge by the time Will left. With luck, he'd forgotten Spike's behavior. Or maybe he'd reported it and left it in the mayor's hands. Will didn't care to risk broaching the subject, so he went home without knowing.

Jesse had heated canned chow mein for dinner. An odd choice, under the circumstances, but he and Adalina wolfed it down. Will took a plate for himself and picked at it. "No luck," he said. "Obviously."

Adalina gave him a sly smile.

"What?"

"We found him!"

"So where is he?"

She thumbed over her shoulder, in the direction of the bedrooms. "Sleeping."

"To be fair," Jesse said, "Adalina found him. I about quit."

The conversation lagged until Will couldn't take the silence any longer. "So?"

"The freeway," Adalina said.

"Three, four miles down the road," Jesse added. "Going west."

Will pushed his plate back. "How the hell did he get there?"

Adalina laughed. "He walked."

"Mighta gone up the on-ramp," Jesse said. "Mighta cut through the trees and hopped the fence. Time we got to him, he didn't know where he was."

It might have been better if they hadn't found him. Inwardly, Will cringed at the thought, but it was only a question of time before his condition became known throughout the town. At least on the road, he might have a sliver of a chance of survival. Here, he was doomed. Maybe not today. Maybe not tomorrow. But soon.

They all jumped when someone hammered on the front door. Adalina slid down in her seat. Jesse pushed back from the table, poised for fight or flight. Swallowing down a rising dread, Will went to see who it was.

Mary Stevenson peered in from the dark, alone, not wielding a gun. Not openly, at least. "Did Spike come home?" she asked.

Will nodded but didn't move to admit her.

"Can I speak with him?"

"He's asleep."

She met his eyes as though gauging his truthfulness. "Then I'll speak with you." She fluttered a hand to suggest he step aside.

Stonewalling would likely make matters worse, so Will motioned her in. She made straight for an easy chair and parked herself in it, then waited for him to sit. Once he was settled, she steepled her fingers in front of her mouth.

A long moment passed.

"I thought you wanted to speak," he said.

"Unless you want to go first."

Will motioned her to take the lead. Not that he didn't know what was coming, but it might be to his advantage to let her say what was on her mind before he tried to persuade her she was wrong.

"Dan Uchida says Spike was at his place today."

"His wife has a sprained ankle. He asked Spike to treat her."

Mary dropped her hands into her lap. "Which he didn't."

"He examined her and prescribed a treatment."

"Before he ran off."

Will neither confirmed nor denied.

"After speaking of being in quarantine."

Will thought for a moment before replying. He wasn't about to deny the truth, but there had to be a way to make it sound less threatening. "I suppose that is—was—an occupational hazard for him. He was a medical researcher."

Cocking her head as though not understanding, Mary waited for further explanation, but Will didn't oblige. "From Dan's vantage," she said, "Spike seemed very disturbed. Mentally unbalanced, even."

"I've known Spike for a while now. He's suffered a lot, so yes, he can seem unbalanced. But he's about as harmless as they come." True, that last bit was a lie, a white lie shading into gray. Spike sometimes seemed moments from homicidal. Still, he hadn't crossed that line, not once.

Mary's eyes bored into Will's, seeking to pierce his soul. He held his breath, waiting for the inevitable. Spike was a lunatic. Dangerous. Rule number one. He must be put down like a mad dog. For the good of the community, he had to die.

"We've all suffered," she said, her voice suddenly soft. "But Will, most of us don't claim we're hounded by demons and aliens."

There was no way to deny that. No way to respond, period. Will waited for her to hand down the inevitable judgement.

But she didn't. "So what is he? Sane? Mad? Borderline? And if the latter, how long until he slips over the line?"

Will truly had no answer. Spike weaved like a drunk behind the wheel, on one side of the line and then the other. He crossed it time and again, but always pulled back before catastrophe struck. What did that make him? Probably just like anyone else. Didn't we all do that in our own ways, even if not so...creatively?

"I think," he suggested, "you should talk to him. When you do, Adalina should be present."

Mary arched an eyebrow.

"He's less vulnerable when she's around."

"That sounds odd. Or disturbing."

"She's like a daughter to him, or a granddaughter."

"I'll take your word for it." Mary rose and looked down at Will as though she was a judge eyeing a convicted criminal from the bench, pondering the severity of an impending sentence. "I'll drop by mid-morning. Don't let him wander off."

Will exhaled his relief. It wasn't over yet, but at least judgement had been suspended. Maybe once Spike fed her his scientific dissertation, she'd be as confused about his status as Will and Jesse were. They hadn't given him the death sentence. Maybe she wouldn't, either.

28

I N HINDSIGHT, it was curious how like the next morning's weather was to that of New York City some three months before. Not quite cold enough for a coat, a touch too chilly for a jacket. High clouds caressing the pale sky. And still. The atmosphere held its breath in anticipation. Will felt hunted. Something prowled the shadows of Newcastle, as it had prowled the canyons of New York, stalking its prey.

Jesse must have sensed it, too. While he spooned instant coffee into a cup, his gaze flickered time and again to the window until he knocked the jar off the counter, spilling dark crystals on the kitchen floor. He muttered a curse but didn't immediately clean up the mess. Something was out there, watching, waiting. Will brought him a broom and dustpan, handed it over in silence. Jesse nodded his thanks. Will understood his unspoken question: *You feel it, too?*

Spike was another matter, but then he always was. His thoughts turned inward, he shuffled to the table and sat as though he'd come to a diner, and the waitress promised she'd get to him shortly. Naturally, she did. Adalina followed close on his heels, looking as bright as the morning sun, and set to work making cocoa for herself and the old man, and instant oatmeal. With pepper, just in case.

Will gave everyone time to eat half a meal before mentioning the inevitable. "Mayor Stevenson will be dropping by soon."

Jesse and Adalina both squirmed. They knew of the mayor's visit the previous night. Will had only told them she wanted to speak with Spike, but no elaboration was necessary. They both knew full well Dan Uchida hadn't hidden his fears.

Spike continued eating, didn't even look up.

"To talk to you," Will told him.

No reaction.

"About yesterday."

Another spoonful down Spike's gullet.

"Do you remember anything about it?"

He set his spoon in his bowl, wiped his mouth with a paper napkin, and finally looked at Will. "No," he said.

"Then it's likely to be a short conversation," Will said. "With a bad outcome."

"I said I don't remember," Spike replied. "I didn't say I'd refuse to talk."

And that was as much as Will could get out of him. Jesse didn't bother trying, and Adalina merely sat by his side, sipping cocoa, downing small globs of oatmeal, silently watching the world—or some small part of it—end.

Mary Stevenson arrived midmorning as promised. By then, the gang was seated in the living room, staring at nothing. Until she knocked on the door, it was the deepest silence Will had ever known, deeper even than the winter mountains at night. He let her in, directed her to a chair, and waited for her to speak.

Which she didn't, not for a good ten minutes. She took her seat, set her bulky black purse on the floor by her feet, adjusted herself for comfort, and waited. The air felt thick with menace even though a whiff of lilac had followed the mayor in. Perfume, naturally, would be as easy to come by as pepper, until it expired. How long would that be? A year? Three? Ten? How should Will know? He'd thrown out the one bottle Sarah left behind the day he realized she wasn't coming back.

"What's your real name?" Mary asked Spike.

Spike blinked at her.

"Spike can't be your real name."

He glanced at Will and Jesse as though accusing them of spilling a dark secret. "Ike Zhao," he said.

"Your family has been in the U.S. for a long time, I suppose."

"They wore 'I am Chinese' signs on their backs during World War II."

Mary nodded as though she'd been there. Not that she could have been. She wasn't *that* old. "You mentioned being quarantined," she said.

"Not to you."

"To Dan Uchida."

Spike shrugged. "I don't recall that."

"Don't you."

"Now and then, parts of my life go missing."

Mary didn't question it. It might have been an everyday occurrence for everyone she knew. "Were you?"

"Was I what?"

"Quarantined?"

"Yes."

"Why?"

Spike gave her a sly smile. "You want the technical explanation or the thirty-thousand-foot overview?"

She matched his smile. Will wondered if being mayor was new for her or if she'd been a politician in her previous life. If new, she'd adapted well. "Let's start in the stratosphere and work our way down."

"I am—I was—a medical researcher. My team worked with potentially hazardous organisms. We had protocols to prevent breaches of containment and to deal with them if they occurred. Quarantining anyone in the facility who was potentially exposed in such a breach was standard practice."

Steepling her fingers in her lap, the mayor gave that some thought. "How often did this happen?"

Spike shrugged.

"Once a year? Twice a year?"

"Only once while I was there."

"And that just happened to result in this." Mary swept her hand around the house, but Will knew she was taking in the whole world. She arched an eyebrow as though waiting for Spike to deny it. When he didn't, she looked at her purse on the floor, squeezed her eyes shut, took a few breaths. "Dan said you called his wife Jun. Someone of that name had something to do with it, didn't she?"

Spike bit his lip. Will wondered why he didn't just spill it. Mary aside, everyone in the room already knew the gist of it.

"Something," he said.

It turned out he didn't need to provide more than the acknowledgement. Mary had already worked it out. "She tried to steal your research. A spy. A Pandora. She opened the box and unleashed hell."

Spike rose and shuffled to the window. He looked out at the world for a long time. Nobody spoke. Will thought they barely breathed. When Spike turned back, tears were tracking down his cheeks. He made no move to wipe them away. "She was too young," he said. "Too inexperienced. Too innocent."

"Hardly innocent." Mary's voice had grown cold.

"The innocence of idealism. She believed the party line. She believed her handler. She didn't know better. She was too young to know better, and she was in love."

"With her handler?"

Spike turned back to the window.

Mary retrieved her purse and settled it on her lap. When Spike offered nothing further, she slipped her hand in. She peered at him as though he was a slug who had destroyed her roses. Then she drew her hand out, and a pistol came with it. She flipped off the safety and aimed for the back of Spike's head.

"Which was you," she said.

Maybe Spike heard the click of the safety. Maybe he knew from the start she was armed. Or maybe he'd been looking for a way out and knew that if anyone could offer one, it was Mary. He stood motionless, waiting for death, his very silence convicting him.

Adalina stretched out both hands in supplication. "Please," she said. "Please don't."

Mary kept the weapon trained on Spike while she scrutinized the girl. "This man," she said, "destroyed the world. Killing him is justice."

"People destroyed the world," Adalina said.

"Adalina—"

"*People* did it. Not one man. All of us. Shoot us all, why don't you? Shoot yourself, too."

Will about interrupted. Insulting Mary seemed a great way to get all four of them killed. Being so young, Adalina knew nothing of power, nothing of how it twisted minds and hearts and relationships. But before he could say anything, Jesse chose sides.

"The kid's right," he told Mary. "Jun had a boss. Spike had a boss. Spike's boss had a boss. Don't matter if it's a company or a country or a little town like this. We're all about greed and power and pride, ain't we? Spike's just a link in the chain. He's easy to take out 'cause he's the weak link right now. But look at him. He's paid his dues. You know why he's sometimes crazy and sometimes as sane as you and me? He ain't just got one bug. He's got several fighting inside him every minute of every day. He's gotta live with that until he dies."

Mary's aim wavered a bit. When she spoke, some of the confidence had leached from her voice. "Be that as it may, he's got a lot to answer for."

Spike did, Will knew that. Yet he couldn't side with the mayor, not now, not seeing Adalina's pleading, scolding eyes. Truth was, Will himself had a lot to answer for. For not holding Sarah closer. For lording it over Jesse. For letting his heart harden to the suffering of others. Adalina's plea was a plea for both mercy and justice. Spike couldn't be blamed for the state of the world, for the state of humanity.

He rose.

He held out his hand, palm up, silently begging Mary to give him the gun.

She didn't look at him.

"The kid's right," he said. "Isn't she?"

That afternoon, a wash of gray clouds stole the blue from the sky, and a drizzle wetted the hills. Mary had neither left nor said a word since Will posed the question. She went onto the deck for a time and only came in once her graying hair grew damp. Then she rummaged through the kitchen and heated herself a can of pasta rings, which she ate with a side of water. Between bites, she picked at the loops with her fork, separating them into sizes, mixing them up again.

She was half done when Spike slipped into the chair opposite her and watched. She was three-quarters done before she said, "There's more in the cupboard."

"I'm not hungry," he said.

"I'm not either."

He blinked at the vanishing pasta. "So why are you eating?"

"It's better than standing in the rain."

Spike thought about that for a moment. He shifted his weight, folded his arms on the table, frowned at her all but empty plate. "Why didn't you kill me?"

"Did you want me to?"

"That's not an answer."

"Neither is that."

For the first time in her experience of him, Spike laughed. It startled her, although she didn't know why. Maybe on some level she hadn't thought him capable of laughter.

"At the time," he said.

That made sense. Standing in front of that window, he had indeed looked done with life. It should have been so easy to grant his wish. "I was looking for an excuse," she said.

"For what?"

"For letting you live."

He laughed again. Twice in one sitting. Amazing. "You're not as ruthless as you seem, then."

Mary set her fork on her plate, sipped some water, tried to decide how to talk about it. Keep it simple? Give Adalina the credit? Start at the beginning? Sum it up, recite the whole novel? She hadn't told anyone, not really, and now it seemed she needed to get it out, but would Spike believe it? It was too strange. Or maybe not. His story was as strange as they came, and she'd only heard a fraction of it.

"I'm a minister."

Spike's eyes widened.

"As God is my witness. A Methodist minister."

"Lost your faith? Or just playing the tough girl?"

That was uncalled for. "People who lose their faith when life doesn't go their way never had much to begin with." Mary paused for another sip of water. "Circumstances led me to strange a place. Led us all there, I guess. As more people gathered, we started asking what happens if the disease hitches a ride to town."

"It's not a disease," Spike said.

She wasn't about to argue classification with a scientist. "We reached a consensus pretty quick."

Spike shuddered as though a chill had gripped him. "So I heard. But why does a minister hold the gun?"

"There's more than one gun in town."

That rattled him further. He left the table for the cupboards and opened one after another as though searching for something that wasn't there.

Mary watched his concentrated aimlessness. "Guns bother you."

He leaned on the counter, refusing to admit it.

Which meant yes. "Sometimes you can't wait for the cops," she told him. "Especially when there aren't any. But it's not as wild west as it sounds. Few people relish the thought of killing someone. Those that do, they're the crazy ones."

Spike leaned his back against the counter and eyed her as though he'd discovered a new life form in his microscope. "That's why they appointed a minister to do the dirty work?"

"I don't *want* the job. But I have leadership experience, so they elected me."

"You shouldn't be the executioner."

"Nor should you."

Spike closed his eyes. "I have a long history of it," he whispered.

Mary figured he was speaking metaphorically. Spike hadn't killed anyone, not directly. But Lai Jun, whoever she was, had clearly been his lover. Maybe he had seduced her to gain control over her. Maybe it had been a fling, or even a genuine relationship. She likely hadn't been the first. A male college professor and certain of his female students—an old story. Did Spike have a wife? Did she know about his affairs? Had he killed her over and over with them? Mary told herself to stop that train of thought. Aside from being weak inference, she might be doing him a grave disservice, and that was wrong. Immoral. She hadn't lost her faith, but she'd certainly lost her bearings.

"Nobody is beyond forgiveness," she said, as much for her own sake as his.

Opening his eyes, Spike met her gaze and held it for a long time. It felt absurdly like a staring contest. "I don't believe that," he said. "But I'm not looking for forgiveness."

"What, then?" Mary asked.

"A way to say—" Spike shook his head and looked away.

She held her tongue, knowing that the rest would spill out in short order. He couldn't keep it bottled up much longer.

And it did. "How sorry I am," he finished.

Now that they had stopped running, life took on a curiously normal quality, if it was at all normal for a once-wealthy white guy, a black guy with unrealized dreams, a young teen girl who had lost everything but her soul, and an old man who had nearly destroyed the world to reside under the same roof. It wasn't life as it had been, but it was life. The town accreted more survivors, not a flood but a trickle that built up over the months. Newcastle made connections with surrounding farms, where someone here had survived, someone there had moved in. Spike spun scenarios and juggled calculations, trying to peer into humanity's future. He got varying answers:

The cities were toast, but the country must be thriving.

Population had leveled out, with about the same absolute numbers of survivors in both urban and rural areas.

Small towns had fared remarkably well. They could pull the nation through.

And on and on.

Will figured most of it was numeric fantasy, but the gradual influx of population to Newcastle demonstrated the resilience of the species.

Jesse, too, chimed in. "You know how many mass extinctions this planet's seen? Life always bounces back."

"Not the dinosaurs," Will countered.

"Birds, man, birds."

Whatever. Fact was, by the end of summer, fresh produce would be back on the menu. Will had helped Mayor Mary (as everyone called her now) orchestrate that, among other things. They hadn't been blown back to the stone age, only to maybe the eighteenth century, decorated with bits and bobs of later eras. The skills to make it at that level were out there, scattered among the survivors and spreading as others learned them.

And then in mid-June, not quite five months after their arrival in Newcastle, Will got a surprise.

Evening was pulling its cloak over the sky. Dinner was done. Will and Jesse had gone out on the front deck to watch the stars blink on. One of the advantages of leading a more primitive existence, Will had discovered, was the lack of outdoor lighting. Even in town now, the night sky was ablaze with more stars than he'd ever imagined. Jesse himself had been lost among those stars at first, although he'd soon found his bearings and could point out even the faintest of constellations.

The sun's afterglow painted the west in reds and oranges. Only the brightest stars had so far winked on. Then a brighter pair of lights lit up the road, headlights creeping toward them, hesitating, turning into their drive.

They squinted into the light, behind which was an extended cab pickup of undetermined color.

"You recognize that truck?" Will asked.

"Not me," Jesse replied.

The engine silenced. The headlights winked out. Doors squeaked open, and human figures slid out, one from the driver's seat, two on the passenger side. One of the passengers, a slight figure, took a few halting steps and looked up.

"Will?" a familiar voice called. "Jesse?"

The two of them nearly tripped over themselves springing from their chairs and leaning over the railing. "Daffodil!" they cried simultaneously.

Daffodil laughed. "I told you I'd find you!"

Will and Jesse all but ran through the house, down to the garage, and out to meet her. Will braked at the last minute, but Jesse scooped her up in a bear hug. She laughed and clung to him for a moment before pushing him back and grabbing Will's hands.

"Don't go all formal on me," she chided.

Heat rose from his core and engulfed his face, but he gave her a halting embrace. Over her shoulder, he recognized her companions: Carolyn and her son Jared. So Daffodil was still tagging along with them, or they with her. He recalled the warning he'd given her about Jared's intentions, and her confident reply: "I'll handle him." Those were the last words they'd spoken to each other. Question was, how had she handled him? Or, maybe, how much?

Jared still wore that grin, a bit softened now, as though pleased Daffodil had been reunited with her old friends. Even Carolyn had lost her edge, although when she spoke, she disguised the change well: "I'm surprised you two are still alive."

Jesse laughed. "Us, too," he said.

Daffodil was still clinging to Will's hands. "We stopped at every town along the way," she said. "We didn't see anybody 'til we got here. I asked about you, and Mayor Mary told us where you were. She said we could have the house next to yours, if we wanted."

Will squeezed her hands. "That would be...good. If you want."

She flashed an impish grin. "In fact, the next three houses are empty, right? You and I could have one to ourselves."

The flash of heat returned.

"You're embarrassing him," Carolyn said. She winked at Daffodil. "Serves him right."

Daffodil winked back. "I think he needs me. And Jesse needs some space for a change. A house by himself might do him good."

"We ain't alone," Jesse said. "We picked up some stragglers."

"Oh yeah? Who?"

"A bright young lady and an old doctor who..." Jesse glanced back at the house. "Who ain't all there all the time."

Carolyn pinched her lips in apprehension. Jared snapped to attention, as though ready to be called into battle.

Daffodil hooked her arm through Will's. "Cool," she said. "Let's meet 'em."

The soft glow of candlelight filled the living room, casting vague, guttering shadows on the walls. A small fire sputtered in the fireplace. Spike, standing just left of the firebox, was studying the writing on a dry erase board he'd placed on an easel, absently rolling an open marker between his fingers. The smell of the marker diffused through the room. Papers were so scattered about his feet that he could barely move without stepping on them. Will recognized some of them as pages from his stash of survivalist printouts.

Adalina was seated on the floor, cross-legged as though in meditation, but her eyes were fixed on Spike. She was the one fixed object in his world these days. Whatever his state of mind, he never mistook Adalina for an alien, a demon, an enemy. Whatever she told him, he implicitly believed, which over the past few months may have kept him from harming others and bringing a death sentence down upon his head. The community got used to him, came to know when to seek his help, when to keep fifty feet back, and understood that so long as Adalina was there, somehow it would be all right.

Although his back was to Will, Jesse, and the newcomers, he somehow sensed their arrival. Capping the marker, he turned, eyes at first on the floor, then slowly raised his head and took in each of them in turn.

"You're fifteen minutes late," he said. "I don't restart my lectures for stragglers."

Carolyn and Jared's mouths dipped into pensive frowns. They had never looked so much alike as in that moment. Will would have laughed if the situation wasn't so dicey. Daffodil cocked her head in amusement.

"Sorry, Doc," Jesse said. "What's on the syllabus today?" He motioned everyone to take a seat on the sofa and the easy chairs.

Spike waited until they were all settled. "I've been demonstrating the use of a flux-matrix model to describe the alien incursion. As you know—as you should know—the incidence of sightings has been on the decline. We must therefore factor in—"

"Not aliens," Adalina said quietly. "The disease."

Spike scratched his cheek. "Young lady, I've told you before. It's not a disease." His face had a stern cast, but the words flowed soft.

"It's not aliens, either."

"Who ever said it was?"

She shrugged as though it didn't matter.

Looking at the newcomers again, Spike backed up a step and almost knocked over the easel. "Who are you?"

Will did the introductions. "Some people we met before we found you. This is Carolyn and her son Jared, and this is Daffodil. Daffodil was a nurse in Nevada."

Spike and Carolyn sized each other up. They might have been preparing for a gunfight. Jared tensed, but Spike seemed oblivious to his presence. Then the old man's gaze shifted to Daffodil, and he seemed to shed a couple of decades. He stood straighter, smiled for a change, and might have been on the verge of asking her for a date. "A nurse," he said. "I could use a nurse."

Daffodil gave him a coy smile, signaling she knew his type. "You look healthy enough to me," she said.

"Not for myself. For my work. The townsfolk pressed me into service as a physician, which I'm not."

"No? So what are you?"

He grinned at her. Then the twinkle left his eyes and his smile slipped and he turned aside. "Nothing," he said. "Nothing, anymore."

And that gained him a nurse, because Daffodil's curiosity refused to be denied.

Prying it out of him took another half year. Will and Jesse knew some of it—all of it, they thought—but they hadn't thought too hard about it. Daffodil weaseled it out of them over time: Spike's work as a medical researcher, the therapies he and his colleagues were developing, genetic engineering, crossing the blood brain barrier, the biological "bottles" and the medications they were meant to deliver, Lai Jun, the theft, the breach, the release of the organisms, the quarantine, Spike never seeing his family again, the chaos his creations had churned up in his brain.

But Daffodil knew there was more. She could tell by Spike's deflections and casual disregard for her questions. Secrets lie interred in his mind.

Meanwhile, the town had grown to respectable size. Most of the housing had been assigned. People of all backgrounds had drifted in, and old knowledge gradually resurfaced, sometimes kept alive by someone with the interest or background, some by trial and error. The resilience surprised Will. He felt all but useless. Mayor Mary kept him busy creating and overseeing plans, but always plans executed by others possessed of true skills. Carpenters and plumbers and other tradesfolk knew more about building and maintaining a town than Will did, even a town lacking the infrastructure they all took for granted. Jesse, too, for that matter. Jesse dabbled in everything. He even took up metalwork alongside an older man who had spent some years as a craftsman in Colonial Williamsburg before crossing the continent to help an ailing uncle with his farm.

And then, on a cool, quiet day in mid-November, not quite a year after their world died, during an afternoon when Spike and Daffodil hadn't been summoned to tend any sick or injured, the old man decided to plant a vegetable garden. The waning of the year failed to tamp his enthusiasm. Armed with a shovel from the garage, he began digging a small plot in the back yard.

From her house next door which she'd been sharing with Will for a few months, Daffodil spotted him hacking up the ground and piling bits of it in a line. "Hey Will," she called. "Spike's being weird again."

Will emerged from the office he'd set up in a spare bedroom. He came beside her and, arms about each other, they watched Spike work. "Whatever he's doing, Adalina will get him back on course," Will said.

They watched Spike turn and tamp and scratch lines in the soil, watched him deposit seeds from a packet, watched him cover the seeds. Adalina didn't appear.

"Let's talk to him," Daffodil suggested.

Will didn't care to. Spike might be wasting his time, but at least it was a peaceful waste of time. But she tugged him, insistent, so he acquiesced. They reached Spike about the time he was unreeling a hose.

"Hey, Doc," Daffodil said.

He ignored her and attached a sprayer to the hose.

"What did you plant?"

"Seeds," he said. He dropped the hose and went to turn on the spigot.

"What kind of seeds?"

Returning, he set the sprayer to "cone" and began watering.

"Whatever was in the packets," he said. With his toe, he nudged a haphazard pile of empty seed packets. He had scratched four rows in the soil and filled them all.

Daffodil picked up the packets and shuffled through them. "Carrots. Marigolds. Sweet corn. Tomatoes. Columbine. Nasturtium. Lettuce." She released them, and they fluttered to the ground. "All mixed together in there?"

"There is wisdom in randomness," Spike said solemnly. "The universe is built on it. Without it, there is no diversity, no beauty."

"No chaos," Will suggested.

Spike shot him an irritated glance. "You don't understand the world very well, do you?"

Probably not. Not anymore. "I used to."

"My life got pretty random sometimes," Daffodil said. "How about you, Will?"

"Not so much." Only once, really, only when Sarah vanished. But that was an eternity ago, and now he had Daffodil. If he could keep her.

"And you, Doc?" Daffodil asked. "Has your life been a row of mixed seeds?"

Swishing the stream of water back and forth, back and forth, Spike shook his head. "Don't try to be clever, Nurse."

"Lai Jun wasn't an aberration, was she? There were others."

He released the handle and the stream stopped. Drops of water dribbled out. Spike turned his eyes heavenward to a few high clouds in the west. "I think that's enough. It'll likely rain tomorrow."

"See," Daffodil went on, "I know your type. Always hungry. I recognize it, because it's me." She gave Will an embarrassed smile. "It was me."

Spike tromped back to the house to turn off the water. Returning, he squeezed the sprayer handle to release the pressure.

"How many were there before her?"

"You have an irritating reserve of curiosity," Spike snapped. "Did you keep score? Neither did I."

"Right. Randomness. A lot of it. And that led to..." She extended a hand, palm up, inviting him to finish the thought.

"This ridiculous nickname," he grumbled.

Will felt a flush of embarrassment, but Daffodil laughed.

"And disaster, once *they* showed up."

Here come the aliens again, Will thought. But this time, he was wrong.

Spike dropped the hose on the ground and gazed into the hills beyond the yard, beyond the town. "You know how governments recruit insiders?"

Will hadn't a clue, nor he supposed did Daffodil. It wasn't like either of them had access to government secrets. Or even particularly sensitive trade secrets.

"If you're an adventurer," Spike said, "they offer adventure. If you're broke, they offer wealth. If you have secrets, they offer to keep them."

Daffodil picked up the end of the hose and removed the spray nozzle.

Still looking to the hills, not noticing her action, maybe not noticing anything anymore, Spike continued. "My secrets had to be kept. From my wife. From my family. But Jun was merely too innocent. Her eyes...they haunt me when I'm sane and torment me when I'm mad. She would have done anything I asked, for no reason but that it was me asking. She didn't deserve…" His shoulders drooped, then his head, then his whole body. He sank to his knees and began weeping.

Daffodil sat on the cold ground by his side. "What happened to her?"

"She wasn't the thief. She was the mule. She didn't know what I'd given her, didn't know it wasn't supposed to leave containment. It was bad luck, a random inspection, and the fool guards dug out the samples, opened the sealed containers, and exposed everyone. They called me to assess the situation. Assess! What could I do? I rushed everyone back into containment, had the facility locked down, but…"

It wasn't quite the story he'd told Will and Jesse, but it ended the same. The details hardly mattered, except maybe to Spike.

Spike closed his eyes and rocked back and forth, back and forth, keening.

Daffodil put a hand on his shoulder. "But what?"

"I didn't know why they called me. They didn't say, so I didn't rush. I didn't show up for probably thirty minutes. When I got there, they had Jun in a little room to the side. She was in a plastic chair, crying. She looked up at me. Her eyes…her spirit was crushed. She knew what I'd done to her. She couldn't know why, couldn't know it was to spare my wife the agony of my betrayals. But she knew what I'd done. After that, nothing mattered. She spent the rest of her life dead." He shuddered. "And so have I."

30

SOME THINGS nobody ever knew. Will figured that was for the best. The exact nature of the disease, that was one thing. As towns began to link up and share information, it became clear that while humanity would survive, many of its accomplishments would lie dormant, waiting to be rediscovered by future generations. By then, most of the clues would have faded into oblivion. Yet, a fresh start could be made. People no longer existed in semi-isolated monocultures. Survivors drawn from every segment of society had been thrown together in new tribes that were defined neither racially nor regionally but by their basic humanity. Who knew? Maybe that would stick. Will hoped so. He, at least, would never look down on anyone again, no matter where they came from, no matter what they looked like, no matter what they did to earn their keep.

Spike, though, had one last secret, one he kept until near the end, which wasn't long in coming. Nobody noticed his decline, not even Daffodil, although Adalina had lost some of her sparkle, so maybe she knew. Spring had returned to the foothills. The weather warmed, the rains diminished, the farmers were predicting a good crop. And Spike asked his closest companions—Will, Jesse, Adalina, and Daffodil—to visit him one evening.

He had a fire going in the fireplace, no other source of light lit in the house. From somewhere, he had dredged up a plastic half gallon bottle of tea and poured everyone a glass. Will thought that funny. Here they were, maybe an hour and a half from Napa Valley, and they were drinking tea. But that was Spike. There was never any knowing what he'd do.

He wasn't having one of his episodes, though. He was fully in command of his faculties that night.

"Don't be alarmed," he began. "But I'm dying."

No sound, no thought even, rose in protest.

"The battle in my head is laying waste to my body. Appetite failing. Insomnia. An odd arrhythmia."

Daffodil leaned forward. "Why didn't you tell me? I can help—"

"It's what I want."

Adalina extended a hand to him. Haltingly, he accepted it. "Don't be sad," he told her. "You've done me more good than you'll ever know."

"I'm not sad." Her voice quavered as she said it. "Well, maybe a little. But you'll still be with us. I'll pray for you every day, and you'll be there."

Spike shook his head and looked away.

"I will. I promise."

Will found it hard to be critical anymore. He still wasn't a believer, but he had to admit, the universe no longer looked as random as it once did.

"If you like," Spike said. He sniffed, straightened, and determination filled his eyes. "I have nothing to bequeath but this. Will, Jesse, and Daffodil: watch over my honorary granddaughter. She's a special young lady. And mark my words: if you don't, and if there *is* an afterlife…" He paused, and his lips turned up in a devilish grin. "…I'll send the aliens after you."

Jesse had been taking a drink and almost choked on it. Wiping the drips from his mouth, he laughed. "Go ahead and try, Doc," he said. "*I* know where the pepper is!"

Spike lingered on, hiding his decline as best he could, but as August turned to September, he fell into a sleep from which he never woke. Four days later, he was gone. Most of the town turned out for his funeral, and then life moved on. Lamps were being lit earlier and earlier, farmers began planning for the harvest, warmer clothing was pulled from storage and cleaned. And Will noticed a moodiness overtaking Jesse, which was strange because a new arrival in town, a young Korean lady named Cindy Im, who had ridden in on horseback—from Folsom, she said—had been spending considerable time in his company.

Jesse's disquiet waxed and waned for months. Fall turned to winter, winter to spring. Will and Daffodil started a garden of their own. One late August day, Daffodil was called to tend an elderly patient. Will was in the garden harvesting whatever was ready when Jesse stopped by. The younger man watched the operation for a time, lips pinched in a frown, hands shoved in his pockets.

"Feel free to help," Will said with a glance over his shoulder.

Jesse remained where he was, an onyx statue scowling at the produce.

"Or not. What's up?"

With a sigh, Jesse went to a tomato vine and inspected the fruits. He picked one and gave it unnecessarily detailed scrutiny.

Will straightened and stretched. He didn't care to admit it, but age might finally have found where he lived.

"Got a question," Jesse said, then quickly added, "Which you don't gotta answer."

"Ask away. After all that's happened, I doubt anything you ask could offend me."

"It' ain't so much offense as..." Jesse made a vague motion but couldn't catch the word that had eluded him.

"It's okay," Will assured him.

Which didn't seem to assure him at all. He kept studying the tomato. "When Sarah left." He gave Will a quick sidelong glance, then focused on the red orb once more.

"Go on."

"You said you dated a few women after."

"In a manner of speaking. Nothing that went anywhere."

"How long before you did?"

Oh. Lynn had vanished from Jesse's life about twenty-one months before, presumed dead, no way now to find out for sure. He hadn't spoken of her openly for a long time, but he must have mourned her every day and night for most of those months. And then Cindy Im rode into his life. She wants him. He wants her. But Lynn...she was his world, until the world shattered, and he'd clung to the shards ever since, Cindy notwithstanding.

"There's no right answer," Will told him. "For me? Four, five months. It went nowhere, I guess, because until I discovered Daffodil, my heart wasn't truly in it. But Sarah left me. Lynn didn't leave you. She was taken from you."

"I just can't..." Anger contorted Jesse's face. He cocked his arm to throw the tomato halfway around the world. Then he slumped and dropped it on the ground. "I know we had no choice, but I keep asking what if. What if I'd looked longer? What if we hadn't left the city? What if, what if, what if!" He stomped on the tomato. Red mush leached out from beneath his boot.

"Same here," Will said. "Maybe everyone who loses someone does. As if we really could change the past. We can't, though. The past is fixed. But the future..."

Jesse lifted his boot and stared at the mess he'd made. The red flesh of the fruit, squished to pulp. The seeds released by his violence waiting for a rain or someone's hands to work them into the ground.

He cocked his head. "Huh," he said.

He gathered himself up and with a mock salute left Will to his gardening.

Will watched him go. Then he pondered the seeds.

How about that, he thought. *Another bullet on Jesse's resume. He's become a philosopher.*

Thank you for reading! Please leave a short, honest review wherever you purchased this book. I greatly appreciate it, and it will help others discover my books.

Afterword

KATHLEEN HAD a better head for history than I, but at least once—maybe *only* once!—my memory triumphed over hers.

Penitence was spawned by a short story of the same name, a story she thought I had written in the late 1990's or early 2000's. By my reckoning, it had been a decade earlier. One day a year or more after she passed away, I pulled that manuscript from the filing cabinet and found a note on the folder, penned in Kathleen's elegant hand:

READ! (to p.33) 12/14/91 kl

An unusual note. Kathleen read and edited all my stuff, but she didn't normally date her work. I can only speculate as to why she did so this time. The short story "Penitence" captured her interest, less for the plague I had unleashed than for the themes of contrition and redemption. And she was taken by the opening scene, in which William and Robert (who morphed into Will and Jesse for the novel) discussed their predicament on the porch of a mountain cabin as winter encroached.

Her attraction to these elements notwithstanding, the writing itself wasn't that good. In those days, I was still groping toward publishability. But it was a start, and the idea sank its teeth into me and wouldn't let go. For two decades, I had novelization in the back of my mind. We didn't much discuss it over the years, but I knew Kathleen wanted to see it happen. And I wanted to do it for her. Alas, I started too late. She was gone long before I completed the first draft.

The timing wasn't just unfortunate. It was bizarre. I started the project in the second half of 2019, less than a year before COVID tore through the world. "I'm writing about a pandemic," I told people, "but it has nothing to do with *this*." They would laugh. I said that for several years while the tale turned into a beast that fought me the whole way. Indeed, I only got my bearings after two false starts, and by then I was immersed in *A Day for Bones*.

And then Kathleen succumbed to her illness. In the end, she never saw one word of *Penitence*, the novel. It saddens me that she missed it, but her love of the story drove me to complete it. You see, I wrote it for her as much as for myself. I don't know for certain what she would have thought of the result. A lot changed in the transition from short story to novel. I even had to sacrifice her favorite scene, although its ghost haunts the tale: Will and Jesse trapped in the ProMaster in the snow; Jesse and Daffodil on the cabin porch near Devil's Peak. But I hope she would have loved the novel as much as she loved the short story.

I think she would have. It's even possible she helped me write it.

Dale E. Lehman
Chase, Maryland
April 12, 2024

About the Author

DALE E. LEHMAN is an award-winning writer, veteran software developer, amateur astronomer, and bonsai artist in training. He principally writes mysteries, science fiction, and humor. In addition to his novels, his writing has appeared in *Sky & Telescope* and on Medium.com. He owns and operates the imprint Red Tales. He and his late wife Kathleen have five children, six grandchildren, and two feisty cats. At any given time, Dale is at work on several novels and short stories.

To learn more about Dale and his stories and to subscribe to his newsletter, visit https://www.DaleELehman.com.